PRASE FOR 'THE WA[ ] AND JOHN IR[ ]

'A small community, a chance encou....., - -g ...) --- --g-- --- the Bear is a rip-roaring adventure that is both insightful and humane. Nuanced, compassionate and funny, this tale of love and revenge is one of my favourite books of the year.' - Carys Bray, Author of 'When the Lights Go Out'

'Suffused with warmth and charm. This is what good storytellers do in the face of the climate crisis: choreograph a dance between the vast and the tiny, between the global and the human. I was completely invested and utterly gripped.' - Shelley Harris, Author of 'Jubilee' and 'Vigilante'

'A novel full of warmth, wit and wisdom. John Ironmonger weaves another charm of a story' - Essie Fox, Author of 'The Fascination'

'This is a tremendously enjoyable book.'
- Marianne Levy, INDEPENDENT ON SUNDAY
on 'The Whale at the End of the World'

'It's a love story of sorts and, above all, it's about the innate goodness of people and our connections with the wider world.'
- PRESS ASSOCIATION on 'The Whale at the End of the World'

'A gentle and uplifting tale of warding off apocalypse in a remote corner of Cornwall . . . charming.'
- FINANCIAL TIMES on 'The Whale at the End of the World'

'This novel, set in Cornwall, will restore your faith in humanity.'
- ELLE UK on 'The Whale at the End of the World'

THE WAGER
AND THE BEAR

JOHN IRONMONGER

First published 21st February 2025 by Fly on the Wall Press
Published in the UK by
Fly on the Wall Press
56 High Lea Rd
New Mills
Derbyshire
SK22 3DP

www.flyonthewallpress.co.uk
ISBN: 9781915789341
EBook: 9781915789358
Copyright John Ironmonger © 2025

A CIP Catalogue record for this book is available from the British Library.

For Amalie and Oli and Theo

Some say the world will end in fire,
Some say in ice.
From what I've tasted of desire
I hold with those who favour fire.
But if it had to perish twice,
I think I know enough of hate
To say that for destruction ice
Is also great
And would suffice.

Fire and Ice by Robert Frost

THE WAGER

1. What a day it was to be back

What a day it was to be back in St Piran. This was summer as God had designed it. A Cornish summer. The sun hung high in a clear blue sky with just a touch of haze upon the horizon. Boats in the bay seemed becalmed, like little islands of solitude on a flat, forgiving ocean. The hedgerows all the way along the cliff path hummed with honeybees and glittered with butterflies. Wildflowers were in blossom. Birds were about their business in song. Herring gulls in full voice soared high above everything, as if directing events below, calling down their commands from the heavens. If there was a breeze, it was a gentle one, carrying with it the salt-fresh smells of the ocean. It was the kind of day that might linger in the memory, filed away somewhere as, 'a perfect summer day'.

Tom Horsmith, nineteen years and eleven months old, in the final hours of his teens, wearing new jeans ripped at the knee, and a t-shirt as yellow as the sunshine, arrived in the village on foot. He carried a pack on his shoulders and wore soft leather boots on his feet. He had walked the cliff paths, four miles from the bus-stop in the town of Treadangel, and every step of the way felt magical, as if the earth was struggling to contain its bounty and was forced to share every new odour, the buzz of every insect, and the musical call of every bird.

The city robs you of these pleasures, Tom thought. It sends you underground. It squeezes you into unnatural spaces, rations your air, and washes away the colours of nature. You have to watch every footstep on a cliff path. The route winds, and there are rocks, and roots, and steps to negotiate, stiles to clamber, sheer drops, and views that will take your breath away. But in the city, every footstep is the same; you just walk. You wait for the lights. You cross. You weave between people, avoiding the gaze of strangers. You glance into the windows of shops. You walk. The soundscape of the city is motor engines, and sirens, and hooters. And voices. But here, Tom thought, there are only the gulls.

How good it was to be back.

From the field gate of Corin Magwith's farm Tom could see the village; a collection of grey, slate rooftops, some aligned this way, and some another, as if they were a child's bricks after a tantrum, or relics of a shipwreck, scattered and abandoned at the head of the bay after a great storm. Whitewashed houses. Grey stone walls. Just three boats in the harbour. Small boats. But it was mid-tide. Other craft would be out at sea, pursuing the shoals. Tom shielded his eyes with his hand and looked out. There, beyond the headland, was Daniel Robin's little ketch, simple to recognise with its front wheelhouse and red paintwork. And there, on the horizon, was that Peter Shaunessy's new boat? *Piranesi?* 'Best boat in the water,' Benny Shaunessy would call it. Hard to tell at this distance. Maybe, Tom pondered, he could find work with Peter and Benny. Summer on the boats didn't feel like too much of an ordeal. Not when the weather was like this. He could catch fish. He could pull in the nets and pack the fish in ice. He could help with the winching and the winding, and the carrying.

Or maybe he would find an easier job in the village. One with less carrying. Anything would do. It was only for three months. His final year at university would start in October. He drew in a deep breath of warm Atlantic air. Perhaps he didn't need to work at all. Not yet. Not for a while. He had some modest savings. Maybe he could enjoy the sunshine. Make his money last. He could sit on the harbour wall with a book. He could sleep in the sun. It wouldn't be a bad way to spend the summer.

He swung the field gate closed and started down the path towards St Piran.

2. A great many legends are told...

A great many legends are told of the village of St Piran; so many, it is difficult, sometimes, to sift the truths from the fables. There are those in the village (just as an example), who say the ancient stone boulders that mark the two ends of the harbour wall are the mortal remains of the fishermen, John Brewster and Matthew Treverran, who were turned to stone (and justly so) for playing dice on a Sunday. Others will tell you that the harbour walls themselves are nothing but the open arms of a *knocker* – a Cornish demon from the tin mines at Botallack – who drowned in the waters of Piran Bay while fleeing from St Michael after a violent dispute at cards. These are the kinds of stories you will hear if you spend time in this village, if you have an honest face, and if you have the patience to listen. There are some in the community who still, to this day, hide the body of a cockerel in the coffin of a loved one. The fowl will be revived in the next world, and his appearance will remind St Peter of his denial of Christ, for it was as the cock crowed that Peter committed his mortal sin. The memory of this, and the attendant shame, will tempt the saint to be merciful when he judges the deceased. So goes the logic. It is not unusual for villages in Cornwall to cling to traditions like these, but St Piran, you might well think, appears to have more customs than most. Every Christmas, the children of the village parade up the hill by candlelight beneath the giant effigy of a whale. This, they will tell you, is in memory of a man who saved the village from one of the great pandemics, when he rode onto the beach on the back of a whale.

They are idle tales, the tales told in St Piran. Some, like the tale of the fishermen turned to stone, are brief events. You might have been in St Piran on the day they happened, and still have missed them. One moment John and Matthew, the dice playing fishermen, were flesh and blood. The next instant they were boulders propping up the harbour walls. No one, so far as we know, was there to witness it. Other stories unfold over weeks. Or even months. And then there is the story of the wager and the bear. Once there was a time when everyone in the world knew this story. Or part of it. They will tell you it has something to do with a bear. And it does. But this is St Piran. This is where the story started, and also where it ended. They have their own way of talking about things here. So, for them, this story is perhaps the strangest tale of all. It unfolds not over days (as the newspapers might have suggested), nor weeks, nor months, but decades. It is a story of human lifetimes. Martha Fishburne told parts of the story to the children in Piran School, and in due course some of them wrote down the episodes they could remember. Charity Limber, who cleaned at Marazion House, heard a great deal of the story from Monty Causley, and she told it all to Jeremy Melon, and Jeremy wrote some of it down, but only part of it, for he didn't live to see it all through. There are photographs if you care to look hard enough for them, and a great many accounts in old newspapers, and even one or two older residents who perhaps remember some of it. There was even a film made once, and a stage play, and most school history books of the period and online encyclopaedias have some version or other of the events. But none of these allowed the whole story to unfold. And this, perhaps, is why the tales are still told in St Piran. It hasn't snowed in the village for fifty years, or maybe more, but there are villagers today who still display a snowflake in their windows in June, and this, they will tell you, is to remember the wager and the bear.

It was a long time ago. Over eighty years have passed since Tom Horsmith, still just a teenager, walked into the square with a pack on his back and a smile on his face. His is the name local people remember if they remember any name at all. But every story, in a village like St Piran, will have its hero. Many also have a villain. Sometimes one gets confused with the other. If there was a villain in the story of the ice, it might be as well to meet him now. His name, after all, is the one the rest of the world remembers, and much of the world considers *him* the hero. He wasn't, in truth, a villain. Not really. Neither was he a true villager. He was an incomer. An invader. His name was Monty Causley.

He was a Cornishman, but not, people will tell you, a Cornishman from St Piran. They say that he came from Lostwithiel where his family made cider, although some believe he was originally from Bodmin and his fortune came from tin. No matter. He was the man who owned Marazion House, on the sea front, and Marazion House was central to the game of dice that would play out in the story of the wager and the bear. The house was the most prepossessing dwelling in the village. It was stone-built, somehow part of the very geology of the bay, an edifice that looked as though it might have grown organically from the walls of the cliff itself, like a sort of artificial rearrangement of the rockface, not quite vertical, not quite horizontal, a building that had never seen the pencil of an architect nor the string of a plumb line, but had somehow evolved in segments and parcels, a piece here and another piece there, until, like an elderly relative, it had become a timeless feature of the harbour. Impressive. Compelling. Maybe it had been the first house in St Piran. No one really knew. Maybe there were smuggler's caves behind it, buried deep inside the cliff, concealing long-lost troves of treasure. That is the sort of house it was. A secretive house. A house that told no tales. It seemed to occupy a dangerous hinterland between sea and land, unnaturally low for a seafront building, carved from boulders that might have been the petrified remains of dice-playing fishermen. It stood in a small bay of its own, the sole building at the top of a shingle beach scarcely wider than the house itself. To reach the front door you would need to descend a dozen steps to a stone path that ran along the top of the beach, and from there you would climb up six steps to the porch. No one would design a house like this today, but Marazion defied all principles of good architecture. The stones of the walls were black with age, and green with lichens, and pockmarked with tiny barnacles, and never truly dry. The fine spray from the waves at high tide, and the southerly winds and the ocean squalls, conspired together to give the walls a sheen.

Who would have built a house so close to the water? When the high springtides came, the sea would very nearly reach the front door. There were times, during these occasional tides, when you could not leave the house to venture into the village without getting your feet wet. The steps could be slippery after a storm; but the house must have been built by master masons, for winter storms would come and go, and the summer sun would blaze, and the ocean waves would lap at the doorstep and then retreat. Marazion would stand unchanged, unaffected, unmoved, with all of its secrets still untold. Seagulls roosted on the slates as if the house was just another cliff-face, and here was where they had evolved to be; and from the roofs, with a single leap and a dive, they could plunge into the harbour at high tide for sprats, and shrimps, and discarded potato chips. The guttering and walls of the house carried the trails of seagull excreta, all the way around, like spilled paint.

Monty Causley was the third Causley to own Marazion House. His father had owned it before him, and his grandfather before that. But this didn't make Monty nor his parents or grandparents, true residents of St Piran. None had truly *lived* in Marazion House. They were absent landlords, strangers still in the village. The house had been, at best, a bolthole for occasional summer visits, a rare and remote holiday-home. Or else it had stood empty. Monty rented it out to holiday makers. Two thousand and four hundred pounds a week the house could earn in the height of summer. A thousand pounds a week off season. It could, perhaps, have earned more had it been in one of the popular holiday destinations, like St Ives maybe, or Porthcurno, or even Newquay where surfers made the season longer; but St Piran was just a bit too far off the tourist map, just a little too tricky to get to. The village sat at the end of a single-track road with no other way in and no other way out (apart from the cliff paths and the sea). Most of the winter months the house stood dark and unoccupied, locked and shuttered against the storms. And just occasionally, in the spring or autumn, there might be a fallow week where no one had booked, and these were the weeks when, from time to time, Monty Causley and his wife, Carys, would drive down from London and park on the quay.

He was mean. That was what they said about Monty in the Stormy Petrel Inn, where the locals would settle at the end of the day to make a long cider last the evening. He was mean, and that was enough to make him the villain. He was mean, and the wager was a judgement on his meanness. The fact that he only showed up when bookings were scarce was evidence. He rarely drank in the Petrel. He never took coffee in the harbourside café. He didn't often give in to the temptation of a Cornish pasty, or haddock and chips from Kenny Kennet's bistro. He bought very few provisions from Jessie Higgs's shop. He wasn't often seen. He and Carys would bring a box-load of groceries with them from a swanky store in London, and they would carry it down the stone steps, and along the short path, and up the steps to the house, and there, in Marazion House, except on the days when Monty was campaigning for election, they would shut themselves away. For the long weekend (or sometimes even for a week), they would vanish behind the big front door.

'He makes no contribution to the economy of the village,' Jeremy Melon would declare, to no one in particular, in the lobsterman's bar at the Petrel.

'Darling, he rents out his house,' Demelza Trevarrick would say, defensively. 'His tenants spend a fortune here.'

'But all the rent payments go back to London,' Jeremy would counter. 'Not a penny to Cornwall.'

'His wife buys cigarettes in Jessie's shop,' someone would say.

'Once or twice.'

'He does drink in here occasionally.' This observation was from Jason Anderssen, the barman.

'Not often enough.'

Charity Limber would see the Causleys. She was the cleaner at Marazion House. She would call in the mornings to throw open the curtains and to make the beds. Twenty-seven years old she was, newly married and bursting with life, like a new bud on a spring blossom; but Marazion House would subdue her. 'It's cold in there,' she would tell the drinkers in the Petrel. 'Unfriendly.'

'But what do they do all day?' people would ask.

'He sits at his desk and never once looks out of the windows,' she would tell them. 'He has his computers and his phones and all manner of devices. His telephone rings at eight in the morning and from that moment on, for the rest of the day, he is talking, or on a video-conference, or shouting something to somebody down the phone.'

'And what about *her*? What about Carys Causley?'

'She sits in the window with a crossword and a cup of tea, but she barely looks at the crossword at all. She stares out at the sea.'

Of the two of them, Monty and Carys Causley, there was more empathy in the village for her. She, Carys, would at least walk out. She wore silk headscarves tied tightly around her head, even in the sunshine. She walked with her head bent as if there was always a wind, and her favoured walk would be down the right arm of the knocker demon to the shoulder, and then up the other arm, all the way along the harbour wall, to the fingertips, to the rock that some would say was John Brewster. And then back. Sometimes she would walk around the headland to Piran Sands, when the weather was fine, but her walking shoes were not well suited to the shingle and the rocks, and so there she would turn around, back to Marazion House.

How old were Monty and Carys? Well, she was younger than he. And he was somewhere in the inscrutable years between thirty and fifty. And so was she. And that was all anyone knew. Until the wager. They didn't appear to have children. And there were no photographs in the house. This was, after all, for most of the year, a property for holiday-rental. It had been stripped of any personal touches. There were no books of special interest on the shelves. No traces of any hobbies. No artworks on the walls apart from nautical pictures that could have come from any gift shop in Cornwall. Every room was as soulless as a hotel corridor.

'You think the man would at least possess a fishing rod,' Jeremy Melon would say.

'Or a yacht,' Demelza would add.

And this perhaps, was why Monty Causley would have to be the villain of any unfolding tale in St Piran. Not because he was necessarily guilty of any villainy. Not because he was ridiculously rich. But because he seemed guilty of so little else. How can a man live so anonymously, and work so assiduously, and steer so deliberately away from the cliff paths, and the beauty spots, *and* the beaches, and spend so little with local business and *still* be innocent of any offence? This didn't seem right. And in St Piran, as in many a small town, there is a natural suspicion of any native who has moved away. What can their motives have been?

'Never be carelessly, or casually, critical of anyone else's beliefs,' the schoolteacher, Martha Fishburne would tell the children in her class at Piran School. 'Be careful, very careful, before you judge someone because of their politics or their God.'

But this lesson of Martha Fishburne's may have been one instruction the drinkers in the Petrel had missed or forgotten. For there was one offence, in many of their eyes, of which Monty Causley was impeachably guilty. He was a Tory. That was his crime.

Or was he perhaps, a Socialist? This was a long time ago, and although these things seemed important at the time, history can be confusing, and governments and parties did seem to swap and change a great deal during those years, and policies came and went on both sides. Whichever it was, Labour or Conservative, people did get unnaturally exercised about these things, and half of the drinkers in the Petrel bar would feel offended, and would object to Monty Causley because of his politics, and the other half would agree because, Labour or Conservative, politicians could never be trusted. 'If there are two things a politician can do,' Jeremy Melon would say, 'and if one is the right thing and the other is the wrong thing, you can always rely on them to pick the wrong one.'

Monty Causley, we should understand, was not simply a Tory. He was an ass. He was a bloated, self-serving, puppet of a government nobody trusted. At least, he was in the eyes of the drinkers in the lobsterman's bar. He was a naïve Cornishman, who had been idly seduced by power. He was a class traitor.

Truth, of course, is always more nuanced than rumour. How do any of us know, of a politician in the news, how he or she might really think, how smart or stupid they really are, what values they really hold? We make our judgements based on party loyalties, on half-remembered comments from hasty broadcast interviews, on carefully curated photographs from newspapers. We paint a picture of a person we never met. 'You should never judge another person until you've spent a day with them,' Martha Fishburne would tell the children at St Piran School. 'And even that is not long enough. When you judge a person,' she would say, 'it tells us nothing about what they are; but it tells us plenty about what you are.'

But human nature is what it is. For the villagers of St Piran, there would only ever be one villain in the story of the wager and the bear. He was the Honourable Montgomery Hendrick Causley. Member of Parliament for Cornwall South. Guilty as charged.

3. It started with an altercation

We know, quite clearly, when the story of the wager and the bear started. It started with an altercation in the Stormy Petrel Inn. It was summer in Cornwall. Beaches were crowded, and restaurants bustling. The B&B in St Piran, run by Moses and Hedra Penhallow, had re-opened as a hotel, *The Fin Whale Hotel*, with a restaurant on the ground floor serving some customers in the garden and others outside on the harbour pavement. A bistro, *The Beachcomber*, had opened on the site of the old fish-packing station, and Kenny Kennet the owner, short of accommodation indoors, had found space for tables and chairs along the quay, and these were frequently full. The Petrel pub had countered this new fashion for al-fresco dining with tables of its own, and no one had yet agreed upon where the boundary line should lie between the pub's tables and the bistro's tables, and so hotel, pub, and bistro jostled for space and few diners were ever really clear which tables belonged to which establishment. As it was, neither the pub, the bistro, nor the hotel could afford to let any disagreement escalate into a public dispute, for fear that this might lead the county authorities to question whether tables on the quayside were even permitted at all. No one would want that. So, an easy truce prevailed, and the harbourside in summer was as busy as an Italian piazza, with coffee drinkers, beer drinkers, and hungry families, who would lurk waiting for a table when the weather was good, swooping in like seagulls onto chip paper as soon as spaces became available. The old doctor's surgery on Fish Street was now an ice cream parlour. One of the fishermen's houses on the quay sold pasties. There was a fish and chip shop at the top of Piran Walk. '*Today's catch*,' it advertised on blackboards in the square. Little St Piran, that for so many centuries had been a sleepy, forgotten hamlet on the toe of the county of Cornwall, had, in summer, become a chic destination. The natural smells of seaweed, old mud, ocean spray, and fish would now arrive accompanied by the new smells of toasting ciabattas, and cheeseburgers, and lattes. The single-track lane that wound for four miles from the Treadangel to Penzance Road would be blocked with traffic coming in and traffic going out. New passing places had been cut into the hedgerows and benevolently tarmacked by the county council, and a cheerful bonhomie generally prevailed as convoys of cars encountered each other, leading to awkward reversing manoeuvres down the lane to the nearest passing space. After all, this was Cornwall. You expect this kind of thing. Everyone was busy. Everybody was making money. The fishermen sold their fish to the restaurants. The dairy farmer sold his milk to the ice cream maker. The craft shop sold local art works and objéts-trouvés from the beaches. The tiny hamlet had discovered commerce, and now, between Easter and the first red leaves of autumn, it would hum with the activities of visitors.

Even tables in the lobsterman's bar at the Petrel could be hard to find on a summer evening. A day or so after Tom's arrival back in the village, he and Benny Shaunessy found themselves standing with their drinks, unable to find even a table for two.

'We shouldn't complain,' Benny said. 'It's good for the economy.'

A middle-aged man in a faded boating-blazer was waving at them from a corner of the bar, trying to get their attention. He was with a woman with a headful of greying curls, kept in place with a red beret. The man looked like an over-dressed commentator for the Boat Race. The woman looked like an aging doyenne of the Paris catwalk.

'Is that Jeremy Melon?' Tom asked.

'And Demelza. I do believe they've found us a table,' Benny said. He grabbed his drink and steered through the press of evening drinkers.

'Four seats about to become free,' Jeremy said, nodding towards a party of young men who seemed to be getting their things together to leave.

'Darling, it's so wonderful to *see* you!' Demelza said. She kissed Tom expansively on the cheek, and then made a point of holding him at arm's length to survey him. 'You've grown simply enormous. And utterly gorgeous.' She slid into the seat vacated by one of the departing drinkers, barely before the man's bottom had left it. She patted the space next to her, inviting Tom to squeeze alongside. 'How long have you been away?' she asked.

'Two years. Apart from occasional visits to see my Nan.'

'Two years, dear God!' Demelza sighed. 'And you have transformed from a gosling into a swan. It simply isn't fair is it, Jeremy? Young men showing up in the village like this, reminding all the rest of us of our desperate headlong cascade into decrepitude, to say nothing of our fading libidos.'

'Indeed,' Jeremy said.

'You haven't changed a bit Demelza,' Tom said, laughing.

'He's learned flattery as well,' Demelza wailed. 'What hope is left for the poor women of St Piran with this creature in our midst? Jeremy! Would you get us all a drink?'

Jeremy took Tom's glass.

That was about seven o'clock. Or not long after. At seven-thirty, they had another round. At eight o'clock, Demelza bought a round. All four searched through pockets for money to put into a kitty on the table and enough was found for one more round, and then, astonishingly, another. It seemed like the right thing to do. Demelza was drinking gin with bottles of tonic and slices of cucumber. Jeremy had started on ale, but the middle-aged bladder can only take so many pints, so now he was on blended Scotch and water. The young men drank cider. It was the cloudy cider, popular at the Petrel. (The story Jacob the landlord would tell, was that a leg of mutton was thrown into every barrel, and when the meat was dissolved, the cider was ready to drink. Was this true? No one seemed to know. The young men would hold their glasses up to the light to test the hypothesis.)

It was a warm night. Some of the drinkers in the bar dispersed onto tables on the harbour side, once the early diners had vacated. Three young men from Porthcurnow, squeezed into a corner, started to sing sea shanties. A woman sitting across from them played along on a fiddle.

What was the time now?

Late. But it was summer. It wasn't yet dark. In their corner of the lobsterman's bar, Tom Horsmith and his companions were on their sixth, or maybe seventh round of drinks, and this time of the evening, as any barman will tell you, is perhaps the most dangerous for social drinkers. They haven't yet drunk themselves into a stupor. But inhibitions now are paper-thin. Opinions are aired more loudly at this time. Drinkers (young men especially) believe themselves invulnerable at this hour of the night. And so it was, at just this dangerous time, when the fiddle player was taking a break, when a man, alone, came into the bar, and tried to catch the barman's eye.

'Well, I'm astonished,' Tom announced, waving a hand in the direction of the newcomer, and speaking perhaps too loudly, unconcerned whether his words might be heard at the bar. 'Look who it is.'

'And who might it be?'

'No one but the dishonourable purveyor of untruths and deceptions to the unwashed masses,' Tom said. 'Mr Marazion House himself. The Dis-Honourable Montague Causley MP.'

We have, at this point in our narrative, quite a cast of characters assembling in the backroom bar of the Petrel, and it might, perhaps, be helpful to arrange some introductions before the rest of this story develops.

At the top of our list, we have Thomas Horsmith. Tom. We have already met him. Born in St Piran and raised by his grandmother, Nan Horsmith. Brother of Morwenna and Connor. An affable young man. Not especially tall. Not especially handsome. Not wealthy. Not worldly. An ordinary young man then. But a man with fire in his belly. A man with passion, and confidence, and drive, and self-belief. His mother, Kelly, had died with depression when Tom was only six, when Morwenna was seven, and Connor was three. That was how Tom would explain it. *She died with depression.* It's an illness. People die with it. In reality, she went to bed one night and swallowed a handful of ecstasy pills and who-knows-how-many over-the-counter tablets. Morwenna found her body. It was a long time ago. None of the children had been especially scarred. Not even Morwenna. Tom, now, barely remembered his mother. He didn't remember that morning. He remembered instead the funeral at the Church of St Piran, high on the hillside overlooking the village, on a wintry morning with seagulls circling the graveside.

Tom's father was a fisherman from Newlyn, apparently. He was no longer on the scene. All three children took their mother's name – Horsmith. Not one of them seemed to know exactly who their father was, or whether they shared a single father, or not, and Nan was never helpful with details, and maybe she never knew either. Whatever, none of the children, not Tom, nor Morwenna, nor Connor, ever expended any effort worrying about it.

Tom was, at this stage in the story, a student at University College London. Two years of study done. One still to go. *Earth Sciences*. A tough subject. But Tom was, by every account we have, a bright young man. He had promise. He was doing well. London, you might think, is not so far from St Piran. Five or six hours by train to Penzance, an hour by bus to Treadangel, and another hour and twenty minutes by coastal footpath to the village. A slow journey but not a hard one. Why had Tom not stayed at home and spent university vacations in St Piran? Well, these things are often complicated, and they were for Tom. The singular truth was, he could find well-paid casual work in London. Less so in St Piran. Even in term time, a job waiting tables at a Covent Garden brasserie could earn him twice what he could earn at Kenny Kennet's *Beachcomber* bistro on the quayside. And every pound he earned in London was an extra pound for his grandmother and his siblings, for Nan Horsmith was rarely well enough to work. So, Tom was a student by day, a waiter at lunchtimes and again in the evenings, a pizza-delivery-boy at weekends, and an occasional barman and washer-up of glasses when his timetable would allow. He had an early alarm that would wake him at six, and a daily agenda where every minute was accounted for and carefully budgeted. A lecture, perhaps, at nine, on deformation mechanisms in igneous rocks, and another at ten on sedimentary environments and the geological record, time for a very swift coffee with friends, and at eleven-thirty he would be racing down Charing Cross road to reach the Brasserie St George in time for the early diners at lunch. *'For you, madam — Leicestershire blue cheese tart, roasted parsnip, apple and walnut salad, and for you, sir, the braised shin of Irish lamb with portobello mushrooms, Welsh rarebit and wilted rocket. Two glasses of Medoc and a sparkling water. Any starters?'* Then back to campus for a two-thirty practical session on mineral resource estimation that would last the rest of the afternoon, leaving less than an hour to grab something to eat in the kitchen of his flat, navigating around the half dozen students of every race and gender (and none) who seemed to hang out there, allowing fifteen minutes for small talk, five minutes to change into a clean shirt and listen to a track from a new Scandinavian band he just had to catch, then close the door to his bedroom and flip open his laptop. Twenty minutes of emails and social media, forty minutes hammering out six hundred words of an essay on volcanoes and their impacts on climate, until an alarm would tell him to move. Move! It was a thirty-four-minute walk from his flat near King's Cross to the Brasserie St George in Covent Garden. He could catch up on text messages on his phone while he walked. Allow thirty-six minutes in case all the crossing lights were red. '*Tom! You're late.*' 'No Sir, I'm exactly on time.' And look. Here come the pre-theatre diners. 'Good evening, I'm Tom. I'm your waiter for this evening. May I get you some menus?'

Tom, on the day of his twentieth birthday, was a work-in-progress, full of potential, and who could tell what virtues or vices might emerge?

Number two on our list of introductions for the altercation at the Petrel, is local naturalist, Dr Jeremy Melon. Jeremy was forty-nine when the altercation occurred. He wasn't, one should surely say, a man who sought out confrontations, and so his participation in the disagreement was rather out of character. You might say it was the drink talking. Jeremy was the kind of man who would normally engineer an early exit to avoid any unpleasantness, rather than hang around and face the music. He was a man who, generally, sought an easy life. He had run away to St Piran twenty-three years earlier. He hadn't chosen St Piran. He hadn't picked the village out on a map. He had simply climbed into his car one night and had driven until he ran out of road. It was a complicated story. But then most stories are. He had been a teacher – a lecturer – at a university in Leeds, and well, there had been a student, a rather good-looking fellow, and Jeremy had become rather too attached, and one thing had led to another, and it all ended with Jeremy in his car, in tears, driving south. In the years since, details of the incident had thankfully been wholly forgotten, even by Jeremy himself, and the events that brought him to the village were rarely ever mentioned. 'Never look back,' Jeremy would say. And he never had. He had found a niche, of a sort, writing natural history books, contributing to encyclopaedias, and marking student essays for American colleges. His earnings were small, but so were his outgoings. He would paint watercolour pictures of crabs, lobsters, and the denizens of rock pools, and Kenny Kennet would sell these in his craft shop on the quay. So, he managed.

But since life rarely delivers for any of us a wholly worry-free existence, events had conspired to furnish Jeremy Melon with a copious source of worries in the form of Demelza Trevarrick. They made an odd couple. If, indeed, they were a couple at all. Jeremy had always exhibited rather fluid preferences when it came to the bedroom, and Demelza's own predilections were equally variable in these matters, informed by the rather hippy-lifestyle to which she aspired, and by her profession as a romantic novelist. *'I'm doing this for research you understand,'* she would purr suggestively at any man or woman who might be persuaded into anything approximating an intimate embrace. Demelza was St Piran born-and-bred, although no one was quite sure where she had spent her formative years. She had been absent from the village for most of her twenties and almost all of her thirties, and sometimes even in her forties she would be gone for a month, or two months, or a season. But she always returned. *'This town,'* she would say, *'it never lets you get away.'* She would laugh off questions about her past, *'far too murky to share,'* or where she might have lived, *'everywhere darling except Truro,'* or whether she had ever been married, *'you can't possibly expect me to remember every piece of paper I might have signed.*' Her novels, although primarily Cornish in their settings, would often include South of France locations, or encounters in Rome or Milan, and her plots could often drift towards what her publisher would call, 'the pessimistic end of the romantic spectrum,' where the central character finds love, and tragically loses it in the final act, coming to terms instead with life alone. They didn't live together – Jeremy and Demelza – although their cottages were only a short walk apart; but they were rarely seen out of each other's company. So, life alone may have been a choice for Demelza; or maybe not. And who knew what went on in the bedroom of either cottage in Fish Street? These things are best never enquired about.

One further character then, and we will be done with introductions. Benny Shaunessy. Tom's friend. Much the same age. A young man as different from Tom, you might think, as it could be possible to find in this village. While Tom was almost a Londoner now, very nearly a city boy, Benny had rarely found reason to travel much further than Treadangel. He was the son of a fisherman, and the grandson of fishermen, and the sea was encoded in his very DNA. Surely, if you were to track his family back, you would find Shaunessys on boats, hauling in nets, right the way back to Noah. While Tom was lanky, Benny was stocky and square. While Tom was restless, Benny was relaxed. Serenity radiated out from him. He could stand all day at the tiller of a boat and never once feel bored. Tom, by contrast, would be itching after just ten minutes. They had been together in the same class at school, Benny and Tom, from the age of five, right the way through primary school, and then on to the comprehensive in Treadangel, and only then, once schoolwork had begun for the first time to feel serious, had any gap grown between them. But these things, when you are friends, when you are *best* of friends, are of very little consequence. Tom would spend longer with his books than

Benny. That was the simple difference. It was the way they were. Benny would watch the world out of the classroom window. He would follow the seagulls across the sky until they were out of sight over Piran Head. 'Benjamin Shaunessy, would you be so kind as to honour us with your presence,' the schoolmaster would say. But it was hard. In his mind, Benny could always hear the sea. He could feel the movement of the waves beneath his hard school seat. The rise and fall of the ocean. He could smell the spray. And so, in increments so small they were hard to notice, Benny slipped behind while Tom pulled ahead. No matter. No matter at all. Learning is only one way a man might make a living. There are many others. And who ever heard of book-reading at sea? Yet brotherhood of the kind a man might have when he has a friend since childhood will survive any sort of gulf. Benny Shaunessy was as staunch and loyal a friend as any Tom might have made in the city. They could go months without seeing one another, but five minutes with a cider at Jacob Anderssen's bar would be enough to put aside any of the unfamiliarity that can grow with separation. They were friends. That was enough. Benny would go to work on his father's boat. Everyone knew that. Tom Horsmith would go off to university and find different ways to earn money, until one day, disaffected and disappointed, perhaps, he would come back to St Piran. Or maybe he wouldn't. But either way the friendship would endure, and when you're nineteen, who cares about these things anyway?

So here we are. In the lobsterman's bar of the Stormy Petrel Inn and the hour was maybe, somewhere around ten, or eleven, or something in between. There were no clocks on the wall. The fiddle player and the singer were off somewhere, taking a break. The evening was winding down.

Benny had a new phone. He was showing it to Tom. 'I'll take a picture,' he was saying.

And it was at just this point when a man walked into the bar from the outside.

'Well, I'm astonished,' Tom said. 'Look who it is.'

The newcomer looked over to see who was talking.

'And who might it be?' asked Jeremy.

'A dishonourable purveyor of untruths and deceptions to the unwashed masses,' Tom said. 'Mr Marazion House himself. Our rarely seen and never heard from member of parliament – the dishonourable Mr Montague Causley MP.'

That was how it started. If it hadn't been half past ten at night. If they hadn't found money for the kitty. If there hadn't been mutton in the cider. If Tom had been facing the other way.

Monty Causley seemed to draw himself higher with the insult, stretching out his neck like an offended goose. For a moment, he froze in this position, lips pursed, chin extended, eyes blazing.

Time slowed down. An odd silence radiated outwards from the epicentre of the bar, so that even revellers who had not even heard the insult fell suddenly quiet. A woman's laugh from a distant corner sounded curiously like an intrusion. Causley turned and fixed Tom with a gaze; and at this point, there was no going back. Every eye in the bar was upon them. You cannot retreat from a bar-fight with your dignity intact. Not in the dying hours of the evening.

'That is a very serious allegation,' Causley said, coldly. 'To call a man a liar. To his face. Do you have any evidence to substantiate your accusation? Or is this libel, pure and simple?'

Jeremy Melon broke in. 'It's not strictly a libel,' he said. 'I think you'll find *libel* has to be written down. Perhaps the word you're looking for is *slander*.'

'And he didn't actually use the word, *liar*,' Demelza added.

'Well, I think you'll find the expression *purveyor of untruths* is a synonym of the word liar,' said Causley. 'So it amounts to the same thing. Either way he should prove it, or retract his statement, or see me in court.'

Fighting-talk, humidity, self-righteousness, and cider. A lethal combination. Tom rose out of his seat.

'Tom, don't...' said Jeremy.

'Well, I must apologise for using a synonym,' Tom said, 'when I should have used a much more direct word.' He pointed a finger at the politician, and half turned so he was addressing not just Causley, but most of the drinkers in the bar. 'This is the man who, as a councillor, promised us a daily bus service from Treadangel. Has anyone here ever seen a bus in St Piran?' He raised his eyebrows. 'A lie, then. This is the man who, campaigning for parliament, told us he would get export tariffs lifted on Cornish fish sent to Europe. Has he done this?' He turned back to face the MP. 'Have you done this? No. A lie. And, Mr Causley, don't I remember you telling us, if your party was elected, the cottage hospital at Treadangel would be saved from closure? You've been in power three years. The hospital closed in February. L. I. E. You promised us shorter hospital waiting lists. You promised us more tax relief for rural businesses. You promised us shore defences on the cliff paths. You promised a big new investment grant for South Cornwall. Do I hear an "L"?'

'L,' echoed several voices from the bar.

'Do I hear an "I"?'

'I!" A louder response this time, as the drinkers in the Petrel figured out what was going on.

'Do I hear an "A"?'

'A!'

'R?'

'R!'

'What does that spell?'

'LIAR!' cried the voices of the drinkers.

'There is your synonym, Mr Montgomery Causley,' Tom said, referencing the crowd with a flourish of his hand. He looked pleased with himself. 'Are you going to sue the whole bar?'

Causley looked flustered. 'None of those accusations are fair,' he protested. 'They weren't lies.'

'Oh no?' Tom was enjoying the support of the crowd. 'Then what were they?'

'They were aspirations,' the MP said. 'They were issues I promised to fight for. Issues I *did* fight for. If you promise your parents you'll pass an exam, you are promising to do your best. If you fail the exam, it doesn't make you a liar That's the language of politics. You promise to fight for causes you support. You won't win every fight. You know that. I know it. The voters know it.'

Tom looked unconvinced. 'So, you promised to fight for all these things, but you lost *every* fight. Is that what you're saying? Either you're a liar, or you're a rubbish politician then. And if you promise to pass all of your exams, and you fail every single one, doesn't that start to look like a lie?' He glanced at the crowd.

'LIAR!' came back a chant. 'LIAR.'

Causley was bristling now. 'And what is your special relationship with the truth that gives you the right to point the finger?' he demanded. 'I work hard for this constituency.'

'You earn a fortune from your family interest in North Sea Oil,' Tom said, ignoring Causley's riposte. 'You keep a house here, and a riverside apartment in London, and a villa in Italy... so three houses... and you spend what, one week a year here? Two?'

'My work is in London.'

'And your constituents are in Cornwall. How inconvenient for you. But you're right. Broken promises don't make you a liar. They just make you untrustworthy. And anyway, you know what? I don't care about any of those things. I don't care about your broken promises. I just care about the *one big lie* you tell people.

The biggest lie of all.'

There was a sound in the Stormy Petrel of a collective intake of breath. A sense that this little bar-room spat was about to ramp up a level.

'You're a climate-denier, Mr Causley!' Tom jabbed his finger towards the man. 'You peddle a very dangerous lie. You deny climate change.'

At this, Causley's expression morphed from a scowl into a wide smile. This accusation had pleased him. He gave a loud and rather awkward laugh and took two steps towards Tom, so the two men were standing face to face. 'So that's what this is about? All that self-righteous truth-and-lies stuff? All that drivel about bus routes and fish? I've hurt your precious feelings because I tell the truth about climate change?'

'You don't tell the truth. You tell lies.'

'Ahh... I'm so sorry.' Causley's tone was sarcastic now. 'Have I caught the poor delicate snowflake on a sensitive day? Can't you take a little intellectual rigour applied to your cherished beliefs without descending into cheap ad-hominem insults? Or do we all have to worship the woke gods of global warming and extinction without questioning them?'

The force of this response seemed to rob Tom Horsmith of some of his energy. He appeared to gulp, and Causley used the pause to press home his advantage.

'I don't deny science, young man. You know what I do deny? Lack of nuance. Simplification of complex issues. That's what I deny.'

Perhaps if Monty Causley had left it here, everyone would have returned to their seats, angry and a little bruised, but largely uncowed. Dignity would have been maintained. The crowd in the Petrel would have gone back to the serious business of drinking as much as possible before the closing bell, and the incident would have been quickly forgotten. But Causley was the Member of Parliament for Cornwall South. He had debated with the best. He had crossed verbal swords with the Prime Minister and batted away questions from Nick Robinson on the BBC. He could make mincemeat of this upstart youngster, and he intended to show the assembled company just how devastating he could be. And perhaps it would help to remember that climate-change-denial, a rare perspective these days, was common enough in the bars and debating chambers of the time. Even American presidents had been known to hold such views. 'I don't believe it,' one president famously said, when asked about a climate report. A Russian leader mused publicly that climate change might not so bad for his country. 'Two to three degrees wouldn't hurt,' he said. 'We'll spend less on fur coats, and the grain harvest will go up.' With such high-level support, Monty Causley was wholly confident of his position. 'You shouldn't try to argue if you don't understand the science,' he snapped, sharply, and condescendingly. 'So, here's a little fact for you to go away and consider. Volcanoes. You know what a volcano is, don't you? Pointy thing with smoke coming out of the top.' He laughed here at his own wit. 'Well, do you know how many active volcanoes there are in the world?' He paused to help drive his point home. 'Tens of thousands,' he said. 'Tens of thousands of volcanoes spewing out carbon dioxide. Every single day. Ten times as much CO^2 as all of humanity, with our trucks and our cars and our power stations, produces every single year. So get back in your box and concentrate on catching fish, or whatever it is you do, and leave me to enjoy my drink in peace.' With this, Causley took a step back. The argument was over, so far as he was concerned. A smile played across his lips. Perhaps he was imagining the drinkers in the bar relating the story to their families when they got home. *'Causley wiped the floor with him,'* they would say. *'Left him speechless.'*

Unfortunately for Monty Causley, Tom Horsmith after seven pints of Jacob Anderssen's cider was not altogether speechless. As Causley stepped backwards, Tom followed, pinning the MP up against the bar. 'I've never heard more idiotic errors in my life,' Tom said. His voice was raised. 'I do happen to know what volcanoes are, Mr Causley. You got one thing right. They *are* pointy things with smoke coming out of them. But there aren't ten thousand active volcanoes. There are forty-six erupting today. Forty-six. There were fifty-three that erupted last year. Through all human history, we know of five hundred and sixty volcanoes, and we have names for all of them. And in the Holocene epoch, which goes back around eleven thousand seven hundred years, there have been one thousand, four hundred and thirteen volcanoes. So not ten thousand, Mr Causley. Forty-six. And do you know how much carbon dioxide these put into the atmosphere? Somewhere between two hundred million tonnes and three hundred million tonnes a year. That is a pretty big number. You're right. But humanity is pumping out sixty-five million tonnes a day. A day! We overtake the volcanoes in just three days.' Tom poked a belligerent finger into Causley's sternum. 'You shouldn't try to argue if you don't understand the science,' he said.

There was something of a cheer from surrounding drinkers at this remark. And this time, Tom should perhaps have let matters lie. But he wasn't done. 'The world is warming. The ice caps are melting. Within fifty years,' he said, 'your precious Marazion House will be underwater.'

Causley, who had been rather on the ropes during Tom Horsmith's litany of facts, now grasped at this prediction as a way to recover some lost ground. 'Not a chance of it,' he spluttered. 'They've been telling my family this for years and I've hardly ever had a drop of water beyond my front step. Except in the very big tides.'

'Well then, why don't we make it a bet?' Tom said, theatrically. He turned to see if he was still earning the approval of the crowd. 'I bet you in fifty years from today at high tide, you won't be able to sit in your front room without drowning.'

Causley laughed. 'How is that even a *bet*? If you make a wager, someone has to win something, and the other party has to lose something. Otherwise it isn't a real bet.' He leaned towards the younger man. 'So I tell you what. We could make it a real wager if you want to. It is midsummer's day today. By chance, it happens to be my fortieth birthday. In fifty years, if I live that long, I will be ninety. I will sit for an hour at high tide on my ninetieth birthday in my front room in Marazion House. If it is under water, then I will drown. But there has to be an equal and opposite jeopardy for you, young man. So, if I survive your promised rising of the waters, then you must take the same risk. Isn't that fair? You must walk into the sea and drown.'

'Don't do this, Tom!' This was Jeremy talking. He came up to the young man and put a hand on his shoulder. 'Leave him be.'

'No!' Tom shook Jeremy's hand away. 'I shall take his bet.' He gave a youthful smile. 'There's a very odd coincidence here. We share a birthday, Mr Causley. I am twenty. Today. Midsummer's day. So in fifty years, I shall be seventy. And you shall be ninety. And if you don't drown, then I will.'

There was a moment. It was almost silent in the bar.

A loud ring came from one corner of the room. 'Last orders please!' It was Jason Anderssen calling.

Monty Causley extended a hand. 'Happy Birthday,' he said.

Tom's hand rose up to take the handshake. 'And Happy Birthday to you, Mr Causley,' he said. 'I'm Tom Horsmith.'

'Call me Monty,' the older man said. For an instant, the two men made eye contact. 'Let me buy you a drink,' Causley said.

'Mine's a gin and tonic,' called Demelza.

Someone in the bar started a round of applause. 'Order whatever you like,' Causley said. 'I may as well get one for everybody.'

And that moment of reconciliation and bonhomie should, perhaps, have been how the incident ought to have ended, and all should have been forgotten, and the details of the wager just a vague memory from a night of heavy drinking. Except that Benny Shaunessy, just a few moments earlier, had pressed a button on his phone. 'I caught that all on film,' he said. 'And mine is another cider.'

And while the crowd pressed around the bar for drinks, Benny Shaunessy clicked a few more times on his screen. 'I've posted it,' he said.

But no one appeared to have heard him. And no one, that night, among the crowd from the Stormy Petrel, gave the wager any more thought.

By midnight, however, Benny's post had been copied and reposted thirty-one times.

By the next morning, it had become a phenomenon.

TWO YEARS AFTER THE WAGER

1. Lykke

Nan Horsmith opened the front door of her cottage on Cliff Street at twenty minutes past four in the morning, when the village was still as silent as the grave, and well before the sun had even shown its face. She was wearing a cotton nightdress. She wore no slippers. She stood, swaying slightly, surveying the doorstep with dismay. A look of concern spread across her face, and her hand began to shake. 'There's no milk!' she called into the house, her voice echoing in the still morning air. 'In't no milk. The milkman 'int been.'

Tom Horsmith emerged, stumbling down the stairs, pulling a T-shirt over his head as he came. 'Nan? What's the matter?'

'There's no milk,' Nan announced, pointing to the doorstep for evidence. 'Look. He in't been.'

Tom laid a hand on his grandmother's shoulder and steered her gently back into the front room. 'Nan, what's the time? It isn't even half past four. Everyone's asleep. The whole village is asleep. You should still be in bed.'

'But there in't any milk,' she protested.

'The milkman never comes before seven. You know that. And he only comes on Tuesdays and Fridays.'

'Then 'ow are we to make breakfast?'

'We make it at eight, Nan.'

Nan Horsmith stopped to consider this. Something clearly wasn't adding up. She shook her head. 'He always comes at twenty past four,' she said. 'George Garrow. Every day. E's as regular as clockwork.'

Tom led her slowly towards the stairs. 'George has been dead for thirty years, Nana,' he said. He exhaled a slow breath, like a sigh. 'Go to bed, Nan.'

'But what about breakfast?'

'I'll buy a pint from Jessie's shop. She's open at six.'

'Six is it?'

'I'll make you breakfast at seven.'

A figure appeared at the top of the stairs, the gangly form of a youth in sleeping shorts but no shirt. 'What's up?'

'It's OK, Connor,' Tom said. 'Nana's coming back to bed. Something woke her.' He started up the steps, moving Nan as if she was a mannequin, both feet on one step, then both feet on the next. 'She's had another one of her turns.'

'She thinks young Mr Garrow is still alive,' Connor said. He came down the stairs to help. 'She does this from time to time.'

'I know.'

'We can get milk from Jessie's. She opens at six.'

'Except on the days when she oversleeps,' Tom said.

'I'll get it,' Connor said.

'That's OK. I'll get it.'

Later, they sat on the bottom step, the two brothers, sharing tea in a chipped mug. The house was quiet. They spoke in soft voices. 'You should get another three hours sleep,' Tom said. 'You'll be knackered for work.'

'I will.' Connor Horsmith was as thin as a broomstick. His eyes seemed shadowed from lack of sleep.

'I'll drive you to work if you like,' Tom said. 'Save you having to walk all the way to the bus.'

'Thanks.'

And later still, at around twenty to five, or just a little earlier, wide awake now and ready for the day, Tom walked alone down the quay and stood hard up against the sea wall, looking out towards the first draft sketches of the sunrise, a smudge of raspberry red like a watercolour stain on an artist's palette, way out to the east among the morning mists. The sea was still dark. Like a velvet cloak all the way to the horizon. Nothing much was stirring. Even the seagulls were still asleep. The tide was low. The fishermen would be all abed.

Yet, how magical St Piran was at this hour, Tom thought. Like rough, unsculpted shapes in a grey mist, the village had yet to emerge into the glare of the day. Occasional streetlamps lit the quay. They cast an orange glow along the fronts of the whitewashed buildings. The shadows were soft and long. Here and there, up among the dark houses that wound up the headland from the harbour, was a light at a window; but this wasn't a community that rose any earlier than it needed to, and when tides were low and a day of work beckoned, it made sense to steal every minute of sleep the night provided.

He stood on the end of the quay. Alone. The saltwater scent in his nostrils. No sound but the *slap slap* of waves on the breakwater.

It felt like an enchanted place, as if the map of the headland and its narrow streets and beach and harbour was somehow encoded into his genes, and when he inhaled, a tiny part of the town was subsumed within the morning vapour and metabolised into his bloodstream, and when he exhaled, a small portion of his own being returned to the village. An exchange of sorts. A sort of contract. An understanding that part of him would always belong here among these ancient stones.

He turned to look back out to sea. The stain that was the rising sun had grown. For a long time, he watched it, the colours leaking into the mist.

And then, behind him, a *tap, tap, tap*. The sound of feet upon flagstones. He didn't turn around. Not at first. The noise seemed like an uncomfortable intrusion into his reverie. There were precious few times when he could experience St Piran completely alone; and now it seemed, one of those moments had passed. Or had been stolen.

Tap. Tap. Tap.

The sound of a woman's walk. A hard shoe on the stone quay.

He turned. Perhaps, after all, it was a friend. An acquaintance even. He caught her eye – the woman with the hard shoes and the *tap tap* footsteps. But no. She was a stranger. A tourist. He could tell that at a glance. A narrow figure in black. Tall. Hooded. Breathing morning steam into the air. She swayed as she walked, as if she were listening to some secret rhythm. *Tap tap*. But now, without intending to, he had looked directly at her; eye contact had been made, and now it would be impossible not to speak. In broad daylight, and among the summer crowds, they could pass each other without a word, or even without a glance. But it was dawn. It was an enchanted time. They were two figures, alone, on the harbour side, dark shapes against the swell of red in the eastern sky. Silence would be uncomfortable.

'Hi.'

The shortest of words. The minimum of effort. He nodded as if this syllable was all he had to say. She could reply with a, '*hi,*' of her own, and then their conversation would be done. Over. No need for anymore. The swell of the Atlantic could do the talking for them. And then, maybe, she would walk away, back into the grey from where she had come.

'It's sunrise on the summer solstice,' she said, as if this was important.

He nodded. 'Yes,' he answered. 'I suppose it is.'

'Did you come out here especially to see it?'

'No,' he said. And then, because this seemed like too brief an answer, he asked, 'Did you?'

'Where I come from, there is no summer solstice,' was her reply.

She seemed faintly oriental. Or maybe not. He found himself looking at her, his curiosity piqued by her comment. No summer solstice? So was she from the tropics? She had narrow eyes, but her long braided hair was earthen, not black. The colour of chalky soil. Unusual, he thought. She was young. Lissom. An energy had been captured in her form.

She breathed again, another lungful of mist. Then her eyes widened just for an instant in a moment of recognition. 'It's you?' she said. She sounded surprised. She slid the hood away from her head, dispensing with the camouflage.

He shrugged his shoulders, as if to say, *and who might you imagine I am?*

'You're Tom. From the viral video.' It was an observation. It wasn't a question. Her accent was faintly northern. Not Scots exactly. Not quite Norwegian.

No summer solstice. Where then?

'That was a long time ago,' he said.

'Two years.'

There was a stillness to her. She let her head tip forward. A single small nod. In the soft glow of sunrise, she had the beauty of an alabaster statue. Her tongue touched her lip and drew back. The still light of a St Piran dawn transformed her into the figure of a goddess.

'Who are you?' he found himself asking. An awkward question. What answer could he possibly expect?

'My name is Lykke,' she said. 'May I stand with you to watch the sunrise?'

And already he had forgotten all else. The milk he had yet to buy. The breakfast he had promised to make. The lift he had offered to his brother. His life. His occupation. His universe. Thus quickly, sometimes, love comes into our lives unannounced. It isn't always an interloper. It doesn't always duel with our wits and our emotions. It doesn't always make unreasonable demands of us. Sometimes love will come and stand beside us to watch a sunrise.

Which is what she did.

Two strangers. They didn't know then that they were in love. They only knew that life could deliver surprises. They couldn't hear their raised heartbeats or smell their musky odours. They couldn't read the signs. Not yet. And so they didn't speak. For a long minute, and then two, they stood in silence and watched the orb of the sun, heavy with meaning, float slowly above the ocean. And for the second of those minutes, Tom fought an almost uncontrollable urge to take her hand. Lykke. This girl who had emerged from the darkness.

Then, at last, she spoke again. 'You weren't entirely honest about the volcanoes,' she said. She wasn't looking at him. Her gaze was still on the far horizon.

The comment caught him unawares, dragging his thoughts back to earth with a bump. Were they to stand here and discuss volcanoes? Really?

'Why?'

'You ignored all the undersea volcanoes.'

Ah. This. 'Seamounts,' he said. He too kept his eyes on the sunrise. 'You're right. I didn't want to confuse the argument.'

'There are thousands of them.'

'Maybe millions. Nearly all extinct. But they don't change the mathematics. We still think humans emit about sixty times the CO_2 of all the volcanoes in the world – including the undersea ones.'

'All the same,' she said, 'you might have spared the poor man a little humiliation if you had acknowledged it at the time.'

Tom opened his mouth to reply, and then he caught himself. He was about to defend his action. He might have said he had no obligation to spare the feelings of a climate denier. Or words to that effect. But something about this curious conversation made him stop. The young woman wasn't challenging his conclusions. Only his lack of empathy. So instead he said, 'Perhaps you're right.' It felt like the right thing to say.

Maybe it was even the truth.

'Why do you dislike him so much?' she asked.

'Who?'

'The politician.'

'Do I dislike him?'

'I think you do,' she said.

And once again they stood in silence. A different sort of silence. Tom felt slightly bruised by the exchange. Lykke was not the first stranger who had cornered him to talk about the video, but no one, until now, had thought to suggest he might have taken a kinder approach.

'Am I allowed to dislike his politics?' he asked her after a while, avoiding her eye, and trying not to sound too defensive.

She shrugged. 'You're allowed to dislike whatever you choose to dislike,' she said. 'It's your choice. Just don't be surprised if people ask you why.'

The day was growing brighter.

'Be careful that hatred doesn't consume you, Tom,' she said. 'I think you're a better person than that.'

'I think, perhaps... you're a better person than me,' he said.

'I don't suppose we will ever know,' was her reply.

In the east, the sun was a huge yellow disc, radiating fingers of light across the sea. They watched the glow of colours reflecting in streaks between the waves.

'Have you ever been fishing?' he asked her. His heart felt like a loose animal in his chest.

Her reply was almost a laugh. 'I come from a family of fishermen.'

'Do you?' Was that good or not? 'I was going to ask, perhaps, if you wanted to go fishing. Later this afternoon. Maybe midday. When the tide is up. My friend Benny has a boat. He calls it the *best boat in the water*.' He was gabbling. He pointed to a small trawler in the harbour, resting on its side in the shallow mud. 'There. *Piranesi*.' He gave a shrug of his shoulders. 'But I suppose if you come from a family of fishermen...'

She looked at him and there was an unexpected warmth in her expression. 'I would enjoy a ride out on the boat,' she said. 'I think I would enjoy it very much. But I ought to tell you, I don't eat fish.'

'You come from a family of fishermen, and you don't eat fish!' Tom sounded incredulous.

'I know.' She gave a smile. 'I am a mess of contradictions.'

'Then maybe we should do something different,' he said.

'Can I make a suggestion?'

'Of course.'

'Before our boat trip, if we have time, I would like to visit a wildflower meadow. Do you know any near St Piran? We don't have these in my hometown.'

'I can take you to my favourite spot,' he said. He was thinking of the way the cliff path wound out of Treadangel woods into the summer meadows. There would be buttercups and harebells and oxeye daisies. Nan would collect lavender there in June. There should be wild poppies, sweet peas, and red campion flowers. And the butterflies would be all at work. And the grasses would be long. 'It's the best time of year to see it.'

'I should like that very much.'

For a long moment they looked at each other.

'There is one thing I should probably say,' she added.

He held his breath.

'After all,' she said, 'the only things I know about you are from that video.'

'Yes?'

'Happy birthday,' she said.

2. Poppies

They lay on their backs in the deep grass, close, but not too close, their heads not quite touching, looking upwards into the cloudless blue of the summer sky.

'This is the most wonderful thing I could imagine,' Lykke declared.

Wonderful? The meadow ground was stony and uncomfortable beneath them. Grass stalks dug sharply into their backs. There were retinues of ants exploring the foraging opportunities provided by their bare limbs. Wonderful?

Yes. Somehow it *was* wonderful. The meadow was bursting with life. A fat bumble bee with a loud buzz hovered briefly above them, and then was gone. There were butterflies and ladybirds, and the calls of songbirds and gulls. There was a bank of wild poppies. Everywhere smelled of summer. Of pollen and hay and mysterious flowers.

'I could lie here all day,' Lykke said.

'We can stay as long as you want,' Tom said, and in that moment, he knew this was true.

'I should love to live close to a meadow like this one,' Lykke said. 'I would come to lie here every day. Imagine all the creatures that live here.' She sat up and looked out across the field, the little oasis of grassland and wildflowers where they lay, the tall trees of Treadangel Woods on one side and the ocean cliffs to the other. 'I think the Garden of Eden must have been like this.'

'It surely was,' Tom said. 'I always say there is no more beautiful place on God's earth than Piran Head.'

'Then you're lucky to live here.' She was lying back down.

'I know.'

He propped himself up and surveyed her. 'May I kiss you?'

She closed her eyes. Slowly. 'Are Englishmen always so polite?'

'Cornishmen are.'

'You may.'

Afterwards they held hands, unselfconsciously, as they picked their way down the cliff path to the village. Polly Hocking saw them from the garden of the vicarage, and she gave them a wave. Demelza Trevarrick was climbing the hill as they were coming down. They passed on the cobbles, and Lykke was resting her head on Tom's shoulder.

'Thomas Horsmith,' Demelza purred approvingly, 'you have such impeccable taste. Who is this young goddess?'

'This is Lykke Norgaard,' Tom said, unable to conceal the smile that had colonised his face.

'Norgaard?' Demelza said, sweeping up Lykke's hand and planting a kiss upon her knuckles. 'Is that a Danish name?'

'It is,' Lykke said.

'In St Piran, we have a special place in our hearts for Danish people,' Demelza said.

'Thank you.'

'Demelza is our local celebrity,' Tom said. 'She's a famous novelist.'

'Pah!' Demelza waved this compliment away. 'Tom is already way more famous than I shall ever be. Are you enjoying St Piran?'

'I'm loving it.'

'I do hope you're not planning to take this lovely creature back to London with you Tom,' Demelza said. 'Not immediately. I want us to get better acquainted.'

'I have to leave tonight,' Lykke said. She looked crestfallen at this.

'Well, I would urge you to rethink,' Demelza said. 'Both of you. There are times,' she said, 'when staying is absolutely the right thing to do.'

It was a perfect afternoon. The sun shone all day. They took the promised trip around the bay on *Piranesi* with Benny at the wheel. Tom pointed out the smugglers' caves, and showed Lykke the beach where once a whale had washed ashore, and in the distance, they saw dolphins playing in the spray.

They bought ice creams, and they walked together to the very end of Piran Head and watched the gulls circling. They sat on the headland and let their arms wind around each other. There were shearwaters skimming over the waves and kittiwakes almost motionless in the ocean breeze. It is possible, however, that Tom and Lykke didn't notice these things. Highly likely, you might think.

What an opportunist human biology can be. We can be puppets, we frail humans, dancing to the pull of its strings. We can live on this earth for two decades or more, we can meet ten thousand people, and all this while our hidden hormones bide their time, absent from our lives until a moment comes, unheralded and unexpected, when they flood our fragile frames with their unfamiliar beckoning. Lykke Norgaard had awakened in Tom a kind of circuitry he hadn't known was there. The contours of her face. The music of her voice. The light in her eyes. These felt like missing jigsaw pieces in the puzzle of his life, as if the space had always been there and only one face could ever fill it, only one voice, only one being. 'I want to know everything about you,' he told her.

'And me, you,' she answered.

And human biology, wanting more, could not be satisfied with this. There was a role now for hands, for lips, for bodies. For touch.

All of this beneath the June skies of Piran head, with the call of the seagulls, and the soft grass, and the scent of the sea all around them.

But every day has to end. Time can be a cruel mistress. A taxi pre-arranged and inevitable, rolled onto the quay at a quarter past six and pulled up outside the Fin Whale Hotel. Tom stood erect like a statue, like a bystander, while Lykke and her suitcase were closed away and the doors were slammed. As the taxi drove away, he blew Lykke a kiss. She may not have seen it.

At around eight in the evening, the solitary figure of Thomas Horsmith might have been seen in the lobsterman's bar at The Stormy Petrel with a single glass of cider.

'Drowning our sorrows are we, Tom?' Jason Anderssen the barman remarked. 'Has it been a hard day?'

'It's been a perfect day,' Tom said. But his voice sounded far away.

Jason wiped the bar with a cloth. He wiped it again. He was a man fully able to decipher the complex language of unspoken sighs from solitary drinkers at a bar. This is a skill set that barmen possess. 'Is it a girl?' he asked.

'A girl?'

'I saw you with a girl.'

'It isn't a girl,' Tom said. 'It isn't anything.'

'Where's Benny tonight?'

'Fishing. On *Piranesi*. They'll be out all night.'

'Ah.' Jason wiped the beer taps. 'Would you like some advice?' he offered.

'I don't need advice, Jason,' Tom said. 'I just need a quiet drink.'

'Today's your birthday, isn't it?' Jason asked.

'Everyone seems to know my birthday.' Tom looked down into his drink.

'Well then,' Jason said. 'I'm allowed to offer advice on a customer's birthday. You have to consider it a birthday gift and be grateful for it. That's the way it works.'

Tom issued a sigh like a surrender. 'I already know what your advice will be, Jason.'

'You do?'

'*Talk to Demelza.*' He fixed the barman with a look. 'That's what you were going to tell me, isn't it?'

Jason hung his cloth over a beer tap and smiled. 'Happen it might have been.'

'Well,' Tom said, 'I don't need Demelza's advice and I don't need yours. What I need,' he said, holding up his glass, 'is a steady supply of cider and a little thinking time.'

It was quiet in the bar. But the evening grew busier as early diners from the Beachcomber Bistro and the Fin Whale Hotel repaired to the Petrel for after dinner drinks, and locals began to make an appearance. At around nine o'clock, with the lobsterman's bar feeling almost full, a barstool was pushed up to the bar right next to Tom, and a woman lifted herself onto it. 'A gin and tonic, and a whisky with ice,' she called to Jason.

'Good evening, Demelza,' Tom said.

'And another cider for the birthday boy!'

There could be no escape from the ambush. Demelza was on one side, and Jeremy was right behind him.

'Happy birthday, old chap,' Jeremy said, accompanying this benediction with a rueful grin.

'And where, pray, is the Danish goddess?' Demelza asked. 'Miss Norgaard?'

Tom waved a hand almost nonchalantly. 'I would imagine,' he said, 'she is on the night train to London.'

'The night train to London,' echoed Demelza.

'So far as I know.'

'And after that?'

'And after that, who knows?' Tom said. He was shaking his head. 'Off to wherever she has to go, I suppose.'

'Off to wherever she has to go?' Demelza made this echo sound simultaneously unlikely and outrageous. 'Wherever. She. Has. To. Go?'

'Yes.' Tom was avoiding her eye. 'Demelza, I know you want to turn every village encounter into one of your romantic stories, but you don't need to do that with me and Lykke. Please. I would rather you didn't. We only met this morning. We spent a pleasant afternoon. I showed her around the village. And now she has had to go. There you have it. Not enough material for a novel, is it?' Tom took a drink of cider and put his glass back down with rather a heavy thump.

'I see,' Demelza said. She turned to look at Jeremy. 'Darling,' she said, 'would you mind awfully taking a seat at that table over there?' She nodded at a table for two in the far corner of the room. It may have been the last unoccupied space. 'I shall come and join you in five minutes. Ten minutes at most.'

'If you say so my love,' Jeremy said. He knew when he was being dismissed. He laid a hand on Tom's shoulder. 'Good luck,' he said.

'I don't need it,' Tom said.

'I rather think you do.'

With Jeremy away, Demelza moved her barstool so their shoulders now touched. 'How long have you known me, Tom?'

'Is this how your advice starts?'

'How long have you known me?' Demelza was not to be shaken off. 'Tell me.'

Tom sighed. 'All my life I suppose.'

'Can you trust me?'

'Of course.'

'Good. So here's the thing, Tom. You know about volcanoes. I know about people. You could say, people are my expertise. People *in love* are my expertise.'

'I'm not in love,' Tom said. It was almost a groan. 'Like I said, we only met this morning.'

'Why was she here? In St Piran? Is she a holidaymaker?'

'No,' Tom said. 'She was in Cornwall for a conference. Yesterday. In St Ives. You probably read about it. They're campaigning for a big marine park. They want all the coast of Cornwall and Devon to be protected. Like a big National Park, but at sea. Lykke was one of the speakers, I think.'

'You think?'

'She was,' Tom corrected himself. 'She was one of the main proposers of the idea.'

'A national park?' Demelza said.

'At sea.'

'No fishing allowed?'

Tom paused and dropped his gaze. 'No.'

'And what would Peter and Benny make of that? Or the Robins brothers? Or the Bartles?'

'I don't know,' Tom said. His voice was quiet. 'I haven't asked them.'

'I see,' Demelza said. She seemed to be assimilating this information for a moment and then she brushed it away with a hand. 'No matter,' she said. 'She's a campaigner then, this Lykke Norgaard? Zealous perhaps? Passionate?'

'I suppose so. She's writing a book'

'A book?' Demelza raised her eyebrows. 'Makes her interesting, doesn't it?'

'She's interesting anyway,' Tom said.

'Tell me why,' Demelza said. She held his gaze. 'Tell me why Miss Norgaard is so interesting. I want to know.'

Tom blew out a mouthful of air. 'She's an environmentalist...'

'Like you?'

'No,' Tom said. 'Not like me. I'm the kind of environmentalist who shuts himself away in his room and writes essays about glaciers and gets into stupid arguments in the pub. She's the kind of environmentalist who changes things; who gets laws changed; who sets up research foundations; who gets countries to create marine parks. She persuaded the Danish government to set aside three thousand square kilometres of farmland to plant trees for biomass heating schemes. She's writing a book about the melting ice shelf in Greenland. She runs an organisation that wants to save the world. Literally. She fills lecture halls all around Europe, and when she speaks, her audience cries. I've been reading all about her on social media. She has millions of followers. She is a very rare thing, Demelza. So no, she's not like me at all. She belongs way up here.' He held his hand high above his head. 'While I'm way down there.' He dropped his hand to knee height. 'I don't belong in her universe, Demelza. That's why I don't need your advice. I know you mean it kindly. But I had a really nice day with her, and I should like to remember that day, and not have to argue about it. Not even with you.'

Demelza laid her hand on Tom's shoulder and spun him on his seat so they were face to face. 'So here's the thing, Tom. Listen to this please. This is my expertise. First, I want you to know that was one of the most touching things I have ever heard. And I have heard a lot of touching stories. But leave that aside. It isn't that I want you to listen to. You see Tom, I climb Fish Street every day, up from the village to my cottage, maybe two or three times a day, every day, and most days I meet people coming down – strangers mostly – and I look at their faces, and I say hello. Lots of couples come down that way. I've seen you come down there with girls before. There was Penny Thoroughgood. I remember her. And that girl with frizzy hair...'

'Alice Trevithick.'

'That's her. Amazing legs. Anyway. You get the point. I see a lot of couples. It's the main route down from the cliff path, and every couple wants to walk the cliffs when they're courting. You would be surprised how much I can tell about them. I spot these things. How close they walk. How much in step. How much notice they take of anyone or anything apart from each other. How high they float above the ground.'

Jason appeared with the drinks. Demelza sent him off in the direction of Jeremy's table.

'You say you trust me, Tom. Then please trust me on this. I've seen hundreds of couples coming down from the cliff path. I've never seen any couple so obviously in love as you and Lykke Norgaard.'

'Demelza...'

'Don't try telling me you only met this morning. I already know that. Heaven knows I'm not a great believer in instant attraction, but it does happen from time to time, thank heaven, and you two are the proof. You don't think you belong in her universe. Well I think you do. Do you think she enjoyed the day as much as you did?'

Tom looked down. 'I hope she did.'

'Well I'm here to tell you she did. I could read it in her face. Is she in an existing relationship?'

'No.'

'Are you?'

'No.'

'And are you planning to stay in touch?'

Tom shook his head. 'We thought it would be too difficult,' he said. His voice was cracking slightly.

'Too difficult!' Demelza said, her tone suggesting complete exasperation.

'We had a lovely day. We thought we could keep it as a special memory.'

'Why are young lovers so dense?' Demelza asked. 'A special memory? Dear goodness.'

'She lives an impossible distance away,' Tom said.

'Mars is an impossible distance,' Demelza said. 'Denmark isn't.'

'She's nearly five years older than me.'

'Oh dear! Five years!' Demelza snapped, with a heavy tone of sarcasm. 'Five years! Just as well you scrapped the whole thing then.' She held Tom close so their faces almost touched. 'Seriously? When did that ever matter? Ever? Anne Hathaway was eight years older than Shakespeare. Brigitte Macron was...'

'I just think perhaps you're making too much of it,' Tom said, interrupting her. He was still shaking his head.

'Tom Horsmith, do you think I'm a fool? You're sitting in the Stormy Petrel drinking on your own which is something you never do, something no one should ever do, and what's more it's your birthday. Does it hurt?'

Tom blinked. 'Does what hurt?'

Demelza looked at him in the way a teacher might survey a schoolboy unable to spell a simple word. 'Do *you* hurt?' she said.

'Is it painful?'

'Demelza, I...'

'Does it hurt?'

He dropped his gaze. 'Some,' he said.

'Some?'

'A lot.'

Demelza made a sound like a hrrmph. 'At last we're getting somewhere. What are you doing at the moment?' she demanded. 'Are you working?'

'I've just finished an MSc degree.'

'So you're not in full time employment?'

'Not exactly. I'm helping Benny and Peter on the boat.'

'That doesn't count.' Demelza was clicking her tongue. 'How long is she staying in London? Lykke Norgaard? Before she goes on to *wherever it is she is going*?'

Tom gave a heavy sigh. 'She isn't staying in London,' he said. 'She's flying tomorrow. Heathrow to Copenhagen. And then onwards from there.'

Demelza gave a snort of irritation. 'Darling, you don't make things easy for us do you?' she said. She slid off the barstool and took his arm. 'Leave that there,' she said, pointing at the undrunk cider. 'Come with me.'

'Really, Demelza, you don't need to do this.'

'I can't remember a single time when I've needed to do it more.'

They threaded through the crowded bar to Jeremy's table. 'Don't drink that, darling.' Demelza snatched the whisky glass from Jeremy's hand. 'You need to keep a clear head.'

'A clear head?'

'You're driving.'

'Driving?' Jeremy looked startled.

'This silly ass has drunk too much cider to drive himself,' Demelza said.

'And where are we going?' Jeremy was rising from his seat.

'Exeter Airport,' Demelza said. 'We need to get Tom onto the six am flight to Heathrow.' She turned to Tom. 'Go and chuck some clothes into a bag and get back here in ten minutes,' she said. She gave him a shove.

'Really, Demelza, I...'

'Don't argue with me. Go!'

There was a moment. And then Tom was out of the bar. There was almost a spring to his step.

'Thank God Jason had the good sense to call me,' Demelza said. She took Jeremy's arm. 'Go and get the car,' she said. 'If we can't get him on the early flight, we'll have to drive him to London. I'll explain on the way.'

TEN YEARS AFTER THE WAGER

1. That damned video

His Majesty's Government's Department for the Environment and Climate – the awkwardly named DEAC – occupied a building in Marsham Street, London, ten minutes' walk south and east of the Houses of Parliament. Symbolically, for any member heading there on foot, this would be the opposite direction from the route taken by those members setting off towards Whitehall, Downing Street, and most of the great offices of state. Right away this said something about the status of Environment as a government department. It was, you might have said, just a little out of mind. Despite this, however, Causley did the ten-minute walk with a smile on his face. Who cared if DEAC was seen as a backwater? He was a minister. A fully-fledged member of the cabinet. For a man whose career had seemed blighted for too many years, this was reward enough.

He strode purposefully across Parliament Square towards Westminster Abbey. This was the best part of the walk. There in the square were statues of several great luminaries. He always enjoyed seeing them. Benjamin Disraeli was there, looking rather stern in his Victorian robes. There too was Abraham Lincoln, and

Nelson Mandela, although Lincoln was unaccountably consigned to the less auspicious side of Parliament Street along with David Lloyd George. Two difficult provincials perhaps. A statue of Millicent Garrett Fawcett always drew Monty's uncomfortable attention to the dominance in the square of male figures. The great suffragette campaigner bore a banner which read, 'COURAGE CALLS TO COURAGE EVERYWHERE,' an inspiring, if abstruse call to arms. *'Audaces fortuna iuvat,'* Monty would whisper to himself as he passed her. His family motto. *Fortune favours the brave.* Mahatma Ghandi was there, looking solemn. Like Disraeli, he too was dressed in robes – just simpler ones. He was in Parliament Square in recognition for his struggle for the independence of India. Winston Churchill, garrulous and leaning on a stick, had a prominent place *despite* his resistance to the independence of India. Monty Causley reflected, as he always did on this walk, on the diversity of human endeavour and endurance on display. Like every politician who ever crossed the square, he would flirt with the unfathomable idea that one day, maybe, he, Montague Causley might be memorialised here. But the thought never lasted long. He had the Department of the Environment and Climate to wrestle with. An exciting new brief. A challenge.

'You know why you got this job, don't you?' colleagues would quip, eternally amused by the delicious irony of it all. 'It's that damned video.'

That damned video. All these years later it still haunted him. Only a week ago, an opposition politician had risen to his feet in the House, during an environment debate, and had intoned, *'The new minister shouldn't try to argue if he doesn't understand the science,'* and the comment had earned its traditional bellow of laughter – not all of it from the opposition benches. Memories could be long in politics. He had learned to adopt a weary expression on these occasions, like a schoolteacher with an impossible child.

'The honourable member should get himself some new jokes,' he had replied acidly, but this too had earned a laugh from much the same corners of the chamber.

That damned video.

'It has killed my career,' he used to say to Carys. 'I'm toxic. I will never make the front bench.'

Yet here he was, ten years later, with a seat in the cabinet. So it hadn't all been bad. And oddly, just as his critics would say, the video – the *damn* video – had played a part in helping him to secure the job. He had been to see the Prime Minister in February, a few weeks before the last cabinet reshuffle. He wasn't there to ask for a job. He was there from the whips' office on a party matter. But the omens were not entirely bad. They had been friends, he and the new Prime Minister, since their first session in parliament when, both in their early thirties, they had shared an office. Her career had blossomed, however, while his... well, his had not. But Monty had been one of her most vocal supporters in the leadership election. And fortune, as they say, favours the brave. *Audaces fortuna iuvat.* So, he asked her anyway. 'The papers are saying you're planning a reshuffle,' he said, when their meeting had ended. He made it sound more like a question than a statement. He looked at her for a response.

'It's no big secret,' she replied. She offered him a smile. 'There are one or two changes I should like to see. But it's a delicate balancing act. I don't intend to rush it. And I don't plan to do what every Prime Minister has always done before me and drop people overnight into new jobs when they haven't got a clue about the brief.'

'No?' Monty sounded curious.

'No,' she said firmly. 'I want to give new ministers a few months to learn what they can about their new portfolios before making any announcements. That way they can hit the ground running.'

'So you plan to pick a new cabinet and... what?'

The Prime Minister smiled again. 'I shall announce the reshuffle in the summer,' she said. 'Probably the first week in July. But I will let candidates know informally, and completely off the record, this week, or next. That gives them four months to learn everything they can.' She gave him a look. 'And in that time, I still have the right to change my mind,' she said.

'Will there be anything for me?' he asked.

The question seemed to catch the Prime Minister unawares. 'Monty, darling, were you expecting something?'

'Hoping perhaps,' he said, trying not to sound desperate.

'I would love to,' she said. 'I really would. You're a smart guy, Monty. And loyal. And I like you. But I don't have anything suitable for you. Nothing you would be happy with. I have a rather long list of names and a rather short list of vacancies, I'm afraid.'

'Thank you anyway, Prime Minister,' he said. But as he turned to leave, she filled the awkward silence that followed, with an unexpected remark.

'The only thing I have is Environment,' she said, and she laughed as she said it, expecting perhaps that he might laugh along too. 'And we couldn't do that now, could we?'

That damned video!

'Why not?' He turned back to face her, feeling a flushing in his face. 'Why not give me Environment?'

'You *know* why Monty.' She gave him her dismissive expression. 'People still see you as a climate-denier. I can't do anything about that.'

'But that's precisely *why* I would be perfect for Environment! Don't you see? They used to say, "Only Nixon could go to China." Because if Richard Nixon, a hard-line critic of China, could be persuaded to go, then voters would know it was serious. If anyone else went, it would be appeasement. Isn't this the same? If Monty Causley the arch sceptic, can be persuaded to make a case for...,' he waved a hand creatively, '...closing down a coal mine, say, then people will sit up and take notice. Because they will know I wasn't just a pushover for some trendy green agenda.'

The Prime Minister gave him a thin smile. 'Are there still any coal mines?' she asked. 'I thought we had closed them all.' She drew a deep breath. 'You always have a clever answer, Monty,' she said. 'I will give you that.' She turned her attention to papers on her desk.

He pushed a little further. 'So, why not? Why not offer me DEAC? I would be perfect for it.'

'You do know,' she said, 'that every interview you would ever give to the media, no matter what the subject, would be hijacked by that wretched viral post.'

'I know, Prime Minister... but...'

'They would play the clips endlessly. They would ask you about that ridiculous wager. Every single time.' She looked up at him. Her expression was inscrutable.

Monty gave a nervous cough. 'I daresay the young man could be persuaded to waive the bet now,' he said. 'After all, it was nearly ten years ago, we were both young. And he had been drinking, and...'

'And what if he won't? What if he won't withdraw the bet? You'll never be able to give a serious interview without being reminded of it.'

'Well, if he doesn't withdraw, it still helps us,' Monty answered. 'Look at it this way. If I don't want to lose the bet and drown in my own home, and of course I don't, I have to work to keep global warming *down*. That should be obvious really. If I fail in the job, I die. Powerful incentive, don't you think, for doing a good job?'

'Oh, I wouldn't worry about losing the bet,' the Prime Minister said, somewhat dismissively. 'That isn't the problem. You'll never live to ninety anyway. The problem is having it hanging over you. Some stories never quite go away.'

'I see. Well, thank you for your honesty, Prime Minister.'

'If I am ever in a position to offer you any sort of promotion, Monty, I will want you to withdraw from this wager. It's the only way it will ever go away.'

'Yes, Prime Minister.'

'If you can do it mutually by agreement with the young man, so much the better. If he won't agree, you need to back out anyway. Publicly. Everyone needs to see it's over.'

'Won't that make me look weak, Prime Minister?'

She looked at him with an expression that failed to provide him with any confidence. 'Dear God, Monty, this shouldn't be about how you look! Anyway, withdrawing would make you look like the bigger man.'

Causley gulped. 'If you give me Environment,' he said, 'I will cash-out of the bet on live television.'

The Prime Minister seemed to consider this. She nodded slowly. 'OK. Talk to Esperanza,' she said, after a moment. 'Come up with a plan to extricate yourself with dignity, and we'll see what we can do.'

Esperanza Mulligan was the Prime Minister's Director of Communications, a key advisor and political strategist. Causley made an effort not to roll his eyes at the sound of her name.

'So, talk to Esperanza?' he echoed, doubtfully.

'Yes. She is advising me on the reshuffle. Talk to her. Come up with a plan.'

'I will. Thank you. Thank you.' Two *thank-yous*. Was that a mistake? Did it sound desperate? Perhaps it didn't matter anymore.

'You may go now, Monty,' was her reply. The hint of a smile was playing on her lips. And as he was stepping through the door, he heard her say, 'I shall think about it.'

The Prime Minister's advisory team occupied two ground-floor offices in 10 Downing Street at the rear of the building, next door to the Prime Minister's meeting room. They shared, with the Prime Minister's parliamentary private secretary, a conference room with windows that looked out onto the garden. Esperanza Mulligan kept Causley waiting for twenty minutes in an anteroom. It was a small, barely decorated room with four hard chairs. A poster on the wall showed a dishevelled looking Albert Einstein, and beneath him a quotation. *In the midst of every crisis, lies great opportunity.*

Was this a crisis, Monty wondered? It was certainly an opportunity.

A harassed looking PA put his head around the door. 'I'm sorry,' he told Monty. 'Her agenda is running late.'

'I can wait.'

When finally he was admitted, Esperanza was at an oval meeting table tapping keys on a laptop computer. She was a smart-looking woman, perhaps in her early forties, with dark curled hair wound up into a ponytail. She barely glanced up as he entered. 'Causley,' she said in such a quiet voice he might easily have missed it, and she gestured towards a chair. 'Sit.' There were no introductions made and no preamble.

'Shall we watch it together?' she asked, as he sat down. She spun the screen of her computer around so he could see it.

The video.

'Do we have to?'

'I need to remind myself of everything that was said,' she explained. 'It's a while since I watched it.'

And so, for several excruciating minutes, Monty endured a decade-old replay of his encounter in the Stormy Petrel with Tom Horsmith. To make the meeting even more uncomfortable, Esperanza insisted on pausing the film from time to time, even rewinding it when she felt she had missed something, to scribble down a note or to ask a question.

The personal assistant Monty had met earlier, sat at the end of the table taking minutes.

When it was done, Esperanza tapped absently on her teeth with her pen. 'Worse than I remembered.'

'Really?'

'You come over as arrogant, opinionated, bombastic, and idiotic.'

Monty squirmed at this assessment. 'Is that all?'

'Over-privileged, self-centred, and scientifically illiterate.' Esperanza dropped her gaze. 'On the other hand...'

'Yes?'

'On the other hand, the other chap has his failings too.'

'Horsmith?' Causley's spirits lifted briefly at this observation.

'Yes. He looks drunk. It isn't a good look. His hair is rather long. Makes him look like a liberal. Middle England isn't too keen on that. And he's cocky.'

'He really is.'

'But likeable,' she said. 'And that's what matters most. He comes over as likeable. You don't.'

'That's a bit brutal,' Monty objected.

'Monty, I'm not here to spare your feelings. I'm here to figure out if we can neutralise this stain on your career.'

'Right.'

'So this is what we need,' Esperanza said. She turned towards her PA. 'Can you write this down please, Martin,' she instructed.

'Yes, Madam.'

'If the PM offers Mr Causley the Environment portfolio... *if* she does... we will need a new video as powerful and impactful as this one. A sequel, if you like. Same two protagonists. Much more controlled environment. It will need to be convivial, jokey, and self-effacing. Our man needs to come over as modest... yet brilliant, apologetic, with a good sense of humour. He needs to look like someone any woman would take on a date. Or any man.' She stood, turning her back on them both, and she walked to the window. For a moment, she seemed to be admiring the gardens.

The PA stopped scribbling and looked up.

'We will need to coach our man carefully,' Esperanza said, as if Causley wasn't still in the room listening. She turned to look directly at Causley. 'Several months of tough homework.' She raised an eyebrow. 'If you are to be offered the environment job, I want you bang up to date with every fact and statistic and piece of research on climate science. Can you do that Monty?'

Causley hesitated. There was only one possible answer to this question. 'Er, yes. Absolutely. Yes.'

'Not good enough. The PM has put me in charge of presentation. She wants the government's message to be effectively and professionally presented in the media and in parliament. We don't want any amateurs. Which means whoever gets appointed to Environment must be an expert. If you get this job, I will need you on the ball, Monty. Like a contestant on *Mastermind*. Special subject global warming. I shall need you to know every arcane detail. *Every single one*.' Esperanza made a punching motion with her fist as she said these words. 'If Horsmith knows there are 500 volcanoes, you must know every one of their names, and the dates of their eruptions, and the exact amount of carbon dioxide each one put into the atmosphere, and the authors of the scientific papers that came up with the figures, and the names and birthdays of their children. You'll need to be able to recite the dimensions and locations of every major glacier, and the rate of melting, and the depths of the oceans, and when you come up with these facts on camera, you have to be able to do it without screwing up your forehead or rolling your eyes as if you're struggling to remember unfamiliar things. You need to know them instantly, without any effort, just as if you were giving us the capital of France, or the president of Russia, or the date of your wedding anniversary.' She narrowed her eyes. 'When is your wedding anniversary, Monty?'

'It's... er... the ninth of August.'

Esperanza looked unimpressed. 'You need to be a lot quicker than that. If the PM gives you this job, then your first few months are going to be like being back at school. But a lot tougher.'

'Right,' Monty said, trying to sound positive.

'We'll want you and Horsmith back in the same pub, but this time *we'll* be doing the filming, not some drunken fisherman with a cell phone. And we'll need a script for you. Something you can memorise and deliver convincingly, however the conversation develops. Something that will look and sound natural but which will have been carefully crafted and written by a hotshot screenwriter. Would you be able to do that?'

'Of course. Yes,' Causley said, trying to conceal the doubt in his voice.

'You have one job as a minister,' Esperanza said. 'Only one job. Your job is to be totally in command of your brief, so when you do interviews you don't come over as a dick.'

'Really?' Monty looked surprised. 'There must be more to it than that.'

Esperanza let out a snort. 'Welcome to government, Mr Causley. Let me make this plain. There are hundreds of very smart, very educated, very committed people in DEAC. Civil servants who have lived with this brief *all* their careers. People who have read every book available on the subject and attended every major conference for the last twenty years, and even written a book or two of their own.' She raised a finger. 'You would be just one member of a very experienced team. What's more, you'd be the new boy. In any other business, you'd be making the tea. But this is government, and everything is back to front. So yes, your only job will be to look good on the media and to make the Prime Minister look good. You have no useful ideas to contribute, and no policies that haven't already been through a dozen think-tanks. Get used to that. If you still have the PM's confidence at the beginning of July, we will have to make do with you. Do this job well and who knows... you could be Foreign Secretary next year. Or Chancellor. Cock it up and you'll grow old on the back benches.'

Causley gulped. 'I understand.'

'Do you work out?' she asked.

'Work out?'

'In the gym?'

'Er... No.' He shook his head. 'Not especially.'

'It shows. I want you in the gym. An hour a day. On the weights. Let's get some upper-body strength, shall we? And get yourself a tan. Not too much. But you need to look good. Fit. Buffed. You're going to be debating a thirty-year-old. We need you looking good.'

'OK.'

'And someone from my team will be in touch about your clothes.'

'My clothes?'

'You'll be in the pub for this encounter. You won't want a pinstripe suit. Someone from my team will phone you for your measurements. You'll need to look cooler than Horsmith, if that's possible. Fashionable, but not stupid. Trendsetting – perhaps.' She surveyed him as if he were a sample in a jar. 'Maybe a collarless jacket,' she suggested. 'A grey rollneck. Let's wait and see how ripped you get by the summer. We may need to see your arms.'

'Yes, Ma'am,' Monty said.

'Good.' Esperanza turned her gaze back to the window. 'The PM would be taking a big risk with you, Monty. Against my advice, I should add. She clearly thinks you're smart. Don't let her down.'

'I won't.'

There was a moment of silence.

'Are you happy with the plan?'

Monty was brooding. 'I guess....'

'Yes?'

There was something of a gleam in Monty's eye. Ten years of wounded pride was swelling up inside him like a river backing up behind a failing dam. 'It's just... I can't help thinking...'

'What?'

Should he do this? Somewhere in his mind the family motto was still swirling. Courage, in the Causley family, had always favoured the brave. He took a breath. 'I can't help thinking... it isn't enough.'

Esperanza turned back from the window, a curious smile playing on her lips. 'Don't minute this, Martin,' she told her PA. She sat back down at the table and flexed her wrists. To Monty she said, 'Explain?'

Causley's chin seemed to jut out. 'Just that. *It isn't enough*,' he said again. 'Just cancelling the bet; it's not enough.'

'Why not?'

Monty's hand tightened into a fist, and he thumped it down onto the table. 'Because the little shit has blighted my career for ten years with his cocky little viral video. So now what do we do? We give him an opportunity to be a smug prick all over again? I don't think so. I want to do to him what he did to me. I want to humiliate him. I want people to laugh at him every time they see him. I want them to say, *you're the silly ass in that video.* I want him to feel acute embarrassment every time he thinks about it.' His hand banged down a second time. 'I want to destroy him. I want to *fucking* destroy him.'

Esperanza liked this. Her smile widened. 'Don't you like him, Monty?' she asked, her question oozing with sarcasm.

'I want to *finish* him,' Monty said.

Esperanza said, 'Don't minute any of this, Martin.' She held out a slim forefinger to emphasise the instruction, until the PA acknowledged the gesture with a nod. She turned to Monty. 'I understand how you feel, Monty. You have some personal animosity towards this young man. We can use that passion. But you understand it would be wholly unprofessional of me to give you any advice on how to make Horsmith look foolish.'

'I know,' Monty said. 'It's just...'

'The best thing you can do is to focus on your own performance.'

'Yes.'

She lowered her voice. 'But I will say, Mr Causley, that it will be crucial for *you* to keep a clear head for this encounter. Do you follow me?'

The PA, Martin, looked up from his notepad and gave a cough. 'I missed those last few comments,' he said. 'May I restart the minutes?'

'You may.'

A look passed between Monty Causley and the Director of Communications.

'How are we planning to get Horsmith to agree to a second video?' the PA asked.

For a few moments, Esperanza seemed lost in a reverie. She turned back to Causley. 'You will have to do that, Monty,' she said.

'He'll agree to it. I'm sure of it. He'll enjoy the fame. And if he can't make up his mind, I'm sure we have all sorts of leverage we can use.' She tapped her fingernail on the desk. 'But let's not give him too much notice. We don't want him to have as much time as you to prepare. We won't film the exchange until mid-summer. On your birthdays again, so that it resonates with the original. That will give us four months to get you word-perfect. I suggest you approach him a week or so before.'

'Right,' Causley said. He sounded uncertain.

'You have a problem with the plan?'

'No. No, not at all. It's just... well, what if he won't agree? He's quite a hot-headed young chap.'

Esperanza gave a knowing smile. 'Find a way,' she said. 'Find a way to persuade him.'

'OK,' Monty said.

'Do it in person. Face to face. Not over the phone. Try not to let him know how much you hate him. Can you do that?'

'I can try.'

Esperanza looked satisfied with this. 'You can combine it with a visit to your constituency.'

Causley gave a nervous cough. 'I don't believe Horsmith is in Cornwall now. Not right now.'

'Then where is he?'

'I'm not altogether sure.'

'Not to worry,' Esperanza said, and she gave a rather fetching smile. 'Wherever he is, I'm sure Martin can track him down.'

'Splendid.'

'Let's hope he isn't at the far ends of the earth.'

2. Ultima Thule...

It was snowing. But only gently. A flurry of soft white flakes, like petals of apple blossom, was blowing east to west across the road. Just a gentle warning of something altogether fiercer.

The first Tom Horsmith saw of his visitor was a figure in a yellow arctic immersion suit standing unsteadily next to a big Mitsubishi all-terrain vehicle. The visitor was almost hidden behind a curtain of snowflakes, looking oddly like a lumpy plastic mannequin, covered from boots to head, and fastened from thigh to chin, with a wide black zipper. Not an inch of flesh was visible. He wore black rubber gloves that came to the elbows, and reflective goggles that covered the only part of his body that wasn't encased in yellow. He lumbered awkwardly, teddy-bear-like, as if his limbs couldn't bend correctly beneath all the layers. Who could know what kind of human figure might emerge from beneath all this insulation. Tall or short? Fat or thin? Young or old?

It was six degrees below zero. 'Too cold to snow,' Tom's grandmother would have told him. Yet it snowed. The sky was heavy, and the sun was a pale glow, perilously low on the horizon.

Tom's own outfit was hardly more becoming than the visitor's. It was, perhaps, a little less bright, less bulky, and rather more weathered. It was a dull red. The red of a late summer rose. Somehow out of place in this wintry landscape. He raised an arm and waved. He could feel the familiar bite of cold air on his face.

One of the mannequin's yellow limbs lifted for just a moment. Was it a wave back?

The figure was making ponderous steps forward onto the ice pack. Tom turned to look behind him. An azure-blue snowmobile was zigzagging its way through the uneven ice field towards them, its rider coated in orange. The arctic was a riot of colour today, he thought.

He made his way to the figure in yellow. 'Mr Causley, I presume,' he said, pulling his scarf away from his face as he spoke.

'Good to see you again, Tom,' the figure said.

'Please tell me you have some coffee in your car.'

'I... er... I believe I have a thing that is supposed to boil water.'

'And coffee?'

'I have no idea. This isn't my car.'

Tom walked round the car, opened the passenger door, and sprung the glove box. 'Coffee,' he said. He held up a jar. 'Daavi always keeps some in here.'

'Do you know how to work the... thing... to boil the water?'

Tom looked at him quizzically. 'The... kettle?'

'Yes... the kettle.' Monty looked annoyed to have been caught out on such a simple word. 'I have no idea how to work it.'

'You have water, I suppose?'

Monty said. 'I don't know what I have. Your man Daavi simply pointed in this direction and sent me off to look for you. I didn't know I was supposed to come equipped for a full Arctic expedition.'

'Well, there's your first mistake,' Tom said. 'Every trip here is a full Arctic expedition.' He held out a gloved hand. 'Welcome to Qaanaaq,' he said.

'Thank you,' Monty said, his voice almost concealed by the cloud of vapour from his breath. His hands were as heavily gloved as Tom's. The handshake felt like clutching at laundry.

Tom said. 'I saw the plane come in. So Daavi met you ok at the airport?'

'Yes, he did. Thank you.'

'And he sent you up here by yourself? That is such an Inuktun thing.'

'I was fine,' Monty said. He gestured. 'It was kind of him to lend me his car.'

Tom shrugged. 'It's the research station's car. So not especially kind. He was saving himself a journey.' He went around the car and opened the back hatch. 'Kettle,' he announced, holding it up. He picked up a plastic container. 'And water.' He pulled a lead from the kettle and pushed it into a socket in the tailgate. 'So. Three days ago, I had a very enigmatic email. A Mr Causley from the Houses of Parliament. Well, well! Not a person I ever expected to hear from. And guess what? You want to pop over to Qaanaaq to meet me. No explanation. It's an awful long way for a brief encounter.'

'Well...' Monty's mouth was opening and closing, but no sound was emerging. He was rescued by the arrival of the snowmobile.

'Are we having a brew?' asked the snowmobile rider, as he lifted himself from the saddle of his vehicle.

'We only have enough for two,' Tom said. 'And technically, Mr Causley is here to see me, so you're gate-crashing a private meeting.'

'Technically, I'm his constituent too, so that means I'm entitled to coffee as well,' the man in the orange snow suit protested.

'I'm sure there's enough coffee for us all,' Monty said.

'Benny,' said the man in orange, peeling his scarf away from his face. He pulled his hand free of his glove for the handshake.

'You're not *the* Benny?'

'*The* Benny!' the man in orange echoed. 'Did you hear that, Tom? THE Benny! From now on, I will only answer to *The Benny*.'

He gave a mock bow to Monty. 'The Benny at your service,' he said.

The tiny arctic township of Qaanaaq, sometimes known as Thule, or New Thule (population 650 or thereabouts, with a similar population of Inuit dogs) was a surprisingly orderly commune of around two hundred or so wooden dwellings and community buildings, in various stages of disrepair, laid out in a rather sprawling grid fashion onto a slightly skewed checkerboard of earth and gravel roads. No one was too close to their neighbour; all houses faced (for the most part) the same direction, south-west (the only compass-setting where you might catch weak warming rays from an afternoon sun; when there was one.) The village sat right on the coast, on a gentle slope that led upwards from a long stony beach to a low range of mountains. It guarded the wide entrance to a fjord, on the north-western face of Kaalaallit Nunaat (the island more familiarly known as Greenland), looking west across 160 kilometres of icy ocean towards Baffin Island. Most houses in Qaanaaq were Scandinavian-red in colour – *falu röd*, the traditional iron-ochre shade used to preserve wooden buildings in this part of the world. Many others, however, had been painted in bold colours – blues, greens, and a whole palette of shades, some bright and new, some weathered and faded. The jolly spectrum of colours felt like a defiant gesture of cheerfulness in a settlement that might otherwise be as bleak as you could imagine. There was an airport, around 4 kilometres to the north of the town on one of the only stretches of land flat enough to provide for a runway; but there was no real harbour for the few dozen small boats. These were pulled up onto the beach when they were not at sea chasing fish or seals. A shallow river split the settlement into two, southeast and northwest, and two pipe bridges linked the separate halves.

There was a church, a school, a playground, a hospital, a hotel, a supermarket, a sports centre, a police station, a museum... all the essential and non-essential social infrastructure of a modern town. And yet it felt oddly artificial in a way a seaside community should not. There was nothing organic in the way the village had grown. Almost every building was rectangular in shape like various sizes of trailer-home or makeshift farm buildings, and the place assumed the feel and charmlessness of a military camp. Which originally, after a fashion, it had been. Constructed in 1950 by the US army, Qaanaaq had been built to accommodate a local population made homeless when the army commandeered the original town of Ultima Thule. It was a self-contained community. Lacking nothing. Except for a dash of humanity, or individuality – and that perhaps, was the singular dimension provided by the colours. Someone, an occupant, had chosen the colour blue for his house. A neighbour had chosen green. Some originality had surfaced from beneath the plain uniformity of a bureaucrat's design.

Most buildings were unmarked. Who needs a sign in a village of 650 people, where everyone knows their way around? The skyline was somewhat dominated by a cluster of huge white oil tanks and water-tanks – essential for survival during the long dark winter. And here and there, scattered among the houses was an assortment of research buildings. Among the most prominent was a Danish infrasound listening station, set up in Qaanaaq in the aftermath of the Strategic Arms Limitation Treaties of the twentieth century. This facility could detect planetary tremors from distant underground nuclear tests. If North Korea tested a bomb, they would know about it in Qaanaaq first. There was the Centre for Permafrost Research – CENPERM - which monitored changes in the ground ice, the Danish Meteorological Institute Geophysical Observatory which was studying weather, and the Greenland Climate Research Centre, whose team spent its time measuring changes in winds and tides. There was a British Antarctic Survey base (despite the fact this was about as far as you could comfortably get from the Antarctic.) They were part of the European ICE-ARC project measuring sea ice. And there was the Glacier Trust Programme that monitored glaciers on the Greenland Ice Sheet.

All in all, these organisations, and occasional others that came and went, furnished Qaanaaq with a curious and ever-changing demographic. The majority population were still Inuktun, natives of north west Greenland, most of them hunters and fishermen, but their numbers were complemented by a small number of scientists and technicians from the various research establishments, as well as a rotation of administrators, medics, teachers, air-traffic controllers and the like, who came to spend time in the world's second most northerly town. These, and most of the researchers too, hailed from the Greenland capital of Nuuk, 1,600 kilometres to the south, or from further afield in Denmark. It was an unusual mix. Several languages were spoken in the town. The local Inuktun tongue, *Inughuartun* was widely used, but many locals also spoke *Kalaallisut*, Greenland's most widely spoken language. Danish was spoken here and there, and English was increasingly common among the research community.

There was an uneasy undertone of distrust as Monty Causley, Tom Horsmith, and Benny Shaunessey settled into the bar of the Qaanaaq Hotel for a late lunch. The three sat at a single table with Causley on one side and the two younger men opposite. They were out of their snow suits and now all three were in chunky jumpers and jeans.

'Well, this is cosy,' Benny joked.

'I should have thought I was the last man on earth you'd go out of your way to meet,' Tom said to Monty.

'Ha ha.' The MP's laugh sounded unnatural. 'What is it they say?' he said. 'Forgive and forget, eh? Forgive and forget.'

'All the same,' Tom said, 'I don't imagine I'm your favourite person.'

'Nor me,' added Benny.

The rather soulless hotel bar was laid out like a cafeteria with parallel rows of tables and benches, but it was busy with a noisy clientele. 'I've never seen so many beards outside a Liberal Democrat convention,' Monty told them.

'They're virtually compulsory,' Tom said.

'Not for me,' Monty said. 'Beards are still a bit of a no-no in politics, you know.'

The ten years since the meeting in The Stormy Petrel appeared to have taken a toll on Monty Causley. His face had developed something of a hang-dog expression, as if the muscles in his face had given up the fight, and gravity had taken control of his cheeks. His neck had grown a new fold, and that too was starting to sag. His hair had thinned beyond the widow's peak he had once sported, to a grey strip like a barren savannah, that swept all the way from his forehead to his crown. He was, however, lightly tanned, reasonably trim, and fairly buoyant in his movements, suggesting a man who had not quite surrendered to middle age; at least not yet.

'Shall we tell you about Qaanaaq?' Tom volunteered, looking at Benny as he spoke, as if this was a double act that the two men could perform.

'That would be helpful,' Causley said, relaxing just a little in his chair.

'Where to start then?' said Benny.

'Some of the Danes still call it Thule,' Tom said. 'You'll still see it as Thule on some maps. *Ultima Thule* meant the end-of-the-world in ancient tradition. The furthest point you could ever travel.'

'It's well named then.'

'It really is,' Benny said.

'So, Benny and I work for the Glacier Trust,' Tom said. 'It's a charitable research organisation – part of the global 1820 Foundation. We're measuring the melting of Greenland's glaciers. It takes us out onto the ice more-or-less every day.'

'Right,' Monty said. 'That sounds... interesting.'

'It is.'

They were flailing around trying to get the conversation going.

'I imagine this bar can get wild at night,' Monty suggested.

Both younger men shrugged. 'Not really. You have to make your drink last the evening,' Benny told him. 'Alcohol is really expensive here. And no one has much money.'

They drank cokes while they waited for food.

'The whole town is sinking,' Benny said.

'The permafrost is melting,' Tom explained. 'That's why the town is sinking.'

It was a curious dialogue. It was an exchange that flipped and flitted between subjects, part briefing and part banter. And maybe part invention. Who could tell? Tom and Benny batted lines back and forward between them as if they had played this game before with many different audiences.

'There's a supply ship twice a year,' said Benny.

'Three times in a good year.'

'How often do you have a good year?'

'We haven't had one yet.'

'But we're hoping.'

'The dogs only work in the winter. They spend the summer sleeping.'

'And scavenging.'

'And making a nuisance of themselves.'

'Everything is melting.'

'Six months of darkness.'

'Bloody cold. I mean, today is a lovely day. But it's June. You go outside without cold weather gear in the winter, you'll be dead in five minutes.'

'Unless you're an Inuit. They can do ten minutes.'

'It's getting harder and harder to catch seals.'

'Why?'

'Because the ice pack is breaking up.'

'The whole place is built on a lie.' This was Tom. 'Erik the Red called it Greenland, because he wanted to encourage people to come and settle here. He should have called it Iceland. It would have been more accurate. But the name was already taken.'

'Erik the who?'

'The Red. I don't think he was a communist. Not that kind of red.'

'Or a Liverpool supporter.'

'So far as we know.'

'What made you come here?' Monty asked. He seemed to be trying to impose some order on the discussion. They were still waiting for food.

'I like palindromic place names,' Tom said. He laughed as he spoke.

'You could have gone to Glenelg in Scotland,' Monty said. 'It's a whole lot closer.'

'Or Wassamassaw,' said Tom.

'You made that up!'

'I didn't! It's in North Carolina.'

The food came. It was cod with rice. 'Oh look,' Benny said. 'It's the fish of the day.' This was clearly an in-joke.

'The piece of cod that passeth all understanding,' Tom said.

'It's always cod,' Benny explained.

They laughed a lot – Benny and Tom. There was a chemistry between the two men, a quick to-and-fro of comic quips. It was gentle, but almost competitive. Like a tennis match. Benny would serve a comment, Tom would return service with a backhand volley, and Benny would come back with an overhead smash. Fifteen-love. They were like brothers. They seemed to read each other's minds.

'What drew you both to climate science?' Monty asked.

'I'm not a climate scientist,' Benny said. 'I'm a fisherman. I'm only here because Tom needs someone to fetch and carry.'

'Someone cheap,' Tom added.

'Someone who won't complain.'

'No one fetches and carries like Benny,' Tom said. 'He is the master of fetching and carrying.'

'I am,' Benny confirmed.

'What drew you to being a politician?' Tom asked.

'I studied history.'

'That doesn't really answer the question.'

'Then what answer do you want? Do you want me to say I went into politics as a way of helping people?'

'Only if it's true,' Tom said.

'Maybe it is true. I don't really know. I wanted a job I could be good at. Same as anyone else I suppose.'

'Well,' Tom said, 'at least that's honest.'

The wind outside seemed to be picking up. The door to the bar opened and a group of fishermen in reindeer and musk ox skins entered, accompanied by a whip of snow. There was a frosting of ice on their moustaches.

'And why are *you* here?' Benny asked.

At last. A kind of serious silence descended on the table. Everyone glanced at everyone else. The meals were eaten. Monty pushed his plate away. 'OK. I came here to ask a favour of you both,' he said. 'You especially, Tom. You'll probably think I'm a little crazy travelling all this way just to beg a favour. Maybe I am.

But I came because I want you to know how important this is for me. And for the world. I hope that doesn't sound too pretentious.'

'Just a little,' Tom said.

'And because, when I ask a favour of someone, I want to be sitting across the table from them, not hiding at the other end of a telephone line. That's a politician thing.' He looked directly at Tom. 'And also,' he waved a hand expressively, 'because I was curious. Curious to see this place. To hear about your work. Who wouldn't want to visit the end of the world?'

'Suddenly I'm nervous,' Tom said. 'What is this favour then?'

'First, I should say I have nothing to offer in return. Not directly. I can ask around some of my journalist friends to see if anyone wants to do a profile of you for a Sunday magazine if you like. A cover story maybe. All about you. About your work. About all this.' He waved a hand to include the bar, and the village, and the whole northern hemisphere. 'Lots of photographs. Human interest. Science. What's happening to the glaciers. Serious stuff and human stuff. I'm sure they'd publish it. It could be good for the Glacier Trust.'

'Happy to do all of that,' Tom said. 'But what is our part of the bargain?'

Causley drew a breath and seemed to be considering how best to do this. 'The Prime Minister is very committed to the environment, you know. She has a very strong, very clear green agenda.'

'Well that would be a first,' Benny said.

'Do you follow the news from the UK?'

'Not especially.'

'May I share something with you in confidence?'

Tom shrugged his shoulders and gestured at the room. 'No one here we can share any secrets with,' he said.

'I'm serious here, Tom. If you repeat this, you will effectively destroy my career.'

'Didn't I already do that?' Tom raised his eyebrows.

'I would rather you didn't do it again,' Causley said.

There was a moment of quiet at the table.

Benny leaned forward to puncture the awkward silence. 'Of course we can keep your secret, Mr Causley. Can't we, Tom?'

'Of course.'

Monty Causley seemed to be contemplating this undertaking. 'Well then,' he said, after a while, 'if you don't follow the news, you may not know that the Prime Minister plans to announce a cabinet reshuffle at the beginning of July.'

'And...?'

'And... she has offered me a cabinet role: Secretary of State for the Environment and Climate,' Monty said.

A second pause, then both Tom and Benny began to laugh.

'That's like... putting Al Capone in charge of the justice system,' said Benny.

'Like making Harvey Weinstein pope.'

Monty Causley laughed too. What else could he do?

'Well congratulations and all that,' Tom said, 'But you're a climate denier.'

'I'm really not,' Monty said. 'But look, we had this argument a decade ago. We don't need to do it again.'

'It's an important argument.'

'I know.' Monty put both hands on the table. 'I'm on your side now. I promise you.'

'But can we believe you?' Tom asked.

'Look,' Monty said. He took a breath. 'Next week,' he said to Tom, 'it will be our shared birthday. You will be thirty. I shall be fifty. Ten years since... the video.'

'*The video*,' Tom and Benny echoed, in unison, exchanging a knowing glance as they did so.

'The video,' Monty confirmed. He hesitated just for a moment, acknowledging their exaggerated grimaces. 'I want to ask you to come back.'

The bar door swung open again and more fishermen came in, blowing lungfuls of steam. It was getting noisy in the bar.

'Back?'

'To St Piran. Both of you.'

Tom leaned back in his chair. He laughed. 'Nice idea,' he said. He shook his head. 'But it isn't going to happen.'

'You and me. Together again. Back in the pub. Whatever the pub is called.'

'The Stormy Petrel. It's your local.' There was a hint of acid in Tom's reply.

'You and me, back in the Stormy Petrel. Face to face. Over a beer. Just the two of us, and Benny of course, and… a TV camera. Think of it as a sequel.' He dropped his voice. 'TV gold,' he said. 'But that's the politician speaking.' He reached out and touched Tom's arm. 'All your expenses will be paid. There and back.'

The two men exchanged another glance. Tom looked suspicious. 'Who will pay our expenses?' he asked. 'You? Or will this be the poor taxpayer?'

'I will pay it,' Monty said. He made a face that seemed to say, *this is not really something I like to discuss*. I'll pay it from my personal bank account. Perhaps I could make it a charitable payment to the Glacier Trust to help with employee travel?'

Tom tipped his head as if he were about to make an important concession. 'OK. Benny's going back to St Piran next week,' he said. 'He'll do it. Won't you Ben?'

'Sure,' Benny said. 'And I'll be more polite than Tom.'

'You're going back to Cornwall?' Monty was surprised. 'For a holiday?'

Benny shook his head. 'Happily, no,' he said. 'My fetching and carrying days are over. For this year anyway. I need to get back to my boat.' He grinned. 'I come here for a month or so every summer just to catch up with Tom. He gets me to work for him. For free.'

'For free?'

'It's slavery really.'

'I beg your pardon?' Tom said, acting as if he were offended by Benny's remarks. 'Free - apart from the cost of the airfare, some very expensive beers, some fine plates of cod, and a month's holiday in a spectacular, unspoiled, resort town.'

'For free,' Benny repeated. 'But it's always worth it, because when I get back to St Piran, it makes me realise how close to heaven it is there.'

Monty raised a hand. 'It's great that you'll be part of this, Benny.' His tone was faintly condescending. 'You're a really important part of the narrative. But we need Tom.'

'We could do it here,' Tom suggested suddenly. 'Here in Qaanaaq.' He slapped his hand down to emphasise his point. 'Let's do it here. Right now. Ben's got his phone with him. He can film us. Let's debate climate change here in Greenland, where it's happening all around us.'

Monty looked uncertain. 'The thing is...' he started to say, 'it isn't as simple as that...'

'Of course it is! What better place to have the debate?'

'Tom!' Monty held up a hand. 'Look, I need to tell you the truth.'

'Aha! A rare commodity. You should film *this*, Ben. The new Environment Minister is about to tell us the truth. We should capture it on film for posterity.'

Ben said, 'I think you should let him have his say, Tom.'

Tom let this reprimand deflate him just a little. 'Very well. Tell us.'

'OK.' Causley sucked in his lip and looked anxious. 'I'm not ready for it,' he said. 'I don't want you to catch me out again. I've only had a few days to get my head around the idea of being a spokesman for the environment. I need to get it right. Not just an off-the-cuff video here. I need a week to get briefed.'

'You think a week will do it?' Tom said.

'I need to understand the science,' Causley said.

This expression, with its echoes of the altercation of ten years before, seemed to take some of the steam out of Tom's tirade. 'Then come back here in two weeks,' he suggested. 'Wait until you get your promotion. We can do it then.'

'No, Tom,' Monty shook his head. 'No one watches to see what trips I make right now. That's because I'm just an unknown member of the whips' office. We're the most invisible people in parliament. But in ten days, I hope, I'll be a minister of state. I shall have a full calendar. Everyone will know where I'm going and why. It takes two days to get here from London. A flight to Copenhagen. Another flight to Nuuk. A third flight here. Then the same rigmarole back. It isn't going to look good if I spend the fortnight of my fiftieth birthday shuttling back and forward to the end of the world. No. This has to look unplanned. Unstaged. Just the two of us. Back in the same bar in the village where we both live. By coincidence, you're thirty and I'm fifty. It's a birthday party. Someone films it. A shaky camera.'

'But this time a different outcome,' Tom observed.

Causley nodded. 'I won't lie to you, Tom. That's the favour I'm here to ask.'

'And how does it end this time?'

'The two of us talk about all of this,' Causley waved a hand.

'Icebergs. Climate. That sort of thing. We bat around some stats on glaciers and sea levels and volcanoes and stuff. We discover we both agree. Then we shake hands...' he blinked, and paused. 'And we call off our wager,' he said.

There was an uncomfortable moment of silence at the table. Tom looked down. 'Is that what all of this is about?' he asked, almost in a whisper. 'You've come all of this way to ask me to cancel a stupid bet?'

'I didn't say it was a stupid bet.'

'You didn't need to.' Tom looked back up. 'It *was* a stupid bet. An idiotic bet. Do you know why?'

Monty shook his head.

'Because I will lose it,' Tom said. He smiled at the MP's reaction and shrugged. 'The world is warming up. Sea levels are rising. That's a consequence of climate change. It is almost irreversible. If the world warms, the oceans rise. There is nowhere else for the water to go. But it's a slow process. Do you know the current estimate for sea level rise? It's four and a half millimetres a year. That's just about a centimetre every two years.' He held up a hand with thumb and forefinger just a little way apart. 'That much,' he said. 'That is how much the ocean will rise in two years. It's probably going to speed up. But it will always be slow. Maybe it will get to a centimetre a year. But even so, in forty years when our bet finishes do you know how much the sea level will have risen?' He held his hands a short way apart. 'About this much. Around thirty to forty centimetres. If things are really bad, it could rise a metre. Either way, it isn't going to drown you in your front room. It won't even get much past your doorstep.'

'Well then...' Monty said, exhaling slowly, with the first hints of a smile appearing on his face, 'you should be happy to call the whole thing off.'

'Should I be though?' Tom shook his head. 'I don't know. This isn't about me, is it? Who cares if I die when I'm seventy? That isn't the issue.'

'So, what is the issue?'

'The issue is the icecaps are melting and the goddamned sea is rising!' Tom smacked his hand on the table in a sudden moment of anger. 'It is fucking *rising*. And it doesn't stop rising when I get to seventy, or when you get to ninety. It still goes on. It doesn't care who wins our bet. It doesn't say, "Oh look, Tom Horsmith is dead, let's turn around and go back down again." It goes on, up and up, half a centimetre a year. Too slow for anyone to notice. Too slow for anyone to give a damn. Until every last bit of ice on the highest mountain and on the coldest continent melts. That's what happens. That's our future, Mr Causley. It doesn't happen in fifty years. That's why it was a stupid bet. Maybe it takes five hundred years. Maybe five thousand. But it still happens. Why can't we see that? Why can't *you* see it? We're on track to warm the planet by three degrees in the next hundred years, maybe by four degrees early in the next century, possibly even five. And up it goes.' He waved his hands upwards to illustrate the trend. 'Once we get to that stage it becomes an unstoppable cascade and God knows what happens then. But one thing is certain. We are fucked. Truly fucked. It's a slow-motion car crash. It's so slow the driver thinks he doesn't need to put his foot on the brake. He thinks he has plenty of time. But it might already be too late.' Tom looked flushed with this outburst. 'You know, the last time the planet was four degrees warmer, the seas were eighty metres higher than they are today. Eighty metres! Do that again and London will be underwater. New York. Tokyo. Maybe three out of every four cities on earth. I won't live to see that, even if I win the bet. Neither will you. But our great-great-great-whatever grandchildren might. Or don't they matter?'

Monty sat forward in his seat. He reached out a hand and placed it on Tom's arm while Tom was still talking. When he had finished, he waited a moment to be sure there was no more. 'This is why you need to do the video,' he said then. He looked Tom in the eyes. 'You need to say these things.'

'But that isn't why you want me to do it, is it, Mr Causley? You want me to save your skin.'

'Yes,' Monty agreed, and he exhaled an apologetic sigh. 'You need to understand this, Tom; that video haunts me everywhere I go. Even after all this time. I can't do an interview on TV without being asked about it. They still play clips of it. I went on *Question Time* on BBC1 and almost everyone on the panel made reference to it. And I know. I get it. I was an ass. I didn't know I was being filmed; I'd had a tiring day. I'd driven for eight hours from London. All I wanted was a quiet drink and instead I got someone calling me a liar in my local pub. I made a fool of myself. But that isn't me, Tom. I deserve a break.'

'And I'm to blame for all this, am I?' Tom asked.

'Not entirely. But partly. I was an idiot, but you weren't exactly a saint.'

Somewhere a mobile phone was ringing. Faces turned to look. 'It's mine,' Tom said, patting his pockets to find it. He drew it from a side pocket of his coat, checking the screen.

'Please... take your call,' Monty said. 'We have plenty of time to talk.'

'That's ok,' Tom said, killing the ringing with his thumb. 'It's only my brother, Connor. If it's important he'll call back.'

'Is he in St Piran?' Monty asked.

Tom nodded. 'Almost. He lives in Treadangel. Just a few miles up the road.'

'Well, come to St Piran next week and you could see him,' Monty suggested. He raised an imploring eyebrow. 'Do you still have other family in Cornwall?'

'My Nan,' Tom said. 'And a sister in Falmouth.'

'Then come and see them. I will pay for the travel.'

'It still isn't going to happen,' Tom said. He pushed his empty plate away and rose to his feet. 'You think this is so important to your career, but you can't spare a week out of your time to come back here. And guess what? I can't spare a week of my time to go and see you. Are we done?'

Causley looked stunned at this. 'Won't you at least stay for coffee?' he asked. 'Let me try to convince you.' He was grasping at straws now.

'You can have a coffee at my house,' Tom said.

'At your house?' Monty sounded uncertain. 'Don't you live at the research station?'

'No,' Tom said. 'I have a house here.'

'Ah. In that case, thank you. Coffee sounds great.'

'Besides, if it will help you to understand why I'm really not in a rush to go back to St Piran, there are three people you really must meet.'

Causley raised his eyebrows.

'One of them is my boss,' Tom said. 'The founder of the 1820 Foundation and director of the Glacier Trust.'

Monty nodded at this. 'I think I know the person you mean,' he said. 'I did a little bit of research before coming out here. Are we talking about Dr Nordberg?'

'Dr Norgaard,' Benny corrected him. 'Lykke Norgaard. Although nowadays she occasionally goes by her married name.'

'I've read about her,' Monty said knowingly. 'Quite a celebrity I understand. Millions of followers online. I even watched one of her videos, you know. Just for some background. Quite a force of nature, isn't she?'

'She is,' Tom confirmed.

'Had her picture in Time magazine – one of the *Next Generation Leaders*. All dressed up in her Inuit furs.'

'You *have* done your research.'

'And she gave the keynote address at the international climate conference, didn't she?'

'She did.'

'Upset the Americans a bit, if I remember. And the Chinese. A bit of a thorn in the side of us government types, eh? Wants us all to turn back the clock. Back to some sort of feudal, bucolic past.'

'Something like that,' Tom said thinly.

'And she lives here in Qaanaaq?'

'She does.'

'And you need her permission to travel?'

'Absolutely.' Tom shot a glance at Benny. 'She's my boss. I need her permission.'

'Well. Maybe I could offer something to make her decision easier. An official meeting with me in London maybe. Once I'm the Minister for the Environment, I mean. That might be helpful to her. Good publicity and all that.'

'You could try.'

Benny said. 'She's an Inuit, remember? They are a tough people. She might be harder than you expect to convince.'

Tom gave a smile. 'Also, you should know, I never travel alone.'

Causley seemed to sense a puzzle was being constructed for him. He paused to gather his thoughts. 'So... apart from your boss, who are these other people I need to meet?' he asked.

Tom held up three fingers. 'Lykke and Ilse and Noah,' he said.

'Ahh,' said Causley, his face reflecting the realisation of what he was hearing. 'Your family?'

Tom smiled. 'Yes.'

'You are married to Dr Norgaard?'

'I am,' Tom said. 'And we have twins. And we travel together.

So, now you understand it could have been an expensive offer you were making.'

'I'll make the offer anyway.'

'And we never fly anywhere without offsetting the carbon.'

'I would expect nothing else.'

'Then perhaps we should go and meet them,' Tom said. He slid his phone back into the pocket of his coat, and at the very moment he did this, it started to ring again.

3. Some say the world will end in fire...

This little window of time, these few fleeting years, during which the first few decades of our story unfolds, would come to be given a name: *the Age of Fire and Flood*. And when the historians wrote their histories, and the analysts offered their explanations, and the apologists contrived their excuses, and the activists pointed their fingers of blame, they would all nonetheless agree with the name. The Year of Fire had become the Decade of Fire. The winter of floods had become the age of floods. Archaeologists of the future, if there are any, will know this time from the layer of ash. Hot dry summers and lingering droughts left forests bare and leafless – like bones in the desert sun. Like tinder. Billions of tons of matchwood waiting for a spark. And sparks were never far away. All around the world, wildfires burned. Forest fires. Brush fires. Grass fires. Jungle fires. Plantations burned. Farms burned. Homes burned. Brazil, and America, and Indonesia, and Malaysia. Greece, and Spain, and France and Siberia. Finland and Lithuania. China and Cambodia. Nigeria and Congo. The planet burned. It was truly a decade of fire, of choking smoke and rising flames and glowing embers; of red sunsets and ashen skies.

And even as the world burned, and even as whole continents were stricken by droughts, elsewhere the rains fell. They fell, it often seemed, where no rain was needed. Rivers swelled and crops drowned. Flood waters swept down valleys and tore down homes. Freak floods and freak fires. Freak storms too, they would say in St Piran, for here at the toe of England when storms blew in from an angry Atlantic, St Piran would be the first place to greet them.

And it was hot. Nearly everywhere was hot.

In St Piran, it was the hottest June since... well since the previous June. Or maybe it was hotter. No one had the energy to measure anymore. Treadangel Woods burned down one afternoon. A small fire on the scale of global fires; but it lifted a dreadful plume of smoke over the headland like a malevolent finger pointing at the heavens, and to many in the village it seemed like an omen.

Demelza Trevarrick, wearing black, sat in a shrinking puddle of cool beneath a sunshade at The Beachcomber Bar, drinking tonic-water and ice. 'Darling, this is unbearable,' she told Jeremy (more than once). 'How is a person supposed to survive in this heat?'

'We're not supposed to survive,' answered Jeremy, rather unhelpfully. 'We're not designed for extreme heat. In fact, our species has a fairly narrow...'

'I don't want to know about our *species,* darling. I want to know what we're supposed to do!' Demelza wailed.

'We're supposed to die,' Jeremy said. 'Thousands died in Cairo, you know, in the last heatwave. And half a city died in Mauritania. What were they supposed to do? And Spain has lost a quarter of a million hectares of vineyards to heat-stress. And Tripoli has...'

'Darling, you're not being helpful.'

'Then I suggest you ask Kenny for more ice.'

It was too hot for conversation. Too hot to be outdoors. Too humid to be inside. The sun was a furnace. Martha Fishburne, the retired schoolteacher, came by, looking as pink as a prawn beneath a black lace bonnet that was too small for her head. 'I feel like I'm one of them spit-roast chickens you see at Sainsburys,' she observed to Demelza.

Demelza was fanning herself with a menu. 'I know what you mean, darling. I feel the fat dripping out of me.'

The heatwave had led to an uncharacteristic lull in activity in St Piran. June weekends were normally busier. It was, after all, high season for businesses along the quay. Out had come tables and chairs for the restaurants and cafes. Blackboards had appeared, with dishes advertised in coloured chalks. *Catch of the day. Mussels. Crabs. Mackerel.* Display-stands had been rolled out onto pavements from the gift shop, with summer hats, and blow-up swim bands, and postcards of whales. Pasties were baking in the shop in Fish Street. But the crowds were curiously absent. 'Too hot to be out for long in the car,' was Jeremy's diagnosis. 'They'll all be at the big beaches.'

Casey Limber, the harbourmaster, was out on the quay inspecting the moorings, wearing only flip-flops and shorts. Charity Limber was shopping in a summer-frock short enough to make a person gasp, with a basket over her arm like a land girl.

'When will it end?' someone was heard to cry.

'I think this is just the beginning,' Jeremy muttered in reply.

'Shall we walk to the church together?' Martha suggested to Demelza.

'Oh darling – don't we have time for one more drink?'

'I think we should set off now,' Martha said. 'It could take a while to climb the hill in this heat.'

Around the corner from the harbour, by the square, where the cobbles of Fish Street began their winding trail upwards, a small group of villagers had gathered to walk together. Jeremy and Demelza joined them. Romer Anderssen carried a battery powered fan, a little plastic propellor that she held rather too close to her face. Jacob, and his son Jason, and several of the men wore dark suits and ties, and their discomfort showed.

'Let's do it,' Jeremy said. It was like a rallying call. The coterie of villagers set off in a disorderly crocodile, an unwilling trail of people unsuitably dressed for the weather, with a steep hill ahead of them.

'Whose idea do we think it was to build the church at the top of the hill when the village was at the bottom?' Demelza complained.

'It must have been a man,' said Jessie Higgs.

At the church, Polly Hocking, the vicar's wife, was handing out plastic tumblers of water along with copies of the order of service to people as they arrived. 'We have to stay hydrated,' she was saying.

'It's too hot for this,' somebody said. But everyone was grateful for the water.

Inside the church, however, it was almost cool. Martha let out a long breath like an engine releasing steam. 'Ooh, that's lovely.'

They squeezed together into the narrow pews. The organist was playing Pachelbel.

'That's young Rosie Moot,' Martha whispered to Demelza, nodding towards the organ. 'She were always musical. Even in Year One. Plays like an angel she does.'

'She does.'

More people arrived. It looked as if the church would be almost full. And then the music stopped. For just a moment. Some sort of signal had made it to Rosie. She was turning pages on her music-stand. A breath, and the first slow haunting notes of Bach's *Come Sweet Death* rose from the organ, and up the aisle came the vicar, the Reverend Alvin Hocking, looking white-haired and fearsome in his clerical robes. Behind him, the funeral procession – the undertakers in their preposterous hats, and the bearers looking uncomfortable in borrowed suits, and the family, unrehearsed and unready, arms around each other. Connor Horsmith and his fiancée Hannah and their little girl; Morwenna Horsmith and her Italian girlfriend Lucia; Tom and his wife Lykke and their five-year-old twins.

'He made it then,' Jeremy whispered.

'So it seems.'

'Lord, thou hast been our refuge from one generation to the next,' intoned the Reverend Hocking. 'Before the mountains were brought forth, or ever the earth and the world were made, thou art God from everlasting, and world without end.'

Afterwards, when Nan was in the ground, the soil had been thrown, and most of the weeping had been done, the party made their way down the hill to the Stormy Petrel. The Anderssens knew how to host a wake. There were tables in the lobsterman's bar laden with refreshments. There were extra staff at the bar. Everyone crowded in.

There are few occasions quite so merry as the party that follows a funeral, and Cornish people know this well. The joviality does not start right away. There are solemn things to be said first, hands to be shaken, tears to be dabbed from cheeks. But a party is a party after all, and after a short while one of the mourners will forget the occasion and break the sombre mood with a loud laugh, and soon there will be more. The Anderssens put jugs of cold cider on the tables to help inject some cheerfulness, and before long the wake had become almost festive.

'We're all so sorry for your loss,' Polly Hocking told Tom, coiling her arm around his shoulder to comfort him. 'She was one of a kind your Nan.'

'She surely was.'

Lykke Horsmith, with one twin balanced on her hip and the other clutching her hand, was pressed into a corner with Tom's sister Morwenna, and Morwenna's partner Lucia.

'It's so lovely to meet you at last,' Lucia was saying.

'You too.'

'You're Danish?'

'I'm half Inuit and half Danish,' Lykke explained. 'I'm a Greenlander. My father is an Inuktun fisherman, and my mother is a Danish biologist. But I've lived in Denmark, and I've studied in Vancouver, and I worked for a while in London. So I feel like a citizen of everywhere.'

Connor Horsmith climbed onto a chair and tried to call for silence by dinging his glass with a fork. 'I just want to say,' he said... *Ding ding ding.* 'I JUST WANT TO SAY...' *DING DING!*

And when at last the party fell silent, he took a breath to acknowledge the moment. 'I just want to say. Our Nan was special. Very special. Yes, of course, she had her issues. And in the end... well... most of you know, she was probably ready to go. Doesn't make it easier though. Not for us who loved her. But here's the thing. Nan was born at Number 12 Cliff Street. She came into the world right there in the front room. She grew up there. She lived there all her life. Barely spent a night under a different roof. And she passed away there. She never ended up in an institution. She'd have hated that. She were never locked away in some soulless council care home in Truro, sitting in a pastel-painted communal lounge all day watching daytime TV and eating mince and gravy. And you know why?' Connor laid a hand over his heart. 'Because this community looked after her. All of us. All of you.' He nodded at the crowd in the bar. 'Jessie, you would pop in every morning to see if there was anything she needed. Martha, you would drop by in the afternoon. Megan, you would call in after your shift at the hospital. Kenny, you would bring her a pasty two or three times a week. Benny, you would drop off a piece of mackerel. Demelza, you would run her into the doctors in Treadangel and pick up her pills from the pharmacy. Everyone was looking out for Nan, because that's what we do in St Piran, isn't it? We've done it before. We always do it. We always will. I know it isn't right to call for a round of applause at a funeral, but to heck, I'm going to do it anyway. Give yourselves a cheer for being the best support group ever.'

With a loud sound of laughter, the funeral party cheered this. Shoulders were clapped. Eyes were dabbed.

'This in't a eulogy,' Connor said. 'We had the eulogies in the church. This is some thank-yous. So thank you to Jacob and Romer for letting us use the Petrel. Thank you to Alvin for a really lovely service. Thank you to Polly for the water and the flowers. Thank you to my big sister Morwenna for help with all the arrangements. And to my big bro Tom... and his lovely family... well thank you for being here. We're a long way from the Arctic Circle.'

There was a second ripple of applause at this.

'And here's a thank-you you might not be expecting. Thank you to Mr Montague Causley, our illustrious MP. He in't here, but you ought to know he dug deep into his own pocket to pay for Tom and Lykke and the twins to fly home for the funeral.'

There were looks of surprise at this revelation, and another burst of clapping.

'I'm not sure you're supposed to have shared that,' Tom called.

'Oh dear!' Connor held a hand to his mouth in mock regret. 'Well, the secret's out now. So thank you Monty. And if any of you wants to buy Mr Causley a drink next time he's in the Petrel, please feel free to do so.'

'He's never been back here since the video,' someone called, and people laughed.

'Well I guess it in't compulsory to drink in the Petrel,' Connor said, 'although Jacob might disagree.'

More laughter.

Connor gave a conspiratorial look, and laid a finger along his nose as if what followed might be a secret. 'And by the way, if you want to understand why Mr Causley has been so generous, well you might just want to be drinking here tomorrow night, when he and Tom will be recreating their famous viral punch-up... although this time, as I understand, it's going to be a lot more polite.'

'Now that,' Tom said, 'was *definitely* not for sharing.'

It was still uncomfortably hot in the back room of the Petrel. Once everyone had spoken to everyone else, and all the sandwiches had been eaten, most of the mourners drifted outside to finish their drinks on the quay.

'I think we hit thirty-eight degrees today you know,' Jeremy said to Benny and Tom and Connor. 'Thirty-eight Celsius.' They were standing together, the four men, cider glasses in their hands, watching fishing boats at anchor on the incoming tide. 'That would be a record for St Piran.'

'Really?'

'It has a name you know.'

'What does?'

'This heatwave. They've started naming them. Like hurricanes. This is Heatwave Danny.'

'Soon to morph into Storm Raheeba,' said Benny, who followed these things carefully. 'Coming our way from the Bay of Biscay.'

'It doesn't feel like there's a storm on the way,' Tom said, although now perhaps it did. There was a certain heaviness in the air.

'It does feel humid,' said Jeremy, nodding.

'It'll likely be a big one,' said Benny.

Four Englishmen on a harbourside talking about the weather. Hardly the stuff that stories are made of. 'Tell me you don't plan to take the boat out in the storm,' Tom said.

'Dad wants to go,' Benny said. 'I've been off enjoying myself in Greenland for a month. So Dad's been on his own. And the catch has been down. We missed a day's fishing today. Can't afford to lay up another day.' He grinned and slapped Tom on the shoulder. 'I promised him. We'll be back before it all blows up. Back for your big moment. Never fear.'

'I almost wish you weren't,' said Tom. 'Half the village will be there now Connor's let the secret out.'

From inside the Petrel, sounds of music were starting to emerge. Someone was playing a fiddle. Faintly, along with it, was the sound of a guitar being strummed. 'Looks like the funeral's over then,' Tom said, finishing his beer.

'Shall I tell them to stop?' Jeremy asked.

Tom and Connor shared a glance. 'Better not,' said Connor. 'That'll be Tim and Ruth Truscott. I told them they could play.'

'In that case,' Tom said, 'we ought to go inside and listen.'

Number 12 Cliff Street felt quiet without Nan. The stairs creaked. Doors squeaked. Footsteps thudded on the floorboards. Tom and Lykke were in the bed that had for so many years been Nan's. The twins were in Tom's and Connor's boyhood bedroom. Morwenna and Lucia shared a single bed in Morwenna's old room. The house had rarely been so full, and rarely felt so empty.

Tom and Lykke spoke in whispers. They lay in bed and did what parents do. They talked about the children. 'Did you see how grown-up Noah looked, walking behind the coffin?' 'I was so proud of Ilse. She behaved so well all day.' 'They haven't fought so much this week. I think all the travel has tired them out.' 'I'm going to plait Ilse's hair tomorrow. It's starting to go in her eyes.' Parent talk. It is the same anywhere in the world. And with twins, there was twice as much to discuss, and even a necessity for equality of consideration. You can't discuss one child too much without swapping to the other. 'Noah is growing so fast now. We need to get him new shoes when we're in London.' 'Do you know what Ilse said to me today?' 'Did I tell you what Noah said?' 'I think Ilse is starting to like English food. At last.' 'Noah ate the whole of that pasty. And it was quite spicy.'

'I want to take them swimming,' Tom said. 'Before we set off to London.'

'Greenlanders don't swim,' Lykke said. 'The sea is too cold.'

'But Cornishmen do. And now they're five they need to learn.'

'Then we shall need to buy them swimming costumes. And they'll only ever wear them once.'

'I shall buy them tomorrow from the gift shop.'

They didn't get a lot of sleep. They lay in bed and listened to the noises of the house. Then later, they crept downstairs together while it was still dark.

'Are you still sure you want to do this?' Lykke whispered. 'You could have a few more hours in bed.'

'Try stopping me.'

Out along the harbour wall they walked in the darkness, hand in hand, to watch the solstice sunrise. 'Happy Birthday,' Lykke said. They stood at the place where first they had met, and they saw the faint glow on the horizon that was the sun. But the sky was grey this time, and a strong wind was blowing in from the West. There would be no clear sunrise this morning.

'It's Storm Raheeba,' Tom told her.

They stayed to watch the dawn all the same. It was almost as magical as it had been eight years before. Daylight grew like an organism in the Eastern sky, the shadows along the harbour wall grew sharper, and the village stretched like a slumbering giant and awoke with its morning noises and lit windows and the calls of early gulls. At around five o'clock, when it was light, a voice called. 'Hey Tom! Lykke!' They turned to see who it was, and there were Benny and Peter Shaughnessy, father and son, waving from the deck of *Piranesi* as she chugged steadily out between the harbour walls.

'See you tonight,' Tom called. 'Come back before the storm.'

'Happy Thirtieth Birthday!'

Ah, thirty. A magical age. Still young. Achingly young. Still agile. Still able to stay up all night to party, or to work, or to make love. Yet thirty can be a lost age. An overlooked age. Too young to be a leader, too old to make a debut. Tom Horsmith, at thirty, occupied that slender slice of life where youthful promise gives way to adult accomplishment. No longer the talented, up-and-coming young climate scientist, now just another jobbing researcher in a whole world of jobbing researchers. The world is bigger when you're thirty. But it often feels smaller. The roulette wheel of life has picked up speed, with its wins and its losses, its achievements and its disappointments.

Better looking now than the gawky twenty-year old who challenged a politician in a pub, Tom had filled out a little. Put on some weight. Developed some muscle. Grown a beard. There was a seriousness now in his eyes, in the set of his brows, in the intensity of his gaze. Marriage and fatherhood. They showed. You could tell by the way he stood, by the way he dressed, by his manner and his movements. He was less impulsive now. The passion was still there, but now, perhaps, he would think before acting. *Pick your battles*, Lykke would tell him. And choose carefully. Life had consequences now. With a family to think about. With bills to pay. Thirty. Three short decades. Was this enough experience? Could you really lay your hand upon your heart at thirty and say you understood the rights and wrongs of the world? Could you pronounce with any authority on religion, or on politics, on gun control, or abortion, or immigration, or war, or censorship, or low pay, or climate change? And yet almost everyone at thirty feels strongly about every one of these things and a hundred issues more, and so indeed did Tom Horsmith, for he still was a man who felt injustice keenly, who saw the world as a battle for great values fought between heroes and villains. 'You can't right all the world's wrongs,' Lykke would say. But even Lykke knew that Tom would nonetheless have to try. It was the kind of man he was.

Yet thirty is an unsettling age. Tom had less confidence at thirty than he had possessed at twenty. He had more perspective now. He had experienced more knocks. And every knock in life is a lesson. *Pick your battles. You can't win every one.* As the solstice sun rose unseen behind a looming grey curtain of storm clouds, Tom resolved once and for all not to pick a battle with Monty Causley. 'I'm going to let this one go,' he told Lykke.

'Good.'

It was starting to rain. Just a few drops. But the drops felt heavy. More would be on the way.

'I've thought about it. A lot. But I can't see what good it can do for either of us to let this wager drag on.'

'I'm pleased,' Lykke said.

'If we can both agree that we have a truly huge challenge ahead of us...'

'...then that would be good.'

'Yes.'

'Then let's get back to Cliff Street before the twins wake up.'

5. St Piran was used to storms...

St Piran was used to storms. It had been a great storm, so it was told, that long ago ripped the gash in the headland creating the bay where the village could be built. It was a storm that once tore the corrugated roof from the lifeboat station and dropped it ten metres away on the quay, scattering debris and timbers all the way down the harbour side. *Smugglers' storms* they would call them in the village. These were the mighty storms, the tempests that once shattered boats upon the rocks and swept ashore treasures from foreign lands. Marazion House, so it was said, had been built with the proceeds of just such a shipwreck. In less enlightened times, beachcombers from Treadangel and Penzance would find their way over the cliff paths to Piran Sands, when the dark clouds of a smugglers' storm began to brew in the Western sky. They would take whatever shelter they could find in the cove and there they would wait to see if generous fortune and gales might deliver them a shipwreck. Barrels of rum from the New World perhaps. Bales of tobacco. Suitcases from passengers with fine jewellery. Bodies of drowned sailors with gold in their pockets. Even once, so it was told, a chest full of silverplate from Argentina.

This would be a great storm. A smugglers' storm. It smelled like it. The air tasted of electricity. The sea was black. It swelled and rolled with menace like a drum being beaten by a giant. Tom, on his own now, out along the harbour, pulled his hood tight around his face. The rain was heavy. It whipped across the bay in bursts like fistfuls of spray flung by an angry demon. It stung. Tom pressed a key on his phone and held it to his ear. No reply. At the harbourmaster's office, he climbed the steps and rang the bell.

Casey Limber answered the door. 'What is it, Tom?' he asked. He let Tom in, and the door slammed behind them in the wind, the whole building ringing with the crash. They stood in the narrow hallway, the sound of the storm violent outside. 'In't seen you for a while,' Casey said. 'Sorry about your Nan.' He led Tom down the corridor into the master's office, a rather cramped space with a single table and windows looking out across the waterfront. Rain was beating against the window. 'Ave you come to tell me it's blowin' a gale?' he asked. 'Happen I've already noticed.'

Tom said. 'I'm worried about *Piranesi*. They shouldn't be out in this.'

The harbourmaster furrowed his eyebrows. 'Benny and Peter?' he asked.

'They went out this morning. Around five o'clock.'

'They'll be out past Botallack Head eight or nine miles or so, looking for sardines,' Casey said. 'Have you called them?'

'No signal.'

Casey nodded. 'In't much of a signal out there. That's true. Still. Weather weren't too bad at five o'clock. Can't blame 'em. High tide was twelve minutes past six. But this storm's come in much faster than they forecast. I'd have expected Peter to turn back when they saw it comin', maybe around seven... not much later if they wanted to get back in the harbour while the water was still high enough.' He tapped his table with a pencil. 'Peter knows this stuff. He's got about two hours each side of the tide when he can come and go.' He glanced up at his wall clock. Nine minutes past midday. 'Let's see.' He sat at a desk strewn with papers and charts. 'They won't come back here,' he said. 'Not yet awhile.

The tide's too low to get back into harbour. Mousehole's the same. They won't want to go all the way to Penzance. They might go north with the wind and try to reach Portreath. My guess though is they'll go up the north coast and look for cover, hope it all blows down. Maybe shelter in Zennor Bay.'

'Thanks,' Tom said. 'I just felt a little worried. That's all.'

'Peter Shaunessey can take care of himself,' Casey said. 'They 'ave a signal beacon. If anything 'appens to them, if the beacon gets wet, it'll send a signal to Falmouth, and Falmouth will call us and the lifeboat stations.'

Tom exhaled. 'Thanks Casey.'

'It'll be hell out there in this wind mind. I wouldn't want to be there. But *Piranesi's* a tough little trawler. Let me know if you get through on the phone.'

'When's the earliest he could come back in?'

'You need to reckon on twelve hours and twenty-five minutes between tides. I figure the earliest she could moor up will be about five to five thirty this evening. High tide at six thirty-seven. I reckon she'll be here any time between five and half eight.'

What a difference a day could make. Twenty-four hours earlier, St Piran had sweltered in thirty-eight degrees of heat. Today the sun was nowhere to be seen. The wind was so strong it was difficult to walk safely down the quay. Rainwater splashed around Tom's ankles as he made a dash from the harbourmaster's house towards the safety of the village.

But there was another call he needed to make.

An old iron handrail embedded in the stones of the cliff guided walkers down the steps to Marazion House. For a second time that morning, Tom stood on a doorstep buffeted by wind and spray. The door this time was answered by a man around his own age, dressed like a policeman or a security guard. 'Better come inside,' he said.

This was the first time Tom had ever stepped into Marazion House. It was a blessed relief from the whipping rain of Storm Raheeba, but immediately he had a sense of having entered another world. At one time or other, he supposed, he had been inside almost every house in St Piran on some errand or on some invitation. He had worked as a teenager delivering groceries for Jessie Higgs. You don't drive to the supermarket in a car if you live in St Piran. You walk to the village store and there you tip a young lad to help carry your bags home. That young lad had once been Tom. For three summers and for many weekends, he had carried groceries up to the big houses on the cliff top, and the narrow cottages on Fish Street, and the apartments on Trevarrow Hill. He had struggled with heavy bags into the echoing holiday houses near the beach, and up the cliff path to the vicarage and the stone fishermen's houses alongside the church. They were all familiar in their own ways. He knew them by their smells and their shadows and their decoration, and their states of disrepair. Some houses were so untidy you had to step around boxes and bags to find your way to the kitchen. Others were neat as pins. Some homes smelled of cooking. Or coffee. Some smelled of cats. Or of fish. Or of babies. Or of old age and decay.

But straight away Marazion House was different. It didn't really smell at all. If it did, it smelled of... what? Clean floors? Vacant rooms? It smelled as if no one had ever shared a meal here, or burned toast, or broken wind, or changed out of wet clothes. The smell was the smell of the outside world. The sea. The cliff wall. The rain.

And the decoration? Well, what had he expected? Maybe he'd imagined it would be gloomy, like a stately home, with dark olive walls and heavy embroidered drapes; with rugs from Arabia, statuettes of goddesses, and paintings of ancestors in huge gilt frames. There would be high ceilings perhaps, and a grand staircase with a chandelier and carved oak balustrades. But there were none of these things. The hallway could have been the foyer of a provincial accountancy office. Magnolia paintwork and carpet tiles. Wood stained a kind of corporation brown. Functional furniture.

The young man who had greeted him leaned heavily against the front door to close it. 'You don't want to be out for long in that,' he said.

'I'm Tom Horsmith,' Tom said.

'I know who you are.'

He was shown into a room at the back of the house. Plain. Furniture from IKEA. Plastic stackable chairs around a long table. It was a low-rent meeting room. Nothing that looked especially comfortable. A single picture on the wall was a cheap print of a painting of a Cornish harbour. Mevagissey by the look of it. Neither Monty nor Carys was there, but moments later the door swung open and a woman carrying a black leather document folder came in, followed by a man carrying a coffee jug. The woman wore a pencil skirt with a faint grey stripe. She had black hair coiled up in a bun. She looked like a civil servant. She even walked like one. She extended a hand. 'Good to meet you, Tom,' she said. 'I'm Esperanza Mulligan. I work for the Prime Minister.'

'Hell of an opening line,' Tom said. 'I bet that gets you a good table at Blakes. I should maybe work on my own version. I'm Tom Horsmith. I work for the planet.'

She didn't smile. 'I don't think that would work so well,' she said.

'Esperanza?' he said, testing out the name.

'Yes.'

'It means *hope*,' he said. 'I guess we could all do with some of that.'

'I'm sure we could.' Her tone suggested that this direction of the conversation was now closed. 'Thank you for coming,' she said.

'Not a problem,' Tom said. 'Monty paid for the trip.'

'Perhaps,' Esperanza suggested, 'it might not be prudent to mention that to anybody. Not everyone likes their acts of generosity to be advertised.' She turned to the man who had accompanied her. 'This is Kemal. He's our AV wizard.'

'AV?' asked Tom as he shook the man's hand.

'Audio Visual,' Kemal said. 'Cameras, sound, lighting. That sort of thing.'

Kemal did look more like an AV wizard than a government employee. He sported a very short beard, and he wore a T-shirt with the face of Einstein and a formula on the front. 'I'm here to make you look good,' he told Tom.

'Right,' Tom said, uncertain whether or not to thank him for this act of kindness.

'Mr Causley isn't here yet,' Esperanza said. 'He's on his way from town.'

Town. It was the trendy urban way of talking about London. Tom felt an unfamiliar sense of discomfort. He didn't belong here. Not among these slick Whitehall types with their fashionable names and city-chic idioms. *Esperanza, I work for the Prime Minister.* He had dropped by to check in with Monty. It was what they had agreed. Yet now he had the sense of much larger machinery whirring facelessly behind the walls in a world where security men answered the door and AV wizards distributed coffee and slick, suited advisors with black leather folders worked for the Prime Minister. 'Shall I come back later?'

'No.' Esperanza's tone was firm. She gestured towards the table, and she pulled out a chair. 'Just a little chat.'

The three of them slid onto inadequate chairs.

'I need to be sure you understand why you're here, Tom,' Esperanza said. Her tone was the tone of an overbearing aunt, determined to ensure that her young charges knew how to behave in polite company. 'I know you've talked about it with Monty, but if you don't mind, I should like to go over it all again. Just to make sure we're all on the same page.'

'That's OK by me,' Tom said. But he could feel his mind wandering already. It was as if the very act of sitting at a meeting table and trying to appear focussed had contrived to make him lose focus. He was still tired. He hadn't slept much. Not for four days. Outside the window he could hear something battering against a wall in the gale. What was it? *Bash. Bash. Bash.* A door crashing maybe. Or a loose window?

Esperanza said. 'So this is how it will work. We have hired out the backroom bar in the pub. This is a private function so we should have it all to ourselves. We won't let people in or out unless we know who they are. We don't want any hecklers. I don't suppose we shall have too many local people there. It's dreadful weather today and nobody knows you and Monty are planning to be there, so we should be reasonably undisturbed.'

'About that...' Tom said.

'We shall have four cameras there,' Esperanza continued. 'One will be on you, one on Monty, the third will be a wide shot of the two of you, and the fourth will be for general crowd-reaction shots.'

Crowd-reaction shots? 'I thought we were going for the shaky, handheld camera look. Like the last time.'

'We can make it look shaky and handheld if we want to,' Esperanza said. 'We can do that in post-production.'

Tom shrugged. The sense of discomfort was growing. *Bash. Bash. Bash.* Outside the wind was still thrashing something against the house. 'OK,' he said. 'If that's how you want to play it.'

'I do. There will be lighting rigs at the back of the room. Not too bright. Warm lighting. Not so many shadows as last time. There will be a make-up artist there to make sure you don't look too pale. It'll all be very subtle. Don't worry. And you will be miked up. But we'll keep the microphones hidden to make it look more natural.'

'More natural,' Tom echoed. None of this sounded particularly natural to him.

'Good.' Esperanza seemed pleased with this. 'So it all starts with you and Monty at the bar. A cheerful hello. Look happy to see him. He offers to buy you a drink. You accept. And when the drinks come, he asks you about your work on the glaciers, and you give him a short answer, and the whole thing rolls on from there. He's just a touch shorter than you, so we've adjusted one of the bar stools to make you look about the same height.'

'You've adjusted a bar stool?' Tom said.

'We cut a few inches off the legs,' Kemal replied.

'I see.' Tom could feel a rising sense that all of this was very much bigger than he had anticipated.

'Will you be wearing that T-shirt?' Kemal asked.

Tom glanced down. He was wearing a black polo shirt, rather faded in places from too many cycles in the washer. 'I suppose so.'

'Please don't,' said Kemal. 'Black is not a good colour for TV. It sucks up the light. Makes it hard to get contrasts.'

'White?' Tom suggested. White made him think about Qaanaaq. The glacier. The landscape of perfect whiteness. The whip of white snowflakes against a white sky.

Kemal and Esperanza groaned in unison. 'Even worse,' Esperanza said. 'Far too vivid. It will be the only thing viewers see. Wear something pastel please. Blue if you have it.'

Tom tried to remember what clothes he had packed. Was there anything blue? He was remembering the perfect blue Arctic summer skies over the sound, looking south towards Baffin Bay.

'Get there at five please. No later. That will give you an hour to relax. Get settled in. We will film the whole encounter, from when you arrive in the bar to when you leave, but don't worry about what you're saying or doing. All we need you to do, is to have a conversation with Monty when he arrives, which will be a short time after you. A friendly conversation. I don't mind how long it takes. If it lasts an hour, two hours, whatever. Don't worry. We can edit it down to three or four minutes. If you give an answer you don't feel happy with, just say, "Let's do that one again," and have another go. But it is important that you give Monty time to speak,' Esperanza said. 'Don't interrupt him, and please don't belittle him. If he gets a fact wrong, correct him gently. This isn't about point-scoring this time.'

Choose your battles. 'OK.'

'And the most important thing of all is to cancel the wager. Are you clear about that? We need a handshake. A strong handshake please. *Let's cancel that stupid wager. Yes let's.* And you shake hands.'

But now his mind was roaming. There were too many other things to think about. Benny and Peter out at sea. Nan cold in the ground. The glacier. It felt like a friend he'd left behind; he could see it in his imagination, a mountain of ice. So huge. So indomitable. And yet so fragile. Lykke. He was suddenly worried about leaving her in Cliff Street with the gale all around them. And the twins. Always the twins. There was never a moment when he wasn't worrying about them on some level. 'I should be going,' he said.

'Not yet, please,' Esperanza begged. 'You've only just got here. We have a lot more to go through with you...'

But his anxiety was rising, and it didn't seem right to be there. Sitting in a meeting in St Piran, as if this was a conference room in Westminster. He rose to his feet. 'I need to go.'

'Tom!'

What was it? Was it the wind, so violent just the other side of the window? Was it the abrupt way the four walls and the low ceiling had begun to feel like a prison? He glanced at Esperanza and then at Kemal, 'I'll be there,' he said.

Bash bash bash.

'Have we said something to offend you?'

'No.' Yet he was offended. He just wasn't sure why.

'Five o'clock then?'

There was no reply for this. He pushed back his chair and he was gone. Back down the corridor. Back into the empty hallway. And out of the front door into the arms of Storm Raheeba. The smugglers' storm. The ship wrecker. It took two hands on the handrail to get steadily down the steps to the beach and up the steps to the quay. St Piran was being pounded by a wind as strong as the storm that had torn the headland in two. Yet everything inside Marazion House had felt strange. And everything outside felt normal.

*

'Tom. I need you to relax.'

Lykke Horsmith had strong hands. The hands of a fisherman's daughter. She took her husband's shoulders and steered him firmly into an armchair. Nan's armchair. The chair by the window.

'I'm OK.'

'You're not OK.' She crouched beside him and put her face close to his. 'You've had a tough week. You had three days of travel. You buried your Nan yesterday. You were up at half past four this morning. It's blowing a gale. And you've got politicians doing your head in, pushing and pulling you this way and that.'

'And Benny's somewhere out there, in all of this,' Tom said.

'That too.'

'And it's my fault he's out there. My fault for keeping him in Qaanaaq so long, so now he feels he needs to go out even in a storm.'

'Babe. It isn't your fault.'

'And I need to prepare for this thing with Causley. I should be making some notes.'

'You need to sleep.'

But how could you sleep in this wind? They ate lunch in Nan's narrow kitchen, with the twins sitting on the pastry shelf because the room would only fit two chairs. They ate pasties from Kenny Kennet's pasty shop, and helped themselves to homemade scones from Nan's pantry. 'The last of Nan's scones,' Tom said, holding one up for inspection, a great bubble of sorrow welling inside him. He could feel tears growing in his eyes.

'Then close your eyes, and remember the taste of every bite,' Lykke said.

'But they're not her best,' Tom said. 'She used to make wonderful scones. Once. When I was a boy. These are too dry. A little bit stale maybe.'

'All the same, Nan would have been happy to know her scones would be feeding you and the twins.'

'She would.'

Lykke Horsmith. Tall for a Greenlander. 'Danish genes,' she would say as an explanation. Still, height could be an advantage. She could wear high heels and look fabulous. But she rarely did. She could enter a room with a retinue of men in tow, and no one would be in any doubt who was in charge. That might have been her height; but it might equally have been her bearing. She was a woman of rare poise and confidence, and it might have seemed, if you were in the presence of Lykke, that there was nothing of consequence that she couldn't do. Ski down a glacier. Tackle a polar bear. Converse in Chinese. Solve a quadratic equation. Perhaps she could do none of these things; but no one would be surprised if she could do them all at once. She was a rare, and rather unusual being. *A goddess*, Tom would say of her. The things you might ask of an ordinary mortal, you would hesitate to ask of Lykke. 'Can you bake a cake? Can you fly a plane? Have you ever written a book? Did you ever visit Moscow? Do you know Greta Thunberg?' *But of course*, you would think. This is Lykke. She existed on a plane where mere mortals could only walk in her shadow. And yet, what was she? A tall Greenlander. An Inuit fisherman's daughter who could gut fish and skin a seal and carry on a conversation even as she did so. A woman who once had her photograph in Time Magazine, who now could fill a great hall with people yearning to hear her speak. A woman who could captivate an audience almost to tears in a language that wasn't her own. 'She's still a mystery,' Tom would say to friends. 'Even after eight years and twins.'

'My dear, you don't know how lucky you are,' Demelza had told Tom, at Nan's funeral party, when Tom recounted this to her. 'The last thing you want is to know everything about your lover. Mystery is the spice that keeps us going back for more.' And even as she said this to Tom, Lykke drifted up to them with her eyebrows arched, as if she knew a thrilling secret but would never tell.

Lykke, already something of a celebrity among climate activists, was the founder and director of *The 1820 Foundation* – an environmental charity – and of its research offshoot, *The Glacier Trust*. This made her Tom's employer. She was also, at just thirty-four, a research fellow at Copenhagen University, the joint-author of an academic book on glaciation, and the sole author of a hugely popular paperback, *'How to Reset the World to 1820.'* This last work was a fanciful, if imaginative, proposition for rewilding the planet, regrowing forests, and repopulating wild creatures to something like their status in the year 1820 – a year that Lykke identified as perhaps the last pristine year on Planet Earth. 'An unspoiled planet,' she argued in her book, 'is the most valuable gift we could ever leave to future generations.' The 1820 Foundation was an organisation dedicated to this proposition. As part of this project, she was the part owner, Tom had discovered (on the day they first met), of a disused coal mine in Poland. 'Why in the world would you want to own an empty mine?' Tom had asked her. 'Because it won't always be empty,' she had replied. 'We call it the *Upside-Down Mine*. Instead of digging coal out of it, we are filling it back up again.' She had explained the idea to Tom, on that very first day, as they lay in the meadow by Treadangel Woods, looking up at the high clouds drifting across the summer sky like wisps of wool from lambs' tails. The project, she explained, would convert sustainably grown trees and domestic biomass into charcoal using microwaves; the charcoal would be compacted, and this would be used to slowly refill the mine. 'This is why we call it the Upside-Down Mine,' she told him. 'We are miners in reverse. We are unwinding our destruction of the atmosphere one lump of charcoal at a time. Every gram of carbon I use in my life, I will repay, back into the mine. So will a hundred thousand others. The only way we can really be sure of taking carbon out of the cycle is by burying it underground. So that is what we are doing. One day, I should like every disused coal mine, oil well, and gas field, to be refilled like this. All around the world.'

'Won't that take forever?' Tom had asked her, nervous that she might see his question as a denial of her idea.

Lykke had simply smiled. 'It took two hundred years to dig up all the coal, it could take a thousand years to put it all back.'

One thousand years! But that was the kind of woman Lykke was. Tom was starting to learn this on that day in Treadangel Woods. Lykke thought big. She had ideas that might start as small as a seedling and grow as large as a forest. Ideas that might take a century. Even a millennium. Ideas she would never (could never) live to see fulfilled. But her ideas possessed a form of life, a resistance to rejection or dismissal, and an ability to self-perpetuate and to evolve into stronger forms, like a stubborn virus that would infect an audience so that they too, might go away to infect others. And something, always, in her manner, in her way of speaking, in her unwavering self-belief, made people listen.

Lykke was a woman whose calendar appeared to bend to accommodate her movements, rather than the other way around; never unduly stressed by the requirements of her different roles, she balanced her responsibilities with the skills of a juggler, and she never dropped a ball. Academia. Motherhood. Writing. Speaking. Administration. Research. She lived in her own hometown of Qaanaaq on the northern tip of Greenland, just about the least convenient location in the world for a businesswoman or an academic, and yet she seemed to have more hours in her day than an ordinary mortal, rising early, and retiring late, and operating all of the hours in between with such well-oiled efficiency, she could be a marvel to observe. She could take a phone call, while feeding breakfast to the twins, and typing a report on her computer, and perhaps, as she did these things, part of her mind would be solving a problem or planning an agenda. Tom had been, from the day they had met on St Piran Quay, entirely in her thrall.

'I have to be in London tomorrow, night,' she told Tom. 'I shall be speaking at the Institute for Oceanography. We need to take the ten-fifteen train from Penzance. There won't be time for that swim, I'm afraid, and I doubt you'll be able to do it today.' She nodded at the window where they could hear the rain lashing on the pane. I'll prepare the lecture on the train. I've booked us seats with a table. Perhaps you can keep the twins entertained on the journey. Oh, and Jeremy has offered to run us to the station at nine thirty.'

'Well. Good,' Tom said.

'We're all booked into a family room at the Tavistock Hotel. You can take the twins and show them London.'

'We have to get tonight over with first,' Tom said. He was trying his phone. Making a call. 'Benny!' he said as the call was answered. 'Ben?'

There was a faint sound that might have been a man's voice, but it was swept away by the noises of the storm.

'At least he's answering,' Tom told Lykke.

'You need to trust him,' Lykke said.

'I would trust Benny with my life,' Tom said. 'But it doesn't stop me worrying about him.'

*

Five o'clock, and curiously the Petrel was full of drinkers. Esperanza was already there. So too was Kemal the AV man, and several new faces – camera-operators, and sound engineers, and a man in a yellow sou'wester and shorts carrying components of a lighting rig. Tom and Lykke were the recipients of a cheer when they came through the door.

'What in heaven is going on here?' Esperanza demanded of him. 'I thought we had this place booked for ourselves.'

Tom shot a glance at Jacob Anderssen who was there wiping down tables.

'You only booked the lobsterman's bar,' Jason Anderssen explained, pointing.

But even the lobsterman's bar was full of drinkers.

'Word must have gotten out,' Esperanza couldn't conceal her annoyance.

'It's a village inn,' Tom said. 'What did you expect?'

Outside the pub, the storm was still raging. Sheets of spray were whipping along the quay.

Connor and Hannah were there already. 'I'm worried about Ben,' Tom told his brother.

'He'll be fine.'

A pint of cider appeared on the bar in front of Tom. 'For you. Just to relax your nerves,' Esperanza said. She stood and watched as he took a first sip. 'And whatever Ben and Lykke are drinking.'

'Two more the same please.'

'On the way,' Jason said.

Ah, St Piran. No troubles lasted here for long. Tom found himself smiling widely for perhaps the first time since he and Lykke had kissed on the quayside at dawn. 'Jason,' he said, as he took a long mouthful of the cider. 'You are a miracle worker.' He raised the glass as if this was a toast. 'You. And my brother. And this town.'

And for the next hour, as Esperanza and her team fussed, and fidgeted, and adjusted furniture, and did sound tests, and manoeuvred lighting, and chased people away from the tables, Tom rediscovered the tranquilizer that was the Stormy Petrel Inn. Jessie and Jordy Higgs arrived directly from closing the village store. They hugged Tom so hard he could scarcely breathe. 'He used to carry boxes for us,' Jessie told a bemused camera operator. 'Best delivery boy we ever had.'

Jeremy and Demelza came and claimed a table in the lobsterman's bar. 'Darling, this is the exact table we were sitting at when they did the first video,' Demelza told Esperanza, as she pushed past to take her seat. She laid a novel down on the table with its cover showing. 'Try to get that in shot,' she told Tom. 'It's my latest.'

And so they came. Modesty and Ardour Cloke, Alvin and Polly Hocking, The Magwiths, The Bartles, the Penhallows, and the

Penroths, and the Truscotts, Lacey and Elin Shaunessey, and the Moots, and both Robins brothers and their wives with their five tall teenage sons. 'Good to get out of that wind,' they would say, as each one of them threw shut the door, and their heads would turn, and their eyes would scout around the room until they found Tom. 'Lovely service yesterday,' they would say, those who had been there to bid farewell to Nan. 'Nan would have been proud.' Or those who had missed the funeral would say, 'Thomas Horsmith, as I live and breathe,' as if seeing him there was a huge surprise. 'It does a feller good to see you. I'm so sorry about Nan. Can I buy you a drink?'

'I'm already well looked after,' Tom would reply. But he would greet them anyway and they would slap his back. 'Good send-off yesterday, was it?' some would ask, 'for Nan?'

'Thank you. Yes.' An unfamiliar giddiness was starting to assail him, as if his brain had come loose from its moorings.

'You look tired,' Lykke told him.

'I *feel* tired,' he said. His limbs were leaden. He sat heavily in a chair and tried to keep his eyes open.

'Promise me something,' she said. She gave him a soft kiss on his forehead.

'Anything.'

'Don't do anything stupid,' she said.

Don't do anything stupid. He tried to focus on the words. Did they even make sense? Everything felt confusing, as if words, and ideas, and people, were somehow melting into a mist.

At six o'clock, the pub door opened and in stepped the protection officer Tom had met at Marazion House, now in a plain grey shirt and black combat trousers. The man glanced around to establish that all was well, and then he held the door open. In came a stadium's worth of wind, and following behind came Monty and Carys Causley, beneath a dripping golf umbrella.

Monty's outfit, pressed chinos, a soft, green pioneer's shirt and a dark-olive Craghopper gilet with ample pockets for emergency provisions, lent him the appearance of a tropical explorer. The effect was somewhat diminished by the brown-leather briefcase he carried. Nonetheless, the arrival of the Causleys perked everyone up, especially Esperanza. 'Excellent, excellent,' she called, 'can we all take our places, please, and stay there. No camera phones, please.'

Young Danny Robins was already filming.

'Please. No cameras.'

'Says who?' Danny demanded in the entitled tone of an insouciant teenager. 'The police?'

'This is a private function.'

'It's my local.'

The protection officer stepped in. 'I am the police,' he said, 'and you don't have permission to film in here.' With a swift move, he had Danny's phone in his hand, deleting whatever the young man had filmed.

'You can't do that.'

'I'll keep hold of this until we're done,' the officer said, slipping the phone into a pocket. 'Any others?'

There were no volunteers. The officer nodded at Esperanza and she called, 'Places, please.'

'Good luck,' Lykke whispered to Tom.

'Thanks.' But the room seemed to be swimming.

'Love you,' Lykke said.

'Love. You. Too.' What was happening?

'Good to see you again Tom,' Monty said unsteadily. He held out a hand. He looked every bit as nervous as Tom was. 'Shall we sit here?'

Tom picked the shorter barstool. He seemed to remember something about legs being cut off. Or cut short. A make-up boy patted his face with powder. 'Just to stop you glowing.'

He felt as if he was already glowing. 'What if I want to glow?'

'Then this will stop you.'

This all took an uncomfortable few minutes. The room was moving as if a slow-motion earthquake was in progress.

'OK,' Esperanza called at last. She cast an eye towards Tom and then she gave Causley a knowing look. 'Roll.'

Something was up. But what?

'Just one minute!' Tom held up his hand, feeling as he did so like a schoolboy in front of a teacher. 'I just need. I just need. I think. A glass of water. Please.' His mouth felt unfeasibly dry.

'I'll fetch you one,' someone said.

'Thank. You.'

'And roll…'

'I like the cider here,' Monty said, sounding very much as if this were a rehearsed opening remark. 'Jacob makes it himself, you know.'

Cider. They were talking about cider. The man never drank in here. Yet here he was praising the cider. Tom struggled to suppress a feeling of anger. *Pick your battles.* 'Yes,' Tom said, looking away. 'I know.'

'Can I get you one?'

'I've had one.'

'Let me get you another.'

A deep breath. 'That would be very kind.'

Two ciders miraculously appeared on the bar.

'Cider,' Tom said, feeling the need to add something to the conversation. 'Jacob makes it himself, you know.'

'I know.' There was an awkward silence. 'Ten years,' Monty said, with rather forced joviality. 'Who would have believed it eh? Ten years since we last met here in our local pub.' He raised his pint.

'Well, you're a busy man,' Tom said. *Busy, busy*, he thought. *Busy, busy.*

'You too, by all accounts. I understand you've been working on glacier research. That must be interesting. You must tell me about it.'

'Well yes, I should love to.' Oh God. This was awful, Tom thought. His brain was closing down. And somewhere he could hear music. Or was it the wind? And where was Benny? And the light from the camera was unnaturally bright. And none of this was comfortable. He couldn't imagine anyone watching this online. *Glaciers*, he thought. Glaciers. I need to tell him about the glaciers.

And then, as if to rescue them both from the torture, the door of the bar burst open and there in the doorway, with grey rain sheeting behind him and the wind tearing through, stood the harbourmaster, Casey Limber. 'I need help!' he called urgently. 'Anyone who knows boats! We have a trawler coming in with a broken rudder. We need several hands.'

'Benny!' cried Tom. He was off his barstool, and already his head felt clearer.

'Leave it, Tom,' Esperanza called. 'There's plenty of people here can help.'

'I'll be back when it's done.'

'Tom!'

'No point trying to stop him.' This was Lykke.

'Damn him!' This was Esperanza. 'It was going so well.'

'Was it?'

Tom was already out of the door, and with him the Robins, fathers and tall sons, and Mark and Trevor Bartle, and Joshua Penroth, and several Magwiths, and Charity Limber and Polly Hocking. In the space of just a few moments, the bar had almost emptied, apart from the film crew and the Causleys and a few older bystanders.

'Well, there was a turn-up,' Demelza said.

'Keep rolling,' Esperanza said to the cameras. 'And follow me.' She leaned towards Monty, still on his taller stool. 'Come with me. You're coming to help.'

'Me?'

'Yes, you.' She grabbed his arm. 'If there's a rescue out there, it's going to be you doing it.'

Monty reached out to grab his briefcase.

'Leave it!' Esperanza commanded.

'I can't leave it,' Monty said, looking aghast at the suggestion. 'This is my ministerial case. If this gets lost or sold to the press, I'm mincemeat.'

'Bring it then,' Esperanza said. 'But hurry.'

And now they were all outside in the storm, a bar-load of drinkers on a slippery quayside in the pouring rain and slicing wind, each person grabbing the handrail to walk into the gale.

Halfway down the harbour arm, there was *Piranesi,* the wrong side of the wall, looking precarious in the swell, and the waves there were as high as the breakwater, and often higher, crashing over the harbour-wall like artillery. The trawler's engine was churning like a tractor, chewing spume and pouring it out, white and frothy, from its stern. In among the giant waves the boat looked small. Insignificant. Flotsam, tipping this way and that way on the unforgiving ocean.

'He can't get into harbour,' Casey called to the straggle of volunteers. 'The wind's too strong and he can't steer. He's going to smash on the rocks if we can't get a line to him.'

Between the high stone wall and the fishing boat, the rocks were huge and unforgiving. On the deck of the little trawler, Peter was fighting with the engine and Benny was coiling up a rope to throw. But the challenge was clear to see. The engine, at full throttle, could barely keep the boat off the rocks. A dozen metres further along the harbour wall, the rocks ended and there the trawler could perhaps be pulled up safely, closer to the wall, and maybe towed around to the mouth of the harbour if there were enough hands to pull, and there it might possibly be drawn into safety. But if they stayed where they were, the engine would surely fail them soon. The boat would smash on the rocks.

Benny flung the line, expending effort like a javelin thrower. The rope rose in the air, and twisted like a dying animal, and then, seized by the gale, it flew sideways and fell uselessly into the waves, well short of its target on the shore. This wasn't going to work.

'Tie something to it,' Tom yelled. 'Something heavy.'

Danny Robins came running up the quay with a rope of his own. 'Throw this,' he said. He handed the rope to Tom.

It was a light rope. There was surely no prospect that this would carry through the wind to Piranesi. 'I need a weight on it,' Tom shouted. Anything.

Around him, the gaggle of volunteers began searching. The harbour side was not a helpful environment for suitable missiles. Once there might have been lifebuoys here. But they had been removed a long time ago. What then? A discarded lobster-pot? Too big. And too awkward. A rolled-up strip of tarpaulin. Impossible to throw in the wind.

'Use this.'

Something was thrust into Tom's hand. With the salt spray in his eyes, he could barely make out what it was. But it was heavy enough. And compact. And it had a handle.

'Thank you!'

And the rescue itself then happened so quickly, many of those there would have to embellish the tale in the months and years to come. It took just seconds to lash the rope to the briefcase, and just a single throw to launch it. Like a discus hurled by an athlete, the brown-leather case with its payload of ministerial papers, rose above the waves, trailing the rope behind it, and, lifted by a mighty gust of wind, it almost flew the last few metres like a graceful creature in flight, right into the waiting arms of Benny Shaunessey.

And now twenty people, or maybe more, had hold of the rope on the harbour. As Benny lashed his end to the cleat, Casey began to bark out instructions. 'This way! This way!' He was leading them towards the harbour mouth, away from the rocks. It wouldn't be easy. The trawler's engine was fighting against the wind, and waves were still hammering the quayside with geological ferocity. 'Pull! Pull!'

It was like the superhuman effort the men and women of St Piran had once made to rescue a stranded whale. Tom had been just a boy at the time, but he remembered it well.

'Pull! Pull!'

The trawler stalled slightly, and the bow rose high on the crest of a colossal wave.

'Pull!'

And now they were past the rocks. Safety beckoned.

'Pull!'

And then an enormous wave. A huge, huge, breaker. It appeared from nowhere, and the force it brought with it would be cataclysmic. A gulf opened up in the ocean to provide it with passage. Tom saw it coming, like a great creature looming out of the haze, and he felt his grip on the rope relax. His head was swimming. It would be nothing, he thought. Just water. Only water. What harm could water do?

'Hold tight!' Casey screamed. 'Hold tight!'

It was a titanic wave. Immense. It crashed against the harbour wall like a battalion of tanks and the whole structure seemed to shake. It broke over the heads of the men and women hauling the rope and it came down as an avalanche, a shoal of water, like a hundred bathtubs released from a height, and almost everyone clung tight onto the rope or onto railings, knuckles white, as drenched if they'd all been bathing.

Not everyone was able to stay upright. Some were knocked like ninepins and were sent sliding down the harbour paving, clutching at railings for safety. Tom was one of these. He was lifted clean off his feet and swept towards the harbour side in a torrent of water. There was a beauty to it, he thought, as the wave overwhelmed him. There were patterns in the paving stones. There were colours in the spray. It engulfed him so completely he could perhaps have swum. And thinking this made him throw up his arms like a swimmer.

Music. He could hear music.

But only for an instant. His head struck hard against a black iron capstan and everything went dark. He dropped into the harbour like a sack of stones.

All the while, the noises of the storm, and the cries of the villagers were almost deafening. Yet somehow, miraculously, the great wave had picked up the trawler, like a cork in a white-water cascade, and had carried it in precisely the right direction, directly into the harbour, right between the open arms of the knocker demon, right between the petrified remains of John Brewster and Matthew Treverran the card-playing fishermen, and with a push from the wind and from its own engines, and a pull from the ropes and the soaked Cornish crowd, *Piranesi* swung and came almost to rest, right at a mooring on the leeward side of the wall.

A great cheer rose up. Benny flung his line and this time it was caught and wound around the same iron capstan where Tom had struck his head.

'We've lost a man!' someone shouted.

Lost a man? How? Who?

'Someone went in the water!'

And now everyone was at the quayside.

'There! There!' A figure was floating awkwardly, face down, like a broken toy.

'It's Tom,' someone cried. 'Tom Horsmith!'

And straightaway, a splash; before anyone had a chance to think, before the name had been fully spoken, someone leapt in. Madness! The sea in the harbour was quieter than the open ocean, but still it rose and fell like a great and dangerous machine.

'That's Lykke,' someone said. And sure enough it was, long-limbed, dark-haired, striking out into the swell, arms flailing.

A second splash, this time from the boat. Benny Shaughnessy had plunged into the water, with his yellow high-vis lifejacket still on. A third splash. Casey Limber had joined them. There was a gasp from the crowd on the wharf. Would there be any more?

'Can you swim?' Esperanza asked Monty.

Monty reacted with an alarmed look. 'Well, yes,' he said, 'but really I don't think...'

'Just get in there! You need to be part of this story. Wait.' She glanced down the quay to where Kemal and the camera crews were crouched in the lee of the harbour wall, cameras still running. She gave Kemal a nod. 'OK,' she commanded. 'Now!'

And so a fourth splash. The Right Honourable Montague Causley whispered something to himself, made a short run – just three unsteady strides – and executed an awkward take-off from the harbour side, his arms whirling in the rain and the wind. As he sailed through the air, a camera flashed, and then another, and now there were four rescuers in the water and a fresh wave coming in from the sea.

On the jetty, Esperanza was on her phone. 'Larry,' she was shouting. 'Larry? I need you to get me the editor of the News at Ten.'

And in all the melee and all the commotion, with the real-life drama of a rescue unfolding before their eyes, with waves still crashing against the harbour, with men and women pulling ropes and others shouting instructions, with camera operators crouching to get their best shot, and with the rain still beating down like the great storms of Genesis, three things happened. One was a dreadful, tragic thing. The second was a glorious heroic thing. The final thing happened unnoticed, and unreported, just a hundred metres away.

The press would report the first two incidents, but not the third. '**MINISTER IN DARING DOUBLE RESCUE**,' was the headline in the Times of London on the following day. Few newspapers could resist a photograph of Monty Causley, dripping wet in the rage of the storm, his hair in snakes across his face, hauling the limp body of Tom Horsmith up the boat ramp. '**EXTRAORDINARY COURAGE AS MP RESCUES THE MAN WHO HUMILIATED HIM**,' read the Daily Mail.

Every newspaper also took space to report the accompanying tragedy. '**CLIMATE ACTIVIST DIES IN STORM RESCUE**,' reported the Daily Mirror.

Lykke Horsmith. Tall for a Greenlander. Nothing she couldn't do. Ski down a glacier. Tackle a polar bear. But Greenlanders don't swim. She would say as much herself. There aren't too many swimming pools in the small frontier towns along the western coast where Lykke had been raised. Lykke could, Tom would later recount to the inquest, manage a few desperate, uncoordinated strokes. They had been together in shallow hotel pools on holiday, and Lykke could windmill her arms and stay afloat for a while. But the panic would take her quickly, and she would end up clutching onto Tom. So what had gone through her head when she jumped into the heaving swell in the harbour that day? 'It would have been instinct,' Demelza would tell Tom. 'She wouldn't have stopped to think. She saw you face-down in the water and she leapt right in to rescue you.' All this, Tom would know, was true. Lykke wouldn't have hesitated. She didn't.

She jumped into the water, and moments later as she tried to swim, she was passed by Benny, and then by Casey and then by Monty, strong swimmers all, and all eyes had been on Tom, the broken toy, and the crowd had followed up the quay as his rescuers dragged him the full length of the harbour wall, twenty metres or more, with the harbour waters rising and falling dangerously like a monstrous piston, until they reached the boat ramp. And somewhere, somehow, in amongst the melee, Lykke had sunk beneath the waves, unseen. Perhaps she slid out of sight behind *Piranesi*. Maybe the current caught her and dragged her down. Who can know? But too many moments passed before someone saw her lifeless shape, like a sea creature wallowing beneath the surface, like a sleeping harbour seal; and the rescuers plunged back in, right then, Monty too, but this time to no avail.

And while, the next day, Tom Horsmith was waking in a hospital bed to find stitches across his scalp and learning the news about Lykke, and while the press and TV crews were descended on the little village of St Piran to film on the quay where the tragedy had happened, talking to villagers and visitors who had seen it all, the third incident somehow escaped attention. It was an event that normally might have been seen as insignificant, especially after a storm as wild and dangerous as Storm Raheeba. But unannounced, and unreported, we shall never know if it might have created a stir. The incident was this. The storm surge that sent the *Piranesi* safely into the arms of St Piran Harbour, and cracked Tom Horsmith's head against the capstan, also breached the flood defences around Marazion House. The front room was half a metre deep in water.

TWENTY-FIVE YEARS AFTER THE WAGER

1. Some say in ice...

Seen from the rib, from a short way out to sea, the glacier was rarely silent. It creaked like a giant walking on floorboards. It snapped. It popped. It rumbled. And every now and again, with a sound like an ominous drumroll, blocks of ice would crack away and cascade down the cliff face. Chunks of ice the size of houses. They would slip, and fall, and crash into the waiting ocean. The sea would swell, and the waves would radiate outwards; giant ripples in an icy pond. At first, the ice would sink, propelled by the gravity of its fall, but moments later, as if it were alive, it would re-emerge from the ocean like a creature rising from a sleep, and it would turn and tumble, this way and that, looking for equilibrium in the water; as it did so fragile pieces would snap off, and they too would perform lesser pirouettes in the cold Arctic sea.

Ilse Horsmith, nineteen, willowy, with hair as black as pitch, and eyes like jasper, steered the rubber boat deftly through a morass of floating ice, with just a touch every now and again on the electric outboard motor and the merest flick of her hand on the rudder.

Her passenger sat in the front of the rib, with a fat Nikon camera held to his eye. Photographing. *Click. Click.* 'Is this as close as we can get?' he asked Ilse.

'It's as close as my dad will let me go.'

Click.

'How high is it?'

'So this glacier is about a kilometre deep,' Ilse said. 'That's about half the average depth of the Greenland ice sheet. It's like three times the height of the Eiffel Tower.' She touched the motor and the rib crept forwards. 'This is Qeqertat, a medium sized glacier. Around five to ten billion tonnes of icebergs calve off it every year. It's about one sixth the size of the Jacobshavn Glacier, which is the one the tourists go to see in Disko Bay.'

Click. The passenger lowered his camera. 'Wow!' he said.

'Jacobshavn is the big one. That's where the iceberg that sank the Titanic came from. That calves around thirty to fifty billion tons of ice in an average year.'

'I can't even imagine that amount of ice,' the man said.

'I guess you don't see many glaciers, huh?' Ilse said.

'Not many.'

It was a seascape of unimaginable, ethereal beauty. The flat ocean was a patchwork of swirling blues, some areas dark, and some pale, and some almost green, or turquoise, as if an artist had splashed every blue from a watercolour paintbox onto a pure white canvas, and crusted the surface with pack ice. The backdrop was the great precipice of the glacier, and behind it, a horizon of white mountains fading into a clear blue sky. Only the cracks and pops of the glacier disturbed the majestic solitude of it.

'It's extraordinary,' the man said. He looked as if he was hunting for the right word. 'Otherworldly.' He pulled his hood away from his head and took a deep lungful of air. 'I simply can't describe it,' he said. 'It's glorious.'

'It impresses everybody,' Ilse said.

Two dozen metres away, silently, a blue-black shape slid briefly above the crust of ice, describing an arc with its gentle curving motion, barely causing a ripple on the surface, and glinting in the thin sunshine as it did. Ilse pointed. 'Do you see that?' she asked.

'What is it?'

'A fin whale.'

Click. Click.

'The second largest creature on earth.'

'Amazing.'

As effortlessly as it had appeared, the whale arched back beneath the ice and was gone. Ilse's guest watched the space where it had been, and for a while the two sat and gazed out over the cold seascape to see if it might reappear.

'Will it come back?'

'Maybe. There is no way to tell.'

The man turned his gaze back to the glacier. 'Do you ever see icebergs calving?' he asked. 'Really massive ones?'

'Sure,' Ilse said. 'Not really massive ones – but some pretty big ones. All the time. If we stay here long enough, we'd see one.' She pointed to a blue-tinged iceberg floating to the west – a hill of ice drifting slowly southwards. 'That one came off this morning.'

'Is that a big one?'

'Medium, I'd say. Maybe thirty or forty metres high. And remember, you only see one tenth of it. It will extend three hundred metres or more under the water.'

'I remember that from primary school,' the visitor said. He nodded to himself. 'And that's a medium sized one?'

'Yes.' Ilse twisted a throttle and the rib manoeuvred forwards through the ice field. 'In 2010, a piece broke off the Petermann Glacier, around four hundred kilometres northeast of here. It was around 250 square kilometres. That's about three times the size of

Manhattan.'

The man nodded, impressed. 'Was that the biggest ever?'

'The biggest from Greenland,' Ilse said.

'And what happened to it?'

'It crashed into an island,' Ilse said. 'And it broke up.' She revved the motor and started to turn the boat around. 'These little bits of ice are called growlers,' she said, pointing. 'If it's smaller than the boat, it's a growler.'

'And if it's larger than the boat?'

'If it's larger than the boat it's a *bergy bit*. Unless it's as big as a cruise liner. Then it's an iceberg.'

Click. Click.

'If it's a big chunky lump of ice, it came from a glacier. It's freshwater. But if it's a flat slab like a floating pavement, it's usually sea ice. That's where the sea froze in the winter, and now bits of it are floating south into Baffin Bay.'

A short way off, to the south, a second rib was shadowing them. A black, military-looking inflatable. And maybe a hundred metres to the north another, much larger steel-hulled, red and white naval vessel sat silently in the sound. A dozen or more people in this ship were watching them with cameras or binoculars. Someone on the deck raised a hand to give them a wave. *Are you OK?*

The man raised his hand. *OK.*

'It's quite natural for a glacier to break up,' Ilse said. 'That's what's supposed to happen. We want it to happen. A glacier is a river of ice, and it flows like a river, only slower. When it reaches the sea, it crumbles into icebergs, and the bergs float south, and they slowly melt, and the cold water sinks, and that draws warm water up from the south, and that keeps Europe warm. That's the Gulf stream.'

'I see.'

'It's a good thing. The problem isn't there.'

'No?'

'No. This is the spectacular end of the glacier, but it isn't where the glacier is melting. Not just here anyway. It's melting all over. All along its length. All through. It's melting on top, and underneath, and it's hollowing out inside. It's like an ice cube left out in the sun.' Ilse had clearly inherited her father's passion, and even, perhaps, a touch of his anger. 'Greenland has one hundred and twenty-five glaciers,' she said. 'And they're all the same. And they're all melting. And not just the glaciers. The whole ice cap is melting.' Her tone had slid very slightly from informative to judgmental.

Click.

'You had better take me back now,' the man said, giving her a sideways look that seemed to acknowledge her accusing tone. 'I can sense them getting anxious on the ship.'

'OK.'

'Besides, tomorrow morning, I shall have the excitement of your father taking me to walk on the glacier, and in the afternoon, your brother is taking me to plant trees.'

'You'll enjoy both those things.'

'Thank you, Ilse,' the man said. 'Your father was right to leave me in your very capable hands.'

'Thank you, Prime Minister.'

*

'The End of the World Tour Company' had its head office in Nuuk, the capital of Greenland. The office was a small room in a nondescript, blue-painted timber cabin, not too far from the seaport. But it didn't need to be large. Not much went on there. Much of the time there was no one in the office at all, and the door remained locked; but it seemed right, nonetheless, for the business to have a pied-a-terre, with a Nuuk mailing address, a telephone number, a plaque above the door, and a logo on the window. The owner and founder of the End of the World Tour Company was Thomas Horsmith. The other principal shareholders and directors were Ilse, and Noah Horsmith. A family concern then. This was its tenth year of operation. Trade was brisk. The business model was simple, and it worked well. Travellers would book their tours online. There wasn't a great deal of choice. The website offered a one-week, carbon-neutral, adventure tour of Greenland. A seven-day, Arctic-fantasy quest. One night in a Nuuk hotel with a chance to experience nightlife in the island's capital, one night in luxury camping cabins up on the ice cap, and three nights aboard a converted icebreaker working its way back and forth between Disko and Qaanaaq. The sixth night would be spent in the Qaanaaq hotel. The final full day would include a flight to Nanortalik on the southern tip of Greenland and a trip to the Qinngua Valley, where the tourist party would camp and trek. Qinngua Valley is the greenest spot on Greenland. Here each tourist would be handed a spade and a tray of seedlings and would be invited to plant trees before the flight home. Twenty trees, Tom would tell them, would comfortably offset the carbon used on the trip. Most holidaymakers would set to this task with enthusiasm and would generally plant more trees than their allotted number. The week's agenda also offered dogsledding, snowmobiling, a chance to see the Northern Lights, a visit to an Inuit settlement with an opportunity to try building a traditional igloo, kayaking among the icebergs, a visit to an ice fjord, a seal encounter, whale-watching, polar bear spotting, a bird-watching trip to see colonies of little auks and guillemots, and a snow-shoe trek to visit a glacier.

'That just about covers it,' Benny had said to Tom, when Tom showed him this itinerary for the first time. 'Not much else for tourists there. Apart from endless games of scrabble during the long winter night, or seal hunting, and I guess no one wants to do that anymore.'

It proved to be a popular programme. Parties of a dozen, generally couples or singles with a sense of adventure, aged anywhere between eighteen and way above sixty, would fly into Nuuk on a Saturday, or a Wednesday, and at any one time, between June and September, there would be two active groups, staggered by three or four days, working their way up the western coast from south of the Arctic circle at Nuuk, to a point well north of Qaanaaq, before setting off south again to plant their trees.

The tour organised for Prime Minister Causley was not to be the full week. Instead it was a two-day, digested agenda, a specially tailored trip for Monty Causley, two protection officers, three political advisors, a parliamentary private secretary, a coterie of civil servants, and an invited press corps of around twenty. A Royal Navy Class 1A1 icebreaker, HMS Endurance, was the floating home for much of the party.

'Good to see you again, Tom,' Causley said, affably, as the two men shook hands on the deck of the naval ship in front of the assembled press and attendees. Photographs would show the two locked in a handshake, sporting unnatural smiles, and framed against the perfect background of the bay, the ice wall, and the clear blue sky.

'You too, Prime Minister,' Tom said.

'Your daughter gave me an absolutely splendid trip to the glacier,' Causley said. 'She's a credit to you. She really is.'

'Thank you, sir.'

They posed for pictures, holding the handshake for longer than was comfortable.

'Are you two friends now?' called a journalist from the press pack.

'Have you abandoned your wager, Prime Minister?'

'Are you planning any dramatic rescues, Mr Causley?'

'Ha ha.' Causley responded to the press with a wide, affected grin. It was an expression that had become a familiar feature in photographs during his premiership. It was a look that would allow him, as now, to avoid awkward questions by presenting the smile, as if this was answer enough to the issues of the day. *Smug*, some commentators would call the expression. *Supercilious*, others would say. It was, perhaps, a rather forced configuration of the face, like a rictus applied by an undertaker to a corpse. For those who shared Causley's political views, the look was broadly seen as genial, an indication of optimism and a warm heart; those of the opposite political persuasion were more inclined to see the grin as a sinister leer, and an unwelcome suggestion of arrogance.

Tom had never seen the smile in the flesh, although he had observed it often enough in media reports. There was, he thought, something faintly fearsome about the smile. As the two of them were united in their long handshake, he turned to look away, with a grin of his own for the press. He hoped his own face was rather less alarming.

'I believe you're planning to say a few words,' Monty Causley said. He said this quietly, almost in a whisper, not even looking at Tom as he spoke, the handshake still in progress, his lips barely moving. A politician's trick perhaps. A way to drop an aside without alerting anyone who might be watching.

'Just a few, sir.'

'Will they be polite?'

'Yes, sir.'

'Good.'

It was too cold to be on the deck for long. Not quite freezing, but a chilling breeze was coming down the sound from the north. Too warm for full Arctic snowsuits, but cold enough to chill feet and fingers. All the same, there was a diplomatic protocol to these occasions, and this had to be followed, regardless of the temperature outside. For this event, someone had clearly determined that official pleasantries would take place on deck. Photographs would be better there. So that is what happened. Coats were worn. Gloves were available for anyone who needed them. Everyone was breathing steam in the cold, still air. One by one, presumably to a pre-agreed agenda, there were more handshakes, with more dignitaries, more forced smiles, more official photographs. The Prime Minister shook hands with a local Inuit leader, and they exchanged a few words. The Greenlander made a joke and Causley laughed in the right place. There followed a short speech of welcome from the Prime Minister of Denmark, and a few warm remarks from Causley, including an effusive thanks to the people of Greenland, then at last, to a general murmur of approval, Tom took to the microphone. Several cameras flashed.

'Thank you, Prime Minister,' he said. 'And thank you to our Danish hosts. And thank you to the navy for letting us borrow your ship. Now, as most of you know, Prime Minister Causley and I have... some history.'

There was laughter at this. Tom held up a hand to quieten it. 'I can never, ever, forget that ... on the last day we met, I lost my wife Lykke. I feel her loss most grievously still, today, and every day. I miss her. I will always miss her. I wake in the morning, and every day I must come to terms with her loss all over again. You all know the tragic events I'm referring to. You will know, too, that one of the people who risked his life to save mine was Monty Causley. I thank him for that.'

He paused to allow a short burst of applause.

'It isn't an exaggeration to say that climate-change killed Lykke. The combination of a record heatwave, and an unseasonal hurricane, were part of the circumstances that led to us all being on St Piran harbour that day. We know that these extremes of weather are caused by us. By humans. By our insatiable demand for cheap energy. This has been a hard lesson for us to learn. But we all grow older, and most of us grow wiser, and these days, despite our early differences, I believe that Prime Minister Causley and I are broadly on the same side. At least so far as our response to the climate emergency goes. And where we're not on the same side...' he took a sideways look at the Prime Minister who stood at the microphone alongside him, 'I hope to have a chance to try and win him over. I'm delighted,' he said, 'that Mr Causley has seen fit to accept my invitation to visit Greenland, to take a look at the work of the Glacier Trust, and to help draw the world's attention to the cliff-face of climate change, which is here...' he tapped the wooden lectern with his middle finger, 'right here in the Arctic.'

Afterwards, when they were all indoors, warming up, an aide came to find Tom as he stood in the small on-board refectory, holding a black coffee in a Royal Navy-branded china cup. 'The PM will see you now,' the aide told him, casting her face downwards to avoid eye contact. The aide was young and female. She wore a navy-blue knitted jumper that came right up to her chin.

'Where is he?'

'I'll take you to him.'

HMS Endurance felt just like any other ship, but with better paintwork; like something recently disgorged from a foundry, it was a cold metal environment, of hard metal corridors, steep metal stairways, and clanking metal doors. It smelled of fresh paint and lubricating oil. Uniformed sailors on board stood to attention like toy soldiers when they passed. One fresh-faced sailor even saluted. Tom wondered if he was expected to salute back. He was shown into a small office, and there sat Monty Causley, smug and comfortable behind a metal desk, as if this was just another back room in Downing Street. A male parliamentary colleague, looking unreasonably young, perhaps an intern, perched on a chair in a corner of the room, unintroduced, and to all purposes absent from the conversation. The female aide gave a nod to suggest her work was now done, and she stepped outside and closed the door.

Causley didn't stand up. 'Horsmith! At last we meet again properly,' he said. There was a hint of Churchill in the way he spoke, as if he were modelling himself on the wartime prime minister. 'Away from all the press and what-not. It is very good of you to invite us up here.'

'Not at all, sir,' Tom said. He wasn't directed to sit, but there was a chair opposite the desk and so he took it anyway and lowered himself down. 'It is my pleasure.'

Causley sat back and made a steeple with his fingers. 'Good for your business I suppose? Publicity and all that?'

'That's not why we invited you.'

'No, no, no,' the PM brushed this thought away impulsively with a flick of his hand. 'I understand that. All the same. You were once a scientist and now you're an entrepreneur. A tour-operator, eh?'

'I still run the Glacier Trust, sir, and I'm a trustee of the 1820 Foundation. But these days, I get younger chaps to do the fieldwork. The travel business is a kind of side-line. It helps us to draw attention to the work we do.'

'Of course it does. Of course.' Causley gave the kind of smile which seemed to suggest he didn't believe this story for a moment, but was happy to go along with the fiction. 'Our fates seemed to be entwined, don't they, old chap? First there was that wretched wager, and then that awful storm...'

'About that, sir. I never really had a chance to thank you properly.'

'Pfft,' Causley dismissed this comment with another wave. 'You just did – to the press,' he said.

'I know, sir. But you had the courage to jump in. And you helped me out of the water...'

'My dear chap, it was fifteen years ago. I was lucky to have been a bit of a keen swimmer in my youth. I don't imagine I could do it now, by the way. Anyway, as I see it, we did each other a favour that day. The press was quite kind to me.'

'Less kind to me,' said Tom. 'They thought I was drunk.'

'Well,' said Causley, sitting back in his chair and rocking like a benevolent uncle, grinning rather wider than perhaps he should. 'Water under the bridge, eh?'

Tom blinked, as if the metaphor had somehow stung. 'Yes, sir.'

'Anyway, Horsmith. That's not why we're here is it? Two lads from St Piran. You and me. Two Cornishmen?'

'Sir?'

'We're here to do some good, eh. Isn't that right? To draw the attention of the voting public to everything that's happening up here in the Arctic. By the way, what are your politics, old chap? Do you mind me asking? You can be as honest as you like. I can work with opponents as well as supporters, you know.'

Tom took some time to ponder this question. 'I would say my attitude towards political parties is much the same as my attitude towards tattoos,' he said, and he offered Causley a smile. 'I fully approve of them in principle. But I have yet to see one I like enough for me.'

'Ha!' Causley liked this answer. 'I feel the same about political journalists and French presidents,' he said expansively. 'But don't repeat that. I just need to know you're not an outright enemy, Tom. I can take a certain amount of opposition, but if we are to do this thing... go out on the ice together... look at glaciers... that sort of thing, well, I need to know you're not going to trip me up or anything. Or to try to use anything that happens out there against me. Politically, I mean.'

'Why would I do that, sir?'

Causley surveyed him, nodding slowly. 'I don't know, old chap. That's why I have to ask.'

Tom looked reflective. 'My only objective is to honour Lykke,' he said, 'and to help draw public attention to the catastrophe that is overtaking the ice fields.'

'Well, that's good enough for me then,' the Prime Minster said. There was an awkward pause. Causley looked at Tom. A long, hard stare. 'We've come a long way haven't we, Horsmith, since our little spat in the pub all those years ago?'

'I guess we have.'

'There was a time when I thought it was going to haunt both of us for the rest of our lives. And yet, now, here we are, eh? Twenty-five years on. You have a successful travel business, and I have a rebellious cabinet, and a falling currency, and price inflation, and huge demands on me, all the time, to go greener. That's partly your fault, eh? The going green bit.'

'I rather hope some of it is,' Tom said.

'Anyway!' Causley slapped his hand on the metal desk. 'We have more photo-opportunities to come. And the press is loving all this by the way. You can tell your charming daughter she made the BBC lunchtime news. I suspect she'll be on the front pages tomorrow.'

'I shall warn her.' Tom gave a respectful nod.

'So now I have a few hours of meetings.' Causley glanced towards the silent aide. 'Oliver has a whole list of people I need to meet. And then, as I understand it, tomorrow morning you and I will be back in the cold weather gear and off to visit the glacier.'

'We will, sir.'

'Splendid. I shall look forward to it.'

'Me too, sir.'

'In the meantime, I'm going to ask Oliver to introduce you to my director of communications.' Causley indicated the silent aide again, with a turn of his head. 'I know this is principally a fact-finding trip for me, but it does help if we feed some raw meat to the media every now and again to keep them happy. Good press is helpful for us both, eh?'

'Yes, sir.'

'She's a very capable lady. Slightly formidable. But she gets good results. I'd like you to spend a little time with her. Get to know her. Get her views on how we can both make a big success tomorrow. Oliver, can you take Horsmith and introduce him to Esperanza?'

'Esperanza Mulligan?' Tom raised his eyebrows.

'You know her?'

A shadow seemed to fall across Tom's eyes. 'Yes, sir. We have already met.'

*

He found her downstairs on a lower deck, supervising as equipment was loaded into an inflatable ready for the next day's adventures. She didn't notice him. Not at first. 'Those items – in this boat,' she was barking, pointing at members of the entourage.' She turned towards Tom, who had appeared alongside her. 'Hello?'

'You're Esperanza Mulligan and you work for the Prime Minister,' Tom said. He held out his hand.

A look of recognition appeared on her face. 'And you're Tom Horsmith and you work for the planet,' she replied.

'Not much has changed then,' he said.

She looked directly at him. 'Except your life was turned upside down and I spent nine years with our lot on the opposition benches.'

'That can't have been fun.'

'Let's talk,' she said. She turned to a young man who was standing, sentry-like, with a clipboard beneath his arm. 'Robin!'

'Yes, ma'am.'

'Make sure everything gets loaded up, will you? We won't have much time in the morning, and I want the press and the PM out there ready to go.'

'Yes, ma'am.'

She turned back to Tom. 'So, Mr Horsmith?'

Tom bit back the impulse to say *yes, ma'am*. 'So, Miss Mulligan?'

'I probably never told you how sorry I was about your wife.'

Tom shook his head. 'No,' he said. 'You didn't.'

'Well, I am. Very sorry.'

There was an uncomfortable silence. 'Monty just called it *water under the bridge*,' Tom said.

'An unfortunate choice of words.'

'Very.'

'Did you ever remarry?'

Tom shook his head.

'Are you dating?'

'No.'

'Pity. Still, I won't try telling you to move on. I suspect too many people may have done that already.'

'They have.'

They walked along the deck together and found a spot away from eavesdropping ears, where they could stand, holding onto the rail, looking out over the soft blue and green waters of the bay towards the great glacier. She hadn't changed much, Tom thought. But there isn't too much to change in a person between the ages of thirty and forty-five. Or between thirty-something, which she must have been on that night in St Piran, and maybe still forty-something now. Or maybe fifty. She looked a little more careworn, perhaps. A touch heavier. A victim of too many clandestine Westminster dinners, perhaps, trying to appease parliamentary plotters. Her hair was greyer now. In parts. Or perhaps it was streaked deliberately. A highlight of grey to signify maturity. She wore blue denim jeans and dark Hunter wellingtons and the kind of grey padded jacket that could have been tailored for those rare days in the calendar when the lady of the manor pretended to muck out the stables. The whole outfit looked as if it had been designed and fitted specifically for this trip.

'What's your angle, Tom?' she asked him, glancing around to make sure they could talk freely. Her manner was quite abrupt.

'My angle?'

'Everyone has an angle. I do. Monty does. You do. Everyone knows what they want out of this little jaunt today and tomorrow. I know what I want. What about you?'

Tom shrugged his shoulders. 'I really don't have an angle,' he said.

'Bullshit! You invited Monty here. You wrote him an open letter and you posted it online. You didn't do that because you wanted to renew an old friendship.' Esperanza fixed him with an uncompromising stare. 'This isn't a criticism, Tom. I expect you to have an angle. I just want us to be clear what it is. That way we can try to make sure we all win from this trip. You, and me, and Monty. So what is it? Publicity for your little tour company? Helping to save the planet? What?'

Tom looked away, out across the turquoise waters of the sound, to where the great ice island of Greenland lay slumbering. A solemn seascape of utter solitude and beauty. A scatter of ice chunks, *bergy bits*, was drifting towards them. He drew a deep breath. 'Lykke was a Greenlander,' he said, quietly.

Esperanza sucked on her lip. 'Yes. I think I knew that.'

'But I'm still just a newcomer here. A foreigner. Even after twenty-two years. They tolerate me here because my children are half Greenlanders. And because Lykke was well loved.' He turned to look Esperanza fully in the face. 'You want to know my angle? Lykke is my angle,' he said.

'I don't understand.'

'I don't expect you to. Are you a parent?'

Esperanza shook her head. 'No.'

'Then I can't answer your question. It's a quarter of a century since I argued with Monty in the bar of the Stormy Petrel. I was a different person then. It feels like a lifetime ago. I'm not fighting that battle anymore. It's a battle we've already lost.'

They stood looking out together, all four gloved hands holding the cold metal safety-rail. A piece of ice the size of a car was drifting gently towards them.

'Which battle aren't you fighting, Tom?'

'The climate crisis battle. The battle against boneheads who think it's all caused by volcanoes or sunspots. The battle to convince people we need to do something. Not so many people deny climate change anymore. Now they just shrug their shoulders and say, *too bad, there's nothing we can do about it.*'

'That's a pessimistic view.'

'Is it? We've known about global warming for decades. The first COP conference was in 1995, for God's sake. Way before I was born. Al Gore made a big deal about it in 2006. Remember him? An *inconvenient truth*, he called it. *Too* inconvenient, as it turned out. We're on a rowing boat heading towards a massive waterfall, and the people at the front of the boat are yelling for us to stop, but the people rowing the boat are all facing backwards, and they can't see the falls. *"What's all the fuss? We'll set some targets,"* they're saying. *"We'll ease up on the rowing in ten years or so. Some of us. Others might keep on rowing just as much as they are now. But there's not much we can do about them. Maybe this waterfall will go away if we don't think about it.*" I'm not the same person anymore, Esperanza. Perhaps I am a pessimist. Perhaps I'm just tired of it. Because do you know what part of me says now? *Fuck it!* We've lost. And if all the people who give a shit about the planet manage to change anything, maybe they'll get us all to slow the climate collapse down by ten years or so. But what's the point of that? If humanity hangs on, it will be a miserable shitty existence for the next hundred thousand generations. What does ten years matter either way?'

'I see.' Esperanza said.

'But another part of me says NO!' Tom banged a fist down onto the guardrail in a moment of visible anger. 'NO! Do not go gently into that good night. Rage, rage against the dying of the light. That would be what Lykke would want. That's why I have to continue with her work. Her vision. Her vision was a return to a pristine world. A world before we started to screw it all up. And that's why this is about Lykke. You want to know my angle? That's what it is. It's anger. It's rage.'

Esperanza gave him a bemused look. Her mouth turned up very slightly at the corners as if she had found this outburst puzzling.

'That isn't what you wanted to hear is it?' he asked.

'Not exactly. I don't know how we help you with that.'

'You can't.'

Beneath them, the car-sized berg was colliding in slow motion with the ship. Fragments of ice were being thrown up like scattered jewels in an argument. They had to step back from the rail for a moment, to prevent themselves being showered by ice.

'It's like a *Titanic* moment,' Esperanza said.

They leaned over the rail to watch the ice floating past. The bergy bit was sliding down towards the prow.

'So, what do you want Monty to do?' Esperanza asked, when the moment had passed.

Tom let out a long sigh. 'He should have asked me that twenty-five years ago.'

'What would you have told him?'

'What *should* I have told him? You should read Lykke's book. Of course she hadn't written it then, but all the solutions are in there and they are the same now as they were then. Ban the sale of coal, oil, and gas with immediate effect. Or, at the worst, with one year notice. I should have told him that. Fund a program to plant a trillion trees around the world. Tax the sale of meat and dairy products tenfold so a burger that costs a pound would cost eleven pounds. Three quarters of global farmland grows feed for livestock. Scrap the livestock and plant forests of native trees, wherever sheep or cattle used to graze. Scotland is practically a desert. Fill it with trees. Cumbria. Northumberland. Much of Wales. Sheep-wrecked. Most of Northern Ireland. We don't need pretty chocolate-box landscapes. We need trees to capture carbon. Fund farmers to make it happen. Stop using cement that isn't from carbon-neutral production. Come to that, stop government procurement of *any* product or service that isn't from carbon-neutral production. Invest in carbon capture and storage. Fund research into green hydrogen as a fuel. Perhaps use some of the land we waste growing food for livestock to grow biofuels. Stop massive factory-trawlers from denuding the oceans. Make half of our coastal waters into protected zones and police them. Harvest our sustainable forests, convert the trees into charcoal and then bury the charcoal back into all those empty coal mines, and keep on doing that for centuries until the mines are full again.' He paused, as if all the energy had left his body with this list. He shook his head. 'Force every company and the richest ten percent of people to publish an accurate annual audit of their carbon footprint and if they aren't net-zero, make them pay to sequester carbon until they are. Invest in ambitious geoengineering projects to reverse all the damage we've done. Rewild the planet. And here is the most important thing. Give the world notice that we will stop doing business, *any business*, with any country that doesn't do much the same thing."

As Tom spoke, Esperanza was shaking her head, almost laughing at this catalogue of demands. 'Tom, Tom, Tom!' She put her hand on his arm. 'Do you have any idea how demented that sounds?'

'You asked me what I should have told him when I was twenty.'

'You were pretty crazy then, when you were twenty,' Esperanza said. 'Any one of those things would have bankrupted us, Tom; would have risked driving us back into the dark ages. You know that.'

'And you still don't get it, do you?' He pushed himself away from the guardrail and started to move off down the deck, but Esperanza's hand on his arm stopped him. He turned to face her. 'You know what really will drive us into the dark ages?' he said. '*Not* doing those things. That's the real risk. If CO_2 rises high enough, Earth will lose the ability to form clouds. That should scare the shit out of us. Two thirds of the planet is covered with clouds. Clouds reflect away a heck of a lot of sunshine. Without them, our forests die, our crops dry up, and we heat up by another eight degrees. Maybe more. Game Over. And we're losing clouds now. It has started. I wasn't being crazy, Esperanza. I was being truthful.'

'OK.' She was looking at him the way a nurse might survey a dangerous patient. 'No one is a climate denier anymore, Tom. I get it. Monty gets it.' She waved a hand. 'Everybody gets it. We just need to be practical. Shooting people who eat meat isn't a practical suggestion. It isn't helpful.'

'I never suggested that.'

'You effectively did.' She looked at him with a curious expression. 'Am I safe letting Monty out on the ice with you?'

He shrugged. 'Seriously?' he said. 'Are these ideas really so dangerous? What is this? Maybe you should arrange for a man with a gun to join us, so if I start raising treasonous ideas like planting forests, he can shoot me before Monty gets to hear them.'

'Don't be flippant, Tom.'

'Who's being flippant? It was you who just accused me of wanting to shoot people who eat meat.'

'Well it certainly sounded as if you felt that way.'

'Well then, you tell *me*, Esperanza – what is *your* angle? Is this really a fact-finding trip for Monty? Or is it just a photo-opportunity? Is that all it is? Maybe it's just a way to remind voters about his heroism, rescuing me from the storm; after all, that was a long time ago and most people have forgotten it now. Maybe they need a little reminder before the next election. Is that it?'

Esperanza gave him a look. 'It can be all of those things at the same time,' she said. 'And still be a fact-finding trip.'

'In that case,' Tom said, 'don't get nervous about letting Monty Causley learn a few truths. We'll be way out on the ice field. Your guys with cameras will be a quarter of a mile away. Sure, there are dangers out there on the ice. But good ideas aren't among them.'

'OK,' Esperanza said. She reached out both hands to hold Tom at arm's length. 'Write that list of ideas out and drop them to me in an email.' She handed him a card.

'I'll do it tonight.'

'I need to give you your suit. You had better come with me.'

Tom looked puzzled. 'My suit?'

'Your snowsuit. What you'll be wearing tomorrow for the glacier visit,' Esperanza said. She gave him a stern look.

'I already have my own cold weather gear.'

'Not for tomorrow you don't. Follow me.' She led him down a steep flight of steps and then another, then opened the door to a cabin that had been repurposed into an office. Two black, zipped suit bags hung on hangers from a wall hook. 'This should be your size,' she said. She lifted one of the bags and tossed it towards him.

'There is really no need,' he said.

'There is every need,' Esperanza said. 'We don't want tomorrow looking like a holiday camp. It isn't *amateur-hour*. This is what the navy tell me is a state-of-the-art survival suit. Waterproof. Hurricane proof. Everything.'

Tom slid the zip down a short way. 'It's military winter camouflage,' he observed with a laugh.

'Why is that funny?'

'You won't see us in the photographs.'

'Yes, we will, Tom, don't be awkward. You'll have the sky behind you. It will look amazing. We need you both to dress alike. You and Monty. That way you look like a team. On the same side. And we need you to look professional. Like you mean business.'

'You'd better not lose us then,' Tom said.

'We won't. Be here ready to depart for the glacier at nine in the morning.'

'I shall.'

'Good.'

2. I've done this two thousand times...

There is no sunrise in Qaanaaq in June. There is not even twilight. The sun is up all day. And all night. No summer solstice, as Lykke would have said. This was a June day, and it was bright and clear. The air temperature at what should have been dawn was an almost comfortable four degrees. A perfect day.

'The snowshoes clip onto your boots,' Tom said. 'Let me show you.' He dropped to one knee and expertly sprang the devices onto Monty Causley's feet. 'We don't really need them here. The snow isn't slippery. But Esperanza doesn't want any risk of you falling over.'

The winter camouflage suits were white, patterned with random swirls of dark blue, pale blue, and grey. Monty Causley in his suit looked uncomfortably like a rather large teddy bear. 'Jolly exciting,' he said, lifting a foot to examine one of the snowshoes. 'They're not how I imagined them. I thought they'd be like tennis racquets strapped onto your feet. But these are quite hi-tech.'

'Inuit snowshoes still look like tennis racquets,' Tom said. 'They make them from wood and seal hide. But these are easier to fit. And they'll be fine for us.' He pulled a strap to tighten the shoe onto Monty's foot. 'Also,' he said, 'traditional snowshoes are for soft snow – to stop you sinking. These are more like spikes, to stop you slipping. There,' he said, happy with the fit. He repeated the process with the other shoe. 'They're a lot smaller than an Inuit shoe, but the snow is fairly compacted on the glacier, so they'll be fine for us.'

'I won't go sliding around and making an ass of myself?' Monty said.

'I can't promise that. But don't try walking too fast,' Tom advised. 'And don't take small steps. Walk with wide strides so they don't knock each other. You'll have two walking poles, so you really shouldn't fall.'

They posed for photographs in their cold weather suits and shoes, holding their poles like Victorian explorers. Esperanza was in control of the proceedings, overseeing action like a film director. 'Over there. A little bit more. A little bit more. There.' Her eyes would narrow, and she would shade her face from the glare of the sun with a gloved hand, as if every camera angle carried potential shortcomings. 'The plan,' she told the gaggle of press and officials, gathered on the snow, 'is for the Prime Minister and Mr Horsmith to walk out a short way onto the glacier, just the two of them. We shall have two drones up there taking photographs,' she pointed upward into the perfect blue of the sky, 'and we don't want the snowscape to be a mess of footprints. Ideally, what will look best on pictures, will be a single trail of footsteps going out onto the ice, no other prints around. Virgin snow. Untouched.'

'Absolutely right,' Tom said. 'We'll walk for about ten minutes, so what you'll get is a long-shot view of the two of us a good distance out, maybe half a kilometre or so, an uninterrupted trail of footprints, and ice all around us. It really is the best way to convey the vastness of the landscape, and the sheer scale of the glacier.'

'That sounds splendid, Tom,' Monty said. 'Although maybe ten minutes is a little long to walk.'

'We offer drone photographs like this to tourists, and these are always the ones that end up on the wall. Trust me. This will be a front-page picture.'

'They need to get out onto the main body of the glacier,' Esperanza explained, talking more to the press pack than to Causley directly. 'They don't want to be seen tiptoeing around at the edge. Mr Horsmith assures me it will be safe. We are over two kilometres away from the ice face, so unless a very huge chunk of ice breaks off, we should be okay.'

'We don't want to end up on an iceberg,' Monty said with a jovial gesture of his gloved hand.

The press pack laughed at this idea. 'It would make for some great pictures,' one photographer joked.

They stood in a little cluster on the ice, two dozen people or more, a forest of camera lenses, and a sufficient number of bright coats and woolly hats to fill an outward-bound shop. Every outfit looked new, Tom realised. Everyone here had been shopping, perhaps just the week before, for Gore-Tex jackets in primary colours, and branded fleeces or chunky fair isle jumpers, hats of all descriptions, and fur-lined boots. The stretch of ice bearing the Prime Minister's retinue and assorted media types might have resembled a winter fashion catwalk. Only the navy personnel, in their dark-blue roll-neck sweaters and sensible grey oilskin coats, served to tone down the whole display.

'Most of the glacier is impossible to walk on,' Tom told the assembled gathering. 'As you can see.' He pointed northwards and down the slope towards a violent landscape of jagged ice, steep cliffs, and ominous crevasses. 'That's because the ice is shifting all the time. Where we're standing... here, right now, on the ice cap... this ice isn't moving. This ice has been here for centuries. But over there, the glacier is on the move. It's a river of ice. If it wasn't frozen, it would be one of the world's great rivers — like the

Rhine, or the Ganges. But it is frozen, and so it ends up looking like this alien mountain-range, all peaks, and chasms, crumbling and unstable, all drifting down towards the sea at about a metre per hour. That is half the speed of the Jacobshavn Glacier, but still really dangerous. So we won't be walking much on the glacier itself. And we won't want to get too close to any of these big outcrops because they can collapse, and we wouldn't want to be underneath one when that happens. So we'll be playing it safe. There's a stretch of the glacier, just over there,' he pointed a short way downstream, 'that isn't moving much. It's like a slow bend in a fast river. It's nice and smooth, and it's covered in snow. So it's good to walk on, it's safe, and we shouldn't have to worry about falling down a ravine. We shall walk out on to the glacier for a few metres there to let Mr Causley see it for himself,' Tom said, 'and we shall stay for a few minutes. I want Mr Causley to see how the ice is melting, and we should be able to see some melt holes if we're lucky.'

Cameras clicked.

'Glaciers don't melt in quite the same way an ice cube melts on a pavement,' Tom said. 'The sun melts glaciers from above. Streams and the ocean melt them from underneath. And their own meltwater finds little cracks and runs down into them and ends up melting the whole glacier from the inside. Sometimes you can see great caverns inside.' He held up a hand. 'The Greenland ice cap is one of the great natural features of our planet. By a stroke of luck, geography has given us a massive island in the Atlantic, most of it lying north of the Arctic circle, and over the millennia, this island has developed the most colossal cover of ice. If you walk east from here,' he pointed, 'you would need to walk over ice for 1,500 kilometres before you reach the coast. If you walk south, it is more than 2,000 kilometres to the southernmost point of the ice, or else it is 800 kilometres to the northernmost point. It is immense. Most of the ice is more than two kilometres deep.

And this fantastically large block of ice acts as an air-conditioner for our whole planet. It stops us getting too hot. But by creating the gulf stream, it also stops us getting too cold. We are so lucky to have this amazing place. But its future is now in our hands. The important message for Prime Minister Causley and for your viewers or readers is — *the ice cap is melting.* And that, I'm afraid, is a very bad thing indeed. We might, with a huge global effort, slow it down. We could, in time, stop it. But we cannot reverse it. That will take millennia. For thousands of years, snowfall in winter and melting in summer has been pretty much in balance. Not anymore. Every year, melting now exceeds snowfall. The Greenland icecap will melt and that will have consequences for all of mankind. We need people to understand that.'

They were nearly ready. It would all be over in less than half an hour. A man in a naval coat came and checked their snowshoes, their zips, their laces, their poppers, and their gloves. 'It really isn't all that cold,' Monty said at one point, as the man fussed with his hood and clipped a radio to his belt. 'I'm actually sweltering in all this.'

'We want it to look cold,' Esperanza said.

'And do we really need all this rope?'

'It'll look good in the photographs.'

The man in the naval coat came over to check Tom's kit. He had a face pockmarked with scars from adolescent acne, making him look as if he had survived a bad fire, or a shoot-out in a glass factory. 'I'm the PM's protection officer,' he said dryly. 'My job is to keep him safe at all times.'

'I understand,' Tom said.

'Are you carrying any recording equipment?' the officer asked, casually. 'A camera? A recorder? A mobile phone?'

'I have a phone.' Tom showed it to him. 'I'm not using it to record anything.'

'All the same, I'll keep hold of it until you get back.' The man plucked the phone from Tom's hand.

'What if I need to make a phone call?'

'You won't.' The protection officer slid the phone into a pocket, and made a show of frisking Tom like an airport security operator. He tugged experimentally at Tom's coil of climbing ropes, running his hand along them as if they might conceal an unexpected weapon, and with a rueful grin he unclipped Tom's ice-pick. 'I'll take this, if you don't mind,' he said. 'Just a precaution sir. You understand.'

'I carry it for safety,' Tom said. 'In case we fall.'

'If you fall,' the officer said, 'we'll come for you.'

'I don't much like going out on the ice without the pick.'

'Just a precaution, sir,' the man repeated, with a little more emphasis, as if Tom might not have heard him the first time. His tone suggested there was no room for negotiation.

Just a precaution. In case, perhaps, Tom was overcome with the desire to embed the ice pick into Prime Minister Causley's skull. After all, Tom reflected, the protection officer had probably viewed the viral video too. Everyone had.

No matter. It would all be over in less than half an hour.

'We're giving you a light rucksack,' the officer told Tom. 'There's nothing in it, but it helps complete the image.'

The rucksack was the same white and grey camouflage as the suits. Tom pulled it on.

'One other thing sir,' the man said. 'You'll need a rifle.'

'A rifle?'

'The Greenland police have warned us there could be polar bears on the ice sir. It's just a precaution.'

'You don't trust me with an ice-pick, but you do trust me with a rifle?' Tom said, trying not to sound too sarcastic.

'You won't have the ammunition sir,' the officer said. He seemed unable to resist a wry smile. 'The Prime Minister will have the bullets.'

'Then maybe he should carry the rifle,' Tom said.

'I did suggest that,' the man said. His eyebrows flickered for a moment. 'But apparently it won't look good to see the PM walking around armed. So this is how we will do it. You shall carry the rifle. I will strap it to your back. Should you need to defend yourself against a bear, you will ask the Prime Minister for ammunition, at which point you will load the rifle and shoot the bear.'

'I'm not shooting a bear,' Tom said, aware that a tone of sullenness had entered his voice.

'I hope not, sir. Have you used a rifle before?'

'Yes,' Tom said wearily. 'I know how to use one.'

'Good.' The man seemed pleased. 'It's just a precaution anyway.'

'You seem to have a lot of precautions in your line of work,' said Tom.

'It's how we stay alive.' The officer began strapping the rifle to Tom's back.

Among the press pack and politicians in the roped-off section, a level of restlessness seemed to be setting in. 'We should go,' Tom said.

There were nods all around. No one looked quite ready to give the order. So Tom stepped out of the press area onto a stretch of undisturbed snow.

'Do we have the all-clear?' Esperanza asked the protection officer. 'Then let's do this.'

And they were off. Two men. Two *Cornishmen* Monty would probably say, rather overdressed for the mild Arctic day, walking unsteadily over melting snow. There was a small cheer from the press pack, and cameras started almost immediately. From somewhere came the high-pitched buzz of a drone. The photographs, Tom knew, would be spectacular. The location would be the star. The pure unblemished landscape of snow from horizon to horizon. The distant peacock ocean with its glorious swirling patterns. The fearsome mountains that had shaken off shreds of their ragged icy overcoats to expose the rocky musculature beneath. And there, not so far away, the chaotic dirty river of ice and grit, groaning and straining like a tug of war team.

It felt good to be walking. Good to be back on the ice. Good to grip the walking poles, to feel the rhythm of his legs, to hear the crunch of the snow beneath his feet, to taste the cold breeze. He had done this walk so many times, the heavy trudge from the rough Qaanaaq Road all the way down the hill to the glacier, the landscape felt like an old friend. 'I used to come here every day,' he told Monty, not sure, as he spoke, quite why he was telling Causley this, but glad to have something to say to fill the silence. 'Seven days a week. For the six years I was studying this glacier. I would walk down this very slope, and all the way along,' he pointed, 'all the way to that hut over there. That was my base camp. I used to have instruments positioned out on the glacier to measure ice speed and mass and a whole host of other things. I became obsessed with taking the readings.'

'I'm sure it was valuable research,' Monty said, in the tone of a man who is only really interested in himself. It was a politician's comment, faintly dismissive, not requiring a response.

But Tom, nonetheless, replied. 'I hope it was,' he said. 'I hope it was valuable research.' He didn't look directly at Causley as they walked. 'I still come back here every few months to measure the glacier's progress,' he added. 'But these days, when I look back at all that work, sometimes all I see are tiny dots on a graph in a scientific paper only ever read by a handful of people and I wonder what it was all for.' They walked on a little further. 'Every dot on the graph,' Tom found himself saying, 'was a month's work. And the weather wasn't always as good as it is today.' Had he ever said this to anyone before? Had he even *thought* this before? Was he trying to be self-effacing to Causley, skirting the truth to provide a response that didn't hint of arrogance? Or had the Prime Minister's comment drawn him into revealing a genuine truth, one he hadn't viscerally understood until now?

'Quite a tough life, I should imagine,' Monty said. Another politician's response. He too seemed driven to find something to say.

'Tough? Yes. I suppose it was,' Tom responded. 'Everything is tough up here.' Yet now he thought about this reply, this too seemed less than honest. He would struggle to remember a better time in his life than those six years in Qaanaaq. He had been warmly clothed, and well fed. He had a home, and a wife, and two young children. He had friends. He had an income and a purpose. He had youth and energy and ambition. He had love. He had drive.

And now?

Now he had pain, and cynicism, and loss. Life was unquestionably tougher now. Yet this answer could never be the whole truth either. Time had worked some of its magic. Tom had grieved, as we all must grieve, but not everything in life had been difficult. He still had a family. In among the hard times, there had been good times too. But they were different kinds of times. He and the twins had become a fortress of mutual strength after the death of Lykke. Ilse and Noah, mercifully, had been just five. Younger even than Tom had been when his mother died with depression; and just as his own absent mother did not feature greatly in his adult identity, so Lykke's absence had never become the dark shadow for Ilse and Noah that it had become for him. They had rebuilt their lives together the three of them, one day at a time; they had moved from Qaanaaq to a house in Nuuk, Greenland's capital city, and they had developed a routine there. Few things appease grief more successfully than a routine. Tom took over the management of the Glacier Trust and converted the smallest of his three bedrooms into an office. The twins started at the International School. They did well. They were regular Nuuk kids. They took swimming lessons at the civic pool. Noah learned to play piano and Ilse learned the cello. They played ice hockey and football. They developed an enviable facility with languages, swapping seamlessly between Danish, English, and West-Greenlandic depending upon who it was they were talking to, and which language worked best for each conversation, and they did this with barely a thought, as if it were perfectly normal, something everyone did. They grew tall, like their mother. Good-looking, Tom would think. How proud Lykke would be of them, of the young adults they had become. They were good kids. Honest. Reliable. Normal. They made good friends, and shone at school, and grew to see themselves, their family threesome, as a unit, an indivisible prime number, a gordian-knot of love and dependency that could never be untied. 'How do you cope without a mother?' people would sometimes ask of the twins, and there was never an easy way to answer this. They coped because they could. They coped because they had the strength, and the bond. They coped because every room in their house had Lykke's picture on a wall to watch them, and because Tom would say, 'Your mother is here,' and because that was the Greenlandic way. 'Your mother lives in you,' Greenlanders would tell the twins, and this thin comfort, despite its echoes of the supernatural, resonated with Tom. Of course their mother lived in them. They were her flesh and blood. Her genes. Her complex heritage of bloodlines and languages and cultures. *One day you will see her again,*' they would be told by well-meaning friends, just as Tom had been promised he would one day see his own mother, just as kindly folk in St Piran had assured him would be true of Nan.

'Will we?' the children would ask, after such an exchange. 'Will we see her again?' And how do you answer this from a five-year-old, or, God help us, a nineteen-year-old? 'Yes,' is the easy answer. 'No,' is the more truthful one. Or is it? In the long winter nights in Nuuk, when often the sky was clear of cloud, and the deep black of the cosmos blazed with a billion stars, Tom would feel the same ache of the infinite that every parent has felt, confronted by the impossible prospect of eternity and the small, but very real, challenges of parenthood. 'Do you believe in the soul?' Noah had asked him once, on just such a dark black night, when he, Noah, was just fifteen and starting perhaps to grapple with the great questions for himself.

How do you answer that?

'No,' Tom had replied. 'But sometimes, yes.' It wasn't an answer that allowed for any explanation. He wasn't a man with any religious affiliation. He had grown, like most in St Piran, with a loose attachment to the Church of England in general, and to the Church of St Piran in particular, and with this, to the calendar of pious proceedings and festivals – Advent, and Christmas, and Epiphany and so on through the year, through Lent and Easter and Pentecost, and all the way back around to Advent again, and this casual observance had afforded him exposure to biblical stories and mythology and teachings to the extent where he felt he understood it, and could turn his back on it from a position of familiarity. None of his family were believers. Not especially. Not even Nan, even though she had attended church every Sunday and rested there now, in the graveyard, interred to incantations from the prayer book. Yet perhaps, since Lykke's death, Tom had become more spiritual than he would readily admit. 'Look at the stars!' he sometimes wanted to say on the dark, black nights in Nuuk. 'Out there are billions of galaxies and countless suns all beyond our vision or our imagination.' With all of eternity available, he would think, surely someone, somewhere, someday will discover a way to rewind it all, like re-spooling an old video tape, or reanimating ancient fossils.

So maybe, here and now, the question, *is there anything waiting for us after death?* is an easy one. No. There is no soul. No heaven. No nirvana. Not today. But in a trillion, trillion years, who knows? Maybe in spite of all our doubts, we will all wake up blinking and astonished, recreated in a new and unfamiliar universe, exactly as foreseen in the Nicene Creed. The resurrection of the dead and the life of the world to come. 'Maybe,' Tom would like to have said, 'there will come a time where Lykke never dives into Piran Harbour and the storm never comes.'

It was normal to think like this, Tom knew. When you lose someone and the pain is so great, then any flicker of light in the unremitting darkness is comfort. But he didn't share these thoughts with Noah or Ilse. They didn't need this cumbersome reassurance. Not yet. One day, maybe they might. Or one night, perhaps, when the universe was ablaze with stars. But innocence is precious. So Tom said nothing to Noah. Just put an arm around his shoulder and felt the tears dangerously close in his own eyes.

After the tragedy, the dreadful headlong insistence of day following day, following day, when every hour would bring reminders of Lykke, long Arctic winters could be a blessing. The perpetual darkness seemed, to Tom, to reflect his mood. Deadly cold lingered outside their house like a silent murderer with a long knife. Biding its time. But life, of course, goes on. It's a maxim no less truthful when you discover it for yourself. Day really does follow day. Even in the Arctic. You still have to get up and dress and wash and eat and make polite conversation, and tomorrow you need to do the same all over again, and so it was that necessity and routine began to work their healing. Tom and the twins took to spending winter school vacations in St Piran. No one had wanted to sell Nan's house on Cliff Street; and so the family kept the cottage as a joint possession, a St Piran bolthole. They could, perhaps, have let it out to holidaymakers. But any such intrusion into their childhood home seemed too painful to contemplate, and the effort it would take to erase the memory of Nan from every room, to paint magnolia over her wallpaper, to discard her bric-a-brac and crockery, and to homogenise the house into a soulless B&B was something they never discussed. Instead, Tom and the twins would escape the Nuuk winter and retreat to Cornwall, and there, Tom would lie awake in the bed he had shared with Lykke on her last night on Earth and ponder the cruel mysteries of life and after-life, and wonder if one day, against all the odds, they really might meet again. The shadow that hung over him would always be there. It would follow him like a cloud, a barrier to so many things. A barrier to true happiness. A barrier to friendship. A barrier to moving on.

'But not always tough,' Tom told Monty. 'Sometimes, out on this glacier, I would wonder if I was the most northerly human being on the planet. I don't suppose I ever was. But it often felt like it. And sometimes I would come here on a perfect day, a day like today, and the views would be so beautiful they would hurt. On days like that, I could feel the most sublime happiness. I would see polar bears down there hunting seals in the ice flow. I would see schools of narwhal in the clear waters, and right whales, and huge Greenland sharks. I would see foxes and hares, and the Northern Lights hung like ribbons across the sky.'

They stopped walking and stood for a moment to enjoy the view.

'Do you remember the first time I came here?' Monty asked.

'Of course.'

'Did we stand on that ridge up there?'

'We did. But it was a cloudy day if I remember. Snowing.'

'It was.'

They resumed the walk. A drone flew close overhead and Tom suggested they turn to give the photographer the best of the light and the landscape.

'I'm enjoying this,' Monty said, as they posed and tried to look intrepid. 'I didn't think I would. But I am.'

'Good,' Tom said. But he was thinking about what would come next. There were things, he knew, that needed to happen, and things he needed to say. Words that would need to emerge from deep within the dark shadows of his soul into the bright light of day. He hadn't rehearsed them. He had put them out of his mind. It was, anyway, too early to speak them yet. But they would need to be spoken before this enterprise was over. And now that they were on the ice, and the moment drew closer, so a fog of doubt began to assail him. He didn't have a particular plan. It was more of a fantasy plan. A set of imagined scenarios. What if this was to happen? What if that? How would I say what I have to say? There was no fixed future for the next half hour. Any number of things might happen. He might lose his nerve. The ice might misbehave. The clock was ticking. Not yet, he told himself. Not yet.

Crunch. Crunch. The familiar sound of feet on snow. He glanced at Causley, and the older man responded with a smile. 'It makes me think of childhood,' he told Tom. 'Playing in the snow.'

There had never been much snow in St Piran. Flurries perhaps. Dusting on the headland like icing sugar on a pastry. By midday it would be gone.

'On Bodmin Moor,' Causley added. Perhaps he had seen the disbelief in Tom's expression. 'My father had a house there. We would get a lot of winter snow.'

Probably true.

After less than fifteen minutes on the ice, they were there, at the edge of the glacier. Unlike a river which necessarily runs lower than its banks, the glacier at this point on the landscape, ran higher than the surrounding ice. A rocky moraine, like a spoil-heap of stones and gravel, marked the boundary between the glacier and the ice cap. They would need to scramble up a metre or so. 'Here,' Tom said. 'Use your poles.'

They picked their way up.

'You're sure this is safe?'

'I've done this two thousand times.'

'OK.'

Tom held out a hand and helped Monty up, and the two men stood unsteadily. They could hear the cracks and complaints of the ice beneath. 'You're standing on the glacier,' Tom said. His heart was thumping unnaturally fast.

'Amazing.'

'Within the lifetime of my children this could be gone.'

'Indeed.' They shared a look. Maybe neither man felt ready to replay their ancient argument.

It was strange, Tom thought, how this simple walk across three hundred metres of snow had converted Monty Causley from the alpha-male Prime Minister, the commander with his troupe of hangers-on, into little more than an ordinary sixty-five-year-old man. A little overweight. Overdressed. Unsteady. More unfit than he should be. No different in any significant respect to so many tourists Tom had taken onto ice fields. There were no commands Monty could bark here. Authority is an imaginary idea, Tom reflected. It only exists so long as there are people around to believe it.

It was difficult too, Tom realised, to altogether hate someone who was walking alongside you. This was something the Inuktun dog drivers knew. If you hitch two squabbling dogs to the same sleigh, then all at once they are on the same side. Step by step across the ice, Causley hadn't felt like an enemy. And yet, Tom thought, he was. He was an enemy.

Wasn't he?

Was this the moment then?

Perhaps. 'We should pose for photographs,' Tom said.

'You're right. Where should we stand?'

'I think just over there,' Tom pointed at a spot nearby. 'Can you see the melt water? That stream of surface water disappearing into the ice. It's a perfect spot to illustrate how the ice is melting.'

They made their way to the melt hole. In the distance, they could see the forest of long lenses pointing their way. Monty raised his arms and waved his walking poles triumphantly like a mountaineer who has just scaled a Himalayan peak. The drone flew close.

'We should show them we are united,' Monty said. He stood and put an arm around Tom's shoulder. 'No hard feelings and all that.'

They grinned for the distant cameras. An image that would become iconic. It was the picture that would lead news reports for days to come. A human gesture, arms around each other's shoulders like reunited companions of battle. Monty Causley's familiar smug smile. Tom Horsmith's faintly conciliatory expression, his eyes betraying just a hint of his discomfort. Military Arctic weatherwear, with a glimpse of their survival kit – ropes and walking poles and the butt of the rifle; a broadly masculine tableau – cheerful, yet staged bonhomie, rivals reconciled, – exactly, perhaps, as Esperanza Mulligan might have imagined it – two men alone in a wilderness of ice and snow and drifting rocks – united by the emblematic track of snowshoe prints that led all the way out towards them.

'Happy Birthday,' Tom said.

'You too.'

And that was the moment when a cracking sound, like the simultaneous snapping of a dozen firecrackers, sounded all around them.

'What in God's name was that?' demanded Monty, looking startled.

'I think perhaps… it was the ice cracking beneath us,' Tom said. He didn't seem unduly surprised by the noise. He looked at Monty and his expression was impassive.

Monty stared back, with a look of disbelief, his face turning ashen. He unwound his arm from Tom's shoulder and staggered slightly. 'What the fuck?'

The solid ice they were standing on seemed, like Monty Causley himself, to have lost its authority. It was crumbling like sugar, dropping in heavy lumps into a dark secret void, as if Tom and Monty had been standing on the glass roof of a deep well, and the glass had given way.

'Dear God!'

There was a moment of weightlessness, that ineffable instant when the world gives you up; hollowness in the belly, like the point of no return on a roller coaster, when there is nothing you can do except surrender to gravity and fall. The last view the cameras would have of the two men was the moment when, with arms and poles flailing, they vanished in a cloud of ice crystals and snow, swallowed by the chasm and the frozen river.

3. Boat trips around Piran Head...

On the harbourside in St Piran, lunches were being served. Vegan fish fillets were popular in Kitty Kennet's bistro.

'I never thought I'd see the day,' Benny Shaunessey would say, but even he preferred the manufactured fillets these days. 'They're not quite so *fishy*,' he would tell Kitty.

'There in't no bones in them,' Kitty would say. 'No skin neither.'

In the harbour, Benny and Lacey Shaunessey were helping passengers up the boarding ramp from *Piranesi* onto the quayside. '*Tours of the Bay*,' read a sign alongside the steps. '*60 minute boat trips around Piran Head to Smugglers' Cave, Whale Beach, and the National Marine Park*' the sign proposed. '*Dolphin and seal spotting. Families welcome.*'

Fishing was banned along this stretch of the Cornish coast, and this was how it had been for nearly seven years since the creation of the sea park. Some limited licences were available for lobsters and crabs, but fish were protected now. A chance to let populations recover, they had been told. A refuge for wildlife from the relentless depredations of factory trawlers and gill nets. But as the years passed, and as the fish, in time, began to return to the bay, there was, to universal surprise, no great appetite among former fishermen to call for a return to the profession they had abandoned. Fishermen were compensated well enough with government money. 'We've gone from poachers to gamekeepers,' Benny would say. These days he, and other St Piran boatmen, sold their services to the National Coastal Agency as Wardens. Benny wore, from time to time, a yellow lifeguard's jacket with a badge on the pocket. He had an electric motor in his boat, courtesy of a grant from the Environment Agency. He would patrol the short stretch of coastline from Piran Head to Porth Curney for perhaps an hour or so each day when the sun shone, looking for anyone who might be catching fish in the national park, and, like many former fishermen, he topped up his earnings by offering boat trips to holidaymakers. He rarely complained. The money was just as good, the hours were better, and in the winter, he could stay at home when the storms blew. 'It's more family-friendly now,' he would say to Lacey, even though the boys were almost grown and looking for boats of their own. All the same, he would spot shoals close to the surface, mackerel, and herrings, and whiting, and sardines, and from time to time, the old yearning would return.

'Aren't you ever tempted?' Jason Anderssen would ask him. 'Just to pop a line in the water and pull in some dinner?'

Of course he was tempted. The shoals were growing. But with every year, it became easier to resist. He felt a kind of affinity now for the sea fish, as if he, personally, had been responsible for their protection, and now he could take some pride as their populations recovered. 'Look at them,' he would call to the tourists in his boat, when a shoal of fish was visible, silver and animated beneath the waves. 'Mackerel,' he would say, and they would all lean over the boat to take a look.

It was a warm day. Benny shook hands with passengers as they left his boat and he wished them well, and most of them thanked him for the trip. Lacey took photographs for them when she could, snapshots of the whole family on the deck, and she gave each of them a small gift of Cornish ginger fudge made with rice milk cream, and she told them to come back again another day.

Lacey Shaunessey. A fisherman's daughter. Now a fisherman's wife, even if Benny never caught fish these days. And were it not for the marine park and the fishing ban, she would be a fisherman's mother too. Fair of complexion. Wild of hair. Rarely seen wearing anything but blue denim jeans and a T shirt – even in church – even in summer. Never seen wearing jewellery. Or make up. Well, maybe just a touch. 'My soulmate,' Benny would call her. 'Mrs Benny,' Tom would say. She was a woman without personal vanity, without great ambition, without any particular agenda of her own. In her forty-three years, she had left the county of Cornwall fewer than a dozen times, and most of those trips had been no further than Plymouth. A year could pass, from Christmas to Christmas, when she never ventured past Treadangel. She was a woman whose horizons had never risen much higher than the cliff paths on Piran Head, and she was content with that. 'I've never met a happy wanderer,' she would say to Benny. 'All they ever do is sigh over photos of their last trip and itch to go on another. But no one can go everywhere, can they? So they get in their cars, and they drive all the way to St Piran, and they're never happier than when they're here. So why would I want to go anywhere else?'

She had sailed with Benny, once, to France. They went on *Piranesi* for their honeymoon. They didn't book a hotel. They cruised into the harbour in Brest, and they stayed in the little cabin on board the boat, sleeping together in a single narrow berth. They ate French seafood, and they drank French wines, and they strolled up French streets and admired the buildings, and after two days, Lacey told Benny she was ready to go home. So home they went.

It was their habit now, Benny and Lacey, after a tour around the bay with paying passengers, to find a table at Kitty's bistro for a cold drink, and maybe a bite to eat, and today that's what they did, sitting together at a table for two, drinking iced coffee, and eating a vegan fish roll, when a young man came running down the quay towards them waving his hands.

The young man was Joseph Hocking, the vicar's son. He ran up to Benny and Lacey, fully out of breath.

'Joe?' asked Benny. 'Have you run here all the way from the vicarage?'

'It's Tom,' Joseph said. 'Tom Horsmith. Have you seen the news?'

'We're only just done with the midday tour,' Benny said. 'I 'int seen nothing. What's up with Tom?'

'You need to see the news,' Joseph said.

'Is he ok?'

'OK?' The boy looked struck by a sudden thought, as if the enormity of his news had only just this moment occurred to him. 'No,' he said. 'No, he 'int ok.'

They watched it on the television in the Stormy Petrel. A small crowd had assembled in the bar – locals and visitors – drawn in by rumours. Many knew the story already. They had seen it on their phones. All the same, they watched in near silence. 'Breaking News', read the ticker line. 'Prime Minister lost in an ice fall.' The report showed footage of Tom, and Prime Minister Causley, walking confidently away across a wintry landscape. Then, first from one camera angle, and now from another, and then again from the air, the same moment replayed itself on the screen. Perhaps the multiple points of view were introduced to make it more real. The two men embraced. A self-conscious, uneasy embrace. An arm over each other's shoulder. A wave to the distant observers. Almost a gesture of defiance. And then they were gone, just like that, in barely an instant, swallowed by a cloud of ice and snow.

'Holy shit,' Benny muttered.

'They're both from St Piran,' someone said unnecessarily.

'No way they could have survived that,' someone else said.

A sense of shock prevailed in the bar.

'Tom will be OK,' said Demelza Trevarrick, who was there at the bar with a cold gin and tonic in her hand. 'If anyone knows how to survive on the ice, it's him.'

'I don't give much for Monty Causley's chances,' said Jason Andersson. 'Too fat and unfit.'

At the back of the crowd, Benny looked at Lacey. 'I need a word,' he said, in a low voice. 'Outside.'

'What is it, Ben? We can talk here.'

'How many batteries do we have?' he whispered.

'Batteries? What for?'

'For Piranesi.'

Lacey let her face respond before her voice. 'Oh no! No you don't, Benny Shaunessey!' she snapped.

'I have to.'

'We don't have enough.'

'Then I'll borrow batteries from Dan. I'll borrow some from Casey.' Benny was already making his way out of the bar.

'Ben!'

He turned. 'I'm sorry, Lacey,' he said. He took her hand. 'I don't have any choice.'

At the bar, Demelza jabbed Jeremy with a sharp elbow. 'We're following them,' she said, nodding towards Benny and Lacey, who were exiting the pub hand in hand.

'I haven't finished my drink,' Jeremy objected.

'We've no time for that.' Demelza had an instinct for these things. 'We need to go with them.'

'What for?'

'Something's afoot.' Demelza finished her gin in a single mouthful. 'They're going to need our advice.' She banged the glass onto the bar and swept out onto the quay, with Jeremy in reluctant pursuit.

On the harbour side, they made a foursome, a little square with Ben and Lacy at opposite corners, standing by the very harbour steps where Tom Horsmith had once been dragged unconscious from the waves. 'What's this about?' Demelza asked.

'Help me, please, Demelza, he's being crazy,' Lacey said. She turned to her husband. 'I know what you're thinking, Ben. But stop. Just a minute. Take a breath. This is crazy, Ben. Completely crazy.'

'Is it? Because I have to do something, Lacey. If I don't do this, what can I do?'

A crowd of people was moving down the harbour side towards them. Demelza took Benny's arm and steered him down the dockside away from Piranesi and temptation, and away from the Petrel. The foursome moved as one. 'What are you planning to do, Ben?' Demelza asked, a hint of eagerness in her voice.

'To go after him of course,' Benny said. 'To go after Tom.'

'Benny, I love you dearly but this is nonsense,' Demelza sighed. 'By teatime, they'll have found him.'

'And if they don't?'

'Then he'll be dead. And there's nothing you can do. Or anyone. Nothing. I know it's a shock, Ben, but you've got the whole British navy and the Greenland navy and goodness-knows-who out looking for them.'

'Exactly,' added Lacey. 'And don't tell me the Americans aren't up there already with their satellites and God-knows what, and the last thing they need is some poorly-equipped Cornishman showing up in a small boat makin' a nuisance of hisself.'

'They'll have them out in an hour,' Jeremy predicted.

'Probably sooner,' Lacey said.

'I know that, Lace.' Benny took his wife's hand and squeezed it tighter than he normally would. There was something of a fire in his eyes. 'I know. But *what if...* eh? What if there is something I could do and I'm not there?'

'There's nothing you can do, Ben,' Jeremy said. 'You need to be realistic.'

Tears were forming in the big fisherman's eyes. 'He'd do the same for me.'

'He'd be sensible,' Demelza said. 'He'd leave it up to the professionals.'

'He wouldn't.' Benny wiped his eye with the back of his hand. 'He'll know I'm coming for him. It'll be part of his plan.'

'His plan?' Lacey sounded confused. 'What are you talking about, Ben? He 'in't got a plan! This were an accident.'

Benny looked at them. 'You don't tell this to anyone.'

Lacey shook her head.

Demelza said, 'This is between us Ben.' And Jeremy nodded. 'You can tell us.'

A family of holidaymakers ambled past them, off to explore the harbour with shrimping nets and buckets. Benny dropped his voice to a whisper. 'Tom doesn't fall through the ice.' He looked from side to side to protect this clandestine information. 'I don't know how else to say it. He doesn't fall through the ice. I've been with him on that glacier hundreds of times. Same place. No one's more careful than him. No one. He knows exactly how thick the ice is here, and how thick it is there, and how much weight this bit can take and how much that bit. That was his job, you see. Measuring the ice. Lots of places you might fall through on that glacier, specially the rate it's melting, but Tom never does. Never.'

An anxious glance passed between the four of them.

Demelza said, 'So if he does fall through, and he's got Monty Causley with him, you think... maybe it isn't an accident? Is that

177

what you're suggesting?'

'I'm not suggesting nothing,' Ben said. 'I'm saying Tom will have thought this through. He's taking a bloody stupid risk. But you know Tom.'

'I thought we all knew Tom,' Lacey said. 'Now I'm not so sure.'

'He hates Causley. Hates him. Hates everything he stands for. I know what you're thinking – easy-going Tom Horsmith, gets along with everyone. But not Monty Causley. Even I don't understand it. There's stuff he doesn't tell me. Something happened between them. I don't know. All I know is, Tom wouldn't stand on thin ice and put an arm around a man he hates. He wouldn't. He'll have a plan, Lace. That's all I'm saying. And who knows if that plan might just include me and *Piranesi*. Maybe it does. Maybe it doesn't.'

'He'd have told you,' Lacey said.

'No.' Benny shook his head firmly. 'He would never have told me. Never. He would never involve me in this. Whatever it is.'

'Well then.' Lacey stood with hands on hips looking obstinate. 'He don't want you involved. So don't get involved.'

'But he'd *know* Lace. He'd *know* I'd come. We've been best mates for more than forty years. He wouldn't need to tell me. He'd know.'

They stood on the harbour side, the four of them, an anxious quartet in a conspiratorial huddle.

'Would your boat get that far?' Demelza asked.

Lacey shot Demelza a look.

'Of course,' Benny answered. 'I'd need to recharge the batteries on the way, but it can get there. Easy.'

'It'll take you a month,' Lacey said. Some of her initial anger had dissipated.

'Six days,' Benny said. 'If I average twelve knots, I can do five hundred kilometres a day. I'll take two sets of batteries. Each one will last me a day. One day to Waterville in Ireland. I'll charge the batteries there. The Gulf Stream going north will give me a couple more knots. Two days from Waterville to Nanortalik in Greenland. Easy. They know me there. Three days up the west coast of Greenland to Qaanaaq. Plenty of little harbours to recharge. I could maybe do it in five days if the weather is good and winds are steady.'

Lacey was looking at him, an expression of frustration on her face.

'I've done it before Lace. You know I have.'

'Only as far as Nuuk.'

'Well, I might not even need to go that far. You might call me up and tell me he's been rescued.'

Above them, seagulls were calling urgently. *Haak Haak.* It was the soundscape of St Piran. 'Don't say I can't go,' Benny said. 'Please.'

'I'm not letting you go on your own. And in't none of the boatmen will go with you in high season. And your Dad in't well enough to do it. And I've got the boys to look after.'

No one spoke for a moment. Then Jeremy broke the silence. 'I'll come with you,' he said.

All eyes looked his way.

'Are you sure?' Demelza said.

'I know my way around boats,' Jeremy said. 'If anything happens to Ben, I'll be there. And with an extra hand on the tiller, we can keep going full speed even when one of us is asleep.'

Lacey blew out a long reluctant breath, and Benny knew this was her consent. 'Are you happy with this?' she asked Demelza.

'Nothing to do with me what Jeremy does,' Demelza said. But there was a gleam in her eye.

'Take warm clothes,' Lacey said.

'We will.'

'And leave your tracker on.'

Benny nodded.

'You go and talk to Casey,' Lacey said to Ben. 'Tell him exactly where you're going. Exactly what you're doing.' She looked at Demelza. 'We'd better go pack these daft buggers some bags.'

4. I think I know enough of hate...

It wasn't a vertical drop, and the fissure was not too deep. They fell for a very short way and then, remarkably, they were captured by the stream of meltwater as it gradually levelled out, and their downward descent became something like the experience of a flume slide at a waterpark, a helter-skelter tunnel of wet ice, slicing almost horizontally in a shallow rivulet of cold water into the hidden heart of the glacier. There was nothing to grab onto. The meltwater had created a perfectly frictionless slide, burrowing into the crevasse, and it was terrifying, and breath-taking, and unbelievably fast. The tunnel dropped dramatically from time to time, and as it dropped, the cavern grew darker, and the two falling Cornishmen were flipped and spun in the cold wet gloom, like driftwood logs in a waterfall.

'Jesus Fucking Christ!' That was the reaction of the Right Honourable Montague Causley, Prime Minister of the United Kingdom and Northern Ireland. His cry echoed in the narrow ice-tunnel like the scream of a teenager at a fairground.

Behind them, as they fell, a second sound followed them, an ominous sound, louder even than Monty Causley's cry, although they may not have heard this during their headlong descent into the glacier. It was the noise of several tons of snow and ice pursuing them into the chasm. The top layer of the glacier was collapsing down the melt hole behind them. Ice was shearing off the wall in shovel-sized chunks and crashing down the slide. Pieces came rushing past them like an avalanche.

So they fell. At heart-stopping speed, they shot down the channel, random objects in the ice fall. The tunnel levelled out in places to a shallow incline, but even here there was no stopping their forward momentum. For what seemed like an age it continued like this, a long straight slope, an almost benign (at times) stream of meltwater, leading them further and further from the melt hole, until, almost in darkness, they hit a bank of snow buried deep beneath the surface, and here they stopped. A gentle conclusion to their long precipitous descent.

'Dear God!' Monty called. His voice sounded strange in the cave-like space.

'Are you in one piece?' Tom was not far away.

'I don't know.'

'Any broken bones?'

'I don't think so.'

It wasn't totally dark. Their eyes were adjusting. There was a soft, opalescent glow from above, barely enough to see by, but enough to provide some comfort.

'Where in God's name are we?'

'We're in a melt hole,' Tom said, sitting up and brushing snow from his coat. 'That little stream of meltwater has created this. Extraordinary!'

'How far have we fallen?'

'Who knows? Probably not as deep as it feels. Otherwise it would be darker. Judging by the light, I'd say we're maybe twenty metres down. Like a six-storey building, perhaps. But that isn't our main problem. The more significant issue is... we've come a very long way from where we started. That was a really long tunnel. It felt like we were sliding for a kilometre or more. We're lucky. It could have taken us much deeper.'

'Lucky!' Monty Causley didn't make the word sound especially propitious. 'We could have been killed.'

'That's what I mean by lucky.' Tom stood up. 'Be careful,' he said. 'It is very slippery. But there is room to stand.'

The gloom was lifting, as their eyes became used to the low light. They were in a cave of sorts. The cascade that had delivered them was a stream of icy water dropping into a lake of meltwater. Tom fumbled in his pocket and drew out a penlight torch. He shone it around.

'Wow!'

It was almost a cathedral in the ice. A huge empty space glowing pale blue in the gloom. The torch wasn't bright enough to illuminate the far side. Above them the *drip drip* of meltwater from a thousand points on the ceiling was almost like rain. Beneath them a clear, shallow lake had formed, fed by the stream and the dripping water. The two men stood on what seemed to be the only level platform not underwater. Their progress down the tunnel had been interrupted by a bank of what had appeared to be snow, but what was, on second examination, more like slushy ice.

Tom shone the torchlight this way and that.

'A melt-hole, is it?' The fall had transformed Monty from the sixty-five-year-old tourist with childhood memories of snow, back into the irascible prime minister with a need to assert some authority. 'And how, exactly, do you intend to get us out?'

'I don't think we can,' Tom said. 'We may have to wait for a rescue.' He avoided shining the torch at Monty. Instead he killed the light. 'We should save our batteries.'

They stood together in the faint blue gloom, recovering their breaths from the fall. The silence was almost total. But not quite. The glacier was still creaking. Ice was still snapping. Water was still dripping. Yet, it felt quiet. Ethereally quiet. Running water, but not a breath of wind.

'How long do you think before a rescue team gets here?' Monty asked. A sense of anxiety sounded in his voice.

'If they're quick,' Tom said, 'I suppose they could be here quite soon. Say, five minutes to run across the ice to the point where we fell. Then if they're brave enough to jump, they'll do the same slide we just did. How long were we sliding? Three minutes. Four maybe. They would come out there.' He pointed to the place in the gloom where they had made their own entrance into the cavern.

'And if they're not brave enough to jump?'

'They'd be mad to jump. They don't know what's down here. They could be jumping to their deaths. So, it could be a while. If they come down on ropes, it could cost them an hour or so. Unless...'

'Unless what?'

'Unless the noise we heard when we fell was the tunnel collapsing in behind us.'

They both stood in silence contemplating this idea.

'An ice cave isn't like a rock cave,' Tom said. 'It's a very temporary thing. Some last for years. Decades, even. Others only a few weeks. Especially on a moving glacier. It isn't particularly strong.'

'Thank you for that kind reassurance.'

'Just saying. If the tunnel collapsed behind us, then our situation might be more serious. Have you checked your radio?'

'Good idea,' Monty said. He unclipped the device from his belt. 'Hello! Hello! Anyone there?'

A hiss from the radio. Not promising.

He tried again. A little louder this time. 'HELLO! HELLO!'

Still just a hiss.

'I don't think they can hear us.'

'We're under a whole lot of ice.'

Perhaps they were both in shock. Shock from the fall and euphoria from survival. They stood and tested their limbs, surprised not to have been injured, enjoying the unexpected pleasure of being alive.

Monty Causley stretched out his arms. 'I'm afraid I lost my walking poles.'

'Not to worry. I still have mine.'

'Lucky we were well padded.'

'Yes.'

It was growing lighter. The cold blue of the cavern was becoming more visible as their eyes adjusted. 'If you stay here,' Tom suggested, 'I'll explore.'

'What is there to explore?'

'A way out, maybe.'

Walking in the cavern wasn't easy. The ice was treacherous, and everywhere was wet. Even in spiked snowshoes it felt unsteady. Tom stepped off the ledge into shallow water. He tried the torchlight again, holding the light above his head. The space they were in now looked less like a monumental building and more like an organic widening of the tunnel, like an unnaturally fat metro station; where the platform of the station would be the ledge where they had ended their fall; the rails (if it had been a metro) would be submerged beneath the lake of water, and the train tunnels at either end would hold the stream of water flowing through. Walking in ankle-deep slush, Tom made his way upstream towards the point where the tunnel entered the cave. He shone the torch into the opening. 'I don't think we'll get back out this way,' he called back. 'A lot of ice fell with us. It's going to be impossible to climb without an ice pick.'

He walked back to Causley who was still standing in the spot where he had landed. 'Do you have an ice pick?'

'Not one that know about.'

'We could try downstream.' Tom shone the torch into the gloom. 'It would risk taking us even deeper into the glacier, and closer to the ice face. But it might give us a way out.'

'When you say the ice face...' Monty asked, 'do you mean...'

'I mean the terminal face of the glacier. Where you were yesterday with Ilse in the rib. Where the icebergs break off into the sea.'

'Right...' Monty sounded anxious. 'And you think we're close to the ice face?'

'I don't know. But we came a very long way and look...' Tom turned off the torch and pointed. 'There seems to be some light from that direction.'

Sure enough, the glow downstream seemed faintly clearer than the glow upstream.

'If that's the terminus of the glacier, then all we have to do is wait for a day or so and we'll drop into Baffin Bay,' Tom said.

'Would that be a good thing?'

'The drop would probably kill us.' Tom lit the torch again and shone it around. 'And nine times out of ten we'd end up in the underwater portion of the iceberg, and if that happened, the tunnels would flood, and we'd drown. Look.' In the beam of light, not far from where Monty stood, a large flat rock jutted partly up from beneath a blanket of ice. 'We might just have somewhere to sit down.'

They cleaned ice from the rock using their gloved hands and they lowered themselves down. Not exactly comfortable, and a little lower than they might have liked. But it would do as a seat. For a while at least.

'I bet it's a media circus up there,' Monty said.

Tom almost smiled. He was trying to imagine the panic that must have set in when the Prime Minister vanished into a hole in the ice. There would have been a collective gasp, and all-hell would have broken out. 'Esperanza will be freaking out,' he said.

'I wouldn't be so sure,' Monty said. He was taking off his gloves and rubbing his hands together for warmth. 'There's nothing Esperanza loves more than a crisis.'

'Really?'

'Really. *In every crisis is a great opportunity.* Einstein said that, apparently. Or something like it. It's Esperanza's secret for success. She uses that quotation a lot. It's what media people want you see. Big stories. Crisis stories.'

'Crisis stories,' echoed Tom, his mind jumping back to St Piran and the storm.

'Oh yes. Think of the headlines we'll get now. *Prime Minister visits a glacier.* That's not a big story. It's a tough one to sell. Everyone knows it's all staged for publicity. Editors aren't interested. Normally it would be a quite a way down the news agenda. Maybe the fourth or fifth story on the six o'clock news, if it's a slow-news day. That's why there's such an emphasis on getting spectacular pictures. Newspapers like big dramatic photographs. That can move the story up. But, *Prime Minister disappears into a glacier.* Now you're talking. That's the top story. That's exactly what Esperanza wants.'

Tom mused on this. 'I thought Esperanza's job was to make you look good.'

'It's much easier to look good in a crisis. If you handle it right, you're the hero. If you don't – well it's the crisis's fault. Would Kennedy have looked so good if he hadn't had Cuba? Thatcher if she hadn't had the Falklands? The refugee crisis was great for Angela Merkel. It could be a small crisis or a global one. It doesn't matter. It's how it makes you look. That's what Esperanza cares about.'

A silence followed this.

'Don't we have a global crisis already?' Tom asked, after a while. He turned to look at Causley. 'Or do you still think none of this is real?' He waved his hand towards the ceiling of the cave and the *drip drip* of melting ice. 'Maybe none of this is really melting. Maybe it's all a manufactured crisis. Maybe it's all volcanoes.'

Causley looked irritated by this. 'We're not being filmed this time, Tom. You can spare me the bleeding-heart environmentalist stuff.'

'So it isn't a crisis, then?' Tom asked.

'For God's sake, Horsmith, don't you ever let go? It's twenty-five years since we had this argument. In that time, look what's happened. We have electric cars now. Everywhere. Wind turbines. Everywhere. There's a wind turbine on Piran Head. Looks bloody awful. But it's there. We hardly burn a lump of coal now. Anywhere. Some planes are flying using hydrogen. We're rewilding big chunks of the country. Covering the place with trees. We have a marine park in Cornwall and Devon. I don't know what else you would have me do.'

'And yet the world still puts fifty billion tons of carbon into the atmosphere every year.'

'That's the world, Tom. Not us.'

'Not us.' Tom looked away. 'And yet we trade with the world. We buy all the comforts of our lives from countries that are still burning coal and oil. Doesn't that make their emissions *our* emissions? Doesn't that make us responsible?'

Monty Causley looked exasperated by this. 'For Christ's sake, Horsmith. We've just survived a headlong fall into a glacier. There are other things we could talk about. Our lives are probably still at risk, and you want to talk about world trade? Get a grip, man!'

'What about *Prime Minister killed in glacier fall?*' Tom suggested softly. 'How would that headline play?'

Causley gave him a look. 'We're not dead yet.'

'We could die down here.'

'Exactly. I'm pleased you can see the seriousness of it. Or, more likely, we could get rescued.'

Both men exhaled. A tone of anger had entered the conversation.

'Let's not fight, Tom. Not here.'

'I wonder which outcome Esperanza would prefer,' Tom said. 'Maybe it would be better for the news agenda if we died.'

They sat on the rock, not facing each other. It was cold, but not uncomfortably so and they were still warm and dry in their snowsuits. There was no wind. Time passed.

'No signal on the phone,' Monty said, at one point.

'Just when you'd love to read the headlines,' Tom said. There was still a hint of acid in his voice.

Another silence. A longer silence. Monty was getting restless. He was checking his watch. 'They should be here by now. If your five-minute estimate was right, they'd have been here long ago.'

'So we know they didn't jump in after us. Or they couldn't.'

'So how long do you think they'll be now?'

'I don't know. Looking at the icefall, it could take days.'

'Days?' Monty looked alarmed. 'Perhaps we should make a noise. Some kind of noise. Let them know we're here.'

'I doubt it would help. But I have a whistle somewhere.' Tom rummaged in his pockets. 'Here.' He passed the whistle to Causley.

Causley blew a tentative blast. Then a louder one. The walls seemed to soak up the sound. 'You're right,' he said. 'I don't suppose they can hear that.'

'They can't.'

'Then how will they find us?'

'They'll figure something out,' Tom said. 'They have ground-penetrating radar at the CENPERM base in Qaanaaq. Maybe they'll use that to find us. Or dogs.'

'Dogs?'

'Plenty of dogs in Qaanaaq. Some of them might be quite good at sniffing us out.'

This idea seemed to please Monty. He perked up a little. 'That's good,' he said. 'So if we allow ten minutes for someone to have the idea, ten minutes to drive to Qaanaaq, ten minutes to round up suitable dogs and their handlers, ten minutes back, and ten minutes to get them all the way down the tunnels to find us. That's less than an hour.'

'But the dogs won't rescue us,' Tom reminded him. 'They might find us. But they'll still need to send guys down the tunnel with ropes, and then they have to pull us out. That could take some time.'

'True.'

'And think about this from Esperanza's point of view. She won't want you rescued too soon.'

Just as the suggestion of dogs had boosted Monty's spirits, so this notion succeeded in quenching them. 'You're probably right,' he said, letting the thought sink in. 'She'll want to wait a full news cycle. She won't want to have us missing for the midday bulletin but rescued by the six o'clock news.'

'So what will she want?'

'Knowing Esperanza, she'll want to keep us down here until after the News at Ten tonight, so people go to bed thinking we're missing – probably dead – and they won't catch news of our rescue until breakfast. It'll be a bigger story that way.'

'In that case,' Tom said, 'I wouldn't keep checking your watch.'

*

Monty checked his watch. 'Thirty minutes,' he announced. 'We've been down here half an hour. I can't imagine what must be going on up there.'

'Panic, I expect,' Tom said. 'Also recriminations. And everyone getting their excuses in early. I mean, how do you lose the prime minister of a G7 country right underneath the noses of the world's press? How do you do that? Heads are going to have to roll, don't you think? You'll have to sack Esperanza Mulligan.'

'Sack her? I couldn't possibly sack her. Anyway, this isn't her fault.'

'Oh, I think you will sack her,' Tom said.

It was an awkward remark. The two men exchanged a glance. Causley looked discomforted by the comment. In any other situation perhaps, he would have snapped back at such impertinence. Here, under the ice, maybe things looked a little different. He chose a neutral response. 'We could freeze to death down here,' he said, turning the subject back to their own survival.

'Not for a day or so,' Tom said. 'The temperature here is a pretty steady zero degrees – or just a little higher, and we're well insulated.'

'I'm wet,' Causley pointed out.

'No, you're not. All your stuff is waterproof. Only the surface layer is wet. Are you cold?'

'I suppose not. Quite warm, actually.'

'Well then.'

Monty shifted his position on the rock.

'But you're right in a way. We could certainly die down here if we stay here long enough. We could starve. Or else the roof could cave in and crush us under a million tons of ice. That's just as likely.'

'Are you trying to depress me?'

'I'm trying to be realistic. The likelihood of rescue down here might be vanishingly small.' He looked directly at Monty. 'We might need to get used to that idea. If the tunnel collapsed behind us, they'll have a real challenge getting down to us. Even assuming they can figure out where we are. I'd say they're very unlikely to guess we slid such a long way. They'll probably end up searching the area all around the melt hole, and not finding us. Then they'll widen the search, and they still won't find us. We slid a very long way.'

'So what do we do?'

Tom exhaled a long, slow breath. 'I'd say we should wait a little longer. If we don't hear anything, I suggest we try our luck following the meltwater downstream.'

Causley was silent for a while. Then he said, 'I thought you said that route would take us to the face of the glacier.'

'I hope so.'

'A dangerous place?'

'Very.'

'I'm sure we'll have heard from a rescue team within an hour,' Monty said.

'An hour,' Tom said. 'Then we're agreed.'

They sat for quite a while without speaking. Monty checked his watch again.

'There is something perhaps we could talk about,' Tom said, after a few minutes had passed in silence.

'I don't want to be lectured about global warming.'

'Not that.' There was another pause. An uncomfortable one. 'I thought perhaps we could talk about the last time we met,' Tom said. 'In St Piran. Fifteen years ago.'

'Oh dear goodness,' Causley said, his tone betraying some displeasure. 'Let's not rake that up, *please*. I try not to think about that day. It was a terrible tragedy, I know. But we have to move on, old chap. We can't do our living in the past.'

'The thing is,' Tom said, 'We're never going to get such a good opportunity to talk about it, are we?'

'We don't need to talk about it, Horsmith. There's nothing to talk about.'

'But I think there is,' Tom said. He felt curiously unafraid. 'You see, I've been over the events of that evening in my mind a thousand times. I've replayed it, you know. Every minute of that day. Funny, isn't it? It isn't like trying to remember a day fifteen years ago, because I've thought about it so often, I can still remember most things pretty clearly. A lot of things about the day confuse me, though. Why did I get up so early? Why was I so unprepared? Why did I get so little sleep? What was the matter with me that day?'

Monty shifted uncomfortably on the seat. 'I really don't think it helps anyone to go over it, Tom. We were all stressed that day.'

'Were we?' Tom asked. 'Were you stressed?'

'Stressed? Of course I was stressed. The first time we'd met in the Petrel, it almost finished my career.'

'Ah yes,' Tom interrupted. 'It did, didn't it? I don't suppose I thought about that too much at the time. I was just a kid, really.'

'You were twenty.'

'I know. But I never gave much thought to the damage I'd done to you. I enjoyed all the exposure Benny's video got. I was twenty. Who wouldn't have enjoyed it at that age? You see, for me it was just a victory in a pub debate with a climate-denier. For you though, it must have been... much more devastating.'

Monty looked down. 'In some way... I suppose.'

'And do you know who helped me to see that? Do you know who made me grow up and recognise for the very first time that there were two people in that argument? It was a girl I met on the harbour at St Piran. Two years later. She pointed it out to me the very first time we spoke. It was one of the first things she ever said to me. I'd never felt guilty about it up until that moment. I hadn't given your feelings a second thought. But she made me feel some responsibility. She made me step back and see how it must have looked for you. Do you know who that was, Mr Causley? It was Lykke. The girl I married. The woman who got swept away in the storm.'

'Tom, we really don't need to have this conversation.'

'But I think we do.' Tom's voice grew louder. 'I think you *know* we do. I think somewhere inside you, you've been waiting to have this conversation just as long as I have.'

'Maybe that's true, Tom, but this is hardly the place!' Monty waved an arm to indicate their predicament. 'For goodness sake, old chap, we should be talking about how we get out of here.'

'Oh, we will. I promise you we will. I think I know how we'll get out of here. But help me out with this first. Think back to that day, Mr Causley. Fifteen years ago. The second time we met in the Petrel. It was different, wasn't it? When we met the first time, I caught you unawares. You weren't expecting an ambush. But that was what you got. So the second time everything was under control. Your control. You had the cameras. You had the lights. You had your people there. You had security men confiscating phones, and deciding who to let in. You had time to prepare. It should have been a shoo-in for you.'

Monty gave a shallow cough. 'I rehearsed hard,' he admitted.

'Yes.' Tom's voice sounded a long way away. 'I bet you did. But it still wasn't going to be enough, was it?'

'What do you mean?'

The silence in the cavern felt almost overwhelming. There were no creaks or cracks from the ice. Just the drip of melting water into the stream.

Tom stood and faced away. 'I've been over every minute of that night in my head,' he said. 'Over and over. And over. And do you want to know the most disturbing thing?'

Monty shook his head slowly.

'The most disturbing thing,' Tom said, 'is that I don't remember it. None of it. I've seen video clips. But it's like watching a stranger. I don't remember anything after arriving at the pub.'

'You did strike your head pretty hard,' Monty said.

'I cracked my skull.'

'Well, there you are.'

'But that doesn't explain it. Not entirely. I remember *going* to the Petrel. I remember walking there through the wind. I remember seeing Jacob there. I remember him giving me a drink. But nothing else. Why not?'

'Head injuries can be funny things.'

'Can they? For years, I blamed myself for Lykke's death. Why did I let go of the rope? Why did I let myself get swept onto that capstan? I was too tired. I was too unprepared. Maybe I drank too much. I should never have agreed to the stupid reunion in the first place. And for all these reasons, it was my fault that Lykke drowned. Everyone else kept hold of the rope. Or if they didn't, they still managed to stop themselves being washed into the harbour. But not me. Not me. I was to blame. That was the only explanation I could think about for fourteen years.'

Monty's mouth opened as if he was about to speak, but Tom held up a hand to stop him. 'I need to tell you a story,' he said. 'I think we have time for it.' He looked around the cavern as if listening for sounds of a rescue and gave a shrug to show that no one was coming. He drew a long breath. 'About a year ago,' he said, 'my son Noah brought his twin sister home from a party in Nuuk. It was a birthday party. One of the kids in their class at school was eighteen. Nothing unusual. But it had been a pretty wild evening by the sounds of it. Quite a few kids. More alcohol than there should have been. There's no minimum age for drinking in Greenland, but that doesn't stop most parents setting boundaries for their kids. There were probably some drugs there too; and people they didn't know well; maybe people they didn't know at all. That's pretty scary for a father. You can't relax while your kids are at a party. Especially not when they're eighteen. You want them to have fun. You want them to be teenagers. Secretly, you even want them to misbehave. A little. It's about growing up after all. But all the same, you spend the whole time worrying from the moment you drop them off until the moment they're back safely home. Well, you see Mr Causley, I was that dad. Even though I knew my kids were sensible, I was always scared of something happening when I wasn't there to help them. I guess that's something all parents get. Maybe single parents get it worse.' Tom exhaled slowly. 'Anyway,' he said, 'this was a night when all my fears seemed to come true. It was in May. The weather wasn't too bad. It was actually quite early in the evening. Maybe around ten. Ten-thirty. Noah and one of his friends came home carrying Ilse between them. I saw them coming down the road. She had one arm over each boy's shoulder. She wasn't walking. Her head was sort of slumped down. I couldn't see her face. They were dragging her feet just above the ground. I thought right away she was drunk. But Noah was pretty insistent she'd only had one drink. So I bundled her into the car – I was panicking now – and I took her to Queen Ingrid's Hospital.' Tom drew a breath. 'Anyway, long-story-short, she was fine. She was ok. And the doctor was a guy I knew. A Canadian. He told me she'd probably been drugged. A date-rape drug, he said. That was a very scary thought. If we wanted to know for sure, he needed to take a blood sample right away, because apparently these things don't hang around in the blood stream for long. And so I said *yes*; they did a test, and the doctor was right. Rohypnol. That's what it was. A really nasty drug. Guys slip a powder into a girl's drink and... well...' He let the idea linger for a moment. 'Lucky for Ilse, she was with her brother; he saw her passing out, and he brought her home. We never found out who drugged her.'

Tom paused again. He turned so he was almost facing Causley, his gaze somewhere in the middle distance. 'But the strange thing for me,' he said, 'was how, the next morning, Ilse had no memory of anything. She remembered arriving at the party. She remembered the first drink. And that was about it. And when she told me this, I immediately thought, *that happened to me once.*'

Tom stopped talking. He stood and seemed to gaze into the gloom of the cave.

Causley said, 'What are you trying to tell me, Tom? Are you suggesting you were drugged?'

The younger man was caught in a deep thought. 'We're in a tricky spot here aren't we, Mr Causley?' he said, emerging from the reverie like a surfacing diver. 'The fact is, I don't like you, and I'm guessing you don't like me. We don't need to pretend down here. But we do need to work together. Like it or not, our chances of survival will be better if we cooperate. So let's talk about how we escape. I think we both know the tunnel collapsed behind us. I don't think we can expect anyone to come for us anytime soon. That means for the next few hours we're going to have to work together. You and me. We're going to have to be a team, right?' He turned towards Monty and raised his eyebrows as if seeking agreement. 'We can hate each other, but we need to trust each other. Completely. Otherwise we're going to die. We're going down there.' He pointed towards the exit stream from the cavern. 'We're going to follow the meltwater right the way to the terminal face of the glacier, and when we get there, we're going to use your radio to call for help. And if the radio doesn't work, we'll need to find a way to climb up to safety. Either way, you need to trust me, and I need to trust you.'

'OK.' Monty looked pale.

'So don't lie to me, Mr Causley. Please don't lie to me. Don't do a knee-jerk politician's lie to save your skin. No one is filming us. This is between you and me. It stays down here, with us.' He caught the politician in his gaze. 'Unless you lie. Do we understand each other?'

Monty's mouth hung open limply, like a fish.

'So don't ask me if I think I was drugged. You're insulting me. That doesn't help us to build trust. Just come out and tell me the truth.'

There was a silence in the cavern. The ice creaked. Causley was breathing heavily.

'Whose idea was it?' Tom asked. Time, in the cavern, was slowing down. The drips were stopping. The air wasn't moving.

Neither man spoke for a while. Then Monty gave what sounded like a low groan. 'It was Esperanza,' Monty said, in a voice so quiet it was almost hard to hear him. 'It was her idea. She put the powder in your drink.' He closed his eyes. The next admission would be difficult. 'But I approved it.'

Tom seemed to inflate. One of his arms was shaking beyond his control, as if attached to a machine. 'You approved it? You fucking *approved* it?'

'Indirectly… yes,' Monty said. 'I asked her for a way to put you back in your box. She talked about drugging you.'

'What the FUCK were you thinking?'

'I'm sorry. I'm really sorry. I wasn't trying to hurt you,' Monty protested. 'I was trying to confuse you. That's all. I had no idea if it was even going to work. Honestly.'

Tom's eyes were red. 'But it did work, didn't it?'

'Almost,' Causley whispered.

'Esperanza got her crisis.'

'Yes.'

'And Lykke died.'

A long pause. 'Yes.'

The air in the cavern was heavy and hard to breathe. No one spoke for a long time.

'And when we get out of here...?' Tom asked at last.

'I will sack her,' Monty said. He let the idea float away into the fading light. 'And I shall resign,' he added.

'Good.'

There was another long moment.

'Do we trust each other now?' Monty asked.

'I suppose we do.'

'Then perhaps we should go.'

Tom stood silent. Then he turned on the torch. 'This way,' he said.

5. Never let your partner fall…

They tied a length of rope between them, and another, longer rope to one of the walking poles, and they jammed the pole lengthways between the walls of the tunnel as an anchor. There seemed to be the slightest breeze of cold air down into the void. 'Have you ever been climbing with ropes?' Tom asked.

'No.'

'There's one rule. Don't ever let your partner fall. If you feel me falling, brace yourself as hard as you can, and grab the rope in two hands because it will tug you really hard. Keep your elbows bent and use your arms like shock absorbers so your biceps take as much of the shock as they can.'

'Got it,' Causley said.

'I'll do the same for you.'

'OK.'

Tom pushed the torch into his breast pocket, so that the beam of light shone upwards. 'We have around thirty metres of usable rope,' he said. 'Not a lot, I'm afraid. And we need to double the rope, so we can pull it after us. Otherwise we'll lose it. So that means we can descend around fifteen metres. After that we need to find another anchor, we pull down the rope, and we go again. Another fifteen metres.'

'I understand,' Monty said.

'There's no coming back.'

'No.'

'If the rescue team make it to the cave, they'll see our footprints,' Tom said. 'They'll know where we've gone. But if they never make it to the cave, well at least we might make it out on our own.'

'Let's do it,' Monty said. He sounded almost ministerial. '*Audaces fortuna iuvat!*'

Tom found himself nodding. The Prime Minister was perhaps a tougher character than he had suspected. This realisation came as a surprise. 'I don't suppose you do this sort of thing very often.'

'It's a lot easier than answering questions in the House of Commons,' Monty said, looking directly at Tom. 'And a lot less dangerous.'

'I'll go first,' Tom said.

The space in the cave tapered away towards a narrow slit, where a thin stream of water was flowing away down a steep tunnel. Would they even fit down there?

'We should go feet-first,' Tom said. He lowered himself into a seated position, and Monty dropped down heavily behind him.

'I'm not as nimble as you,' Monty cautioned.

'I'll try to bear that in mind. Try not to slide this time. Dig your feet in where you can. Let's go slowly.'

So it started. The meltwater had created another treacherous fissure, and once again they were in a tunnel with no idea what lay ahead. They inched forward, feet first and faces upwards. There were rocks and gravel here and there, and these helped to provide footholds. Progress was slow, and after fifteen metres they pulled back the rope. The walking pole was left behind. A convenient rock provided a second anchor, and they were off again.

'How much further do you think?' Causley was clearly tiring.

'I really don't know.'

The tunnel opened into another cavern, not dissimilar to the first, and they took a rest. The radio still wasn't working, and if anything, it was getting darker.

The second walking pole was pressed into service as an anchor, and they set off again. This time the slope was less severe, and after fifteen metres, Tom managed to recover the pole by shaking the rope. They scrambled on without a rope for a while. The tunnel began to get wider and higher. They reached a point where they could stand up and proceed on foot, ankle-deep now in icy water. This cheered both men up. It felt like progress. Tom shone the torch ahead and they could see the tunnel wide and tall stretching out in front of them.

'I think it's getting lighter,' Tom remarked after a while. 'We could be getting close to the edge.'

'Close to the edge but further from the rescue party,' Monty replied.

A short while later, a faint shaft of light became visible ahead. 'Daylight!' Tom called back. They were still roped together, but now they were side by side, standing fully upright as water rushed past their feet. Sure enough, as they manoeuvred around a bend, there, about twenty metres ahead, was a cave entrance, and beyond it the bright promise of daylight.

'This is the most dangerous point,' Tom cautioned. 'We should stop here and call for help.'

Monty unclipped the radio from his belt. He lifted it to his face, and he would, surely, at the next moment, have depressed the call button and contact might have been made. But at the very instant, when he ought to have made the call, a noise assailed them – a *crump crump* noise like the sound of heavy ordnance on a battlefield. Low frequency noise. Noise from some distance away. But a sound that seemed to shake the ice where they were standing.

'What in hell's name was that?' Monty exclaimed.

'I have no idea,' Tom said. He had never heard a sound like this before on the ice. 'Could they be blasting somewhere up above us?' This didn't feel likely, but no alternative candidate for the noise came to his mind.

CRUMP CRUMP

'They're trying to blast us out!' Monty cried.

WHOOOM!

A huge bang. It shook the ice so hard Tom and Monty were thrown off their feet.

'What the hell do they think they're doing?' the Prime Minister shouted, scrambling back up.

WHOOOOOM!

This time the cave seemed to tip to one side. Monty fell forwards, his hands held out to cushion his fall. There is no elegant way to tumble on wet ice in a glacier cave. He fell awkwardly and slid forwards in the stream until his progress was caught in a sudden jerk by Tom hauling back on the rope that now stretched between them like a taut umbilical cord. The sudden interruption of motion caused him to drop the radio. It flew out of his hand and skidded away in the stream of water. 'Oh shit, my radio!' he called.

The radio, it seemed, had been designed to float, but this feature that could perhaps have been a lifesaver if anyone were to drop it at sea, became a liability when the device was dropped into a fast-flowing stream. The current took it and swept it out of reach.

'Leave it,' Tom said.

In moments it was gone.

'Now what?'

As if in answer to that question, the ice beneath their feet issued a groan like the fingernail of a monstrous giant being scraped along a board.

'That doesn't sound good.'

'It doesn't.'

The noise was growing in volume. And now it was more than a noise. It was a shaking and trembling that shook the whole cavern.

'We should get to the exit. NOW!'

Chunks of ice were dropping from the ceiling. It was raining ice. The walls were cracking.

'NOW!'

Still roped together, they scrambled and crawled as fast as their muscles would take them, assaulted from above by a barrage of falling ice. The world seemed to be moving. Like the launching of a giant ship on a slipway, the glacier was sliding, gathering speed. The noise now was deafening. Ice was cracking with a sound like the explosions of an artillery battalion.

'Hold on!' Tom shouted.

'What to?' There was nothing to hold, so Monty Causley took hold of Tom. The glacier was falling faster than they were. They were like loose objects in a plummeting elevator, lifted off their feet and thrown into the air, and as they fell, the ice was turning and there was sunlight above them streaming onto them through the entrance to the cave. *CRASH!* The roof behind them collapsed.

An instant of hope. A great swathe of blue sky. They were outside. Tom wedged his walking pole into a fissure of ice and shouted back to Monty. 'HOLD TIGHT!'

And then the hope was gone. The glacier was calving into the ocean, and it hit the water with a million tonnes of mass behind it. A colossal calving. It crashed into the waters of Qaanaaq Bay like a super-tanker at full speed, sending a tidal impact-wave in all directions, and so great was the force that the whole iceberg vanished for seconds beneath the water. For the two Cornishmen, this was surely the most dangerous moment of all. Ice cold seawater flooded into the cave and even as they realised what was happening, they were dragged mercilessly underwater and submerged in freezing blackness. They barely had time to take a breath. And now they were drowning. And the ice beneath them was turning.

6. There's been some kind of ice fall...

Who could have imagined that the tiny community of Qaanaaq, perhaps the most remote settlement on the planet, would find itself the centre of a global news story? A routine photo-opportunity for a beleaguered politician had turned into the kind of juggernaut that captures the news agenda from time to time, leaving every other story jettisoned in its wake. News editors from New York to Sydney were frantically rolling maps onto tables. Where the hell is Qaanaaq? How do I get a crew there? Where is our nearest reporter?

Around two kilometres from the cliff face of the glacier, the phones of every member of the press corps began to ring within moments of the disappearance of the Prime Minister. Journalists, photographers, and cameramen who might have expected a whole career without a hint or sniff of a global scoop, suddenly found themselves at the heart of the maelstrom. Editors were barking instructions from their offices to reporters they had possibly never met. 'Get down there.' 'Follow them.' 'Find them.' As a naval rescue team set off on foot towards the point where the two men had vanished, they were pursued by an Inuktun tracking team, sightseers from Qaanaaq, a collection of dogs, and an ill-prepared but equally determined crowd of reporters. The double trail of footprints over the virgin snow was obliterated as the melee swept down the hill towards the glacier. What they found, once they had clambered up the ice shelf, was a shallow depression like a meteor crater and a morass of ice blocking the way.

'There's been some kind of an icefall,' a navy man called, quite unnecessarily.

The crowd stood around to marvel at the icefall, and a sense of shock percolated outwards. Two or three people tried to take charge all at once. A Greenlander who looked important starting calling instructions to local bystanders in his own language. An aide to Prime Minister Causley began shouting commands to the ministerial party, and the navy man was on a radio talking in acronyms. The press stood around looking dazed. One man, either ambitious or foolhardy, started digging in the snowdrift with his hands, perhaps expecting to find a hidden crevasse. On the edge of the crater, Esperanza Mulligan stood looking down at the chaotic scene, with a curious smile on her lips. 'Thomas Horsmith,' she muttered to herself. 'You have outsmarted us.' She put her phone to her ear. 'Keep the drones up,' she said to whoever answered. 'And please get me the Deputy Prime Minister on the line.'

7. For destruction, ice is also great...

Big icebergs typically calve from great glaciers like disobedient slices of bread peeling away from the side of a loaf. The slice tears off and crashes face-down into the sea. Smaller bergs drop in massive lumps from great heights. If either of these had been the fate of the iceberg that calved with Tom and Monty within it, the outcome, for them at least, might have been different. But there are gentler calvings too. These are rarer, but counter-intuitively, they are often the biggest calvings of all. When they happen, it is less like the piecemeal shedding of a sliced loaf and more like the wholescale floating of an unsliced one, as a whole chunk of the glacier loses its grip on the bedrock and slides down the wet slipway into the water like the launching of a liner. It is as if a piece of the island itself snaps off and floats away; and while the impact in the ocean may be dramatic, the effect on the breakaway iceberg itself can be rather less extreme. It can end up floating away in much the same orientation as it entered the water, too wide and too heavy to topple over. With very good fortune, this was what happened with the iceberg that bore Monty and Tom. Having plunged into the sea like a massive tabletop, it rose again, and twisted so the greater mass of it was underwater, in the way, perhaps, that a double decker bus might float nose down, and there it floated.

Miraculously, Tom and Monty were above the waterline.

Just.

The crisis was over. For the time being. The noise had stopped. Above them, remarkably, the sun was shining. So brief had been their submersion in the cold sea, that while their faces had been immersed, their arctic suits had protected them from a soaking. The two men might have looked like bedraggled flotsam from a wreck, but they were still largely dry. They lay like whales on an icy beach, too shaken for the moment to move.

'Are we still alive?' This was Monty.

'I hope so.'

Neither man made any effort to rise. They were waiting for the next calamity. The next crash. The next cascade of ice.

None came.

Monty was the first to sit up. 'They had better make a fricking film of this,' he said.

'Who would play you?'

'A Hollywood megastar. Someone with a square jaw and a solid background in action movies. Someone with at least one Oscar to his name.'

Tom sat up and rested back on his gloved hands. 'You're taking this very well.'

'Well? I've just been swallowed by a glacier, shot down a tunnel, bombarded with ice, thrown off a cliff into the Arctic Ocean, dunked into freezing water, and I've ended up on an iceberg. It's a miracle we're still here. I'll take that very well thank you.'

Tom almost laughed. 'You still have to resign,' he said.

'I don't want the job anymore. I'll get a new job as advisor on the screenplay,' Monty said. 'Can we stand up? We're still tied together.'

Cautiously, they lifted themselves to their feet. They were on a level plane of ice, a plateau, like an icy beach, that rose up into a steep white hill maybe a hundred metres high.

'Can you get a phone signal?' Tom asked.

Monty patted his pockets and drew out his phone. He grimaced. The seawater had done its worst, and the phone was dead. 'No matter,' he said. 'They'll find us now.'

'I hope so.'

'Can we untie this rope?'

Tom looked up at the mass of ice above them. 'I don't think we should,' he said. 'Not yet. We still have some climbing to do.'

'Climbing?' Monty too gazed up at the huge iceberg. 'We don't need to climb. We're safe here.'

'Not for long,' Tom said. 'The berg is going to start to melt. It will be slow, but a platform like this is going to be the first thing to break off. We'll be safest if we can stay on the biggest block of ice. We ought to get as high as we can.' He pointed to a ledge above them. 'We should aim for that.'

'Oh shit!'

'It isn't too high.'

'I had hoped all our heroics were over.'

'Not quite.'

Still roped together, they picked their way gingerly up the slope. It was slippery, but not too demanding. After a while, it became too steep to scale. They had to stop. 'We should be ok here,' Tom said, and Monty collapsed down onto the ice.

The sky was duck-egg blue. The seascape all the way across the sound, as far as a distant and faint horizon, was utterly tranquil and achingly beautiful, the clear vista of an ocean littered all the way across with ice fragments – some large, some small – most, it seemed, casualties from the calving of their own iceberg. From their vantage point on a wide ledge, twenty metres or so above the water, Tom and Monty could see a whole flotilla of bergs of which theirs was undoubtedly the largest, every one of them adrift on a turquoise sea. There was a moment, as the two men made themselves comfortable on the ledge, when they both had to stop, simply to admire the view. They were looking Westwards, out towards the open ocean and Canada, although the distant ice fields of Ellesmere Island were too far away to see.

'What do we do now?' Monty asked, once they had taken their fill of the views.

'We save our energy and wait to be rescued,' Tom said. 'They should find us soon enough now.'

'Maybe the camouflage suits were a mistake,' said Monty.

'I'd be happier in my bright orange survival suit right now. But it doesn't matter. They'll find us. Look out for helicopters or drones. Or boats. And wave like mad.'

As remarkable as it might sound, the calving of a million tons of ice from the terminal end of the glacier into the Baffin Sea had not roused particular attention among the rescuers and onlookers gathered around the collapsed melt hole almost two kilometres away. The glacier, after all, was calving all the time. There was no special interest in this calving, despite its unusual size. The river of ice was moving west at a speed of around a metre an hour. Bits would drop off. This was inevitable. There were more immediate things to think about. One of these things was an attempt they had made to blast open a crevasse about a hundred metres downstream from the melt hole. *WHOOM!* The explosion had thrown tons of ice and snow into the air, and sure enough the crack had widened. A second blast, deeper in the crevasse seemed to have done the trick. A deep hole had opened up. 'We'll get a man down there,' the navy commander had called, and a volunteer had run forwards. Within moments, he was belaying down the fissure. Almost every journalist there was too busy recording this momentous rescue attempt to pay much attention to the distant rumbling of an iceberg crashing into the sea. 'The plan,' a BBC reporter was saying to camera, just before the calving happened, 'is to send a team downstream of the melt hole to look for an alternative way into the cavern where it is believed the Prime Minister and Mr Horsmith may have fallen. Imagine a crevasse running from upstream to downstream. The rescuers will hope to find a way in, and then they can work their way upstream until they find the two men.'

On the surface, a team of Greenlanders had decided upon an alternative plan. They were going to dig. With an assortment of available tools, ice picks, spades, and shovels, they began to pick at the loose ice. Almost every vehicle parked at the top of the valley carried tools of this nature, and very soon more people joined the effort. More cars were arriving too, as the news of the accident became known in Qaanaaq, and with them came dogs and more digging tools. A team of Danish researchers arrived with a ground-penetrating radar set that looked for all the world like a bright yellow lawnmower with pram wheels, complete with a laptop screen attached to the handles. There was a lot of excitement at this. Half a dozen people stumbled across the ice with the device.

'Will this find them?' demanded the Navy commander.

'It depends how deep they fell. This should find any anomalies under the ice down to about ten metres,' a Danish man with an impressive beard told him.

Ten metres. This didn't sound especially far. 'Could they have fallen deeper than ten metres?' This question came from Esperanza Mulligan.

'If they did, they're probably dead,' the Dane said. 'But if they were lucky, they might have fallen into a tunnel and slid a little way downstream. We should search in that direction.' He pointed in the direction of the ocean.

'And if you find them,' Esperanza asked, 'then what?'

'My expertise is finding objects buried in the ice, not in digging them out,' said the Dane. 'But if you want my opinion, I'd recommend a big mechanical digger.'

'Are there any in Qaanaaq?'

'We passed one on the road on our way here. It's on its way.'

'Get searching then,' the Navy man said.

'And let us know,' said Esperanza. 'If you find them, I want to know before any of these do.' She indicated the press pack with a nod of her head.

'If you say so,' said the Dane, his beard waving wildly as he nodded his head.

'I do say so,' said Esperanza.

From the direction of the ocean a rumble could be heard like the growl of a concealed bear. The ground seemed almost to tremble. Quite a few people looked up, some with expressions of alarm, as if this might have been an earthquake.

'Looks like your blasting has broken off an iceberg,' said the Dane.

'Is it anything we ought to worry about?'

'No.'

8. I was never in the scouts...

On the iceberg, an uneasy truce established itself between Monty and Tom. Neither had moved very much since they had settled on their ledge. They were sitting at the base of an ice fall, on a ledge littered with lumps of ice that had presumably crashed down the cliff when the iceberg calved. Moving around on the ice felt perilous. The better idea seemed to be to sit tight and wait for a rescue boat. And so they sat, uncomfortably, a metre or so apart, on the only piece of level terrain they could find.

'Can I make a suggestion?' Monty asked at one point.

'Go ahead.'

'Did they ever teach you this in Scouts? When you have nowhere to lean, you sit back-to-back, and you lean on each other.'

'I was never in the Scouts,' Tom said.

'All the same, we could give it a try. My back is aching.'

'I should unstrap the rifle first,' Tom said.

'We're hardly likely to need it now.'

'We might want to use it to attract attention. Can you unfasten it for me?'

Monty unclasped the rifle from Tom's shoulder and passed it to him. Cautiously the two men manoeuvred into position and leaned backwards. The technique worked surprisingly well. If there was any discomfort, it was more a social unease from the unlikely intimacy of the situation, rather than anything physical. Tom drew up his knees and laid the gun in his lap.

'I always knew my years in the Scouts would prove useful one day,' Monty said.

Tom closed his eyes. There was a lot to think about.

'How fast are we moving?' Monty asked.

'We'll drift south at about two kilometres an hour,' Tom said. He was feeling curiously dizzy. 'It's a thousand kilometres to Disko Bay. We'll go past in about twenty days.'

'So what do we do?'

'We won't have to wait that long. Sooner or later, they'll come looking for us.'

'We hope.'

Time was passing slowly. The world was silent. They sat and watched blocks of ice the size of office buildings drifting along with them in the flat sea. They didn't speak much. The adrenalin, and all the associated biochemicals of crisis that had flooded their systems earlier in the morning were starting to dissipate from their bloodstreams. Heartbeats were returning to normal. Stress levels were dropping.

'Would you mind very much,' Monty asked after a while, 'if I was to take a nap? Just for a short time?'

It seemed like a rather good idea. But Monty had asked first, so Tom simply nodded. 'Lie down. I'll keep watch,' he said.

'Just a nap,' Monty repeated.

'Go ahead.'

'Wake me up if a rescue party comes.'

'I will.'

The older man drew his hood around his head and lay on his back on the ice. 'The damn hood is still a bit wet,' he complained.

'It will dry.'

'I hope so.'

Tom sat forwards and held onto his knees. Causley lay not far from his feet. One kick, Tom thought, would send the Prime Minister off the ledge, down the icy slope, and into the cold sea.

One kick.

Why do you dislike him so much? Lykke had asked him. On another midsummer day. A long time ago.

Do I dislike him?

I think you do.

Do I dislike him? He took a deep breath of crisp, cold, air. Did it even matter anymore? They would be here soon. The navy ribs would soon appear, and this would all be over. Causley would resign. Esperanza would be finished. A fifteen-year struggle for closure would be complete. Almost complete. Except that Lykke would not be there to see it.

Why do you dislike him so much?

I dislike his politics, Tom thought. I dislike the way he appropriates St Piran as his hometown to lend himself a Cornish rural identity. I dislike his smirk. His sense of entitlement. His manipulation of people. His casual dissembling. I dislike the way he so indifferently drugged me to lubricate his own failing career. I dislike the way he leapt into the stormy waters of St Piran harbour to rescue me from drowning, when I already had rescuers aplenty, robbing them of the glory and leaving Lykke to drown. I dislike that he conceals his denial of climate change, because he knows that to do so would be electoral suicide, and I despise the cynical way his environmental policies (of which he boasts) have the most minimal impact on the crisis. I hate that he doesn't recognise there *even is* a crisis.

One kick would do it.

He unzipped his hood and let it fall onto his shoulders. It was a warm day, by Arctic standards. He was on an iceberg, a fairly huge one, drifting at strolling speed down an icy sound towards the open ocean. Every minute was taking them further from Qaanaaq, further from land, further from rescue. They were alone. From his viewpoint, there was no sign of humanity. Not a single boat disturbed the tranquil waters. Where was HMS Endurance? Probably out of sight on the other side of the iceberg, a dozen kilometres away. They might have felt the wake from the calving, but they wouldn't have seen it. If he could clamber up the berg, he could perhaps try to spot an Inuit fisherman if there was one, could try to attract attention. But the wall of ice was impossible to climb.

Where then, were the rescuers? Surely by now, someone would have suggested looking downstream. Surely someone had noticed the calving?

But maybe they hadn't. This was a worrying thought.

By his feet, Monty seemed already to be asleep. What a talent! To sleep so easily. Tom tried to make himself comfortable. It wasn't easy. He resented now, that Monty had laid down and now there was nowhere to lean.

Be careful hatred doesn't consume you, Tom.

A flicker of distant movement in his sightline. What was it? He shielded his eyes with a gloved hand and looked out over the ice flow. There it was again. Not a rescuer. A soft white shape on a floating piece of ice. A bear. Tom had often seen them in this bay. This one was a long way off. It was standing on all fours, looking away from them, scanning the water for fish or seals. One more thing to worry about. But not an urgent thing. Tom began to relax. This could be a long wait.

9. This might be embarrassing…

'This might be embarrassing,' Monty Causley said. He was awake, and once again they were sitting back-to-back like boy scouts. 'I'm going to need to pee.'

'The suits unzip,' Tom said. 'I'll look the other way.'

'I might need to do more than pee.'

'In that case,' Tom said, 'I suggest you go now before the temperature starts to drop.'

Monty scrambled among the blocks of the ice fall and found a concealed spot. He re-emerged some minutes later. 'All done,' he said.

Tom took the opportunity to embark on the same mission. With both of them suitably relieved, Tom picked his way along their ledge to see if there might be a better resting spot among the loose ice of the ice fall. The surface of the iceberg was melting in the summer sunshine, and everywhere was wet. 'Do you fancy some physical activity?' he asked Monty, on his return.

'Not especially,' Monty answered. 'What did you have in mind?'

'There's a lot of crumbly ice here. A bit of an icefall. I thought we could have a go at building a makeshift igloo.'

Causley looked uncertain about this proposition, but he followed Tom, and they stood and surveyed the raw materials.

'We may need somewhere to shelter overnight,' Tom said. 'Especially if the weather turns.'

With no knife or axe available, they used the butt of the rifle to break up blocks of ice, and the barrel of the rifle to shape them. 'This won't be very elegant,' Tom apologised. 'But it doesn't have to last for long.'

It wasn't an easy task. Wet ice kept slipping from their hands. An almost finished wall collapsed into a heap, and they were forced to start again. They used the rifle and the walking pole as props and lashed the wall with ropes to prevent a second collapse. They were lucky that many of the blocks of ice had broken in a regular fashion leaving a helpful pile of rectangular pieces, and these formed the base of the wall.

'This is like one of those team-building exercises we used to do at school,' Monty said at one point. He seemed almost to be enjoying it.

The roof was a miracle of design and good fortune. A perfect block of ice formed the keystone at the centre of the roof. Tom propped himself up, as a human arch, on hands and feet with this large block balanced on his back while Monty found smaller blocks to pack around it. 'This will never work,' Monty said, several times. 'This is all going to come crashing down.'

'Just do it,' Tom said. 'Before my arms give way.'

Eventually, despite his misgivings, Monty was happy with the construction. 'It's going to be now or never,' he said. 'Lower yourself down very slowly.'

Tom eased himself downwards and the roof held. It was an almost unexpected moment of triumph. He wriggled out from beneath the new roof and the two men raised their arms in a gesture of jubilation.

'I hope we don't need it,' Monty said, 'but if we do, it's the finest igloo I ever made.'

It was growing colder.

'I don't suppose you have a secret bar of chocolate hidden away in one of your pockets?' Monty asked.

'Sorry.'

They sucked on lumps of ice to quench their thirst. 'My watch isn't working. What do you reckon the time is?'

'Maybe six pm. Maybe seven.'

The iceberg had rotated slowly on its leisurely drift, and they now had a partial view of the land they had left behind, a spectral silhouette of white hills, now several kilometres away in the gloom of the Arctic summer evening. Rather than lifting their spirits, the sight of land served only to highlight their sense of isolation. The west coast of Greenland is bleak and largely unpopulated. The prospect of a rescue seemed to be fading with every passing hour.

'They'll be looking for us underneath the ice,' Tom said. 'Sooner or later they'll figure out we aren't there. We just have to be patient.'

So far as patience was concerned, however, they had very little option but to observe it. With the igloo built, there was nothing more to do apart from staring at the horizon in the hope of spotting a rescue party. 'How many cartridges do we have for the rifle?' Tom asked. 'We could use the noise to attract a boat if we see one.'

Monty searched his pockets. 'Three.' He passed them over.

'Your man didn't trust me with them,' Tom told him. 'He thought I might shoot you.'

'He thinks everyone wants to shoot me,' Monty said. 'Anyway, you don't need to shoot me. You could push me into the water. It would look more natural.'

Tom lowered his gaze, anxious not to betray his thoughts.

'I am sorry about Lykke,' Monty said.

'I know.'

'I mean it. I am truly sorry.'

'It doesn't bring her back.'

'No.' Monty was silent for a while. 'I once saw a lecture she did,' he said, when the silence had grown too long for comfort. 'An online lecture. One of those ten-minute talks they do. TED talks. I watched it when I was trying to learn as much as I could about my brief as Environment Secretary. I had no idea that she and you were... together. Not then.'

Tom issued a long sigh. 'I watch it often.'

'Yes. I suppose you do. I mean... I would too.'

'*When will the ice be gone?*' Tom said. 'That was the title.'

'Yes.'

The two men sat and looked at the horizon.

'She was dressed in her Greenland clothes,' Monty said. 'For the lecture. She looked amazing.'

'Inuktun clothes,' Tom said, 'Reindeer leather trousers and a musk-ox parka, and moccasins.'

'She looked magnificent.'

'Like a goddess,' Tom said.

'Like a goddess.'

Overnight, the temperature dropped, even though the sun remained stubbornly above the southern horizon. The sub-zero conditions were good for the igloo, freezing the blocks together and converting the crushed ice rubble into solid walls. Tom and Monty took turns crawling inside to sleep while the other man kept watch. It was a difficult night. They were hungry, and uncomfortable, and growing increasingly anxious.

The new day brought a change in the weather. A grey cloud hung low above them and there was more of a breeze. The sea was choppier now. 'I'm going to try to catch us a fish,' Tom said. He showed Monty the ski pole. He had adapted it into a spear by wrenching off the circular stop and tying a rope to the end.

'I might be hungry,' Monty said. 'But I'm not hungry enough for raw fish.'

'You will be,' Tom said. 'Stay here.'

He scrambled down the slope to the platform of ice that constituted a shore. This wouldn't be easy. He tried to picture the way the polar bear would do it, standing as still as a statue, eyes focussed on a small patch of sea, infinitely patient. The water was clear, but there was no sign of any fish. He held the spear above his head, his elbow cocked, and he waited.

After a while, his arm ached. He changed position. Stood still. He had seen Inuit fishermen in this pose, motionless on the ice for an age. He would need the same discipline. The same focus. He tried to relax into a posture which wouldn't cause his arm to ache. One with the elbow bent, at waist height. This was easier. He stood for a long time. No fish.

'Anything?' called Monty from the ice ledge above him.

'Not yet.'

In the distance, his eye was drawn again to the ice floe where the polar bear had been. He imagined he had spotted movement, but when he tried to find the bear, there was no sign. Good. He relaxed a little and then, to his surprise, he spotted a fish. A small fish. With a sudden impulse he flung the spear. It missed the fish by almost the length of an arm. He pulled the spear back out with the rope, but the fish had gone. No matter. There would be another.

There wasn't another. Not for the first hour, nor for the second. By the third hour, even in his snow suit, Tom was starting to feel cold. He decided to abandon the attempt. He needed a break. 'No luck,' he told Monty when both were back on the ledge. Monty, he noticed, had not been altogether idle. He had fashioned some of the crushed ice into two seats – with backs, and even with arm rests. One faced northwest, the other faced southeast.

'So we can both keep watch and stay comfortable at the same time,' Monty said.

'Thank you.' It felt the right thing to say.

'I tell you what,' Monty said, 'I'm so hungry, I could now eat some raw fish.'

They laughed at this. Tom settled into his newly built armchair. 'Very comfortable,' he announced.

From somewhere out of sight, to the east side of the berg, they could hear the unmistakable sound of helicopters, a long way off. Several helicopters. It was a promising sign. 'They must have flown up from Nuuk,' Tom said, 'to help in the search.'

'You know what we need?' Monty asked. 'Paint,' he said. If we had paint, we could paint a huge SOS on the ice.'

'I'll pop down to B&Q,' Tom said. 'Any preference on colour?'

The sun was still up, but it was evening. A heavy tiredness had set in. Tom took the first shift in the igloo. He didn't sleep. Too many anxieties were invading his thoughts. Instead, he closed his eyes and willed his body to relax, and for a short time his tired limbs almost obeyed the instruction. But then he was awake again. He crawled out of the tunnel to discover Monty was not in his chair.

'Mr Causley?'

'I'm here!' Monty was waving from the plateau below. He had taken a stretch of the rope and arranged it into an H-shape. 'For the helicopters,' he called. 'What do you think?'

'Good idea.'

Actually, it *was* a good idea.

'Do you need any help?'

'No. I think I'm done.'

Monty scrambled back up to the ledge and lowered himself into his seat. 'It feels good to do something,' he said.

Monty took his turn in the igloo and Tom was alone again. The sun was low on the horizon. The wind was growing stronger. He pulled his hood low over his face. This was his watch. He would stay awake.

And then remarkably it was morning. He woke to the sound of Monty Causley crunching towards him over the ice.

'Did you drop off, old chap?' Monty asked him.

'I think I must have done.'

'Good. Do us both good. I've just been for a pee. I have such a weak bladder these days. One of the many downsides of growing older, I'm afraid.'

'Right,' Tom said.

'It must have been jolly cold last night,' Monty said. 'It has frozen the igloo into one solid lump of ice. Do you want to take a turn inside?'

'No thanks. I'm OK,' Tom said. He was starting to feel guilty for having fallen asleep.

'Can I offer you some breakfast? Poached eggs and vegan bacon with muffins, crusty white toast with thick orange marmalade, and a hearty cup of English Breakfast Tea?'

'Coffee for me,' Tom said, lifting himself to his feet. 'And Scots porridge oats with honey.'

'A very good choice, sir, if I might say so.'

Tom found himself laughing. He picked up the spear. 'I shall have another go at some fishing,' he announced.

'Right ho,' Monty said. 'I'll just stay here in the office and govern the country. If that's all right by you.'

'Be my guest.'

It had been an unexpected conversation. The rather strained atmosphere that had shackled their discussions since Monty's confession the day before, appeared to have dissipated like the morning mist. Tom rather welcomed the new sense of levity. He set off down the slope, and with unexpected good fortune, within about twenty minutes, he speared a cod. A huge one. It took a lot of effort to land it. Emboldened by success, with plenty more fish still there, he speared a second, but this seemed to alert the shoal, and they departed before he could catch a third. All the same, two fish, each a substantial size, constituted a victory. He carried them up to the ledge, where Monty was lavish with his praise.

'Dear God, they're enormous,' Monty said. 'This is like a seal. It's colossal. I had no idea a cod was so big. What do they weigh do you think?'

'Probably twenty-five kilogrammes or so,' Tom said. 'Each.'

'Gosh! That's the size of decent spaniel,' Monty declared. 'We can feast on this for a month.'

They snapped the useless mobile phone and used a fragment of the broken case as a knife to fillet the first fish. It was a messy business, but there was no pressure of time. 'We should just do the one,' Tom said, 'and keep the second one for emergencies.'

They were left, once it was done, with strips of white meat in a very generous heap.

'Let's pop these into the freezer, shall we?' Monty said. He laid the strips out on the ice and covered them with a handful of ice fragments. 'Tomorrow, we can have crusted cod with lemon and garlic, served with sauté potatoes and marrowfat peas. Today it's cod tartare without the tartare sauce.' He dangled a strip of fish meat over his mouth. 'Shall we do this, young Horsmith?'

'I think we should.' Tom helped himself to a piece.

'Down the hatch, then.'

'Bottoms up.'

They sat in their ice chairs and they looked out over the sea. The skies were grey. 'How far do you think we've drifted?'

'Maybe fifty kilometres or so.'

They each had a second slice of cod. 'Not nearly as bad as you might imagine,' Monty declared. 'One more life experience for the autobiography, eh!'

'The autobiography,' Tom echoed.

'Every prime minister writes one. It's expected.'

'And what will it say? Will it list all your great achievements? Will it explain why you decided to resign?'

There was a short silence for thought. 'I hope it will,' Monty said. 'I would want it to be honest. But – and I know this might be hard for you Tom... I wouldn't want any silly mistakes to overshadow the whole thing.'

'It overshadowed everything for Lykke,' Tom said.

'And I don't expect you to let that go. Just to permit some perspective. That's all. I've tried to do my best for the country, Tom. Really, I have. I know how the opposition paints me, and I know what they say about me online. But I've tried to be a good Prime Minister. I'm proud of the things we've achieved.'

'You don't have to campaign to me, Mr Causley,' Tom said. 'You won't ever win my vote.'

'No. I don't suppose I will.' Another silence. 'What about the immigration force? That was my initiative. Very popular. Universal income for all over-fifties? A big vote winner. Control of inflation. Better access to the courts for young offenders. A cap on parking charges at fifty pence an hour. Free GP visits for school age children?' This was clearly a list Monty had recited before. 'Free emergency care to children and pensioners?'

'Stop!' Tom held up his hand. He was shaking his head forcefully. 'You don't get it do you, sir? All that...all that list... it's bullshit. None of that stuff matters.'

'OK.' Monty held up a hand. He hadn't finished his list. 'Marine parks. You must approve of them.'

'I do,' Tom said. 'But you inherited the marine parks from your predecessor. All you've done is to grow them. And only marginally. And you *still* don't get it, Prime Minister. History won't judge you on your management of a few ragtag refugees. History won't care about inflation. No one is going to contribute to raising your statue in Parliament Square because you made car parking less expensive. Jesus Christ, Monty, if that's the sort of thing your autobiography is going to brag about, then people in two hundred years will look at it and ask, *how could he possibly have got things so wrong? How could he have missed a crisis so immense it will still be causing misery and suffering to every human being on the planet for the next hundred thousand years?* History will look back at this time and there'll only be one political story, one overwhelming narrative – one super juggernaut issue, a billion times bigger and more cataclysmic than every trifling crisis your government has ever faced. And the real failure is, you actually know what the crisis is. You're just too scared to admit it. And do you know what? History will judge you, Mr Causley. It will judge you as one of the great, great villains.'

'And what gives you such a special relationship with history, Horsmith, that you know its judgement long before history itself does?' Causley spluttered. 'I studied history. You studied volcanoes. You know what? You shouldn't try to argue if you don't understand the history.'

Tom gave a sarcastic laugh. 'You're right. I'm not a great student of history. I couldn't recite the order of Plantagenet kings, or tell you who shot Archduke Ferdinand, or explain the Gold Standard. But let me tell you some history I do know about. Do you have time for it?'

'I don't need a history lesson from you, Mr Horsmith.'

'Well, hear me out all the same. I think we have plenty of time. Do we have anything more important to discuss?'

'Very well.' Monty gave a sigh. 'If you must.'

'I must. Here it is. A history story. I call it the Very Strange Story of the Missing Bugs. Stop me if you've heard it before.'

'I don't believe I have.'

'OK,' Tom said. He stood up from his chair and looked at the older man. 'So this is a story about two extremely odd things that happened way back in the past —and one even odder thing that *didn't* happen. The first odd thing happened around three hundred and sixty million years ago.'

'OK, so already you've lost me,' Monty interrupted. 'You can't start a story three hundred million years ago.'

'Three hundred and sixty million years,' Tom corrected him.

'Whatever. That isn't a history story. It isn't a human story. It has no relevance.'

'Stay with me for just a few minutes and let's see,' Tom insisted. 'Three hundred and sixty million years ago, the world was way hotter than it is now. We worry about the planet heating up by three degrees. Maybe even four degrees. But back then, average global temperature was fifteen degrees higher than it is today. So the planet was hot. Really hot. You're right to say this isn't a human story. Humans wouldn't have been able to survive then. Not easily. We wouldn't have been able to live anywhere between say, northern Europe and South Africa. The heat would have killed us. Earth was not a nice place to be. And by the way, there was no ice anywhere; not even at the poles.' Tom waved his hand at the ice all around them. 'You could walk to the south pole in sandals. The oceans were much, much, higher than they are today – maybe seventy metres higher, and here is the important thing – there was eight times as much carbon dioxide in the atmosphere, and that was the killer.' He paused for a moment. 'Earth was the ultimate greenhouse,' he said. 'Like parking your car in the midday sun in Cairo, with the windows closed. Well, anyway, that was when the first curious thing happened.' Tom turned and looked at Monty.

'Plants invented a new material,' he said. 'We call it... wood.' He looked around and tapped on the butt of the rifle for illustration. 'Wood,' he repeated, with some emphasis. 'An astonishing new thing. We are so familiar with it, we overlook just how amazing it is. It introduced two quite complicated new polymers to the world, cellulose and lignin; and it was completely revolutionary. It was incredibly strong for a start. It meant, for the first time ever, plants could grow tall. And so they did. Why wouldn't they? They'd just invented wood. Huge tree ferns would grow up to fifty metres high, that's like a fifteen-storey building; and before you knew it, everywhere was covered in forests. Even here.' He gestured towards the distant hills. 'All around the world. There were billions and billions of trees. Trillions. Huge trees. The Earth became a massive tropical forest from the Arctic down to the Antarctic and everywhere in between. I should love to have seen it.'

Tom looked away, as if inviting Monty to share in his contemplation of this curious world of three hundred and sixty million years ago. 'The next odd thing that happened,' he said, ploughing onwards with his theme, 'was the thing that didn't happen. And what didn't happen - was that nothing could figure out how to eat all this wood. Bacteria couldn't digest it. Nothing could. So far as microbes were concerned, this new material might as well have been steel. There was nothing they could do with it. And the upshot was, none of the trees could rot. Imagine that. Trillions of trees all over the world, and when they died, they just fell over and stayed there. For year after year, and century, after century, and millennium after millennium, the trees just piled up. Or else they'd smoulder away into charcoal.' Tom demonstrated with his hands, staircasing his gesture up to head height and beyond. 'For millions and millions of years. Imagine if plants today were to discover a way to make plastic instead of wood. The same thing would happen again. Nothing would rot them, and they would build up forever. That was what happened back in the carboniferous. There was nowhere for the dead trees to go. It was planetary madness. Surely, you'd think, bacteria would find a way to eat all this wood. Or maybe a fungus would work it out. Or some other microbe. Or a termite. Or something. Anything! But apparently it was a harder task than you'd imagine, because not a single creature figured it out.' Tom paused again. 'That was the mystery of the missing bugs. Where were they?'

'Anyway. After a few million years of this, it started to get serious. You see, all those trees needed carbon dioxide, and it was starting to run low. Most of the world's carbon was now locked up in colossal, monumental, piles of undigested logs. In fact, after sixty million years, it looked like the end for Planet Earth – and it could easily have been. Not only was everywhere dangerously short of CO_2, but taking all that greenhouse gas away made things a whole lot cooler. The climate got much more comfortable. Ice caps began to build up at the poles. And ice at the poles reflects away heat like a mirror. That cooled things even more. We started to get a reasonably pleasant planet to live on. Eventually a very new thing started to happen. Stratocumulus clouds began to form. We hadn't had them before. And the clouds made the world cooler still.'

'But think about it. *Sixty million years*! That's *slow* for evolution. It only took sixty million years between the first tiny mammals and the first humans. And yet, for sixty million years, nothing could find a way to digest cellulose. Nothing! How odd was that?'

'And then, suddenly, hey presto...' Tom waved his hand as if he was holding a wand, 'The third odd thing happened. Three hundred million years ago, along came a microbe that cracked the problem. We don't have a name for it, which is a shame, because we really ought to build statues to it and name streets after it. Because that little bug saved the world. Literally. And from that moment on, every tree that died would rot or burn, and either way all of its carbon would go back into the atmosphere in a beautiful balanced cycle. And that's what still happens today whenever a tree dies; unless a bit of it just happens to be part of the frame for the Mona Lisa; wood eventually gets eaten or rots away, or burns, and every single atom of carbon bound up inside it finds its way back into the atmosphere, ready to feed new trees. It is an extraordinary and very beautiful equilibrium. But we owe our comfortable climate not just to that bug that figured out *just in time* how to eat wood, but to the sixty million years when nothing could. Because for all that time, trees got crushed under the weight of falling forests and they dried out, and they became coal, and all that carbon was taken out of the atmosphere because nothing eats coal. And while all of this was happening, tiny little sea creatures and plants were being converted into oil and gas, and nothing could digest those things either, and this helped take carbon out of the air too. It was an incredible gift to the universe. You say you studied history, and yet you don't know this story, surely the most extraordinary thing in all of history. It's such a fantastically unlikely story, it could almost make me believe in God. If anyone ever shows you a film where astronauts land on a planet with a perfect climate, ask yourself what happened to all their carbon. Because surely this never happened anywhere else. We were gifted a perfect climate. Not too hot. Not too cold. A Goldilocks climate. And we owe it all to our good friend the Carboniferous period.'

'Very interesting,' Monty said.

Tom nodded gratefully. 'But here's the thing,' he said. 'Once microbes had learned to feast on wood, they could never un-learn it. So, when God gave Adam dominion over the world in the Garden of Eden, this must have been the deal: *if you like the climate the way it is, don't burn the coal and oil. Because if you do, there's no going back.* And that, Prime Minister Causley, is the contract we've been busy breaking for the past two hundred years. And that's why history will say you did nothing. We are frogs in a saucepan. All of us. We never noticed the water getting warmer and warmer. And now it's almost too late to jump out. We tolerate the slow erosion of our climate the way a frog in a pan tolerates the rising heat. This year, we lose one percent of our coral reefs. Never mind. We can live with that. Next year, we lose another one percent. Hey. Never mind. And then another. And another. And in a hundred years they're gone and we never noticed it happening. Not just coral reefs. Ice caps. Forests. Meadows. You're the driver of a bus, Mr Causley, a bus packed full of people, stalled on a railway line at a level crossing with an immense freight train racing full tilt towards you, and you've been using the precious seconds to adjust your rear-view mirror.'

10. They breakfasted on frozen fish...

It was day three on the iceberg; they breakfasted on frozen fish.

'I think I'm getting a stomach-ache,' Monty said anxiously, as he let the cold fillets slide down his throat. He was looking pale. 'I didn't get much sleep last night. Did you?'

'We need a new plan,' Tom said. He had been down to the platform and had returned looking concerned. 'We're melting faster than I'd hoped. We can't climb any higher, and in another day or two we could find ourselves underwater.'

'Really? I thought it was quite cold last night.'

'It's the sea that's warm,' Tom said. 'It's probably about two or three degrees. All that ice underwater is melting.'

'Maybe we'll get rescued today.'

'If we're lucky.'

Monty raised himself up, and adopted a Prime Ministerial tone. 'I wondered, perhaps, if we might try something different,' he said. 'I think we need a new strategy. No one has come looking for us yet. They're probably still blasting their way furiously into the glacier, and meanwhile we're a hundred kilometres away.'

'What do you suggest?'

'Look,' Monty pointed out towards the ocean. 'Look at all the floating ice. We should try and find a piece, a flat piece of sea ice, about the size of a small boat. A piece that can support us both. We find a way to catch it and reel it in, we jump onto it, and then we paddle back to land using the rifle as a paddle.'

Tom gave this suggestion a groan. 'There are so many problems with that idea, I can't begin to list them,' he said.

'Such as?'

'Well, number one – how do we catch a floating ice boat? That isn't going to be easy. We can't just lasso one. We could try harpooning one with my ski pole, but I suspect it would just bounce off. Number two – *we jump on board. Really?* We'd probably tip it over and end up in the sea. Unless it was huge, in which case how do we paddle it? Also these slabs might look like floating blocks of polystyrene but they're not. They go down deep. They'd be really hard to paddle. Number three – even if it works, how far are we from the coast of Greenland now? We have no idea. But it could be twenty kilometres or more and I don't think one rifle is going to be sufficient to row a great lump of ice all that way. And we'd still be melting, but we'd be on a smaller iceberg. How would that help us? We wouldn't have our igloo for shelter. *And* if we did reach the west coast of Greenland, what would we do then? We'd be hundreds of kilometres from any kind of settlement. I don't think you've thought this through, Monty.'

The Prime Minister deflated a little with this response. 'I know it won't be easy,' he said. 'But at least we'd be doing something, instead of just sitting waiting for a rescue that might never come.'

Tom looked thoughtful. He said, 'Actually, there may one good thing to say about your idea.'

'And what's that?'

'We might find it useful to have a lifeboat to hand. If we drift close to an island, for example. Or if this big berg starts to break up.'

'There you go,' said Monty. 'I knew it was a good idea.'

'OK,' Tom said, 'Let's try to catch us an ice boat. At least it will give us something to do.' He explained his idea. They would find a block of ice big enough to act as an anchor, and they'd tie one end of the rope around it. Then they would heft this block onto a passing berg and reel it in.

They descended the slope to the platform and began to put this plan into effect. Monty reeled in the rope he had used to mark a helicopter landing. Then Tom secured it to a piece of ice the size of a basketball, and finally the two of them stood together on the very edge of the platform to examine potential escape rafts. There was no great shortage of possible chunks, but most were glacial pieces, not of a suitable size or shape, and what sea ice there was, never seemed to be within throwing distance of the berg. 'This one is just to prove the technique,' Tom called. He swung the boulder of ice around his head and let it fly, twenty metres or so, towards a drifting slab. The accuracy was all right, but the block shattered on impact.

Monty gave a laugh. Tom laughed too.

They pulled the rope back in and found a piece of ice for a second attempt. A shallower throw this time, but the target had drifted too far and his throw missed. After this there were no candidate floaters for a while.

Monty lost interest in the exercise. 'Maybe it wasn't such a good idea,' he said. He climbed back to their ledge and settled into his chair.

Around midday, Tom took a break. They swallowed some more fish and sucked on more ice.

'Do you know something?' Tom said. 'We're halfway through our wager. Did you know that? Twenty-five years gone. Twenty-five to go.'

'I used to think it would be a good thing to cancel it,' Monty said. He was lying down now, on a mattress of crushed ice, looking up into the grey sky. 'Now I'm not so sure.'

'Why?'

'I think the world has forgotten it. I'm not sure we ought to remind them. I rarely get asked about it now. Not since... well, not since the storm.'

'Yet once it was so important to you, you could drug me and let Lykke die.'

'It wasn't like that, Tom. You know that.'

'You're saying it was all an accident?'

'I'm saying no one ever could have foreseen what happened.'

They were drifting into a fresh pack of ice fragments. There was a cracking noise as the berg collided with a chunk of ice the size of a family house. Blocks of ice were falling off and dropping into the sea. Monty sat up and pointed down at them. 'More ice boats for us,' he said.

'Should we do it now?' Tom offered, ignoring the interruption. 'Shall we shake hands and call the wager off?'

'I'm not altogether sure we should,' Monty said. 'Imagine if we survive all this. Well, it will add a little frisson to the story, don't you think?'

'Is that what this is to you? A story?'

'Everything is a story, Tom. One day, this will be a story in the history books; maybe even a movie. You and me, on this lump of ice. Whether we survive it or not. If we do survive... well, it needs a little spice, don't you think?' Monty was staring into the near horizon, his attention captured by something. 'What the devil is that?'

'What?' Tom followed his gaze. 'Oh. That's our friend the polar bear. He's been following us for a couple of days.'

'You saw him before?'

'He's been fishing for seals off the ice floe. I saw him down there looking for food.'

Monty said, 'I thought polar bears were extinct. Or nearly extinct. Or something.'

Tom said. 'They are highly endangered. This is where they live, here on the pack ice, and the ice is melting. The seas are grossly over-fished, so the seal populations have crashed, and polar bears go hungry. Happily, there are still a few around, like our friend here.'

'Is he dangerous?' Monty asked.

'Dangerous?' Tom raised his eyebrows and smiled. 'If you mean, *is he going to come here and eat us?* then probably not. He already knows we're here. He can smell prey more than fifteen kilometres away, and he hasn't shown any interest in us. Not yet. But if you mean, *is he a dangerous animal?* – well he's about as dangerous as they come. He's an apex predator. Very big. Incredibly powerful. Very deadly. If he did decide to come and eat us, we wouldn't stand a chance.'

Monty was shaking his head. 'Yes, we would,' he said. He pointed. 'We still have the rifle.'

Tom laughed at this. '*I* have the rifle,' he clarified. He held it up to emphasise his point. 'We will use it to attract a boat. When we see one. We are *not* going to use it to shoot an endangered bear.'

Monty looked at him open mouthed. 'Unless he attacks us, then we have to.'

'No we don't.'

'If I thought you were being serious....'

'I am being serious.' Tom held the rifle away. 'I told your protection officer when he gave me the gun. I told him I would never use it to shoot a bear.'

'Then why do we have it?'

'I don't know. Something to do with making us both look more macho as we walked out with a gun strapped to my back.' Tom raised his voice, just a little. 'I would hesitate to shoot a seal.

But I would, if we absolutely needed food, and if the seal was our last hope. But look at him,' Tom waved towards the bear. 'He's magnificent. The pinnacle of evolution. Comfortable in sea or on land. He can swim for a week or more in icy waters that would kill us in minutes. Extraordinary. I've spotted bears almost a hundred kilometres from land. It doesn't seem to bother them. He could swim here and climb to the top of this iceberg in no time at all, and it would be easy for him.'

'Then I hope he doesn't try.'

'Keep hoping,' Tom said. 'Because I have no intention of shooting him.'

It grew warmer. The clouds dissipated as the sun rose higher, and by around mid-afternoon, Monty had unzipped the front of his snow suit and was sitting like a holidaymaker almost basking in the sunshine. Tom descended to the platform for a second attempt to capture an ice raft. The waters of the sound appeared to be full of ice, but nothing floated close enough for him to rope it in.

By late afternoon, the sun had turned the iceberg into a treacherous mound of very wet ice. Little rivulets of melt water ran down to form a network of tiny streams. 'Oh bugger!' Monty exclaimed when they settled down for the evening. 'I'm sitting in a pool of water.'

'It will all freeze again tonight,' Tom said.

There was no further sign of the bear. Far away, they could hear the sounds of more helicopters. In the far distance, Monty thought he might have seen a boat, and then lost it. They scoured the horizon for more evidence, but the boat didn't reappear. Maybe it was yet another iceberg.

11. Overnight on the fourth night...

Four nights in, and they were developing a routine. Monty took the first watch and Tom tried to sleep. At some unknown hour of the un-dark night, they swapped around, and Tom took his turn outside, gazing out in the shallow sunlight at the wilderness of ocean and floating ice.

A few hours into his watch, Tom became aware of an odd thing happening. It felt as if they were tilting – as if the sanctuary that was their ledge was no longer level, but was instead tipping them forwards towards the sea. It was a slow readjustment, but already it felt unsteady. They were no longer camped on a secure horizontal ledge, but on a slight slope. There were unsettling noises coming from somewhere within the berg. Tom felt uneasy. When an iceberg breaks in two, Tom knew, it can be dramatic. The two halves will each try to re-establish a floating equilibrium, often turning upside down in the attempt. Any significant break or fracture can upset what is, essentially, a delicate balancing act. If a piece should break off above the waterline, the remaining berg will float higher. But a separation below the waterline will cause it to sink deeper. Tom stood up. His legs were shaky.

Below him, the ice platform that had been the shoreline of their little bay for three days, that had briefly been their anticipated helipad, had vanished beneath the sea. The iceberg had dropped and tilted. Their ledge was now no more than two metres above the waves. Tom called into the igloo, 'Monty!'

The Prime Minister was asleep. Was this important enough to wake him? Tom drew a deep breath. The berg beneath his feet gave a lurch. He was almost thrown down the slope.

'Monty! Wake up!'

The older man grunted.

'Wake up! The berg feels like it's toppling over.'

Monty wriggled out of the door like a moth from a pupa. He grunted. He didn't need an explanation of their predicament. The igloo was leaning forward enough to make everything clear. 'What can we do?'

Climbing upwards was not an option. The vertical cliffs that rose to the peak of the berg had been dangerous to scale before the tilting, but now they overhung perilously, and the prospect of moving any higher was impossible to contemplate. Going down the slope, however, was scarcely more attractive as an idea. The pathway to the shore now ended in water. It was as if they were on an island, and the tide had come in.

Tom said, 'I guess we have to go with Plan B. Your plan. We need a lifeboat.' He half-scrambled and half-slid down the slope. 'Bring the fish,' he called.

There was no sea ice to be seen, but some distance away a bergy bit the size and shape of a nose-down shipping-container was just within reach of the rope. It wasn't an especially inviting contender for an escape craft, floating slightly askew, like a truck that was balanced on its windscreen – but it was the only available ice. Tom threw his anchor and, very gently, he reeled it in.

The iceberg gave another lurch.

'It's now or never,' Tom said. 'Do we have everything? We have to jump.'

'Tom, I'm sixty-five years old,' Monty protested. 'I don't jump.'

There was an ocean gap around two metres wide. They would have to cross it somehow. 'Did you ever do the long-jump at school?' Tom asked.

'Yes,' Monty said, 'fifty years ago, with proper running shoes not snow-shoes, and a nice flat running track.'

'We should take off the snow-shoes,' Tom suggested. He bent and unsnapped the devices from Monty's shoes, and then his own. 'Hold one shoe in each hand with the spikes down,' he said, 'and when you land, jam them down as an anchor to stop you sliding off.' He paced out the limited distance available for a run. 'Five strides and then jump,' he instructed. 'As fast as you bloody well can.'

Monty Causley took two deep breaths.

'Another one for the autobiography,' Tom said.

'It's going to be a heavy volume,' Monty said. He took a third breath. 'Audaces fortuna iuvat!' he cried, and he raised his arms in the air like a prize fighter.

The Prime Minister wasn't built for speed, but there was something of the ox in him as he hit his final stride, a heavy momentum that defied gravity, but only for an instant. His head and arms reached the raft, but his legs fell short. He dug the snow-shoes in with his hands and lay dangling, half-on and half-off the platform. 'I'm stuck!' he called.

'Stay there.' Tom grabbed the remains of the cod fillets, and the whole uneaten fish and pressed these into his empty rucksack. He threw them ahead, and they landed safely. His own jump was barely better than Monty's – an equally inelegant landing, but he was far enough onto the ice to drag himself on. He stood, unsteady, and pulled Monty up.

'I swear that will be the last daredevil manoeuvre I shall ever do,' Monty declared.

The tied themselves together and edged up on all fours to the crest of the platform; once there, they sat astride it, like roofers perched on the ridge of a roof, one leg each side. 'This is the only way I'm going to feel safe on here,' Monty said. They were face to face now, uncomfortable and unsteady on the top of the ice. 'I don't see how we can hope to paddle this.'

'I don't think we can.' Tom sighed.

'This isn't safe,' Monty said. 'I regret this idea enormously. Can we try to get back on the iceberg? At least that's stable.'

Adrift now from the great iceberg, and floating away, they could, perhaps for the first time, get some sense of the size of the refuge they were leaving behind. It loomed above them like a huge white hill, like an island in an infinite ocean.

'This was a mistake,' Monty said. 'We should have stayed there.'

But the wind and currents were already separating them, faster than they might have expected. They watched as the gap grew. 'We'll try to find a better raft,' Tom said, a note of apology in his voice. 'I was frightened we were going to topple over.'

Monty didn't answer. But the great iceberg did. It gave a groan, like the snapping of a giant oak, and then with ponderous slowness, the peak of the hill began to drop, and the whole island of ice started to twist and roll. A wave spilled outwards towards them, and their own block of ice rocked in the wake. The ledge where they had spent three difficult nights, and the igloo of which they had been so proud, sank beneath the waters, and were gone. Having turned, the great berg seemed satisfied with its new orientation. It rose – still a hill of ice – but a different-shaped hill. Sea water flooded down the new valleys.

'Lucky we moved when we did,' Tom said.

'We could try to get back onto it,' Monty said.

But they were already too far away.

'We need to look for sea ice,' Tom said. He pointed towards a broad flat slab of ice two hundred metres or so away. 'Like that.'

'How do we get there? We can't row.'

'We sail.' Tom grinned. 'Slowly,' he said. He unzipped the top of his snow suit and peeled off his jumper. 'We will be the masts, and this will be our sail.'

'It's a very small sail.'

'I did say it would be slow.'

They sat a short way apart and held the jumper between them, flat against the breeze like a sail. There was a light wind, but it caught the garment like washing on a line. 'Hold it firm. Let it fill with the wind.'

'I don't think it's moving us.'

'It will. I'm sure it will.'

Sure enough, perhaps half an hour later, the sea ice was looking closer. They persevered. 'Maybe we could sail all the way back to Greenland like this,' Monty suggested.

'We might have to.'

After an hour or so, the gap had closed completely. No heroics would be required. The little berg bumped up against the platform of ice, and they slid down, and onto it.

There was something quite comforting about this new ice vessel. It was almost perfectly flat, an irregular shape reminiscent of a floating map of Africa, the size, perhaps, of a tennis court, or a small suburban garden, floating about a meter or so above the water. Best of all, it was covered with snow, which made it easy and safe to walk on. They made themselves a camp, roughly in the centre, sweeping up some of the surface snow to use as fresh water, and more to build a bivouac as a shelter from the wind. Tom pulled his jumper back on. He examined the camp. 'Excellent,' he declared. 'Do we have any fish left?'

It had been a strange day. They had shared an unexpected sense of achievement. They had escaped from a tumbling iceberg, had figured out how to sail, had found themselves a more agreeable home, and now, for the first time since they left the glacier, they could see the whole vista that surrounded them, including almost as a mirage on the eastern horizon, what could only be the distant hills of Greenland. They had survived for four days. Surely, they could manage a few more? The sea ice had a feeling of solidity and permanence that the iceberg hadn't possessed. This was an illusion. They knew that. In time, it too would melt. In a few days or weeks, it would be gone. But by then, they would be rescued. So they told themselves.

'I shall spend this afternoon fishing,' Tom announced. 'And tomorrow we should set sail for land.'

It was a bold declaration, but it cheered them both up. Monty worked on improving the camp wall. The snow was too soft to support a roof, but they agreed that the best strategy for overnight might be for the man on watch to bury the other man in snow to keep out the wind. Tom set about looking for fish. This exercise was unsuccessful, but neither of them felt downhearted. Tomorrow, they would sail.

12. The difficulty with sailing

The first difficulty with sailing was the wind. It was a steady north-easterly, sending them south-west when they needed to go east. The second difficulty was the lack of a rudder. They abandoned the idea of holding up clothing as a sail, and instead they tried to construct a wall of snow that might catch the wind. After a few hours of work, it was clear this was not going to be effective. The sea-ice had chosen its direction of travel and was not be persuaded into any other.

Tom and Monty sat at the camp and sucked on frozen fish.

By mid-afternoon, all idea of sailing the platform seemed to have been forgotten. Tom was back at the water's edge with his harpoon. Monty was sleeping. The skies had turned grey. The mood had turned too. They had not spoken for a while. In the cold of the afternoon, a thought that had never been far from either man's mind was beginning to take hold. What if they were never rescued? What if they drifted ever further from land, as their sanctuary melted drop by drop into the warming waters of the North Atlantic? Tom returned from a fruitless fishing endeavour and sank down onto the snow. Soon, perhaps, they would need to fight for space on an ever-dwindling patch of ice. Who would be the first to go, to slide off into the water?

Monty turned in early on the fifth night. He was feeling unwell. Tom sat up, looking at shadows in the gloom. It was a cold night. A night without stars. A night with a penetrating wind. Monty slept the whole night. Tom slept too, sitting half upright on a bank of snow. His feet were cold. His fingers.

In the morning, who knew what the time was? Breakfast maybe? Monty was still unwell. He had to rise to pee, and afterwards he lay back down.

Tom opened his back-pack. 'We have two fillets of cod left,' he said, 'and then we will have to start on the second fish.' He laid the huge fish down on the ice like the prize specimen on a fishmonger's counter.

Neither man felt like more frozen fish. They felt hungry for other things.

'This is how we die,' Monty said. They had no energy between them.

'We don't die,' said Tom.

But the older man was right and they knew it. They might not survive this last ordeal.

'We should drift right past Disko Bay in about fifteen days,' Tom said. 'There are plenty of boats there. Fishing boats. Pleasure boats. Supply boats. Someone will spot us.'

Fifteen days, though. Would their platform survive that long? Would they?

Later that morning, they heard helicopters a long way to the north. The sound lasted for about an hour, and then they were gone.

Around midday, both men were asleep. The sun was thin on their faces. Tom felt a sudden rocking of the ice. He opened his eyes. His hands were clutching the rifle. 'Was that you?' he asked of Monty. He raised himself to his feet and looked around.

Monty made a noise. He had woken and now he had seen what Tom had seen. At one far end of the floating ice stood the bear.

He had pulled himself up and out of the water and was standing on all fours, cautiously watching the two men as if uncertain whether they might represent a threat or a meal, weighing up the possibilities and consequences of each.

'Oh shit!' Monty said, scrambling to his feet. 'What do we do?'

'Make a noise,' Tom said. He propped the rifle beneath his arm, pulled off his gloves and began to clap his cold hands. 'Stand next to me. We will look bigger and more fearsome.'

Clap. Clap. An unsettling sound. *Clap. Clap.*

Monty moved closer to Tom.

'Aaaaaaaarh!' Tom shouted, in the direction of the bear. 'AAAARH!'

'Aaaaarrrr!' yelled Monty.

This intervention had little effect on the bear, beyond initiating a twitching of his small white ears. He rocked on his feet, watching the two men with an unbroken intensity of focus.

From where Tom and Monty stood, the bear did not look especially huge. He was a lank creature, wet and slick still from the sea, his fur more cream than white, his muzzle grey, his eyes like buried coals, his nose shiny and black. When he stretched out his neck, he seemed to grow. When he held up his feet, they were like paddles armed with knives. He was simultaneously menacing and appealing, a contradiction in almost every aspect of his being, a miraculous survivor within this bleak and lifeless wilderness, a soft white creature from the deep, like a dreadful ghost, with claws that could rip a man in half.

'Shoot him!' Monty demanded in an urgent whisper. 'SHOOT HIM!'

Tom shook his head. He stopped his shouting. A curiously normal silence descended on the ice flow, as if what followed deserved to be a silent tableau, where events would unfold without the slightest noise disturbing the arctic solitude.

'You have to shoot the damn bear,' Monty said.

'Why? Our lives are no more valuable than his life.'

'For God's sake, Horsmith, I'm Prime Minister.'

'No, you're not,' Tom hissed back. 'You're an ex-prime minister, soon to be a dead one. If we're not killed by the bear, we'll still die in the next few days. Why take his life when we're dying anyway? He at least has a chance to survive. And you're one human of eight billion. An old man. He is one polar bear of ten thousand. A young male. We've destroyed his habitat. We've destroyed his world. He has never harmed us. But we have harmed him.'

'Shoot the fucking bear, Horsmith!'

'Look how thin he is. He's undernourished. He's as hungry as we are. We've over-fished the oceans and left too few fish for the seals. And now there are too few seals for the bears. Do you have grandchildren, Monty?'

'No.'

'Neither do I. Not yet. But if I should, then by the time they reach your age, the planet will be losing its ability to form high clouds. It's a tipping point. It's called the stratocumulus tipping point. We'll see it in about eighty years at our current rate. Give or take. When that happens, there'll be no high clouds to reflect away the heat of the sun. There'll be less rain. No ice cap. No forests to cool the world. Game over. We'll be gone. And the polar bears will be gone. And pandas and penguins and pangolins and porpoises. And zebras and lemurs and flamingos and tree frogs and pelicans and elephants and giraffes. We'll all be gone. So what does it matter now? If you were a politician with even a sliver of guts or leadership or vision to try and sort things, I'd save you rather than the bear. But you're not, are you Monty?'

Monty looked as if he wanted to respond. His mouth dropped open, but the words wouldn't come.

'Besides,' Tom said. 'I don't particularly want to live in a world without polar bears or pandas, or penguins, or pangolins. Do you?'

Monty seemed to gulp. He was shaking.

Tom cracked the barrel of the rifle and aimed high into the air. 'If the purpose of my life is to save this one bear,' he said, 'then my life has not been wasted.'

On the other side of the ice, the bear gave a snarl. It wasn't a growl. More of a warning. His lips curled upwards to reveal teeth like curved daggers. But he made no move towards them.

'We're not killing the bear, Monty. I've never shot a bear in twenty years. Lykke often used to say a bear would get me in the end. It looks as if she was right.' Tom squeezed the trigger. A bang, so loud and so strange in this landscape of silence. It made the ears ring.

Thirty metres away, the bear was startled by the noise. He leapt backwards, almost lifting all four feet off the ice, and retreated to the edge, ready to drop back into the sea.

Tom cracked the rifle and pressed in a second bullet. Pointed the barrel upwards.

'BANG!'

This time the bear's reaction was calmer. He turned his head slowly, examining the world around him in search of the threat. Then he threw back his head and he roared. A devastating roar. A fierce, rumbling roar. His jaws opened so wide it looked as if he might dislocate the joints.

'Last bullet,' Monty said. 'Shoot him. Shoot him. SHOOT HIM!'

Tom loaded the last round.

'If you fire this one into the air, I'll kill you myself,' Monty said.

Now the bear decided to move. He lowered his head and charged towards them, a gallop of a sort, his jaws still open. Still roaring.

Monty turned to flee. There was nowhere really to go – except to stay out of the bear's way. Tom chose to stand his ground. He turned the rifle around and as the bear lumbered into reach, he swung the butt of the weapon towards the animal as if it was a club. It never hit the bear. A great paw batted the gun away and it flew out of Tom's hands and lodged itself in the snow. Tom fell backwards and as he fell, the bear was on top of him, a huge weight of fur and muscle and anger. The bear's jaws, with its terrible teeth, were directed at his head. In an instinctive move of self-protection, Tom covered his face with his un-gloved right hand and the animal's jaws closed.

It was a moment of the utmost terror. An end-of-life moment. A gory, heart-stopping moment of sheer pain.

The animal's teeth were cushioned by the sleeve of the snowsuit, but this didn't stop their terrible progress. These were teeth that could tear through the leather and blubber of a seal with barely any effort. The soft mechanics of a human wrist were no impediment to their progress. The bear drew his head back, and Tom was lifted up by the force and then dropped back onto the snow, his hand severed completely, gushing blood into his snowsuit and all over the snow.

BANG!

A deafening report. The bear lurched backwards.

Monty had the gun. He had fired. But the bear appeared unharmed.

'This is for you,' Monty shouted. In his hand he held the cod. The un-filleted, whole cod, a twenty-five-kilogramme meal. A big meal even for a bear.

The bear turned his head.

'Come and get it,' Monty yelled. He waved the fish like a lure.

The bear was tempted. He had forgotten Tom already. With extraordinary speed, he lurched towards Monty and the cod.

'Fetch!' Monty called. His arm swung and the fish flew away in an arc — a missile the size and weight of a suitcase, and after it galloped the bear. Both fish and bear entered the water at the same time. A huge splash.

'Jesus Christ, Tom!' Monty was kneeling over him.

All around the snow was red, like the floor of an abattoir.

We needed paint, Tom was thinking. *We wanted paint to spell out an SOS. And all the time we're full of paint. Bright. And red.*

The pain was barely real. It was like a noise so loud you can no longer hear it. And everything was moving. Swirling. In a slow motion of red.

'Tom!'

Once, at Nan's house, he had torn his foot on a nail and bled all the way up the stairs, until every step was wet with blood, and Nan had carried him over her shoulder to Dr Books to be sewn up. He could remember that day. Once Peter Shaunessey had thrown him and Benny off the side of his boat and into the sea and told them if they couldn't swim to shore, they would drown. And so they swam with Peter watching every stroke. Once they had rescued a whale. A beached whale. Everyone in the village was there, pushing and pulling like a single creature. Once he had met a girl on the quay and fallen in love. Once he had cradled twins, one in the crook of each arm.

How dark it was.

'Stay still, Tom. Stay awake. Stay with me.'

Somebody was winding something around his arm. For some reason, the arm hurt.

Once he had been lost on the ice, and she had come to find him. Everywhere had been dark then. It was winter in Qaanaaq. His sense of direction had abandoned him. She found him walking quite the wrong way and she ran across a kilometre of snow to catch him. Once he fell victim to a storm, and holed up in the little research cabin as violent winds and murderous cold rocked its walls, and even then, as the storm could grow no stronger, and the cold was starting to lock his limbs, the door had flown open, and there she had been, frightened for his life.

Where was she now? Now that he was dying?

'I didn't shoot the bear,' a voice was saying. 'I should have done. But I didn't.'

Where was she?

Something was tightening around his arm. The pain was dreadful.

'Lykke!' He was calling her name. 'Lykke!'

'What do you want to say to her, Tom?'

What did he want to say? He wanted to see her. To see her face. To hear her voice. To hold her. To smell her. 'Lykke?'

'She's here, Tom. Say what you need to say.'

And there she was. There again. On the quay. Smiling. Just as he knew she would be. 'Tom. Don't give up, Tom,' she said.

'But I can't do it without you.' His eyes were filled with tears now. Salt tears. Tears that stung.

'You don't have to do it without me. I'm always here.'

Always here.

It was growing lighter. He blinked his eyes. Where was she?

'Stay with me Tom. Stay awake. Stay awake.'

Where was he now? Lying in blood and snow. An ocean of blood and snow. And pain.

He knew this man who was leaning over him. He looked at his arm. Somebody had wound bootlaces around his forearm so tight that it stung. 'That hurts,' he said.

'I didn't shoot the bear, Tom.'

'We're dying,' he found himself saying. 'We're all dying. We're boiled frogs.'

'I know. Stay still if you can. You've lost a lot of blood.'

'We won't jump out until we boil. That's what happens with frogs. You warm up their water and they can't decide when to jump out. Eventually, they boil.'

'Stay with me, Tom. We shall get you back soon,' said the man. His name was Monty. Tom remembered this now. His mind was clearing.

'You didn't shoot the bear?'

'No, Tom.'

'Why not?'

'I don't know. Maybe you were right. Maybe he deserves to be here more than we do. Anyway. We have a saying in my family. Good fortune favours the brave. It doesn't often let me down.'

Tom almost smiled. 'I like that.' There were things he needed to say. He could feel them in his mind, edging towards the front. 'There's something I need to tell you,' he said. What was it? He closed his eyes.

'What is it, Tom?'

'I've forgotten,' Tom said. 'Something.' Thoughts were coalescing like pieces of ice into an ice flow. How much of it was real? 'It wasn't an accident,' he heard himself saying. These words felt good. They seemed to be one step ahead of his brain. He could hear the words and he knew what came next. 'It wasn't an accident,' he said again. 'The melt-hole.'

'I know,' said the man.

'You do?'

'Of course I do. I figured it out.'

'I wanted you to fall through the ice. I wanted us both to fall.'

'I know.'

'I didn't care if we lived or died.'

'Do you care now?'

Did he care?

Once on the headland at St Piran, he had clambered down the steps to the beach in the early morning, on a winter morning, just a short while after dawn, because that was a good time to think about Lykke, and a good place too. He had walked out between the rocks and seen a dolphin in the bay, cresting among the waves, not too far from the shore. Alone. It felt like a sign. *'Is that you?'* he had whispered to the creature. 'Is that you?'

Why is there never any answer? Why could she never reply? Just one word would be enough. Just one.

And then he had heard voices from the village path, and there were Ilse and Noah. Thirteen they had been. They had crept out of the cottage on Cliff Street and followed him all the way to the sands.

'Do you come here to see Mum?' Ilse asked him, and she took his hand like she had done as a child, holding hands to cross the road, holding hands to climb the steps, holding hands to face off a danger.

Noah sat beside him and slid an arm around his waist.

'There's a dolphin in the bay,' Tom told them. But when he looked the animal had gone.

'I think perhaps I do care,' he told the man who was strapping his arm.

The man let Tom's arm down slowly. 'I think this means we're quits,' he said.

'Quits?'

'Evens.'

He was waking. Things were growing clearer. Something in his blood, perhaps, had diffused into his mind, into the odd convolutions and folds of his brain, like strong coffee or a magical elixir. Shapes were emerging from a very thick mist. And he was awake. And everything was clear.

'Let me see.'

Monty released his arm and Tom tried to lift it.

'Careful,' Monty said.

His hand had gone. Not cleanly like a rip from a saw, but roughly, and raggedly, like a bite from a bear. Gone. 'Holy shit.'

'You'll be OK,' Monty said. He had a second bootlace in his hand. 'Better not to watch. Look at the sky. I need to give you one more torniquet.'

He looked at the sky. High clouds. Stratocumulus clouds.

'Here.' Monty pushed a piece of ice into his mouth. 'Suck on this.'

Across the flat blue sea, there were a million pieces of floating ice. No one would ever find them in this.

'I was wrong about you Monty,' he said.

'I know,' Monty said.

'Do you?'

'Yes.' Monty was pulling the cord tighter and tighter around his arm. Soon it would cut right through, and the arm would float away into the sky like a balloon.

'I was wrong too,' Monty said.

'Were you?'

'I've been wrong about a lot of things.'

A final pull on the bootlace. A cymbal crash of pain.

'Talk to me, Tom!'

'What were you wrong about?'

'Oh God. Just about everything.' Monty lowered Tom's arm for a second time. 'I'm going to pack some snow over your wound. Is that OK? Don't move it.'

'OK.' Staying still was easy. 'Tell me. Tell me what you were wrong about.'

'I was wrong about the statues in Parliament Square. They don't put them up for the chap who makes parking cheaper.'

Tom managed a rather tortured smile. 'They don't.'

'They absolutely don't. I was wrong not to listen to you, Tom. Not just you. I was wrong not to listen to everyone who was telling me the same story. I was wrong, because I saw it as an argument I needed to win. A binary thing. Like a tennis match. Someone has to win every ball. Every point. And I always wanted that player to be me. Smash. Smash. That's politics you see. It's tribal. It gets so it doesn't matter what's right or wrong anymore. It only matters that you stay on the same side. My party, right or wrong. Politics doesn't give you any space to compromise. Or to cooperate with the other side. Or to change your mind. I was twenty when I was a climate denier, Tom. Twenty. I have no idea why I assumed the views I held. I just did, and I wouldn't let anyone change them. I'm sixty-five now. God knows, I should be allowed to revise my opinions. Have some kind of an epiphany. But no. No one lets you do that in politics. I wouldn't let myself do it. I had chosen my tribe and my platform and to hell with all the rest. And that's why I was wrong. I should be able to stand up and say "Fuck you all" to anybody I want to say it to. But I couldn't. I was a follower and not a leader. I believed what I was told to believe. And do you know the real irony? It wasn't lack of intellectual rigour that kept me stuck. It was lack of courage. Misfortune favours the cowardly. *Ignavus malafortuna iuvat.* That should have been my motto. I've been a coward, Tom.'

'Not today,' Tom said.

'The funny thing is,' Monty said, 'it wasn't all this that made me see it.' He waved an arm toward the ocean, with its scattering of ice. 'Not in the way you hoped. You thought I'd see melting glaciers and it would prick my conscience. You thought I would see the light, but you didn't know who I was, Tom. You showed me melting glaciers and all I saw was wet ice. When I walked out onto that glacier with you, Tom, however many days ago it was…'

'It seems like a year.'

'A year at least. When I walked out onto that glacier, I had no plans to change my mind. I had a speech half-written already in my mind that would kick the ball down the road. I was going to say how valuable the experience had been. How important it was for us all to face up to our own responsibilities for the climate crisis. In other words, I was going to tell people this was all their fault. Not the fault of governments. I was going to talk about the big initiatives we already have. Electric cars. Wind farms. That sort of thing. But I wasn't thinking about any change in policy. If anything, I was deliberating ways to avoid doing very much. "We're steering a big ship," I was going to say. "You can't yank on the tiller. You have to make small adjustments and the ship will turn." It was an excuse. A fudge. But something *has* changed my mind these past few days. I'm just not quite sure what it was. Maybe it was the solitude. The chance to think. To really think. No phones ringing. No advisors putting their heads around my door. No TV cameras being thrust in front of me. No opposition politicians winding me up.'

'And maybe it was just the perspective. The big picture. You know. Here we are drifting down the coast of Greenland, but we still have another fifteen days before we get to Disko Bay and even then, we're only about halfway down. My world is normally so much smaller. If I need to go to New York for a meeting, I get on a plane and I'm there in a few hours.' Monty paused. 'And maybe,' he said, 'it was confronting our own mortality. We're such fragile beings. I don't think I'd truly seen that before. When you stand so close to your own imminent death, perhaps you start to see things differently. And maybe,' he said, 'maybe it's because I had the courage not to kill the bear.'

Tom lay back. 'Thank you for that,' he said.

'For what?'

'For not killing the bear.'

'Even after what he did to you?'

'He did what bears do.'

'I wonder if all he ever wanted was the fish.'

'Probably.' Tom closed his eyes and let the pain drift through his mind. 'If we ever get through this...' he started to say.

'We will get through it.'

'But if we do. If we really do. There is a project of Lykke's, I wanted to talk to you about it. But well...'

'What is the project, Tom?'

'Lykke originally called it the 1820 project.'

'1820? Like the year?'

'Yes.' There seemed to be a red film over Tom's eyes. He tried to blink it away.

'Tell me about it, Tom,' Monty said. 'Tell me about the 1820 project.' His tone was the kindly, urgent tone of a paramedic keeping his patient awake.

Tom said, 'Lykke would say that 1820 was about the last time the earth was pristine. Truly pristine. Right at the start of the industrial revolution. Before we plundered the planet and melted the poles and wrecked the atmosphere. Lykke's idea was for every country – every *county* even – to pick a dozen key measures and figure out a way to reset them to where they might have been in 1820. So maybe get back to the same number of trees, or the same area of wilderness, or the same population of orangutans, or the same sized flocks of wild birds. That sort of thing. Sequester all the carbon they had used since 1820. Get everything back to 1820 levels. It would be a long project. Maybe it would take a hundred years. A thousand years. But it would engage people. Locally. For a whole planet, the idea is almost too big to contemplate. But for a county? Who knows? It could be do-able. We could do it for Cornwall.'

'And what was the population of orangutans in Cornwall in 1820?' Monty asked.

Tom almost laughed, and the effort brought a violent pain to his arm. He screwed his face up. 'All I'm asking,' he said, 'is if you get through this, and I don't, would you promote Lykke's project?'

'We will both get through this,' Monty reassured him. 'You can run the project.'

'But if we don't. If I don't. Will you promise...?'

Monty said, 'If we ever get through this, I'm appointing you my chief climate adviser. Then you can do Lykke's project yourself.'

'Climate adviser?'

'We need a new approach, Tom. A less confrontational kind of politics. We need to work together...'

Monty's words were growing faint. They were becoming lost somewhere, out over the dark seas, floating out like emerging butterflies, dying in the cold. For Tom, the world was growing dimmer once again. And everywhere was colder. The cold had reappeared like an interloper that had been waiting and quietly biding its time. How cold it was now. There was a coldness in his feet. Coldness in his very bones.

Cold.

Like Nan's cottage on Cliff Street in that cold winter when there had been no oil for the heating. No one had any heat that year. That had been the year of the whale. Or like the storm in Qaanaaq, when Lykke had rescued him, so nearly frozen, his eyelids almost welded together with the cold. Or the cold, so-very-cold-day when a dying seal had taken refuge outside their front door and they had pulled it inside, into the warmth, and like magic they had brought it back to life.

How strange, though, to be this cold. Shivery cold.

On Christmas day in St Piran, they would climb the hill to the church, and the children would carry candles, and they would all sing carols outside, everyone wrapped up against the cold. *God Rest You Merry Gentlemen*, they sang. And *Silent Night*.

How strange to be back in St Piran on such a cold day. A sea bird was circling high above. What was it? He could see it drawing patterns in the sky. Not a herring gull. The wings were too wide. He was struggling to remember the names of birds. A guillemot? No. Guillemots were short and stumpy. Not a kittiwake. Not a puffin. An albatross, then. But who ever heard of an albatross in St Piran?

'St Piran,' he said, feeling the words as they found their way past his tongue and his teeth. 'We need to go to St Piran.'

'Yes, we do,' Monty said. He was nodding. 'We'll go home.'

Home. For a second or two, the word felt unfamiliar. And then it didn't. 'Yes,' he said. Of course they would go home. It was summer in St Piran. There would be butterflies in the hedgerows. Wildflowers on the meadows. Seagulls on the headland. Holiday makers on the beach. There would be pasties, and ice creams and cider. They would be singing sea shanties in the Stormy Petrel. 'We can go on *Piranesi*,' he said.

'Piranesi?' The man called Monty sounded uncertain. 'What is Piranesi?'

What a curious question. 'Surely you know Piranesi? It moors right outside your house.'

Somewhere, far off, he could hear a voice calling, and he knew who it was. It was the naturalist. The man who painted rock pools.

'What are you talking about, Tom?'

'Benny's boat,' Tom said. He blinked and pointed to a shape that seemed to be heading towards them. 'Best boat in the water,' he said.

FIFTY YEARS AFTER THE WAGER

1. And would suffice

There are few things in life quite so reliable as the tides. In they come, when the moon and the earth command them. Out they go at their allotted time. Day or night. Summer or winter. There they are. Trillions of tonnes of water lifted and dropped. And lifted. And dropped.

Tom Horsmith sits on a bench at the highwater mark of Piran Sands and he contemplates the tide. It is already high up the beach. Too high, he thinks. There are two more hours until high tide, yet already the water is at his feet.

When Tom was a boy, an old man used to sit on this bench. An old seaman. He would sit here almost every day. Tom can recollect him with the clarity that comes with childhood memories. The old man would light a pipe, and he would push the stem into the corner of his mouth, and the pipe would bend his whiskers. Then he would lean back, and look out towards the sea. All day he could sit there, in peaceful contemplation. 'What are you looking at, Mr Garrow?' Tom asked him once, and the old man drew the pipe from his mouth and seemed to meditate on the question.

'I'm looking at the sea,' was his reply.

Today Tom was looking at the sea. The sea was breathing. Up. And down. Up. Down. Like an organism asleep.

Seventy. Imagine that.

Sometimes he would sit here with Benny. They weren't old, they told each other. 'Life begins at seventy,' Benny would say, buoyantly. But they could sit here for longer now than they might have done at fifty. Or at twenty.

Tom had bought the cottage in Cliff Street from Connor and Morwenna, and he'd overseen some renovation. 'It's time to start erasing Nan's fingerprints,' he had said. The builders had been in, and they had redone the wiring, and the plumbing, and installed new windows, and repaired the roof, and insulated the walls, and fitted a new kitchen.

Ellie Magwith had moved in twenty-three years ago; into the spare room at first. It was a temporary thing, while Tom was spending most of his time in London. She was a friend of Benny's. She was, as it happened, a school contemporary of them both, just a few years their junior. She had needed a roof over her head after a breakup with a partner, and following a smugglers' storm which tore the roof from the cottage she rented on Tyler Magwith's farm. Tom, in those days, rarely spent more than two or three nights a week in St Piran, so letting Ellie have the spare room had seemed the charitable thing to do, and, well, one thing had led to another, as it must do. You can't share a cottage as small as the one on Cliff Street without some intimacy. Cause and effect. Biology and endocrinology. These things happen, and the long evenings in the little cottage had proven to be a powerful aphrodisiac. Ellie was round, and rosy, with a headful of disobedient curls, a smile as wide as a fisherman's boast, and a hearty laugh you could hear in the square. Tom had fallen in love with her very quickly indeed. A surprise to them both. But not to anyone else. Villages like St Piran understand these things. They know what must happen when a woman moves in with a man. These are things that make the world go around.

When they married, they told no one, except for Benny and Lacey, who came along to the registry office in Treadangel to act as witnesses. They took their honeymoon in St Ives. Not so far away from St Piran. But, as Lacey Shaunessey might have told them, when the whole world wants to take their holidays in Cornwall, why would you go anywhere else?

Ilse and Noah still owned controlling shares in the tour business in Nuuk, but they no longer had much to do with the day-to-day management. There was a CEO in Nuuk who could do that, and she did it very well. The business was a big concern now. They employed more than sixty people. Ilse had married Emil, a Danish high-school teacher with a wide red beard, and they lived in Copenhagen where Emil worked. Ilse was Director of the 1820 programme in Denmark. She was a recognisable face on Danish TV. Denmark, that once prized itself on raising pigs, and cattle, chicken, and mink, now paid farmers to replant forests. It hadn't been an easy transition. But fashions change. Young people didn't eat meat the way their parents did. Ilse would fly to Nuuk a few times each year to keep an eye on things and she still took visitors to see the icebergs at Qeqertarsuaq Island in Disko Bay when she could. But she was settled now. A Danish citizen. Noah had married his boyfriend and he stayed in Nuuk. He, Noah, was a climate scientist. He worked on glacier research. The husband, Carl, was an artist who painted canvasses of Arctic seascapes. It was all good. They would meet up at Christmas in St Piran, the whole Horsmith clan. That was a tradition now. Tom would rent a holiday home and it would fill with people. He had grandchildren now. Axel and Torben. Ilse's children. Soon, he might have great-grandchildren. What a thought that was.

We don't see the world changing. Tom would say this to people. Some changes happen in an instant. A dice-playing fisherman is turned to stone. A bear bites off a man's hand. These things happen in a moment. If you were looking the other way, you might have missed them. But the real changes, the dangerous changes, are the ones that creep up on you. The flock of birds that every year is almost imperceptibly smaller. The landscape of trees that is now a monoculture. The smoke from a distant fire. The air that is just a tiny bit less good to breathe. The summer day that is just a breath warmer.

'We are frogs in a saucepan,' he would tell people, when he was chief adviser to the prime minister. 'We all ignore the heat.'

Ellie would make excellent pasties. Once, he might have called them *vegan* pasties. These days they were just pasties. They didn't need the adjective anymore. Tom had weaned himself off meat and fish a long time ago. 'The last time I ate fish,' he would tell people, 'was a raw cod fillet, frozen in ice.'

'Is that really what you want?' Ellie had asked, when she made her first vegan dish, and served it up to him in the kitchen of the cottage on Cliff Street.

'It's exactly what I want,' he said.

They bought a bigger bed. They were too bulky in their middle age for the double bed that had once accommodated Tom and Lykke. Now they had a king-sized bed, with barely sufficient room to walk around it. Tom lay on the right so the stump of his arm could hang over the edge.

Ellie came to the relationship with a daughter of her own: Meadow. Meadow was fifteen when Ellie and Tom married, but she took Tom's name and, in time, she moved out of her grandparents' house on the hill into Tom and Ellie's cottage. So they were a family. For a few short years. Good years.

His life had been eventful. When you get to seventy, you start to think like that. You start to catalogue the things you have done. There can be a lot of memories to sort through.

The world was a different place. He was sure of that. If you took the twenty-year-old Tom Horsmith, the angry young man who, full of passion, had challenged a politician in a bar, and if you were to drop him into the world of the seventy-year-old Tom, would he recognise the place now? Would he rail at the changes? Or would he be satisfied with all they had achieved? Tom wasn't even sure he could answer that. But he wasn't so angry now. Time had healed him of that. 'Be careful that hatred doesn't consume you,' Lykke had warned him, so many years ago. It hadn't. He was happy about that.

Seventy. The mind is still sharp at seventy. But the body is starting to wind down. There are aches and pains where there should be none. His feet were not so good. His digestion was wayward. A year ago, he had had a health scare. A *Transient Ischaemic Attack*, the doctor told him. A TIA. Frightening at the time. Not exactly a heart attack – more of a mini stroke. 'But you need to be careful,' his doctor said. 'It might be related to your trauma.' She meant the loss of his hand.

He did his best to keep fit. He would walk the cliff paths most days. Early in the morning, he would rise and walk, down alongside the wall to the mouth of the harbour, to the stone remains of John Brewster, and there, if his timing was good, he could watch the sunrise.

He had twice been made a widower. Ellie had died one night in her sleep. Fifteen months ago. He had been away at a climate conference in Berlin. They sent a messenger in to the seminar where he was speaking, to whisper the news into his ear. An embolism, he was told. A blood clot that had lurked somewhere in her system with malign intent, waiting for a night when it might voyage up and into her brain. Not so different perhaps, in its clinical presentation, to his own health scare; except that Ellie had not survived it. A kind way to go, people told him. But her death was a shock and he missed her badly. He slept alone in the king-sized bed and his dreams were rarely agreeable.

He had lost a lot of friends. St Piran was a different place to the village he had known as a child. Most of the familiar faces from his childhood were now gone. Jeremy Melon died with prostate cancer not long after the rescue in Baffin Bay. He had been hailed by the press and TV as a hero, and he enjoyed the brief notoriety. It had been Jeremy with his keen eye for the natural world who, awake at the tiller, had heard the distant sounds of the rifle, had spotted a streak of red on a distant piece of drifting ice, and had steered Piranesi off course to investigate. After Jeremy died, Demelza Trevarrick moved away from St Piran. One night, she was simply gone, and her house was for sale. She had written a bestselling novel, and the proceeds, villagers said, had bought her a villa somewhere in France. Who knew where she was now, if she even still lived?

Benny and Lacey remained. They would never leave St Piran. They were as permanent as the rocks that guarded the harbour walls. Their sons had worked the boats for some years, but tourist numbers had fallen, and revenues had evaporated too. One day, a sad day, Piranesi was sold to a stockbroker with a house in St Mawes. 'It wasn't making money anymore,' Benny told Tom, but he had tears in his eyes as he said it. The stockbroker wanted a weekend leisure boat. Benny motored it around to St Mawes harbour, and moored it there, and he had never had the courage to visit again, to see perhaps if it was still there. Today, the Shaunessy boys were married with children of their own, living somewhere far inland with nothing to remind them of the sea except for occasional seagulls.

We move on. We all move on. Like the sea we keep on breathing. Up. Down.

Tom had worked as a climate adviser for DEAC for sixteen years, long after Monty Causley's tenure as Prime Minister had ended. He took over the running of Lykke's global 1820 Foundation. The Foundation had been seen, by almost everyone, as fanciful at first. Ridiculous even. But his own notoriety as the man-who-had-lost-his-hand-to-the-bear helped him to find an audience, and the backing of Monty Causley was surely the match that lit the kindling. Slowly, the idea took off. 'We don't have to do it all at once,' Tom told the audience for an online TED talk. 'If it takes a hundred years, then so be it. But nothing is so valuable to all mankind as a pristine planet, and if we can recreate that, then we must.'

He lived for the sixteen DEAC years partly in the cottage on Cliff Street, but mainly in a basement flat in Bloomsbury – not all that far from the student accommodation he had shared when he was nineteen. He would walk a similar route to the one he used to walk when he was waiting on tables in Covent Garden – across Bedford Square, along Oxford Street, and down Charing Cross Road; but he would need to go further now, through Trafalgar Square, down Whitehall, past Downing Street and the great buildings of state, and across Parliament Square Gardens. Here the statues of the luminaries looked down upon him as he walked. Gandhi. Disraeli. Mandela. Churchill. He had joked about these with Monty. He would often remember this. *No one ever will ever raise a statue to you for cutting car park fees,* he had said. That, he hoped, would still be true.

He hadn't seen Monty Causley for fifteen years. There was a time when they would meet twice a week in Downing Street, and on various occasions they had been out together to dine in one of Monty's familiar haunts in Pimlico or Chelsea, always under the watchful eye of one of the Prime Minister's security men. But Causley had lost the premiership after seven years, in a putsch led by an ambitious young Chancellor, and straightaway he had packed his suitcases and departed with Carys to live in their villa in Taormina, and only once or twice had Monty's and Tom's paths ever crossed again at occasional government receptions or conferences in foreign lands. Monty and Carys, to Tom's knowledge, never revisited St Piran.

A few years after Monty's departure from Downing Street, a smugglers' storm damaged Marazion House. The sea crashed through the windows and doors on the ground floor, and everywhere was flooded with seawater and foul water, and the tenants (for there were holidaymakers staying in the house at the time) made an excessive claim for damages. It wasn't the first flood to have hit the house, but it was certainly the worst. The lawyers and surveyors advised Monty that he should not let the house again. The risk of flooding was too great. There was a real danger to life. And so Marazion House stood empty. It could not be sold. Monty didn't appear to have even entertained this idea. No *For Sale* sign ever appeared. Instead, boards were nailed over the doors and windows, and there they remained, growing grey with the passing years. Slates slid off the roof. Moss grew up the pointings. Marazion, once the most prominent home in St Piran, had become a civic embarrassment. It was being reclaimed by the sea and the cliff. A residents group raised money for a blue plaque that they fixed up on the wall. The plaque read, *'This is the home of former Prime Minister, Monty Causley, who has allowed it to fall into disrepair, to the shame of St Piran.'* If the sign was intended to embarrass Monty into restoring the house, the action did not succeed. In due course, the sign itself faded and became streaked with seagull excrement. A chain-link fence and a gate with a heavy padlock went up to protect the building from vandals, and (perhaps more importantly) to protect vandals from the building. Several hundred years of construction had been undermined by the storm, and by others that had followed, and even the cliffs into which the house had been built, had succumbed to a measure of erosion that seemed to threaten the building.

'They should tear the place down,' Benny said once to Tom.

'That would cost money.'

'They're a rich family.'

Well, that much was true. But months passed, and years passed, and no one showed up to demolish Marazion House, and after a while it became just another feature of St Piran, a crumbling ruin at one corner of the harbour, pointed out to day trippers on the boats for photographs.

Tom has a prosthetic arm. They made it for him at St Thomas's Hospital in London, and for a while he wore it every day. It straps onto the stump of his forearm, about midway between his elbow and the place where his wrist would once have been. It resembles a hand, and with a mental effort, he can communicate with the machinery that opens and closes the fingers. But it is a lot of fuss just to allow him to carry a coffee cup or deliver a handshake. He has a perfectly good left hand that can do the job. So he has started wearing the prosthesis only for important meetings, and on the days in between he doesn't. He has taken to wearing short-sleeved shirts. They are easier. And now he has retired – well almost retired – he can go a month without taking the arm from its box.

Almost retired. Well. He is nearly seventy. He is allowed to retire. But he still speaks on the conference circuit, although invitations are less frequent these days. And he still advises the international board of The 1820 Foundation, but he no longer draws a salary. He still takes the train to London once a month or so for some event or other. He was interviewed for '*Desert Island Discs*' a radio show where a celebrity interviewee can review highlights of their life, punctuated by eight records of their choice. He chose, among other pieces, the landscape movement from Vaughan William's *Antarctic Symphony*. It would remind him, he told the interviewer, of the solitary seascapes of the Baffin Sea. He chose the sea shanty, 'Cornwall my Home,' (*for this is my Cornwall, and I'll tell you why, Because I was born here, and here I shall die.*) And he chose the Beatles, *Strawberry Fields* because they were a band from over a century ago, because Nan used to like them, and because he could.

So he is busy. He is collaborating on a book about the 1820 project. He has been a panellist on a TV Question Time show. He is due to record a video for amputees to talk through the recovery process they might expect. But time is an odd commodity when you're seventy. You have both too much of it, and too little of it. He is sought out sometimes by visitors to St Piran, especially by young people, who come hesitantly to speak to him at his table in the Petrel, or (if they are bold enough) to knock on the door of his cottage on Cliff Street. They always want to talk about ice caps. About warming. About CO_2. About stratocumuli. About plastic in the oceans. About antibiotic resistance. About species extinctions. They are young, and passionate, just as he had been once. Not so long ago, it feels to him. Even though it has been fifty years. He is patient with them. Always. He lets them buy him a lemonade and he sits on his seat by the empty fireplace, and he talks. He has plenty of stories.

'Are you a pessimist, or an optimist?' a young woman asked him once. She reminded him of Lykke. She was tall with braided hair. She had a soft accent like Lykke. She had Lykke's earnestness. 'What day is it today?' he asked. 'A Tuesday? Then today I'm an optimist. I'm an optimist on a Tuesday, a pessimist on Wednesdays and Fridays, and for the rest of the week I'm not sure.' When she looked at him bemused by his answer, he said, 'I'm optimistic about humanity's ability to find solutions to the crisis. But I'm pessimistic about our willingness to put them into action.' He would lean forward in his seat when he was asked questions like these, and it seemed as if he had a secret he might whisper. 'What you need,' he would say, 'is for my generation, and all its greed, and all its blindness to the crisis, to pass away, and for the future to be given to you. My generation inherited the crisis and we made it worse. We don't deserve to be allowed to repair it. You are the solution. You are what keeps me optimistic. At least on a Tuesday.'

St Piran has changed. In the twenty-five years since Benny Shaunessy and Jeremy Melon set off on *Piranesi* on their rescue mission to Greenland, the little hamlet at the toe of England has retreated, gently, into a fundamentally quieter state of existence. Holidaymakers have stopped coming this far. Who knows why this is? Travel has become expensive. Maybe that's it. Cornwall isn't quite so fashionable. Beaches have slowly lost their allure. Maybe all of these things.

It didn't happen all at once. It has been a gradual thing. Like the warming of the world. Each season has been a little less busy than the season before. The road that leads all the way from Treadangel has become potholed, the passing-places have grown muddy, and the hedgerows have risen higher. An unexpected aura of dilapidation has settled on the village. The whitewashed walls have grown grey. There is a feeling of neglect now. There has been no new vicar for St Piran Church for two decades or more, since Alvin Hocking, the priest, died. For a while a vicar from Treadangel visited for occasional services, but even that small support has long since ended, and the church now stands empty, ghostlike at the brow of the hill – a hollow shadow over the village below. Many of the businesses in the town have closed. The boats and the boatmen have largely gone. The only vessels still in the harbour are weekend pleasure boats, and these don't put to sea very often. The Bistro on the quay, and the ice cream shop have gone. The pasty shop remains open, but for just two hours a day and only at weekends. The Anderssens left St Piran a decade or so ago, and the pub was bought by a Ukrainian couple from Lviv, who spotted the *For Sale* board on a visit to the village. They have settled into St Piran well. They are generally liked. They don't make their own cider. They sell a fizzy German cider called *apfelwein*. It is more popular with youngsters, they say. But it isn't the same.

Tom sits on the bench that overlooks the sands and he reflects on all these things. His mind is a muddle of thoughts today. He needs the breathing of the sea to calm him. But there is a fierce wind coming in with the tide. This isn't a breeze. It has power behind it. It is the kind of wind that can lift a man off his feet and carry him up the beach.

He has a walk to do. He should do it now. He rises from the bench and makes his way along the footpath, climbing the long flight of stone steps that winds up to the headland. It is a tiring climb. He is out of breath at the top.

The churchyard is overgrown with tall grasses and weeds, but villagers have kept the newer graves clear. There is no memorial here to Ellie. He regrets this. The church closed well before she died. She was cremated in Treadangel, and Tom, with Meadow and with members of the Magwith family, scattered her ashes on the farm fields where she had grown up. But there are graves in the churchyard that Tom will often visit. His mother Kelly is here. She took her own life, but that never prevented the church from welcoming her remains. Nan is here too, in the same grave, beneath the same stone. There are old friends here. And in a corner, beneath the shade of the Hornbeam, is a modest grave with a low, white marble headstone.

Lykke Horsmith — aged 34 — taken from us in a storm — an activist for a better world — forever missed.

Somebody has been to the grave. Someone has clipped the grass — perhaps with a pair of hand shears — and has put flowers in the vase. Tom bows his head. Forty years. He has been visiting this stone for forty years. 'What would you say to me today?' he whispers to the shadow of the stone. 'What would you tell me to do?'

He knows the answer. *Don't do anything stupid.* He does not need to hear it. But maybe it isn't the answer he wants.

Someone is in the churchyard. He sees her moving behind a row of graves, a basket in her hand. Charity Limber. She is seven years his elder, but still fresh of complexion with a ready smile. She is here with flowers to visit Casey's grave — a fresh mound of new black soil. She comes to Tom and puts her hand upon his shoulder. 'How are you, old friend?' she asks.

'Much the same,' says Tom. 'And how are you?'

'Much the same.'

This is how they are in St Piran. And this is the reply when age starts to rob you of your agility. *Much the same.* They talk for a short while. They share a few old memories. Then Tom bids Charity farewell and he carries on his way. He walks down the hill, over the cobbles, and into the village. It is a warm enough day, despite the high wind, and there are people out and about their business. Most of them say *hello, how are you*, and most of them Tom knows.

The wind is picking up. It already feels like a gale. There is a whistling sound as it blows between the waterfront buildings. The new landlord of the Petrel is ushering early diners away from the outdoor tables towards the seating indoors. Tom walks uneasily down the quay towards the stone steps that lead down to a rocky platform and then wind upwards to the front door of Marazion

House. But the steps and the rocks are already underwater. The tide is rising steadily today. The approach to the house is treacherous. All the same, he steps into ankle deep water and feels the sea soak into his socks.

There is a wire fence all around Marazion house, fastened onto steel poles sunk into the concrete. Before you reach the front door, there is a gate, usually sealed with a padlock. But there is no padlock today. Someone has removed it. Someone with a key. Tom lifts the latch and the gate swings open. He is in water almost up to his calves.

He isn't wearing his prosthesis today. For a moment, he regrets this. But it is too late to go back.

He steps up to the front door. The water is rising; and there is still an hour until high tide. He tries the handle, and the door, unlocked and unlatched, swings open in the wind like a sail. It is a heavy door, and the hinges are rusty. It squeaks like a wounded animal. Tom has to lean hard to close it against the wind. He walks through the hall, splashing through water, and he pulls open the door to the front room.

The boarded windows make the house gloomy, but not altogether dark. Enough June light streams in through gaps in the planks to light the room. There is no furniture. There are no pictures. No rugs. No drapes. Nothing to say this was once a family home. But maybe it never was.

'Hello, Tom.'

'Hello, Monty.'

The old man is there already. He is sitting on the floor, in the very centre of the room, uncomfortable, curled forward like an ancient embryo, looking ready to topple. He is dressed for a colder day than today, a rather formal attire with a coat, a tweed jacket, a waistcoat, a shirt, and even a tie. There is something almost comically tragic about him, marooned in his fine dress in the derelict ruins of his once-great house. Old men should not sit on the floor. Especially not old men who once led a nation. There is an indignity about it, countered only by the dignity of his dress. He sits in several centimetres of water, and so his legs and arms are wet.

'No protection officer with you today?' Tom asks. He raises his eyebrows.

'I haven't had one for years,' Monty says. 'Not a good use of public money.' He raises his shoulders. 'Who would want to threaten me anyway?'

'You look well,' Tom says.

'Looks can deceive.'

They survey each other. One old man, and one very old man.

'It's good to see you, Tom,' Monty says.

'You too.'

'I knew you would come.'

'Did you?' Tom looks surprised. 'Well, I nearly didn't. I thought about it. I thought perhaps you were in Spain – or wherever it is you live these days.'

'Sicily. That's where I used to live. I haven't lived there for fifteen years.'

'Oh.' Tom is surprised. 'Then where...?'

'The Causley family home is in Bodmin.' Monty leans on the heel of his hand. His whole hand is under the water. 'Up on the moors. The old ancestral seat. We all end up there eventually, we Causleys.'

'I see.'

'I came here in a self-driving taxi. I rather like them, don't you?'

'I use them when I need to.'

They are rediscovering each other in a conversation about taxis. 'How long was the trip?'

'About an hour and a half, I think. Maybe more. I wasn't watching the time.'

'May I sit down next to you?' Tom asks.

'Of course,' Monty lifts his stick off his lap and indicates a place with a tapping motion. 'If you don't mind getting wet,' he says. 'There's a trick I learned when I was a boy scout. Did they ever teach you this in Scouts? When you have nowhere to lean, you sit back-to-back, and you lean on each other.'

'I was never in the Scouts,' Tom says. He lowers himself down. 'Didn't we do this once before?'

'I think perhaps we did.'

They manoeuvre to find the least uncomfortable position, and carefully they lean back.

There is no weight to Monty now, Tom realises. He has shrunk. And he is frail. A gust of wind would blow him over.

The water is cold, but it isn't freezing. Tom lets it soak into his trousers. He feels like he did as a child, when he and Connor would paddle in the rock pools, netting for shrimps. Home they would come with soaked clothes.

'Do you ever think about that time?' Monty asks him. 'That time we spent on the ice floe, you and me?'

'I think about it every day,' Tom says. He holds up the stump of his right arm. 'I have a regular reminder.'

'Ah yes,' Monty says. 'Of course you do. Insensitive of me to mention it.'

'Not at all,' Tom says. 'How about you? Do you ever think about it?'

There is a quietness in the empty room. Monty's breathing is heavy and watery. 'It has never left me,' he says. 'Do you remember the igloo?'

'Of course.'

'When I think back on my life's achievements, I can't help myself thinking about the igloo.'

'It was magnificent.'

'It surely was.'

They sit, back-to-back, in the rising water. The wind is squeezing through the planks with a murmur and a rattle.

'When is high tide?' Monty asks.

'About an hour.'

'Then I suppose we shall have to wait.'

Tom answers with a grunt. His legs already feel as if the circulation in them is failing. He cannot sit here for an hour. 'We don't have to sit here at all,' he says.

'Well, *you* don't,' Monty says. 'But I do. As I recall, the bet was for me to sit in my front room for an hour.'

Tom doesn't reply. He is feeling an ineffable weariness. He has waited far too long for this day. Now it is here, it somehow feels unreal.

'Funny isn't it,' Monty says, 'how all the world has forgotten our wager. Apart from me and you.'

'The world thinks we called it off,' Tom says. 'You told the press…'

'I told the press our wager was history,' Monty says. 'They asked me the question, and I said you and I were resolved on the matter, and now it was ancient history. They drew their own conclusions. I didn't remind them that history is something, invariably, that you can't go back and change.'

'I thought we agreed to be quits, though,' Tom says. 'Honour even on both sides.'

'Only in respect of our mutual indiscretions,' Monty replies. 'Not in respect of our wager.'

'Well, we could scratch it now,' Tom says. 'We are older and wiser. We could shake hands. We could go and have a fizzy cider in the Petrel.'

'Sadly, I can't drink anymore,' Monty says. 'My doctor won't let me. It doesn't agree with my constitution.'

'We could have a cup of tea.'

'You make it sound almost agreeable.'

'It could be.'

The water is lapping at their legs. There is the salty smell of ocean.

'How high have the waters risen?' Monty asks. 'Since our original wager?'

'Much more than we expected,' Tom says. 'The Antarctic melt has been catastrophic.'

'How high?'

'Almost a metre. But today is a spring tide. A high one. And there is a strong southerly wind blowing. I think we might see a tide about two metres higher than we would have seen fifty years ago.'

'And how high will that be?' Monty asks. 'In this room?'

'No more than knee-high,' Tom says. He illustrates with his good hand. 'You will survive it.'

Clatter clatter. The planks on the windows are rattling in the wind. Outside the weather is developing into a storm. Inside the water is eddying and swirling as waves crash against the front door.

'What now?' Monty asks. His voice sounds frail.

'What now?' Tom echoes. *What now indeed?* 'One of us drowns. Or else we shake hands and we put this all behind us.'

'I don't mean that,' says Monty. 'I mean what now for the world?'

'Every year gets a little bit hotter,' Tom says. 'Every year the sea gets higher. Every year there is more CO_2. Every year there is less ice to reflect sunlight. Every year there are fewer clouds. We reach the stratocumulus tipping point in about five or six decades. The planet will no longer be able to form high clouds. We will cook. The world will cook.'

'And the polar bears will be gone.'

'And the pandas. And the penguins. And the pangolins.'

'All of them.'

They sit, back-to-back, reflecting on this.

'In the end,' Tom says, 'it's just a stupid wager. It isn't a legal contract. We don't have to be here. We're grown-ups. Neither of us has to die. We can get up and walk away.'

'In truth,' says Monty, 'I am finding it rather cold. I thought I'd become used to the cold when we were on the iceberg, but the water is chilling me.'

'Me too,' says Tom. 'Shall we call this off?'

But neither man makes any move to stand. Outside, almost lost in the roar of the wind, they can hear the sounds of children running along the quay looking for shelter from the storm. Raised voices. Laughter.

'Did you ever have grandchildren?' Monty asks.

'Two. Two boys. Axel and Torben.'

'I think perhaps I met them once.'

'You did.'

'You're lucky.'

'Very.'

'Did you ever remarry?'

'Yes.' Tom gives a sigh. 'But I'm a widower again.'

'I'm sad to hear that. Carys died last year. Did you know?'

'I saw it on the news. I'm sorry.'

'No need to be sorry. She was eighty-six. Not a bad age really, is it? She was ready to go,' Monty says. He looks at Tom. 'Does anyone know you're here? Is there anyone who knows our wager still stands?'

Tom shakes his head. 'Only Ben.'

'Benny?' Monty looks anxious. 'Benny? Will he show up and try to interrupt us?'

'He is in hospital in Truro,' Tom says. 'He is having a new knee. In any case, I made him swear he wouldn't try to come. I told him I would be OK.'

'Good.'

'He wasn't easy to convince,' Tom says. 'But he won't break his word. Even if he could.'

'Good.'

'So, what now?' Tom asks. 'How long do you want us to sit like this?'

'Don't be in too much of a hurry, Tom. I've thought about this moment almost every day for fifty years. Haven't you? I don't particularly want to rush it. I've played this scene in my head. I know how it goes from here,' Monty says.

'Well, so have I,' Tom says. 'I've thought about every eventuality. And I know how it goes too.'

'Really?' asks Monty. He sounds a little surprised. 'Then why don't you tell me... how do you think this scene unfolds?'

'I come to Marazion House, and I discover you here,' Tom says. 'Just as I have. Just as I knew you would be. You are determined to make a point. Because you're stubborn. Because you want me to know you were right. You want the *world* to know you were right. Because I deserve a lesson. All of which is understandable. You *were* right. I *do* deserve a lesson. So what happens? We sit together in the water, and we have this conversation we're having now, until eventually you let me talk you out of it. That's how this scene works. I need to be the one who concedes. I lost the wager. But we're gentlemen. This isn't an old-fashioned duel to the death. So we shake hands, and we go for that cup of tea. That's the only outcome. It's the only one that makes sense. If you insist on making me drown, then history will look badly on your legacy, and you care about history, don't you? My death would be a stain on your record. It would look almost like a murder. They will never raise your statue in Parliament Square if you have blood on your hands. So what do you do? You need to be seen to be magnanimous. You want me to beg you. But that's OK. Because whatever I say, and however I say it, you eventually relent, and we cancel our wager. That's how this scene ends, Monty. It is the only way it can end. The only question is, how cold and uncomfortable, and wet, do we have to get before you pick up the script?'

A long silence follows this pronouncement. Eventually Tom fills it. He leans forwards and lifts himself back onto his feet, leaving Monty alone on the floor. The water is higher than his ankles now. It is almost up to his calves. 'Shall we agree then?' he asks. 'Shall we shake hands now and get on with the day?' He holds out his good arm. 'I can help you back up.'

But Monty makes no move to stand. Instead, he lets his head drop a little further. 'You haven't asked me,' he says. 'Ask me how I see the scene unfolding.'

Tom lets out an anxious sigh. 'Very well. If you must. Give me your version.'

'One of us has to drown, Tom. That's how I see it. That's how it is. You're wrong about history. I studied history. You didn't. You studied volcanoes. You once told me you couldn't recite the order of Plantagenet kings or tell me who shot Archduke Ferdinand, and that's OK. You don't have to be able to do those things. But don't try to use history as your alibi if you don't understand it.' Causley's breathing is laboured. Talking seems to be expending his energy. He gulps for air – a deep rasping breath. 'Let me explain to you about history,' he says. 'History is about *stories*. More than anything – that's what it is. It has very little to do with the order of kings, or dates, or treaties. It's about stories. Stories we can tell. Stories we remember. Stories with a message. We remember Joan of Arc because she was burned to death. If she had died peacefully in her sleep, who would know her name now? The story has to have an end that satisfies the build-up. Otherwise, it isn't a story. We remember Scott's expedition to the South Pole more than we remember Amundsen – even though Amundsen got there first. Why do we do that? Because Scott has a better story, even though he perished in the cold. And that's how it will be with us. If we walk away now and have tea at the Petrel, no one will remember our story. They may remember how we got lost on an iceberg. How one of us was attacked by a bear. But is that how you want our story to be told? Where is the message in that story? I always thought you were the passionate one, Tom. You were the one who wanted the message to be shouted from the rooftops. Don't try to tell me you wouldn't feel a huge sense of disappointment if, after all this time, we just gave up on the story. Because if we do, there's no going back. You know that don't you? We can't put this off to next week, or next year. It is today. Now. This is the hour we promised. This is where our story needs to end, Tom. Not with a whimper and a cup of tea.'

Tom is swaying slightly on his feet. His chest feels heavy.

'This will be a St Piran legend,' Monty says. 'A global legend. People will talk about this forever. But only if one of us drowns.'

'But what if I refuse to drown?' Tom asks. 'I don't even know if I can. I don't believe I would have the courage to take that lungful of water.' He is anxious now. He has known Monty would be stubborn. He even expected some resistance. But the old man's calm assurance is disturbing him.

'But you don't need to drown, Tom,' Monty says. 'I thought you said you had thought this through. Every possible scenario.'

'I have.'

'Well then. Ask yourself this. Who really lost this bet?'

'We have almost an hour to find out.'

'Nonsense. We know the answer now. Look about you, Tom.' Monty waves his stick at the disintegrating room and decaying walls. 'Look at this house. It's uninhabitable. It's a ruin. I'm sitting in water. If I had foreseen this fifty years ago, would I have counted it a victory for my position? I don't think so. The oceans have risen. Just as you told me they would.'

'Not by as much...' Tom starts to say.

But Monty interrupts him. 'Pah!' he says. 'We weren't arguing about centimetres. We were arguing a principle. Were we recklessly endangering our world with policies that allowed the ice caps to melt and the seas to rise? Yes, we were. I was wrong, Tom. You were right. History will take your side.'

'But that isn't the bet. You can't drown yourself. The rising waters have to drown you.'

'And so they shall. But if we are to act like lawyers here, dissecting the definitions of words, I will remind you of what was said. *I will sit for an hour at high tide on my ninetieth birthday, in my front room in Marazion House. If it is under water, then I will drown.* Is my front room under water, Tom?'

Tom squeezes his eyes closed for a moment. He breathes deeply. 'Yes,' he says.

'Then I must drown. That was my undertaking. And I am a man of honour, Mr Horsmith. Equally, I cannot be helped. Not by you. Not by anyone. That would invalidate the bet. I cannot sit here for an hour, Tom, leaning on my hands. My shoulders are too weak. My stomach muscles cannot do it.' He sinks down and now he is lying in the waves, propped up on his elbows, partly floating.

'I won't let you,' Tom says. 'This is nonsense. I won't let you drown, because of a fifty-year-old drunken bet.'

'Yes, you will. Don't worry, Tom. I have left a letter with my lawyer explaining what I intend to do. This won't come back on you. But don't try to stop me, Tom. Rescue me and I *will* demand that you drown. I will call it in. Like Shylock. I will insist on my winnings. Think of Lykke. Think of your twenty-year-old self. Think of that passion you had.'

Tom is standing over him. 'And you should think of your legacy,' Tom says. 'You were a good Prime Minister. You did more to address the climate crisis than any leader before or since. If you want people to make statues of you, you shouldn't jeopardise that. No one will make a statue of a suicide.'

'I don't want a statue, Tom. I want a story. A story will last far longer than a statue. Besides,' Monty says, 'I don't want to live in a world with no polar bears. No penguins. What were the other things?'

'Pangolins,' Tom says.

'Or pelicans.'

A wave brings more water in. It washes over Monty's face.

'Still forty minutes to high tide,' Monty says. He closes his eyes.

Tom drops to his knees. 'I'm sorry, old friend,' he says. 'But I can't let you do this.'

'How can you possibly stop me? You only have one hand.'

'Twenty-five years with only one hand teaches you how to cope,' Tom says. He feeds his left arm around the old man's back and under his arm. 'I'm going to lift you now,' he says. 'I would appreciate it if you were to help me by standing.'

'No!' Monty's coat and clothes are heavy with water. He is not cooperating. He pulls his arms tight around his chest.

Tom struggles. With his single arm, he cannot get a clear hold. He strains to stand but Monty responds by leaning backwards into the water, and now they are both almost submersed. 'I'm taking you,' Tom cries. 'Don't be idiotic! I'm not going to let you drown.'

It has developed into a struggle. A fight between two stubborn old men, soaked and cold. Monty is resisting with what little strength he has. Tom is fighting back, and a man of seventy has an infinite advantage over a man of ninety, despite a missing arm. They slide across the floor and the waves froth up around them and Tom gets the hold he has been trying for, behind his opponent with an arm around his chest and his hand clutching the collar of the coat. It is an effort to get up; but his grip is tight and now he has the older man on his feet like a wet, woollen mannequin. But then they are over again, back on the floor, back in the water, and he will have to do it all a second time. Who will tire first?

'Leave me die,' Monty implores him. 'I want to die in here. This is how it has to end.'

'No!' Tom has the hold a second time. This time he stands, and leaves Monty sitting, still in his grasp. The struggle has tired them both. Tom can feel his own heart straining with the exertion. 'You're coming with me,' he says.

The fight seems to have left Monty Causley. He lets Tom drag him across the floor like a sack of fish. His face looks grey. 'Don't do this, Tom.'

'I have to!'

They are out of the front room and into the hallway. It is darker here. 'Hold onto me,' Tom commands. He is going to need his good hand to open the front door. Which means he will have to let go.

Outside the wind is howling like the spirit of a Cornish demon.

'Hold on!' Tom releases Monty and the old man falls back into the water like a deadweight. Tom stretches forward to pull open the door, but before his hand even reaches the handle, the latch drops and the door opens and a surge of water pours in like a tidal wave. Both men are thrown backwards.

Someone else has opened the door. Framed in the rectangle of light, with spray and sunlight all around her, is the silhouette of a woman in jeans with long white hair blowing in all directions.

'Lacey!' yells Tom. His voice is almost blown away by the force of the wind. 'Help me!' He staggers forwards and clutches at her arm.

'What's going on Tom?' Her expression is fierce.

'Help me!' He looks towards Monty, now face down in the water. 'We have to stop him from drowning.'

As he speaks, a wave rolls in through the door, and Tom loses balance and falls.

'Oh God!'

This isn't over. Not yet. The undertow from the wave pulls at his legs and he is dragged out of the door on to the very top step – a step slippery with seaweed. This might, he thinks, be the last thing he knows in this life, as the great undefeatable forces of wind and sea, the violent and malevolent intentions of the smugglers' storm, drag him down from the steps into the froth and spume of the ocean and onto the dreadful rocks of Piran Bay, rocks that stand like a stack of knives guarding Marazion House.

But Lacey has grabbed him. They fall together down the steps. Weightless, as the water retreats beneath them. Tom lands first. Lacey just above him. He lands with a hideous crunch, on hard, sharp, rocks, and he knows at once he has broken his right shoulder. He recognises the sensation of trauma. Blood is spilling out into the foam.

Who cares? This is his damaged arm. They struggle like a single organism to stand.

'Come.' She is leading him away from danger towards the shelter of the harbour wall. They crunch forward unsteadily on the slippery shingles, until they can scramble up the steps to the harbour. They collapse together on the wet quay. The blood from his shoulder feels warm against his skin.

'I've broken something, Lacey,' he says to her.

'Yes, you have: every promise you made to Ben,' she says. She is sitting up and looking at him. 'You told him you'd be safe.'

'Well, he promised me he wouldn't try to stop me today.'

'And so he hasn't.' Lacey stands with her hands on her hips. 'But he knew you'd have a plan, Tom. And one of us had to be part of it.'

'This wasn't a plan,' Tom gasps. He nods his head urgently in the direction of the house. Go and get Monty.'

She turns towards the steps. 'You stay here. Don't do anything stupid.'

Don't do anything stupid. Lykke had said that to him once. He sinks back in pain. Maybe they will cut the whole damned arm off. He doesn't need it.

He watches Lacey navigate the steps to Marazion House, clutching the handrail. The front door is open, banging in the gale. He wasn't expecting this. He hadn't imagined Monty wanting to drown.

It is a long time before Lacey reappears. When at last she does, she is alone.

EIGHTY YEARS AFTER THE WAGER

1. Torben

'I never knew my grandmother,' Torben tells the crowd. He is on a wooden platform, and there are several thousand people in the square. He leans on a lectern for support. His voice is amplified. It comes back to him from speakers in the trees. 'But my grandfather would talk about her all the time. I was always a little afraid of my grandfather. He would show me the stump of his arm. *I lost my hand*, he would say, *when it was bitten off by a bear*. That's a fairly terrifying story when you're eight years old.'

The crowd is in good spirits. They are willing him on. They reward his story with a generous laugh.

'I am told that I *did* once meet Montague Causley, but I was only three, so, alas, I have no memory of the great man that I can share. So I shall, instead, share with you some statistics from the 1820 Project – an idea of my grandmother, Lykke Horsmith, that was championed by my grandfather, Thomas Horsmith, and converted into a global political reality by Prime Minister Montague Causley. A project I am privileged to lead.' Torben unfolds a piece of paper. 'One hundred and six countries have now signed the 1820 pledge.'

There is applause for this.

'Those countries have together planted nine hundred and ten billion trees which pushes us over seventy-five percent of our target. More than 15 million square kilometres of land have now been rewilded. Nearly ten thousand species of plants and animals are no longer on the red list.'

Greater applause.

'It gives me huge pleasure to welcome to this stage to unveil this statue... my grandfather, Thomas Horsmith.'

Tom is helped up the steps. He is a small man. A very old man. His beard is white.

He greets Torben with an embrace. He bends a little as he walks, but at the lectern he straightens to accept the appreciation of the crowd. 'I should like to read you something,' he says. He takes a pair of spectacles from his pocket and carefully puts them on. 'This is something Lykke wrote for an address she gave to a climate conference in Gottingen,' he says. 'Seventy years ago, if you can imagine that.' His voice is unsteady and shallow. The voice of a very old man.

He reads from a small book. 'Imagine if you can, a wild meadow in summer,' he reads. 'You come across it on a countryside walk, and straightway its beauty takes your breath. It is a clearing in the woodland – not too large – a rolling hectare perhaps, rich with wildflowers and meadow grasses, visited by bees and butterflies, home to mice and voles, and spiders, and frogs, lizards, and weasels, and badgers, and hedgehogs, moths, and ants, and woodlice, and ladybirds, squirrels, and newts. And more. So many creatures live here. Far too many to list. Imagine the songs of the birds that feed here, and the whoosh of wings from the bats and owls that swoop at night.' He lowers the book for a moment. 'It might help to remember,' he says, 'that these words were written by a woman who grew up on the north-west coast of Greenland, where very few of these things are found. Maybe,' he says, 'this is why she found them so precious.' He takes up the book and reads on. 'A red deer passes through this meadow and grazes on the sweet, sweet grass. A vixen makes her home in a burrow beneath an oak tree and there she is raising a litter of cubs. Imagine the trees that take root around the clearing, the moles, and earthworms that burrow beneath the soil, the beetles, and termites, the wasps, and the midges, the slugs and the snails. There are mushrooms and toadstools here and all manner of microscopic fungi and yeasts and living things for whom this little oasis of wilderness is the whole universe. Imagine the tall waving grasses, and the mosses, and the saplings, the brambles, and the nettles, and the dandelions. Can you smell the wild garlic? Perhaps you can detect the scent of lily-of-the-valley, and honeysuckle? Can you find cow parsley, orchids, and buttercups, and primroses? One little patch of land. One tiny spot. And yet there is more richness, beauty, and eternal satisfaction in this small piece of meadow than there is in any art gallery or museum on Earth. I should rather leave this single meadow to our children than all the artworks in Paris. And the world will be infinitely poorer for the loss of this meadow. Poorer than it would be if all the works of humankind were rendered into dust. We owe this to our children. To our grandchildren. To protect the meadows, the woodlands, the jungles, the savannahs, the oceans, and the ice caps. We owe our children the pristine world we were given. It is our duty. It should be right at the top of every action list we write. It should also be our joy.'

Tom puts down the book. He looks around the square at the faces. 'I am ten years older now,' he says, 'than Montague Causley was when he died in the storm at St Piran. My hundredth birthday was last week. When you get to one hundred, you reflect on the changes you have seen in your lifetime. Not all of them are good. But this is how it has been for a dozen generations. Ever since the early years of the industrial revolution, every generation has bequeathed a poorer world to its successors than the one it inherited. Poorer not in material possessions, or knowledge. But infinitely poorer, as Lykke wrote, with the loss of every meadow and the with felling of every tree. I hope mine will be the last generation for which this is true.'

Tom stops talking. He looks across the crowd. He nods his head slowly. 'This will be the first statue raised in New Parliament Square,' he says, 'since Parliament itself and all the existing statues were moved here to Birmingham to escape the floods.' He turns. A short distance away, there stands Nelson Mandela, cast in bronze; close by is Millicent Garrett Fawcett with her suffragist banner, COURAGE CALLS TO COURAGE EVERYWHERE. And there is Mahatma Gandhi. And there is Robert Peel and a host of former Prime Ministers. Churchill. Palmerston. Disraeli.

Behind Tom is a monument shrouded in a white cloth. 'Perhaps we should have provided a meadow,' he says, 'but let this instead serve to remind us.' He pulls on a rope and the cloth falls away from the statue like the billowing of a raincloud.

There she stands, in her Inuit reindeer trousers and *Kalaalisut* musk-ox parka, fringed, and patterned with stripes, and decorated with beads, with the hood thrown back. A proud and confident Inuktun. She is tall. She has narrow eyes and long braided hair. Her expression is determined. She has beauty and she has poise. The soft glow of the summer sunshine transforms her almost into the figure of a goddess.

FIRE AND ICE

This novel is a work of the imagination. No character is based on a real person, and no situation is based on a real event.

The original idea for the story came from my brilliant agent, Mark Stanton. I told him I wanted to write a climate change novel, and he sent me an email in February 2021, describing a scenario he described as a cross between *Not Forgetting the Whale* and *Local Hero*. He called it 'Not Forgetting the Iceberg.' Not much remains of his original story, alas, except for the iceberg. But for that, and for all his other help and extraordinary support over the years, thanks Stan.

Around 10 percent of the land area of Earth is covered with ice. Most of it is in the ice sheets of Antarctica, but around 10% is in the northern ice caps over Greenland and in other glaciers around the world. If all of this ice was to melt, sea levels would rise around seventy metres. On current form, it will all melt. In time. A 2021 study published by Potsdam Institute for Climate Impact Research in Germany explains that the melting of enough ice in Greenland alone to raise sea levels by a metre at least is already certain and irreversible.

The threat to clouds that Tom describes to Esperanza is a genuine concern. If atmospheric CO_2 levels exceed 1,200 parts per million, it could push the Earth's climate over a tipping point. This would see clouds start to break up, and, according to research published in the journal *Nature Geoscience*, this could trigger another 8°C rise in global average temperatures. The 2019 paper is titled, *'Possible climate transitions from breakup of stratocumulus decks under greenhouse warming,'* by Tapio Schneider, Colleen M. Kaul, and Kyle G. Pressel.

The concept of the boiled frog is a rather unpleasant metaphor. Al Gore used it in his climate change movie, *'An Inconvenient Truth.'* The idea is that a frog dropped into hot water will immediately jump out, while a frog in water that is slowly heated won't notice and will eventually boil. Happily, it seems the legend is broadly incorrect. Frogs are smarter than we imagine and will escape from the saucepan if they can. But the metaphor is useful nonetheless to describe the apparent inertia humanity has displayed towards our warming world.

Despite the overwhelming scientific consensus that the world is warming, climate-denial has often been a reasonably tolerated (and often almost respectable) position. Donald Trump tweeted in 2012 his belief that climate change was a Chinese plot to make the US less competitive, and at a rally in 2015 called it 'a money-making hoax.' A former UK finance minister, Lord Lawson, gave an interview to the BBC in 2018 where he claimed that "average world temperatures had slightly declined." In 2016 every Republican US presidential candidate questioned or denied climate change. The British botanist and TV presenter David Bellamy is on record as saying, 'man-made global warming is a myth.'

I am grateful to Esben Lyager, an air traffic controller at Qaanaaq Airport, for reading my chapter on Qaanaaq and advising me how it might be improved. Among the host of insights he gave me, he told me that many houses in Qaanaaq don't have a water supply. 'There's no plumbing in Qaanaaq,' he told me. 'The spillage is dumped right in front of the houses.' He also told me, 'In the summer we get our water supply from the shallow river that divides the town. But it stops running early September. Until the sea ice is thick enough to carry the front loader (usually in January) our water comes from those tanks. When the ice is thick enough, the front loader drives to an iceberg, takes a big chunk and returns it to the ice melting plant in town.' Thanks Esben.

Some readers might recognise '*Piranesi*' as the title of a brilliant novel by Susanna Clarke. I loved the novel, and I borrowed the name because it seemed perfect for a St Piran boat; but I'm happy to say I have Susanna's blessing for this. Thank you, Susanna.

I always bother Dr Jon Bloor when I need medical details for a story. It is so helpful to know a doctor who answers the phone. Thanks Jon.

The 1820 Programme is not real. I rather wish it was. The idea was inspired by a real initiative – '30 by 30' which, if adopted, would commit nations to setting aside 30% of land and sea for nature by the year 2030. The plan, developed by the Convention on Biological Diversity (CDB) was set up following the 1992 Earth Summit in Rio de Janeiro and to date it has been signed by every UN member state apart from the USA. Despite this, according to New Scientist in April 2022, all 20 goals set for the last decade have been missed. Which is depressing.

Charcoal sequestration is an idea that is gathering attention. Traditional carbon capture simply slows down the release of carbon burned in power stations, but burying charcoal from sustainable sources (known as 'biochar'), or mixing it into soils, may be the one technique that effectively removes carbon forever from the environment. The International Biochar Initiative has a target to produce one billion tons of biochar a year.

My son Jon, a journalist, travelled with me to the west coast of Greenland (on a carbon neutral trip) to help me research this story. Jon is also a hugely helpful reader. Thank you, Jon. And thank you, Daniel Jonssen, a Greenlander, who took us to the Greenland ice sheet and the glaciers. It was amazing.

A special thank you to Isabelle Kenyon and the amazing 'Fly on the Wall Press' for their incredible talents, and for taking a chance on me and this book.

Finally, as always, thank you, Sue. For everything.

About the Author

John Ironmonger was born and grew up in East Africa. He has a doctorate in zoology, and was once an expert on freshwater leeches. He is the author of The Good Zoo Guide and the novels The Notable Brain of Maximilian Ponder (shortlisted for the 2012 Costa First Novel Prize and the Guardian's Not the Booker Prize), The Coincidence Authority and The Whale at the End of the World (an international bestseller). He has also been part of a world record team for speed reading Shakespeare, has driven across the Sahara in a £100 banger, and once met Jared Diamond in a forest in the middle of Sumatra. He's on X at @jwironmonger

About Fly on the Wall Press

A publisher with a conscience.
Political, Sustainable, Ethical.
Publishing politically-engaged, international fiction, poetry and cross-genre anthologies on pressing issues. Founded in 2018 by founding editor, Isabelle Kenyon.

Some other publications:

Your Sons and Your Daughters are Beyond by Rosie Garland

The Process of Poetry Edited by Rosanna McGlone

The Soul We Share by Ricky Ray

The Unpicking by Donna Moore

Lying Perfectly Still by Laura Fish

Modern Gothic - Anthology

And I Will Make of You a Vowel Sound by Morag Anderson

The Dark Within Them by Isabelle Kenyon

The Others by Sheena Kalayil

Man at Sea by Liam Bell

Snapshots of the Apocalypse by Katy Wimhurst

Demos Rising Edited by Isabelle Kenyon

The Devil's Draper by Donna Moore

The Truth Has Arms and Legs by Alice Fowler

Climacteric by Jo Bratten

The State of Us by Charlie Hill

The Sleepless by Liam Bell

Social Media:

@fly_press (Twitter)

@flyonthewallpress (Instagram and Tiktok)

@flyonthewallpress (Facebook)

www.flyonthewallpress.co.uk